To Jenni

SO MANY PATHS

Grace Farrant

Grace Farrant

Pen Press

First published in Great Britain by Pen Press

All paper used in the printing of this book has been made from wood
grown in managed, sustainable forests.

ISBN 978-1-78003-522-2

Printed and bound in the UK
Pen Press is an imprint of
Indepenpress Publishing Limited
25 Eastern Place
Brighton
BN2 1GJ

A catalogue record of this book is available from
the British Library

Cover design by Jacqueline Abromeit

To my daughter, Helen

Grace Farrant's short stories were published in magazines for a number of years before she began writing novels. Her first novel, *The White Rose Weeps*, is set mainly in Yorkshire where she lived as a child. *So Many Paths* is set in East Anglia where she has lived since university and getting married.

Her career includes teaching languages and serving as a magistrate. Learning languages has always been a passion and she is now adding Italian to her other languages. She says that she inherited this fascination from her Armenian mother who was a gifted linguist.

Grace enjoys being involved in the local community giving talks to various groups including those involved in creative writing. She has a daughter, a son and four grandchildren and lives in a fifteenth-century farmhouse in a Suffolk village.

Using her knowledge of legal procedures she is currently working on a detective novel.

Chapter 1

"Annie! Move yourself!"

Her mother's voice carried up the stairs to the room Annie shared with her sister, Eileen. Still not yet five in the morning, Annie could hear her parents moving about in the room below.

Like many others in Densbury, Annie lived in a house specially designed for the weaving industry in an area of East Anglia where small towns and villages had grown up based on this work. The houses were tall, plain buildings with the middle storey which had been designed in the nineteenth century to hold the massive loom operated by outworkers for the local mill. Some of the poorer weavers operated looms in badly ventilated, unheated sheds in backyards.

Now that powerful steam engines had been installed in the factory to drive the looms, outworkers were no longer needed. Annie's grandparents slept in the room where they had once operated the loom. Annie's mother often used to say how she had woken up before five to the sound of the rumbling of the loom and had fallen asleep to its growling lullaby. The pay was poor and the toil backbreaking, but in that part of England in the late eighteen hundreds and early nineteen hundreds, the only choice was either weaving at home or working as a farm labourer.

There had been one brief period of prosperity towards the end of the nineteenth century, when the crinoline enjoyed again a brief flirtation with fashion, London dressmakers demanding haircloth for stiffening the wide petticoats and flounces, giving

Densbury home weavers much needed work. The fashion had soon faded, leaving the industry in the doldrums yet again.

"Can't you hear your pa and me up already and you still lying abed?" Her mother's voice carried the threat of a good thrashing if Annie did not make haste to get ready for work.

Annie leapt out of bed ready to pour the cold water in the ewer into the large china bowl, but nothing came out of it. She shuddered as she poked a finger in the top of the jug. "Oh no!" she muttered, her teeth chattering. "Frozen again." Her breath came out in white wispy clouds. Shivering in her flannel nightdress, she watched her breath hanging in the air. "Misty white, that's what Miss Turkentine would call that colour." All discomfort forgotten, she stood entranced by the beauty of the pattern her breath was creating in the cold morning air.

"Be quiet." Her sister Eileen, still only ten and at school, pulled the blankets over her head until just a few strands of her straight brown hair were visible. "You and your colours. I want to go back to sleep."

Annie sighed, "Don't forget it's your turn to feed the hens and clear out the grate in the kitchen." She pulled off her nightdress and threw it on a chair. The coldness of the water might have dictated how long her morning ablutions took, but her mother had drummed it into her that thoroughness was not to be sacrificed to speed. Her ankle-length brown skirt and long-sleeved blouse would be covered later by a huge shawl voluminous enough to keep out the worst of the weather. She tugged on her brown leather boots flinching as the realisation dawned that they were now too small and pinched her toes over her thick stockings A hasty flick through her shiny black curls and she was ready. " All the same I wish I was you."

She had loved her time at the Board School, doing sums, learning her times tables and practising handwriting, all of which came easily to her. She had dreams of going to the places with the strange-sounding names on the huge globe of the world which Miss Turkentine used to twirl as she pointed out countries and their capitals. Once she had asked Miss Turkentine if she had ever visited any of these foreign lands.

"Only in my thoughts," Miss Turkentine had replied. "That is all I need."

Annie had thought it a funny answer. One day, I will really go across the sea, she used to tell herself. But the greatest day had been when Miss Turkentine had given her some coloured chalks and told her to draw her favourite flower. Annie chose to draw a bluebell, as the only flowers she had ever seen were the wildflowers dotting the meadows and cornfields; nothing more exotic bloomed in the barren backyard of her cottage. Annie had never forgotten the look on her teacher's face, a look of wonderment bordering on veneration as the realisation dawned that she had a pupil with the seeds of artistic genius in her class. Each tiny detail of the intricate petals of the bluebell Annie had chosen to draw had been so skilfully outlined that the flower seemed real enough to pluck.

Miss Turkentine had struggled for a time to find the right words and then had said very quietly, "I have some paint and brushes at home. I'll bring them in for you to use."

Ever since that day, Annie had lived for Friday afternoons when she was allowed to do real painting while the rest of the class cut up bits of coloured paper or drew on their slates with chalk.

And now, she had to be up at five every morning to go with her mother up to Baythorpe Hall, a massive Victorian pile, home of the Gladwells. It had been constructed for size and show, its architect having no regard for the extra work his design demanded from the small army of women required to keep it clean and warm. After one week, her hands were red and sore. Annie gazed at them ruefully. Would these fat, red fingers ever be able to hold a paintbrush again? No good worrying about that, she told herself. All the dreams from her school days were lost, swallowed up in the huge, steaming coppers filled with the washing of the Gladwell household.

"Consider yourself lucky they agreed to take you on," her mother had said. Beatie Claydon had lived under the shadow of her husband's loss of a job for over a year and now it was happening. The new steam engines at the factory meant that fewer outworkers were needed and he was struggling to be taken on at the mill. Fearing her mother's wrath if she wasted any more time, Annie rushed downstairs to grab a slice of bread and a cup of tea.

"Hurry up and let's get going," her mother ordered. She pushed her wispy brown hair under the protection of her shawl. "Half past five we're due to start and if the kitchen isn't scrubbed down by six, we'll both get turned out."

Mother and daughter crept out of the cottage which was one of a long row in the centre of the town, just a few hundred yards from the mill which Will Gladwell's father had set up fifty years previously and which was the main employer of both men and women for miles around. As the two went out of the back door, the cold East Anglian wind lashed their faces with its icy whip. Annie copied her mother, pulling her scarf up over her mouth and bending her head down in order to protect her eyes, which were already streaming with tears in the cold winter's morning.

They passed the church surrounded by the neatly well-tended graveyard where generations had been laid to rest. This was the church of Saint Michael and All Angels, its all-embracing name defying any other church to attach itself to a celestial being. The chapels in the town pretended not to need outward signs of their connections with the Almighty. The Ebenezer Chapel and the Wesleyan Chapel were proud to boast their nonconformist roots. Regularly on Sunday, Sir Rowdley and his family came to worship and enjoy the slavish adulation of the congregation, which was their rightful due. In retaliation,

William Gladwell's father had joined the Nonconformists, liberally endowing an opulent chapel, known as the Old Independent, a touch of defiance in its title. Workers at the factory patronised the chapel, whilst local shopkeepers and other members of the lower middle classes worshipped at the church. Factory workers curtsied to the Gladwells on Sunday whilst the shopkeepers bowed to Lady Rowdley. As weavers, the Claydons attended chapel more out of a sense of self-preservation than concern for their immortal souls.

Beatie and Annie made their way to the outskirts of the town, passing the shops and finally reaching the wider street where the doctor, dentist and tradespeople lived with their families and one maid-of-all-work. It was hard going climbing this unmetalled road, which led out of the town and to the Gladwell estate. Neither Annie nor her mother spoke, still covering their faces against the biting wind and avoiding the deepest puddles and mud. It was almost half past five when, half frozen, the two ran the last few yards to reach the back door to the kitchen.

The housekeeper at Baythorpe Hall held on to her job by treating the domestics harshly, making sure they did not pause for a rest. As the live-in head of the domestic staff, she was treated with a degree of deference by the maids afraid for their livelihood.

"That Mrs Golding doesn't like me, you know that," Beatie warned her daughter, "so mind what you have to say when she's about."

"'Course I will, I'm not stupid," Annie told her mother.

"Less of that," her mother reminded her, "you've still got a lot to learn. Come in and wipe your feet."

Glad to be out of the cruel wind, the two entered the warm kitchen heated by a huge shiny black range. "I don't know where we'll start this morning," Beatie said. "They had those friends of theirs down from Norfolk this weekend, so there'll be more than ever to do."

"And a lot of filthy pigs they are," Annie said.

"Annie! Don't you let anyone hear you say things like that!" Beatie was shocked. "They're the gentry and our betters so don't you forget your place."

"Gentry or not, they're still pigs. I don't care what Pastor Briggs says at chapel about us knowing our place."

Beatie was troubled. Getting Annie taken on at the Hall had not been easy. She should have known that her daughter's rebellious spirit would not accept easily the daily grind of drudgery, working for people she considered no better than herself. Where she got such strange notions baffled Beatie. That was not what she had been brought up to think. We must accept our station in life as ordained by God, is what the good Pastor Briggs instilled into his congregation each Sunday. Why Annie failed to follow his teachings, was beyond her mother. There were times when she feared her daughter might easily take the road to damnation as Pastor Briggs called it. There was little joy in his weekly sermons, which consisted of listing all the activities certain to lead members of the congregation straight to the doors of Hell itself.

The housekeeper greeted them with a snapped, "Right, so you've decided to put in an appearance at last."

"We're early," Annie began to protest, swallowing what she meant to say as her mother's elbow dug into her side.

The comment did not go unnoticed by Mrs Golding. Her grey eyes narrowing in spite, she turned on Annie. "Now, let me see where you can start." She paused for effect. "I know, you can see to the washing. Some of the gentlemen who stayed were a little ill during the night. The linen will need swilling down and scrubbing with cold water outside before you can put it in the copper. That should put a stop to your insolence."

Annie gasped. She knew exactly what state the sheets would be in with the so-called gentlemen unable to get to the bathrooms on time. As she commenced the foul task allotted to her, she stared at the comfortable beds, deep carpets and huge wardrobes which gave the rooms such an air of luxury. And this is how my elders and betters behave, is it? she thought. I have to clear up their mess whilst they do no work.

"They should try getting up to a cold bedroom and using the privy at the bottom of the yard," she told her mother, as she passed by her in the kitchen.

"Hush!" Her mother paused in her scrubbing and knelt back on her heels. "Keep those thoughts to yourself before we both get the sack."

"What's all this time-wasting?" Mrs Golding had reappeared. "Haven't you finished the floor yet, Beatie Claydon? And you, Annie, make haste and take those sheets out to the pump and make sure you give them a good swilling."

Shivering and with hands numb with cold, Annie worked the pump, the icy water splashing her boots and soaking the hem of her skirt. She gathered up the dripping sheets and carried them through to the laundry room where the coppers needed to be filled and the gas lit to heat the water. Once washed, the sheets would then have to be put through the mangle. With a bit of luck, they might dry on the linen lines in the cellar. Her task would be to iron them before she went home late that afternoon.

"Come in here, love and dry yourself out," Betsy Palmer, the Gladwells' cook, called out to Annie. "Stand by the fire here before you catch your death of cold." She handed Annie a steaming mug of tea. "Here, drink this."

Annie hesitated. "What about Mrs Golding? I don't want me and Ma to get the sack."

Betsy put a comforting arm round Annie's shoulders. "Don't you worry, my pet," she assured the girl. "She's in with the mistress getting her instructions for the day. I always know when she's on her way down again. I just listen for the creak on the fifth stair."

Annie smiled. With nice Betsy Palmer to look after her, the work was just about bearable at Baythorpe Hall. Betsy took the empty mug from Annie and with a swift movement had washed it in the sink. She gave a wink and a nod to indicate that the dreaded Mrs Golding was on her way back. High-bosomed in black, her sparse grey hair tightly pulled back in a bun, Mrs Golding appeared.

"Now, girl, all the guest bedrooms need the grates emptying and the fires relaid. Miss Lavinia is still resting and her fire needs coal on it."

"Oh dear," Annie said, determined to say the right thing. "Is there no coal in the scuttle in her room? I'll take some for her at once."

The housekeeper rounded on her. "Impudent girl! Miss Lavinia doesn't see to fires herself. Get yourself up to her room at once!"

"I didn't mean—" Annie tried to explain, but was cut off with a sharp reminder to get on with what she was told to do.

The cook pointed to an outhouse some fifty yards from the kitchen door. "The coal's in there, dear. Fill a bucket and take it up the back stairs. Miss Lavinia's room is the third on the right. Don't cross her," she warned.

The coal, gleaming black nuggets, was piled high in the outhouse. Annie stood staring in astonishment at the luxury facing her. Their tiny fire at home was kept smouldering with dry twigs and coal dust. With the rolling countryside acres owned by one or two families and protected by gamekeepers, there was little chance of trespassing to cut a few logs to provide more warmth. Old man Farnel still walked with a limp, a sharp reminder of the shot still lodged in his thigh where a gamekeeper had shown him who owned the vast woodlands. Annie filled the bucket and headed back towards the house, clutching the heavy bucket with both hands before struggling up the narrow back stairs. She carefully closed the door to the stairs, terrified in case she made a noise and woke any of the family still in bed at ten-thirty. A red-patterned carpet covered the long corridor. Annie stood for a moment, letting her cold feet sink into the soft wool. She sighed as she closed her eyes, recollecting the hard floors at home.

A loud voice brought her back to reality. "For goodness sake, get a move on before Miss Lavinia freezes to death." A girl in her twenties, wearing the standard black dress with starched lace collar, was standing by the bedroom door. "How can I give Miss Lavinia a bath when her bedroom is as cold as charity?"

Annie was puzzled. Miss Lavinia wasn't a baby. She had understood her to be about eighteen years of age, so why could she not bath herself? Fancy letting the maid see her with no clothes on, she thought.

Lavinia was sitting up in bed, her dark hair spread out on the silk pillows. With her strong features and dark brown eyes set too closely together, she might have been considered to be quite handsome, but never pretty. The petulant expression terrified Annie. "What is happening in this house this morning?" Lavinia complained. She gestured towards the breakfast tray on her bedside table. "First the fire is nearly out and this tray has not been removed."

Still holding the bucket of coal, Annie stood transfixed. While attempting a curtsey, she dropped several lumps of coal on the pale blue carpet.

"Idiot!" Lavinia yelled. "Do my fire and get out!"

"Yes, ma'am," Annie whispered.

"And don't forget the tray," her maid reminded Annie.

The task of trying to carry the tray as well as the empty bucket was too much for Annie. She had nearly reached the door to the back stairs when the tray tilted sideways, tipping the fine bone china cups, saucers and plates into a heap onto the red carpet. "Oh, no," Annie gasped.

"No harm done," someone behind her said. "Nothing broken."

A young man in pyjamas and dressing gown came out of the bedroom nearest to Annie. "Allow me," he said and proceeded to replace the crockery on the tray. "Hmm," he said, pushing back the thick straw-coloured hair which had fallen over his eyes. "Now, I would say, young lady, that what you are trying to do is impossible. The tray or the coal bucket, but not the two together." His blue eyes crinkled in a smile. "You take the tray and I'll bring the bucket."

"You can't do that," Annie protested.

"Oh, you'd be surprised how clever I am at carrying buckets," he said. "I've never been known to drop one yet."

Annie giggled. "Are you Master Anthony?" she dared to ask.

He nodded. "You're new aren't you? What's your name?"

"I'm Annie, I've been here a week." Suddenly remembering what she was supposed to be doing, she told him to wait while she took the tray down to the kitchen. "Then I'll come back for the bucket."

"No, you won't. I'm just on my way to see Mrs Palmer. She should have made some of her wonderful shortbread biscuits this morning and I didn't have any breakfast."

Annie felt her heart sing. At least not everyone was nasty in this overfed, pampered household.

Anthony Gladwell was Will Gladwell's only son, seventeen and away at boarding school during term time. It was generally taken for granted that once his education was complete, he would spend his days with his father running the Gladwell factory. Rumour had it that young Anthony showed no interest in the weaving of cloth, and raised voices had already been heard coming from the library during that Christmas holiday.

"I do not want to do a law degree just so that I can come back here and spend my whole life in your factory," he had said.

"Yes, my factory," Will Gladwell had thundered at his son. "The factory which pays for your fancy education and lets you spend your holidays doing nothing while I turn out every morning."

The argument had not been resolved and there were those who wondered what would happen when Master Anthony's time at school was over.

Miss Lavinia presented no problems. At eighteen, she was tall and dark with her father's handsome features and already sought after by the young men in the locality. Her father had ambitions for her too. His hints that he expected her to marry into a titled family were unnecessary. Lavinia had inherited her father's driving ambition.

"That is exactly what I have in mind, Papa," she had told him. "I'm not throwing myself away on some country clodhopper."

"Good girl. At least I can rely on you to do what is expected of the daughter of someone in my position."

In his more sombre moments, Will Gladwell wished that his son and not his daughter had inherited his taste for wealth. Anthony spent all his spare time mooning around the estate, indulging his love for painting. Much to his chagrin, Will Gladwell had to admit that his son took after his impractical mother.

"All the same, Thora," he had told his wife, "he is my son and he will join me at the factory."

Thora's heart ached for her artistic, sensitive son. There would be battles ahead, but she would see that Anthony would not be tied to a desk with the ever present clanking of machinery and the smell of engine oil his daily companions.

It was dark by the time Annie and her mother were released from their day of drudgery. As they stepped through the muddy lane leading to their cottage, Annie told her mother about her chance meeting with the son of the house. "He was really nice, helped me with the tray and everything, not at all stuck up like Miss Lavinia."

Beatie gasped, her pale, ashen features reflecting her horror. She stopped dead, faced Annie and grabbed her shoulders. "Oh Annie, you must not get too familiar with young men in their position." Beatie Claydon could not explain her fears to her daughter. "Just do what you're told to do and no more. Speak when you're spoken to and remember, just a simple 'yes, sir' or 'no, sir' is all that is expected of you. If you have to do the fire in the young man's bedroom, do not look at him."

"But why not?" Annie frowned, not understanding her mother's concerns.

"Never mind why," she was told. "I shall be watching very carefully."

Although she would not be fifteen until the summer, Annie's figure held the promise of beauty to come. Her black hair framed her heart-shaped face with its ever-ready smile and twinkling dark blue eyes. Beatie feared for her daughter in the Gladwell household. There were plenty of rumours about maids being sent packing never to be seen again once their pregnancy began to show.

The house was strangely quiet when they arrived home. Fred Claydon was slumped in a chair at the kitchen table. "I tried the mat factory but work is drying up there as well," he said. "I'm beginning to think I'll have to go further, London perhaps, and send what I can home."

"Oh, no, Fred!" Beatie was aghast. Too many men had tried that and fared no better, often not seeing their families for months, if not years on end.

Fred raised his head, despair clouding his eyes. "I'll have another try at the Gladwell factory. It'll mean lining up at the factory gates with the rest and wait to see if I get picked out, but men are coming from miles around looking for work."

Beatie's eyes filled with tears. This quiet man with the gentle smile had won her heart when she was only seventeen. Still in his thirties, his thin drawn features made him appear like a man in his fifties. She knew who would be doing the picking out of the crowds of men outside the factory. Charlie Singleton, now the factory manager, had courted her in her younger days and was furious when she had turned him down and married Fred instead. Marriage to his plain sour-faced wife had not improved his temper. Spiteful by nature, he would enjoy rejecting Fred every morning.

"You know as well as I do what will happen tomorrow morning, if Charlie Singleton is doing the calling out."

Annie listened to the exchange. With no money coming in apart from what she and her mother earned cleaning up at Baythorpe Hall, the rest of the winter would be a cold and hungry one. Please let Pa get picked out, she prayed.

Chapter 2

Annie's fifteenth birthday on the last day in July was no different from any other day, except that she had to work even harder at Baythorpe Hall.

"There's going to be a big do," Betsy explained. "It's Miss Lavinia's birthday, she'll be nineteen the second week in August and there's going to be the biggest party ever."

"It's my birthday today," Annie said.

"Is it now? That's nice." The cook bent down to take some pastries out of the oven. "You'd better be off now then and see what Mrs Golding wants. She is frantic trying to make sure that the house is perfect for the great day, so mind you don't cross her."

Annie could hear the housekeeper's heavy footsteps echoing down the flagged passageway outside the kitchen. Whatever she did was sure to inflame the woman's venom. "I'm coming, Mrs Golding," she called out.

"So, this is where you're hiding," the woman spat out. "If we hadn't got so much to see to in the next few days, I'd give you your marching orders." She laid a hand on Annie's shoulder. "Now, listen to me. I want fires laid ready in every bedroom, all beds made up with the best linen. Mary will show you where everything is. Now, get along with you."

Lugging buckets of coal up the back stairs left Annie breathless and exhausted and there were still the beds to do.

"Get a move on!" Mary, the under-housekeeper was already bearing down on her laden with crisp linen sheets. She modelled her behaviour towards the young skivvies on that of her boss, Mrs Golding. "Do the six bedrooms on the first floor and then the six on the second floor," she told Annie.

"But I won't have time," Annie protested. "Me and Ma are supposed to go home soon."

Mary laughed, giving Annie a hearty poke in her chest making her flinch with pain. "I like that! You've got a lot to learn, you cheeky girl. You'll go home when the work is done and not before. Wait till I tell Mrs Golding."

"Oh, please, don't tell her I said that, Mary. I'll get the work done." Tears rolled down Annie's cheeks, especially when her mother came to find her. "I can't go home yet, Ma," she wept.

Her mother looked anxiously about her. "I can't help you, Annie. I'm not supposed to do any work involving the bedrooms. I'm only here to do the rough work."

Annie watched her mother go out of the kitchen and then returned to her tasks. All this for one spoilt girl's birthday while she spent hers making up beds for the guests. It was long past her tea-time when she finally managed to run down the drive along the lane and through the town to her home.

Her sister Eileen rushed to fling her arms round Annie's neck. "Quick, look what I've made – a real cake with currants in it."

"And here, a present from me and your Ma, love." Her pa handed her a little box beautifully wrapped in pink paper.

Annie opened it, her eyes widening in astonishment when she saw the delicate necklace with its tiny dark blue stones.

"To match your eyes," her pa said proudly.

"But it must have cost so much," Annie protested.

Fred Claydon grinned. "Not too much. Now that I've been taken on at the mill, things are a bit easier."

Her mother laughed. "Charlie Singleton fell over and broke his leg, so the day your dad lined up for work it was his old mate Zak who was in charge of hiring."

"And Mr Gladwell is so pleased he's put me in charge of one section," Fred told his daughter. "From now on, your ma can stay at home and run the house instead of slaving up at the Hall."

Annie's birthday treat suddenly lost its lustre. "Does that mean I've got to go there all by myself?"

Her parents exchanged knowing glances. "Well, you are fifteen now and you've been there a while, so you know what to look out for and that nice Betsy Palmer has promised to keep an eye out for you," Beatie said, trying to reassure her daughter.

Annie was not reassured. Who would protect her from some of Lavinia's friends who, encouraged by their hostess, found it amusing to openly mock her, calling her the little peasant girl? One of the men had put an arm round her touching her breasts, and laughed when she had cried and wriggled free. How could she tell her mother what was happening? She had told Betsy Palmer.

"Just the young gentlemen's ways, you mustn't take too much notice. They don't mean nothing." The horror in Annie's eyes prompted her to add, "And it doesn't do to complain neither. Do as I say, just move away quickly and get on with your work."

Sunday was her day off, a wonderful day of freedom. With her mother at home now, Annie did not have to spend the day doing the washing and cooking. Sunday mornings, they all dressed in the clothes specially kept for going to chapel and taken off again once they were home. Annie liked listening to the organ and singing the hymns, but Pastor Briggs terrified her with his talk of hell and damnation. The Gladwells sat in the front pew, ornately carved unusual for a nonconformist chapel. At the end of the service, Pastor Briggs, signalled to the congregation to stand. He then followed the family at a respectful distance out of the chapel. No one was allowed to move until they had left to be taken home in Mr Gladwell's latest acquisition, a huge Panhard, driven by his chauffeur.

After Sunday dinner and helping her Ma with the washing up, the time was hers to wander and do as she pleased, apart from the innermost desire she had always had since those magical Friday afternoons spent painting at school. Now, with no Miss Turkentine to bring her brushes, paint and a paper, her few leisure hours were filled with frustration. To be able to sit outside in the sunshine for just one precious hour and transfer the beauty of the country scenery to her paper would have compensated for the misery of her work at Baythorpe Hall.

"Why can't I have some of my wages for myself?" she asked her mother one Sunday. "I'd like to do some painting like I did for Miss Turkentine when I was at school. She said I ought to keep it up."

"Keep your wages? Whatever next! I don't know where you get your ideas, I really don't." Her mother shook her head. "It's all very well teachers putting ideas into your head. They can't marry, so they've no notion of what it's like trying to feed a family." She tutted loudly. "We need every penny of the money that comes into this house, so you can forget your fancy thoughts. I'll decide what you need and I'll get it."

Annie ran out of the house, her heart heavy with despair. The bleakness of the back yard reflected the desperation she felt. There was not even the colour of one tiny flower amongst the mud and the concrete. If one had tried to spurt up, pushing its way through the harsh surroundings, it would have withered in the presence of so much grief and poverty. Turning out of the centre of Densbury, she wandered up the hill passing the houses of the better-off tradespeople and that of Doctor Anstruther. Soon she had reached the fields surrounding Baythorpe Hall. At least here she could gaze on the green hedges and listen to the birds singing. She stooped to gather some wild violets almost hidden under the long grass bordering the hedge.

"Hello," a voice called. "I thought you would have had enough of us for one week."

Annie caught her breath, suddenly realising that she had strayed into the grounds of her employer. "Oh, I'm so sorry," She gathered up the hem of her dress ready to flee.

"Don't go." Anthony Gladwell was sitting at an easel. "Come here, Annie, tell me what you think of my efforts."

Shyly Annie peered over his shoulder. He had almost completed a watercolour of the view over the meadows by the river on the western side of the town. She screwed up her eyes and considered his painting.

"Well, speak up Annie, I won't bite your head off."

Annie stared at him for a moment. She hesitated, remembering what her mother had said about the behaviour of young gentlemen and what she was to do in order to avoid unwanted attentions. Surely she was safe enough out here in the field from whatever mysterious danger her mother was trying to protect her.

Anthony was smiling. He stood up and offered her his seat, a small wooden three-legged stool. "Come on, be honest with me."

Annie looked at the painting afraid to say anything which might make him angry.

"You don't think a great deal of it, do you?" he asked.

"It's not bad," she offered. "Quite nice, really."

Anthony threw back his head, letting out a mighty roar of laughter. "Annie, you're wonderful," he said. "Here, you have a go then."

She shrank back. "I couldn't do that, sir."

"Yes, you can and you can call me Anthony – at least while we're away from the house and Papa and everyone."

Annie took the paintbrush and drank in the scene ahead of her. She saw lush meadows sprinkled with the gold of buttercups, the garish yellow of dandelions, and the dark green river flecked with white and glinting in the sun where it escaped from the shadows of the trees lining its banks. Somehow, Anthony's painting seemed flat and lacking the joy of the scenery around them. For the next twenty minutes not a word was said, as Annie, now oblivious to everything, worked on transforming the young man's efforts. Anthony stared in astonishment at the finished painting.

"That is amazing! Annie, you're a genius. Where did you learn to paint like that?"

The sound of dogs barking and horses' hooves interrupted their innocent enjoyment. Miss Lavinia together with her male companion rode up to the pair.

"So this is what you get up to with the maids, is it? You are a sly young dog," the man said. He leant over intending to touch Annie's breast, but Anthony intervened himself between Annie and the Honourable Miles Fanshawe.

Annie recoiled in horror as the hooded eyes gazed intently at her. He reminded her of the picture of a snake Miss Turkentine had shown her class. She gave a little cry of terror as the man tried to push Anthony out of the way. "Let me know when you tire of her," he said, tapping the side of his nose and winking at Anthony.

Lavinia's dark eyes smouldered. "Wait till Papa hears about this." She prodded Annie with her whip. "You'll be getting the sack, you little trollop. Come along, Miles."

The two young artists watched as the horses disappeared into the distance.

"I'd better go." Annie was shaking with fear. "I can't afford to lose my job and if your pa gets rid of me, where else can I work?"

"Don't worry, Annie, I'll see Papa first and I'll make sure that Lavinia behaves herself. She was just a bit jealous if you ask me." Anthony's eyes mirrored his delight at the thought of his sister's jealousy of a housemaid.

"Jealous? Of me?"

"Well, Miles Fanshawe is a catch, being a peer of the realm and all that. Lavinia has rather set her heart on marrying into the blue bloods."

Annie was still frowning. "But what's that got to do with me?"

Anthony laughed, his blue eyes shining. "Didn't you notice how Miles was looking at you? You're so pretty, Annie, there isn't a man in England who couldn't fail to notice it."

"I think I'd better go home." Annie was beginning to feel uneasy at the turn the conversation was taking.

Anthony was immediately contrite. "Oh, Annie, you must think me an oaf. I didn't mean to offend you. Come on, sit down and show me what else is wrong with my painting." His smile was so open and honest that Annie accepted his offer.

"You're so lucky being able to paint whenever you want to," she said.

"Why lucky? I know you have to work up at the house, but what about your days off?"

Annie blushed and hung her head. How could she explain that there was not sufficient money in the Claydon household for luxuries such as paint, brushes and paper?

With sudden insight, Anthony said, "If it's materials, I've more than I can use. It will be back to school before long for me. There's no point in leaving them in my room when you could make use of them."

Annie leapt up. "Oh, no, I couldn't." An instinct of self-preservation warned her not to become beholden to the young Master Anthony. He might smile and be friendly, but what was to say he would turn out to be any different from his sister or, even worse, her suitor?

"Please," he pleaded. "A present from one friend to another." At eighteen, Anthony was still a gentle boy, in many ways younger than his years. First, he cleaned the brushes, wrapping them in a cloth he used to wipe the paint from his hands. The paper was then rolled up to make it manageable for Annie to carry. "There you are, Annie, you'll be able to paint all the time that I'm away and then, when I return, you can give me some more lessons."

The two laughed together at the thought of the fifteen-year-old housemaid giving the son of the house painting lessons.

"Make sure you're here when I come home again," he called out.

Annie watched him as he turned to wave running back towards Baythorpe Hall. "I wish he was my brother," she thought.

Her way home involved negotiating a rough meadow and crossing a stream before she reached the boundaries of the Hall. To take a short cut through the well-mown meadow near to the stables ran the risk of being seen by the grooms and possibly members of the family out riding. Not wishing to risk running into Lavinia and the Honourable Miles Fanshawe, Annie opted for the safe, longer route. She had just reached the stream when the darkening clouds brought the downpour which had been threatening ever since she had left Anthony. Gathering up the hem of her dress, she covered the precious paper he had given her. She told herself that no one would be out in such a storm and therefore no one would be shocked at the sight of her petticoats. With the rain blinding her eyes, she ran alongside the stream until it disappeared into a culvert just beyond the narrow bridge.

The sound of horses' hooves made her catch her breath.

"Whoa!" Miles Fanshawe reined in just ahead of her. "I say, Lavinia, take a look at this. There's Anthony's little maid showing off her drawers."

Still clutching the hem of her dress to her waist to protect Anthony's precious gift, she cowered against the wall.

"What can you expect from her kind?" Lavinia called out, deliberately riding as close as she could to Annie, splattering her dress with mud. "Wait till I tell Mama."

Their laughter rang in her ears as the two rode off in the direction of Baythorpe Hall.

Cold and wet, Annie ran the rest of the way, praying that she would not meet friends or neighbours of her parents. Her dark curls clinging to her forehead and tears mingling with the rain on her cheeks, she wished a hundred times over that she had not stopped to paint with Anthony Gladwell.

"Annie! Whatever has happened to you?" Joe Langmead, who worked with her father at the mill appeared. "Here, child, let me put my coat round you before you catch your death. Thank God I've found you. I just dropped in to see your pa and he told me that you were out so late, he was beginning to worry."

Her teeth chattering, Annie was in no position to protest. Besides, Joe Langmead had all the confidence of a twenty-year-old who had had to fend for himself and his widowed father ever since he had been a small boy. It did not occur to him that Annie would shrink from contact with him. In his eyes, she was the little girl of a workmate and needed his care and protection. His masculine good looks made him stand out from his peers and, if he could have had the pick of any of the girls in Densbury, so far not one had managed to capture his attention. High cheekbones and a strong jawline were not features generally associated with Densbury men, whose round, indeterminate faces made one seem very like another. At well over six feet, his height contrasted greatly with the short, square-shouldered East Anglian men. They would have been surprised to see him suddenly swing the girl up into his arms as if she were a baby and run with her to her house.

Warm and safe, Annie was only too relieved to be delivered to her back door.

"What on earth has happened? Just look at your dress and your boots, child." Beatie Claydon stared at her daughter, whose best Sunday dress was not only soaking wet, but daubed with red, blue, green and yellow paint where it wasn't covered in mud. "Where have you been?"

"I found this little waif by the bridge up at Baythorpe Hall," Joe explained, "so I thought I'd better bring her home."

Beatie seized her daughter by the ear. "You little madam! Haven't I told you to keep away from there. You go there when you're working and no other time. So what were you doing today?"

"Painting with Master Anthony," she whispered.

Before her shocked mother could respond, Joe produced the painting materials given to Annie by Anthony Gladwell and went to hand them over to her. "Here you are, all safe and dry," he said.

Her father lunged forward ready to take them and hurl them into the fire. "You don't take presents from the likes of him," he ground out, furious that his daughter had somehow demeaned herself. The fear of what young high-class men could do with naïve country girls remained unspoken between husband and wife.

Joe carefully hung on to the articles. "Well, I for one would very much like to see what Annie can do with such a fine gift. I hear the young man is off to school again in a week or two, so he won't have any use for them and it seems a pity to waste them. Besides, we get little enough from the likes of him and his family."

It grated on Annie hearing Joe Langmead mocking Anthony's generosity, but at least he was holding her painting materials well out of her father's grasp.

Her parents looked at one another and nodded. "Well, so long as he's not about, I don't suppose it can do any harm," her mother conceded, "but next time you go painting on your day off, you keep off the Gladwell land and take your sister with you."

Eileen let out a wail. "Do I have to? She'll be hours just painting and I want to play with Gladys." She flinched as her mother raised a warning hand to her.

"How about if I go with Annie?" Joe suggested. "I'd be happy to take a book and keep an eye on her, a sort of stand-in uncle, if you like, Fred?"

Annie wasn't sure what a stand-in uncle was, but at least it meant that she kept her painting materials. Looking up to the huge man towering over her father, she knew that she had a champion who would protect her against the detested Lavinia Gladwell and the Honourable Miles Fanshawe.

From that day, whenever the weather was fine on a Sunday afternoon, Joe would call and escort Annie to wherever it was she had chosen for her painting session. Although his friendship with her father had its roots in their work together at the factory, he became a frequent visitor to the house, often staying to Sunday dinner. He had also taken to sitting next to the family at chapel.

One Sunday afternoon, totally engrossed in trying to decide which shade of green best reflected the rolling meadow, she did not hear Joe's question.

"Why don't you give one of your pictures to your ma and pa?" Joe repeated. He had raised his eyes from the book he was reading and was carefully appraising Annie's efforts.

Annie blushed. "They're not good enough for that, Joe," she protested.

Joe was quiet for a moment, then took hold of Annie's hands in his. "Little girl," he said, "one of these days, you are going to be famous. Talent like yours can't stay hidden. I'd like to have one of your paintings framed and then see what your ma and pa have to say."

It was late in September when Joe turned up at the house with a large paper parcel under his arm. He placed it on the kitchen table. "There you are, Mrs Claydon, a present for you, for all your nice dinners."

Beatie stared at the young man. People in their situation seldom gave or received gifts. Slowly she unwrapped the parcel, taking care not to waste any of the string tied round the brown paper. Both the string and paper might come in useful. "A painting, Joe?" She stared at the watercolour landscape in astonishment. "We can't take this, can we Fred?"

Her husband gently touched the painting. "I don't understand, Joe. How could you afford anything like this?"

"You mean we can keep it?" Beatie asked her husband. She looked at the bare walls of the cottage. "I've always wanted some pictures, but there was always something else more important to spend the money on."

Joe winked at Annie. "Well, you'd better get this young daughter of yours to do some more for you."

"Our Annie did this?" There was a moment's silence as the tears ran down Beatie's cheeks.

"Why are you crying, Ma?" Annie asked. "You're not angry, are you?"

How could she tell her daughter why she was crying? Beatie was weeping with despair as she saw Annie's life mapped out for her already. Hard work for little reward, marriage and children with barely enough money coming in to survive on. There would be nothing to spare for luxuries such as art. She ran to hug her daughter, looking over her shoulder at her husband as she did so. After years of marriage, words were not necessary.

Chapter 3

Annie found life at Baythorpe Hall even harder with Lavinia Gladwell always ready to find fault and complain about her to Mrs Golding. When the bell in Lavinia's room was heard to ring, its tinkling tones taking on the venom of its operator, the housekeeper ran up the stairs to see what the problem was.

Lavinia was sitting up in bed, a large white shawl around her shoulders. "Just look!" she screamed. "That wretched girl! She's let my fire go out again. I don't know why we have to keep her on. I shall tell Mama."

"I'll have a word, you can be sure," the woman answered, glad of the opportunity to berate the young housemaid, who besides having too much to say for herself, actually looked her betters straight in the eye instead of keeping her head down with the correct degree of deference.

Annie was shocked when the housekeeper threatened to have her wages docked if any more such incidents occurred. "But the fire was burning brightly when I went in while Miss Lavinia was having her breakfast. Perhaps she accidentally spilt some of her tea in it."

A swift cuff round the ear reminded Annie sharply that she would do better to keep her suspicions to herself in the future. If only she could get to the root of why the girl hated her so much. Annie knew that her work could not be faulted, paying special attention as she did for everything concerning Miss Lavinia. Perhaps it was as Anthony had said; Miles Fanshawe had been just a little too fulsome in his praise of Annie's beauty, or could it be that she resented her brother's friendliness with a housemaid?

"If we didn't need you for the spring cleaning, I'd send you packing right now," the woman told her. "We'll make a start in the morning. All the carpets from the bedrooms have to be taken up and laid out on the grass and beaten. I'll get Alfie to give you a hand."

Even with the help of Alfie, one of the under-gardeners, dragging the heavy carpets, thick with dust down the stairs and onto the lawns, was almost more than Annie could manage. The thin, badly nourished Alfie had barely enough strength to be of much use, muttering angrily that this was women's work and that he should not have been asked to do it.

After three days of the backbreaking work, Annie was in no mood to listen to his whining. "One more word from you and I'll go and ask Mrs Golding to send me a real man to help instead of a useless idiot like you."

With that, Alfie picked up the wooden beaters and set about thumping the carpets until the air was filled with dust, leaving the two of them gasping and choking. "You asked for it," he growled at Annie.

Night after night, Annie barely had the strength to crawl home. There was no maid to run a bath to help ease her aching back. She had to be content with carrying jugs of lukewarm water up to her bedroom, where her sister Eileen gave her a hand to wash the dust out of her hair.

"I don't know why you put up with them all up there," Eileen said, as she tried to untangle the knots in Annie's thick black hair. "When I leave school, I'm going to work in Miss Witton's wool shop. She gave me some wool and told me to knit a little jacket to see what I could do. And guess what! She was so pleased she has promised to take me on. I'll be able to knit baby clothes and things for her to sell as well." She beamed at the prospect of being able to spend her days doing the very things she adored. "So why can't you leave and go somewhere else?"

Annie let out a huge sigh. "If only I could, but I'd have to ask Ma first and be sure of another place to work."

She dared not admit to Eileen what she dared not admit to herself, that she hankered after Anthony Gladwell and lived in hope of seeing him at the house during his holiday. His blue eyes and friendly smile brought summer sunshine to even the greyest of days. He was due back from Oxford for Easter. With a bit of luck, Annie thought, they might be able to resume their painting, so long as they kept out of Lavinia's way. Nice as Joe Langmead was, he did not have Anthony's ability to converse with her on the one thing that made her life tolerable, namely her art. Besides, he was older, too much of a grown-up, unlike Anthony. On the Sunday afternoons when Joe sat with her, he read a book while she painted, making the occasional comment, "That's pretty, Annie, it looks very real." His earlier enthusiasm for her talents had been superseded by a casual tolerance, as if he thought her zeal would evaporate as being part of a childish dream. He would then return to lighting up a cigarette and immersing himself in his book. It was so different when she and Anthony were together. They would discuss the merits of which shade of ochre or umber to use to create a particular effect, or whether they had captured the particular light that day; that was what she missed. With a pang she recollected how they could laugh together. In comparison, Joe was so serious.

Returning to work on Monday brought her back to the reality of her situation. There would be no further day-dreaming about the idyllic hours spent with Anthony. Once the carpets had been beaten, there were still the curtains to hang out and beat, all the corners and cupboards to be washed and dusted, windows thrown open and thoroughly cleaned until the stale odours of winter had been thoroughly eradicated. Annie dealt with the insults and the exhortations to work harder in the hope that

Anthony would soon be back. Once the school holidays were here, she would be able to creep up to their favourite spot from where they could look down on the undulating countryside surrounding Densbury.

"You need not prepare Master Anthony's room," Mrs Golding told her. "He is spending Easter in Florence with some friends."

"He's not coming back at all?" Annie's voice trembled with disappointment.

"No, but that has nothing to do with you," the woman snapped, enjoying the girl's look of anguish. "I'm not the only one here to notice you've got ideas above your station. Just you watch your step," she threatened. Lavinia had already confided her suspicions to Mrs Golding. "In my opinion, it's high time you were put in your place, Annie Claydon."

For once, Annie was too distressed to say anything in her defence. So Anthony would be in Italy, no doubt visiting the art galleries they had spoken of during their painting sessions. He had told her of the masterpieces in the Uffizi in Florence, filling Annie's heart with the longing to see them first hand. He must have known all along that it would be just a matter of time before he went to Italy and that Annie could never in her whole life have enough money to travel further than to the nearest town to Densbury. The injustice of their vastly differing situations struck her so hard that she had the sudden urge to run away and never stop running. If only I could escape, she wished. She made up her mind to talk to her father that evening about the prospect of finding employment as a machinist in the factory, where the money was better and she would be free of Lavinia's malice and her henchwoman. Mrs Golding.

Will Gladwell, always keen to expand his business, had long recognised that there was profit to be made by not only weaving the cloth, but also by making up the finished garments. With this expansion at the back of his mind, he had bought up several acres of land surrounding the mill. The factory housing the looms had been designed with high walls, whose windows set high up on the walls and in the roof let in maximum daylight. The brick walls with no windows allowed for an extension to be added at minimum cost with no loss of free lighting.

Early on, before the turn of the century, he had begun in a small way by training machinists to sew simple smocks for farm labourers and fishermen out of the rough fustian woven in the mill and by outworkers. As a good businessman with an eye to profit, he had first checked the colours required by the different trades. The fishermen were the most particular, wanting reds, blues and greens to distinguish one crew from another. As time went by, he had progressed to more sophisticated materials – finer wools to be made into men's suits and sold in the large London shops. His machinists had to be trained to a high standard to meet with the quality demanded by such establishments, but Will Gladwell, far-sighted as always, engaged skilled cutters and tailors, thus making the work of the women machinists less liable to be faulty and wasteful of material.

"I know I could soon learn," Annie pleaded with her father. "If Hettie Farlie can do it, I'm sure I could." Poor Hettie Farlie had been the butt of the other pupils' jibes at school, rarely a day passing when she did not have to stand in the corner with the dunce's cap on.

Her mother was not so sure. "But that would mean leaving the Gladwells at the Hall. I don't think they would like you walking out on them. What if you leave and then they won't have you at the factory?"

It was on the tip of Annie's tongue to tell her that Lavinia Gladwell was always seeking ways to be rid of her, but explaining to her mother that Lavinia was jealous of a maid's friendship with her brother would have resulted in a major row and possibly a smacked face.

"I'll have to talk it over with your father," was as much as Annie was going to get that evening, but at least it was not a downright refusal.

Fred Claydon's response was a measured, "Leave it with me."

Annie flung her arms round his neck. "Oh, does that mean you'll get me in?"

"Now, now, my girl," he said, smiling, gently unwinding her arms from strangling him, "I can't promise anything, but I'll have a word with Zak tomorrow. His missus works in the machining room. If they need a learner, she might be able to take you on."

Annie could hardly sleep that night at the prospect of getting away from Miss Lavinia and her constant carping and ill-will. To sit at a machine sewing nice clean clothes all day instead of the relentless drudgery of the housework at Baythorpe Hall, was her idea of a working heaven. With a jolt, it struck her that she would not hear news of Anthony's visits home. She would just have to guess the dates of his holidays.

Mrs Golding was not so pleased later that week when Annie broke the news that she was leaving to take up another position. "You ungrateful girl. All these hours I've spent training you as a housemaid and now you throw it all back in my face. How dare you!"

When the time came for Annie to leave, she waited in the kitchen for Mrs Golding to bring her the wages owing to her. The woman finally arrived an hour after Annie was supposed to finish and thrust a few coins into Annie's outstretched palm. Annie stared at the money. Even without counting every coin, she could see that it was barely half of what she was owed. "I think you've made a mistake, ma'am," she said, trembling.

The woman bared her crooked, yellowing teeth in a triumphant grin. "There are deductions for breakages," she told Annie gleefully. "Miss Lavinia tells me that you have dropped her breakfast china on countless occasions, but not wishing to be the cause of you getting the sack, she did not report your shortcomings. Now that you are leaving of your own accord, she felt it her duty to tell me just how much you owed the household."

Annie gasped. "That's not true, I've never broken a single cup or saucer. Miss Lavinia is mistaken."

A stinging slap across the cheek was the response. "Get out, you lying, ungrateful girl!"

Annie turned and ran. The loss of a few shillings was nothing compared with the feeling of release she experienced. Never again would she have to put up with Miss Lavinia's spite. A sudden pang of unhappiness made her stop short. Leaving employment at the Hall would mean that the happy afternoons painting with Anthony would never be repeated, even if Anthony were to spend his holidays at home in the future. Mrs Golding's final farewell still rang in her ears. "Come here again and we'll set the dogs on you!"

Although Annie could not define her feelings at that moment, underlying the relief at escaping from Lavinia and the mean-minded housekeeper, was a determination to seek revenge. "One day," she told herself, as she fled from Baythorpe Hall.

If Annie thought that, by working as a machinist in the factory, life would be easier, she soon found that there were hard taskmasters there too. By speaking up for her, Zak's wife had been instrumental in having Annie taken on as a learner, but she soon let Annie know that nothing less than perfection would do. The first two weeks went by in a haze as she struggled to operate the huge sewing machine. The cloth she was working on seemed to have a mind of its own, constantly slipping out from under the needle and causing her to undo much of the machining already done. There were times when she wished she had not been so hasty in leaving Baythorpe Hall.

"Any mistakes and I'll get the blame for them, so pay attention." Zak's wife Emmy was constantly at her shoulder prodding and criticising. "That seam isn't straight, Annie, keep your eye on every stitch," she told her.

It was not always easy when her eyelids started to droop after ten hours spent staring at the tiny stitches. The women had to be at their machines and ready to start on the dot of six. Lateness by even one minute was punished by a deduction in wages. There was a break for breakfast at eight, but this was missed by the mothers who had to dash out to the alley next to the factory. There, groups of grannies or little girls would be waiting, whatever the weather, until the mothers appeared to breastfeed their squalling infants. Their next feed would be at twelve-thirty when there was an hour's break for dinner.

As a liberal-minded employer, Will Gladwell had had constructed a covered area for nursing mothers, so that they and their babies were, to some extent, protected from the worst of the weather. Conditions in his factory were no worse and certainly better than in most of the similar places of employment for miles around. He took pride in being a kind but firm employer, even going so far as to invite inspectors in to see the standards enjoyed by his women machinists.

What was lacking was any kind of ventilation. With the windows placed so high, the summer months were unbearable. Annie remembered with some nostalgia the afternoons on the lawns of Gladwell Hall when she and Alfie had beaten the dust out of the carpets. At least she got to see the grass and flowers, filling her imagination with pictures of what she would paint on the next Sunday outing chaperoned by Joe. Here her days were spent staring at straight seams. If she raised her eyes for a moment, she saw herself imprisoned by plain, brick walls, while her eardrums were aching with the constant whirring of dozens of machines. Worst of all, was the assault on her nostrils of the smell of engine oil, which often filled her with nausea and which lasted long after she had run home.

One evening in early August soon after her sixteenth birthday, she arrived home to find her parents standing shoulder to shoulder in front of the fireplace in the living room. Unspoken, angry accusations were in the air. Her father was holding a picture postcard in his hand.

"Well, what is the meaning of this?" he demanded.

Annie shook her head. "What is it?"

"This postcard is from Anthony Gladwell. It's," he struggled to go on, "it's a picture of, well… I hardly dare say it in front of your mother… a man with no clothes on, so you'd better tell me what is going on."

In spite of never having seen her father so angry, Annie was overjoyed that Anthony had written to her. "Oh, let me see it." She rushed forward to take it from his hands.

"You silly, deceitful girl," her mother said, intercepting the card and tearing it into fragments as Annie went to take it. "Absolutely disgusting, it is. I don't know what Pastor Briggs will have to say. I wouldn't be at all surprised if the postman doesn't tell him what sort of unspeakable rubbish he had to put through our door." By now she was shaking with rage.

"How dare you have anything to do with that family!" she yelled. "Haven't I told you often enough that men in his station of life are not to be trusted with the likes of girls such as you?"

Annie was at a loss to understand her mother's anger. "But I didn't know anything about this. I haven't seen or heard of him for months, not since I started working at the factory." So Anthony was once again abroad; that was the reason she had not seen him on the rare occasions she had ventured as far as the boundaries of Baythorpe Hall in the hope of seeing him.

"Hmm, that's as maybe," her father conceded, "but you have to promise me that you will not attempt to contact him. This card is enough to show me and your Ma that he has no respect for you. Looking at this shows exactly what his intentions towards you are. You must keep away from him. Is that understood?"

Annie's eyes were swimming in tears at the injustice and cruelty of her situation. She nodded, her misery compounded seeing the torn postcard in the empty grate, symbolic of her shattered dreams. It was hours later as she was undressing for bed, that her younger sister Eileen whispered, "Look what I've got." She delved into her pinafore pocket and produced the fragments of the postcard. "I knew that you were sad about what Ma did with it, so I waited till Ma and Pa were out of the way. I found these bits in the grate. They're not too dirty. If we're careful, we can put them together."

Annie hugged her sister. The two of them had to stifle their giggles as they attempted to form a whole from the scraps laid out on the counterpane. The finished product was as her parents had said, the picture of a nude man.

"Do you think we ought to be looking at this?" Eileen asked, eyes wide open, avidly taking in all the details of the male anatomy. "No wonder Ma and Pa were so cross."

None of the details had escaped Annie either, but she was keen to read what Anthony had to say.

"This is a picture of a sculpture done by the famous artist and sculptor, Michelangelo. His statue of David is the most inspiring thing I have seen in Florence. I wish you could be here to enjoy all the wonderful art. I hope to be painting with you again soon."

He had signed his name in full, so there was no mistaking who had sent the card.

"He must have gone to Florence again," she mused. "Lucky Anthony." Having promised her parents that she would not see him during the rest of August, she was filled with misery. In any case, if he would not be returning from Italy that summer, there was no chance at all of a meeting. In her mind Annie could picture Anthony, his eyes bright with eagerness, bringing to life with his wonderful gift for words, the paintings and sculptures he would be seeing in Florence and Rome. With a feeling of emptiness in her heart which only Anthony and his friendship could fill, she resigned herself to a summer of bleak monotony.

"I'd better sneak downstairs and throw the pieces back in the grate," Eileen, ever the practical one suggested. She took one last glance at the postcard, still assembled on their bed. "Funny, isn't it?" she remarked. "I never knew that boys had all those bits and pieces."

"Hush!" Annie told her, "or we'll both be in real trouble."

Her knowledge of biology had increased since working at the factory with older girls and women. A source of some amusement to the older girls was the huge drum placed in the centre of the weaving shed, specifically for the men to use as a urinal. The chemicals thus produced were an invaluable and free source of the sizing needed for the woven materials. One or two of the girls had taken a peek through the open doors one day and had come back with exaggerated descriptions of what they had seen. It was not long before Zak's wife Emmy had given them all a good telling-off and threatened to report them if they tried that again.

"One word from me to Charlie Singleton and you'll all be looking for other jobs."

As the manager, Charlie Singleton's word was law. Will Gladwell relied on him to keep the workforce in order.

The long, hot summer was further marred by her grandmother's illness. Trudging home after a long day spent machining in the airless workshop, Annie had just reached the end cottage in the row where she lived. A girl she recognised as Isabelle Anstruther, the doctor's seventeen-year-old daughter was standing beside a pony and trap holding the reins. She gave Annie a shy smile. Annie was a little nonplussed at this show of friendliness, but returned the greeting. Isabelle was the only daughter of the town's widowed doctor and spent term times away at boarding school, returning home during the holidays. She was often seen accompanying her father on his home visits to patients.

There was something strange about father and daughter, neither having friends in the town or being members of the chapel or church. In fact, nobody called him out on Sunday mornings, as he was never in Densbury. Rumours abounded concerning his religious affiliations, but as he was such a respected doctor, little attention was paid to them.

"I've seen you painting on Sunday afternoons," Isabelle said, blushing to the roots of her burnished red hair. "You must be very clever."

Annie hung her head shyly. "It's just that I like painting and Sundays is the only day I have."

"Could I come and watch you?" Isabelle asked. Seeing Annie's surprised look at this request, she said, "I'm sorry, I shouldn't have asked. It is very rude of me."

Annie was overwhelmed at these overtures of friendship from a girl who was way above her station. She laid a hand on Isabelle's arm. "Please, it would be very nice. You could help me." Isabelle was certain to have the benefit of good art teaching at her school.

Isabelle smiled. "I will." She nodded anxiously towards Annie's house. "I think you ought to go and see how your Granny is. Papa is with her now."

Annie gasped. "Oh no! Granny's not ill, is she?" She had assumed quite wrongly that the doctor was at a neighbour's cottage.

She flung open the back door to find her mother distraught. Doctor Anstruther was talking quietly to her in the kitchen. "These tablets will help to ease the pain and she will sleep a great deal. If there is any change, send for me at once."

"But what is wrong?" Annie demanded. "Granny has been fine, hasn't she?"

The doctor shook his head. "The tumour is very advanced. She must have suffered without telling anyone. I'm sorry, my dear, there really is nothing more we can do."

Annie raced up the stairs to her Granny's room. Her grandfather was sitting beside the bed, holding his wife's hand and talking in gentle soothing tones.

He placed a finger on his lips. "Ssh," he warned, "Granny's not too sharp today."

Annie knelt by the bed. "Oh, Granny," she said, "why didn't you tell us you weren't well?" Seeing the frail old lady with her yellow, parchment-like skin and dull eyes, filled Annie with remorse. Why had they always taken it for granted that Granny was well just because she had never complained?

"Don't you listen to what the doctor has to say," she admonished her granddaughter. She struggled to raise herself up from the pillow. "Fetch me that box, the one in the bottom of the cupboard, dear."

Annie opened the cupboard door of the huge walnut wardrobe which contained the few pitiful possessions of the old couple. A large box tightly bound with yellowing string was tucked away in the back corner.

"That's the one."

Annie carried it over to the bed, placing it on the patchwork bedcover. "It's a bit dusty, Granny."

"Never mind that, just open it."

It was a struggle to undo the tiny knots, but finally Annie succeeded in lifting up the lid. Inside were bundles of rolled up papers.

Her grandmother lay back on the pillow and sighed. "You're the only one who would understand what all this is about," she managed to utter. "Undo them."

Annie unrolled one of the papers and gasped. "Granny!"

"I used to do them before I married," she explained. "I couldn't afford paint, so they're all pencil sketches." A faraway look brightened the misty eyes. "I loved drawing, but we hadn't any money and I always had to work. I kept them in case the day would come when I might do some more." She looked at them wistfully. "That day never came."

Annie studied the beautiful line drawings of the church, the market square and main street. There were also some wonderful life-like drawings of faces well known to Annie.

"I can't believe it," she whispered. "Oh, Granny, you're so clever. I'll treasure them always."

So that was where her love of painting had come from. Annie felt suddenly guilty. At least she was able to buy a few paints and spend her Sunday afternoons with Joe doing what she liked doing best. Poor Granny, working hard and dreaming of time for leisure which was denied to her all through her life.

"You make sure you do what I couldn't. Husband and children can wait." With thin bony fingers, she clutched Annie's hand with unexpected strength. "Don't waste the gift the good Lord has seen fit to give you. Promise me you'll choose the right path in life."

"I will, I will!" Annie promised. "You'll be proud of me."

"I know I will," was the whispered response. "Good girl."

It was just a week later that the funeral of her grandmother was held at the chapel. There was a brief service in the chapel and later at the graveside. Annie wept as the coffin was lowered into the grave. Her poor grandmother, she thought, half-starved and slaving all her life to raise and care for her family, and yet dreaming all the time of expressing her visions in art. How she would have been mocked if she had dared to share her feelings with her husband or acquaintances.

As the life of the household gradually assumed its normal pattern, Annie continued to meet Joe on Sunday afternoons. Although Isabelle had asked if she might join her, Annie had not really expected her to do so, and was surprised to see her appear at three o'clock one Sunday. She was dressed in a floral muslin dress and was wearing a wide-brimmed straw hat trimmed with matching colours. "To keep away the freckles," she explained later. "I hate my red hair. I wish I had lovely black curls like you."

Joe glanced up from his book, suspicion clouding his dark eyes. He leapt to his feet, pulling off his cap as he did. "Good afternoon, miss," he said, raising an enquiring eyebrow in Annie's direction.

"Isabelle! You've come! This is Joe, my pa's friend. He looks after me when I'm out here."

Joe scowled at the reference to Annie's father. "I thought I was your friend too, Annie," he whispered, but not softly enough.

Isabelle was swift to pick up the hostility in his tone and turned as if to retreat. "I just thought I'd like to see Annie's pictures before I go back to school."

"Come on then." Annie took her hand firmly and sat her down in front of her easel. For the next half hour, the two girls were engrossed in conversation, Annie entranced by Isabelle's stories of the art mistress at her school, who let the girls do exactly as they pleased whilst she carried on with her own masterpiece. The corners of Annie's mouth turned down in a wistful moue. "How lovely to be able to paint all day long without a care in the world. Your art teacher is very lucky."

"Lucky?" Isabelle repeated. "You ought to be there. We really are a terrible class." She became serious. "You mean you want to take up art as a profession?"

Annie didn't understand what her new friend meant by profession. "All I know is that I want to be a painter." She lay down her brush with a flourish. "There! I've said it."

Joe stirred uneasily, no longer engrossed in his book. He frowned, suspicion forging deep furrows between his eyes as he listened to the two girls.

"And what about you?" Annie asked. In her heart she had already foreseen Isabelle's future. Surely Isabelle would marry one of her father's young colleagues and enjoy a comfortable life as a doctor's wife.

Isabelle leaned forward and lowered her voice. "I want to be a doctor, but Papa is against the idea, doesn't think it is very ladylike."

Overawed at the idea of her friend becoming a doctor, Annie stared in amazement. Her Granny's words came back to her. She gave Isabelle a little prod with the dry end of her brush. "You know what my gran said to me, Isabelle? She said I was to follow the path that I wanted to and that I wasn't to get married and have children until I'd done just that."

Isabelle's face lit up. She gave a little dance of joy. "Then the two of us will go to London and make our fortune, just like Dick Whittington. You'll be a famous artist and I will be a doctor, but for women and children only."

Joe's eyes darkened with anger as he saw this vibrant, yet earnest girl fill Annie with impossible ambitions which, if she were to attempt to realise would take her far from Densbury and him. He interrupted their light-hearted chatter with a reminder that it was time for Annie to get back home. Unsmiling he began to dismantle the easel, with a, "Come along now, Annie."

Afraid that his ill-concealed bad temper would put Isabelle off, Annie made her promise to come the following Sunday. "Don't take any notice of Joe. He's being a bit of a grumpy old uncle today."

"Less of that, young lady," Joe told her. "Just you mind your manners."

He stood for a moment watching the older girl disappear in the direction of Belfyon Heights where the doctor lived. "I can't make you out at all, Annie," he said, his rugged jawline set in a determined line. "First you have to go and make a fool of yourself over that Anthony Gladwell and now you want to mix with the likes of that young miss." He placed two hands firmly on Annie's shoulders. "I'm warning you for your own good about her. There are things I could tell you concerning her and her father, but they're best left unsaid."

Her cheeks flaming, Annie recoiled. "Why is it that first Pa and Ma say who I can talk to? And now you're even worse." Tears spilled down her cheeks at what she felt was interference in her innocent friendships. "Can't I have any friends of my own?"

Joe took a deep breath. "I'm sure your parents have explained to you about the young Gladwell lad, but this is different. You'll have to take my word that Isabelle Anstruther will bring nothing but trouble."

They walked home in silence, Annie puzzling over Joe's warning. How could Isabelle bring her harm? She was just a lonely girl in need of a friend, Annie decided. What she did not understand was why a girl in her position did not bring home friends in her own walk of life.

As she took her paintings up to her bedroom, she could hear the voices of Joe and her father in earnest discussion out in the backyard. She peered out of the window hoping to hear what was being said. All she saw were the heads of the two men close together. The voices were too low for her to catch even the gist of the conversation, but she guessed it must have been very serious from the manner in which her father shook his head from time to time.

All through tea, her mother attempted to keep up a flow of natural conversation. "Guess what, your grandpa is off to stay with Auntie Clara in High Stoughton. Won't that be nice for him?" She did not have to add that he was missing his wife so much, that he could not bear to sleep in the same bed he had shared with her for over forty years.

Annie's mind was still so filled with what Joe had said to her earlier about Isabelle that she did not pay attention to her mother's item of news.

"Annie! Are you paying attention to what your mother is saying?" her father asked. Your grandpa is leaving us."

"I'm sorry, Grandpa." Annie turned to speak to the old man. "Will we be able to come and see you?" It was with a shock that she realised that he was looking old and ill since his wife's death. "Aunt Clara will look after you, won't she?" Her agonised plea had everyone laughing.

"Don't you worry about me," the old man said. "I intend to be here for your wedding whenever that might be."

Annie's pink cheeks creased and dimpled as she giggled at the idea. "Granny said I wasn't to get married until I'd done all the things I wanted to do first." She did not add that she intended to remember those words uttered on her grandmother's deathbed and that a promise made to someone dying was sacred.

Still unspoken was the subject of conversation between Joe and her father. "Isabelle Anstruther came to see me paint this afternoon," Annie blurted out. "She's really nice."

"That's as maybe," her father said. "What would she want with you? A doctor's daughter and you working in a factory. There's something funny about her. I mean, why hasn't she got friends of her own sort? It's not normal, her father being a doctor and all that."

Conscious of the fact that she had to tread warily, Annie tried to appear nonchalant. "I expect she was just out walking and wanted to while away the time. She's lonely, I think. She's at boarding school and all her school friends live miles away. They must come from all over England." She was about to add, "Just like the boys at Master Anthony's school," but bit her tongue.

"Lonely or not, I don't want you to get too friendly with her."

"She's very clever," Annie persisted. "She's going to be a doctor."

Joe snorted. "I knew there was something odd about her. Who'd want to go to a woman doctor?"

Annie opened her mouth to protest, but was cut short.

"No argument," her father said sternly. "She spells trouble."

Chapter 4

With no news of Anthony other than what she gleaned from gossip in the factory, Annie determined to put him out of her mind. Occasionally, odd comments would inform her of his progress as a student at Oxford, most of the remarks only serving to enforce the knowledge that she had been a silly little fool ever to imagine that he could be a real friend. University followed by travel abroad to extend his education with money no object contrasted sharply with her life of long working hours and counting every penny.

"I expect we'll be seeing him strutting about the factory before long once Mr Gladwell retires," was one of the remarks overheard.

Without looking up from her machine, Annie interrupted the conversation. "Surely with his money he doesn't have to be a slave to these machines like the rest of us."

The two women laughed. "Ah, but he'll be a better paid slave. Don't waste your pity on the likes of the Gladwells." The speaker glanced over her shoulder. "No more talk of that. I need to keep my job."

The rest of the afternoon, Annie found it hard to concentrate on her sewing and was admonished twice by Emmy. "Just as I thought I'd made a nice little machinist out of you, you go and mess things up. Pay attention girl!"

From time to time, her neighbour in the rows of machines mentioned the August Gala. "You going, Annie?"

The question was superfluous with the whole town turning out for the town's big day on the meadow used as a football pitch in the winter and a cricket pitch in the summer. On August Bank Holiday, one part was given over to a fair and the rest was carefully prepared for the competitions held in front of the grandstand. Although large enough to accommodate several hundred, the centre section was cordoned off and the seats covered with cushions for the Gladwells and their family and friends. Occasionally, the event was graced with the presence of Sir John Rowdley and Lady Rowdley, which meant that the seating arrangements had to be altered in order to conform with the demands of protocol. The Gladwells were allowed to sit in the rows behind Sir John and his family, except when the titled family was unable to attend allowing the Gladwells to sit in the front row. Although the proceedings followed the same ritual year in year out, the day was looked forward to with no diminution in anticipation or enjoyment. With work and money problems laid to one side, the young unmarried girls made sure that they appeared in new outfits guaranteed to catch the eye of the young man of their dreams. This was the day for fun and hopefully romance.

Annie had no such thoughts as she prepared to try on her new gown. In keeping with tradition on this occasion her mother had given Annie most of her pay packet for herself to buy the latest in fashion. A cotton dress in fetching shades of dark and light blue stripes, with the waist higher than had been the fashion in previous years, complemented the blue of Annie's eyes and drew attention to her tiny waist and gently rounded hips. The hat too was the latest and, unlike the matrons' choice of large feathered creations, was a simple deep-crowned straw with a large brim and decorated with a band of ribbon matching the blue dress.

After her beloved grandmother's death, the huge walnut wardrobe which had contained the old lady's treasured drawings together with the old couple's few possessions, had been transferred to the girls' bedroom. The centre panel boasted a long mirror in front of which Annie twirled and preened.

"How do I look?" she asked Eileen.

Eileen took her time, carefully studying her older sister who at that moment seemed to have suddenly become a young woman. "Hmm, sort of old."

At that point Annie was trying to peer over her shoulder to see how the slim skirt fell in tiny gathers to just above her ankles. "Old? What do you mean, old!"

"Just grown-up, that's all." She considered her sister thoughtfully. "Who are you going with then?"

"Well, who do you think, you idiot? Of all the silly questions! With you and Ma and Pa of course."

Eileen's affected air of innocence did not hide a hint of slyness aimed at disconcerting her sister. "Just thought it might be Joe."

"Joe? Whatever made you think that?"

"Well, you go out with him every Sunday afternoon painting," Eileen insisted.

"That's different." Annie kept the thought to herself that the only reason Joe had started to accompany her while she did her painting was so that he could stop her sneaking off to see Anthony Gladwell when he was home. "And in case you've forgotten, he only does that because you were too mean to come with me."

"I wasn't mean. I only wanted to play with Gladys. You couldn't expect me to spend a whole afternoon just sitting still watching you." Eileen paused, satisfied that she had won her point.

Annie continued to admire what she saw as a new person in the mirror. Going to the gala with Joe. How stupid could little sisters be.

"I've seen him looking at you, sort of funny like," Eileen said.

Colour washing up from her neck to her forehead, Annie swung round to confront her sister. "Don't be so silly! Joe's Pa's friend. He's more like an uncle than … " She was just about to say 'sweetheart' when something stopped her. Suddenly afraid of the images the thought was conjuring up, she turned on her sister again. "So, that's enough on that subject."

Sensing victory, Eileen gave a mischievous grin. "And you like him, don't you?"

"Stop it at once!" Annie shouted.

A voice from the kitchen interrupted the girls' row. "Stop your noise and come down here at once, do you hear?"

Annie placed a finger to her sister's lips. "That's Ma. Don't you dare say a word."

The girls crept downstairs, Annie doing her best to conceal the maelstrom of new emotions swirling round in her brain. Beatie Claydon was seated at the kitchen table putting the finishing touches to her gala outfit. Although still in her early thirties, she had seen no need to follow that season's fashions, still adhering to the lower-waisted full-skirted design of previous years. She had made her outfit herself, seeing no reason to waste good money on paying a dressmaker to achieve what she found so easy herself.

"I'm just going to get ready then we can all go off together."

"Joe should be here soon," her husband chipped in, appearing from the kitchen. "I asked him to come with us for company. I believe he's got someone to come in for the day."

"Poor Joe," Beatie agreed. It was well known that Joe's father, Ben, was an invalid and relied on a good neighbour to help when he was out at work all day, or out for long periods such as on Gala day.

As if on cue, Joe knocked at the back door and was invited in. The memory of her young sister's words still in her mind, Annie suddenly saw Joe in a new light. Hitherto, she had dismissed Joe as being simply a friend of the family who was kind enough to help out in supervising her painting sessions. This tall, handsome man, dressed in a close-fitting suit which drew attention to a powerful muscular body, was staring at her with undisguised love shining out of his fine dark eyes. Annie lowered her gaze, putting a hand up to her face to hide her shyness.

The looks exchanged between the two were not lost on Annie's parents. Fortunately, the moment's awkwardness was broken by Eileen, who danced up to Joe. "Look at me, Uncle Joe. Do you like my new frock?"

He picked her up in his arms and said solemnly. "I'm sure you'll be the prettiest little girl there this afternoon."

Amidst the laughter, Annie told her sister to stop showing off and behave herself. "Whatever will Joe think of you?"

Ignoring Annie's warning frown, Eileen smiled impishly. "And what about our Annie? Do you think she looks pretty too?"

"An absolute picture," Joe agreed, turning his head away in an effort to appear nonchalant.

"All ready then?" Beatie asked, suddenly tutting as she noticed a button missing on her husband's jacket. "Oh, no. You'll have to wait until I sort out your Pa," she told the girls.

Eileen's outburst protesting at having to wait a minute longer was forestalled by Joe. "I'll take the girls," he offered. "Any longer and we'll miss the band. They'll be starting off by the Corn Exchange any minute now."

There was a second's hesitation on Beatie's part before agreeing. "Well, just so long as you stay with Joe and Annie and don't go running off." The unspoken message was not that she was afraid of Eileen getting into mischief, but that for the first time she had picked up the signals of a shift in the relationship between Joe and her elder daughter.

As Joe had predicted, the Densbury Silver Band was tuning up at the starting point before beginning its musical procession down the High Street towards the gala meadow. Dancing along beside him and keeping up an endless stream of chatter, Eileen hung on to Joe's hand. Annie was grateful for the narrowness of the pavement and the presence of hordes of excited holidaymakers, forcing her to walk several paces behind Joe and Eileen. From time to time, Joe turned to smile at her, making her heart leap into her mouth and sending new sensations pounding in her body.

Finally, the musicians turned into the wide gateway leading into the grounds, at the same time striking up a rousing rendition of 'Goodbye, Dolly Gray.' By this time, Joe had taken advantage of the fact that they now had plenty of room to walk side by side and had tucked Annie's arm close into his and was pressing her close to his side.

"Mustn't lose my two girls," he said by way of excuse. "Your Ma would never forgive me."

Annie's struggles to think up a suitable reply were interrupted by a cry from the crowds. "They're here!"

The huge Panhard driven by the Gladwells' chauffeur swung effortlessly through the meadow gates held back by two cap-doffing stewards. Will Gladwell and his wife acknowledged the cheers of the crowds with barely perceptible nods of the head.

"Who do they think they are?" Annie stamped her foot.

"Quite the little rebel aren't you, Miss?" Joe said with a laugh. "Don't let anyone hear you say that, if you want to keep your job at the factory."

Lavinia Gladwell was seated at the back. Proud and elegant in a dark purple silk dress with matching hat and parasol, she stared straight ahead of her until a shout from someone behind Annie made her turn her head. The sneer on her face as she caught sight of Annie with a man she had seen in the factory, was mixed with an expression of pure triumph. This delight did not last long as a second open-topped car sped in through the gate, sending swirls of dust into the eyes of the onlookers.

"Oh, there's Anthony," Annie said, immediately regretting her show of pleasure on seeing Joe's grim expression. Her smile soon faded as she noticed Anthony's companion, the Honourable Miles Fanshawe.

Pushed to the front of the crowd by the eager onlookers, Annie found herself almost next to the car and unable to escape Miles Fanshawe's hand as he thrust his arm over the edge of the car door and grasped hers.

"The lovely Annie," he yelled above the roar of the car's engine, just as Lavinia was getting out of her father's car.

Her look of fury was missed by most who were more interested in the young men and in the attentions that one in particular was paying to a factory girl. Annie buried her face in Joe's sleeve, mortified at the shame of being singled out in this fashion, yet grateful that her parents had not yet arrived to witness the incident. It occurred to her later that someone would pass on an exaggerated account of it in any case.

"Don't worry my love," she heard Joe whisper. "You're with me." The words, 'now and forever,' remained unspoken.

"Do you know that man?" Eileen asked. "I've never seen him before."

"Oh, I've seen him when I worked at the Hall," Annie explained trying to sound offhand. "I believe he's engaged to Miss Lavinia." She resented giving the girl a title, but did not want to sound as if she cared about either the Gladwell girl or her hated intended.

The explanation only partly satisfied the astute Eileen, but further questions were cut short as the Densbury Silver Band struck up with, 'God Save Our Gracious King'. One old lady nearby muttered that she kept getting the words wrong, it being only a few years since Queen Victoria had died to be succeeded by Edward the Seventh. "I still keep singing, "God Save the Queen," she told her companion.

The main events of the afternoon then followed with the children competing in the races, running in whatever shoes they possessed, only one or two showing off in brand new black plimsolls. The winner of each race was rewarded with a rosette and a certificate, but all entrants received a tiny bag of sweets prepared by the wives of the gala committee members. Later it was the turn of the young men, cheered on by their sweethearts. There was more at stake here with cash prizes for the first three in each race, giving the winners more to lavish on the girls in the hope of some tangible reward from them once night had fallen.

"Are you going to race, Uncle Joe?" Eileen asked. "I bet you could beat them all."

"What, and leave you two young ladies without an escort?" he said in a half-mocking tone.

Annie could feel his heart beating faster as he held her even closer to his side. "I don't want you to leave us," she whispered to him, partly fearful of what would happen if he were to join in the races. What if the dreaded Miles Fanshawe should reappear? A little voice inside her kept reminding her that she would really love to see Anthony and talk to him, but it was Joe who was by her side and it was Joe who was making her feel special.

Neither Joe nor Annie noticed the departure of Anthony and Miles Fanshawe until it was too late, Anthony pulling up as close as he could in order to speak to Annie. Murmurs of surprise at the young man's interest in Annie Claydon echoed round that part of the meadow where she and Joe were standing. Annie gave a shy smile before turning away. She knew that her parents had seen Anthony Gladwell stop to speak to her and that they would not feel honoured by his attention to their daughter.

"Quick, let's get away from here," Joe growled, glaring at Anthony suspiciously. His hatred of Anthony Gladwell mingled with the fear that Annie was under his spell twisted his features in anger. Annie saw his expression and held even more tightly onto his arm.

"I'm with you, Joe," she reminded him.

Gradually, his scowl changed to a smile. "Now, Eileen, just you watch me win you something extra special on one of these stalls."

Eileen giggled in expectation. "Oh, can you really?" she asked, her voice breathless and excited.

One of the favourite attractions was the test of strength, which consisted of striking a hammer on a heavy weight, the object being to make it rise to hit the bell at the top of the contraption. Cheered on by their workmates and girls, the young men took off their jackets and swung the hammer with all the strength they possessed. It was not until Joe took off his jacket and gave it to Annie to hold that the spectators fell silent. Here was a man with enough power in his muscular arms and body to hit the weight to the top and beyond if need be. Annie felt a surge of pride seeing the looks of admiration on the faces of the other girls and the bitter jealousy of the undernourished young men. 'He's mine,' she said to herself, exulting in the fact.

A loud cheer went up as Joe's mighty blow with the hammer had the bell resounding, proclaiming his physical superiority over all present. The prize, a box of brightly coloured sweets was handed over to Eileen before he reclaimed his jacket from Annie, who helped him on with it, straightening his lapels with a proprietary gesture.

"Well done!" Fred Claydon came up and patted Joe on the back. "It's a long time since I managed to win on that."

"And you're not starting now," his wife told him. "I don't want you laid up with a bad back. In any case, it's time we all went home for a nice cup of tea. We can come down later for the fair and the torchlight procession."

Eileen was dancing around her parents, jumping up and down, her hazel eyes shining with excitement. "Come on, let's hurry up and then we can come back. Joe says he's going to win me that doll on the shooting gallery."

53

"I said I'd try, you cheeky young lady," Joe protested.

Joe left them at the corner of his street, promising to call for them later provided that his father was still able to be left in the care of the kindly neighbour. He did not have to spell out all the tasks he had to carry out for his father, who, unable to walk, had to be cared for like a baby.

"We'll be ready to leave about half past seven," Beatie told him, "but if you can't come up to the house we'll see you up at the meadow."

Annie secretly hoped that he would be able to come and call for them. She was half afraid that one of the older girls from the factory, seeing him alone might attach herself to him. Although ignorant of what could happen, she had the feeling deep down that a more experienced girl might have something to offer Joe that she could not. He was free to go off with any girl he wanted instead of hanging around with a couple of children. Please let his pa be well, she prayed.

Tea was another hasty affair with bread, jam and cake washed down with a large cup of sweet milky tea. Willing Joe to appear, Annie kept her eye on the clock as she forced herself to chew on the huge doorsteps of bread and jam prepared by her mother. All through the meal, Eileen had been sitting quietly barely nibbling on one piece of bread. Unusually for her, she had not said one word about all the interesting items seen at the gala, but stared grimly at her plate. Suddenly, she leapt to her feet. "Ma, I think I'm going to be sick!" With that, Eileen shot out of the back door into the yard. Groaning as if about to die, she heaved up the contents of her stomach, while her mother held a wet cloth to her forehead.

"What on earth has brought this on?" she asked Annie.

"Those sweets, that's what it is." She faced her young sister with an accusing stare. "Don't tell me you've eaten that whole box of sweets Joe won for you?"

Eileen's feeble nod goaded Annie into a tirade on her greediness. "Serves you right, you greedy pig!" was all the sympathy Eileen received. "You didn't even give me one!"

"I'm so vexed," her mother went on. "Now we'll all have to stay in tonight. Just look at her. She's been sick all down her new frock and mine as well."

"Oh, Ma, that's not fair," Annie started to complain.

"It's just as much your fault letting Joe give her all those sweets."

Annie thought better of reminding her mother that they were present when Joe had handed over the sweets. All she could think of was that Joe would go the fair that evening on his own. "I suppose I'd better go and get changed if we're not going out."

"Why?" Joe's voice coming from the back door startled her.

"I've a good mind to box your ears, Joe Langmead, stuffing Eileen with those sweets. Just look at her, will you? Now we can't go to the fair this evening," Beatie complained.

A look of remorse crossed his face. "Oh, no." He turned to Fred. "Look, why don't you all go and I'll stay here and look after Eileen seeing as it's all my fault."

Argument and counter argument followed until it was agreed Eileen would have to stay behind with her parents while Joe accompanied Annie to the fair. It was clear that Beatie was not entirely in favour. "I want her home straight after the torchlight procession. Just you take good care of her, do you hear me, Joe?"

Joe heard and understood the drift of her warning. No longer was he considered the stand-in uncle who watched over their daughter while she painted on Sunday afternoons. He had become a young man showing an entirely different interest in their daughter who was now a young woman.

"I won't let her out of my sight," he promised. "Come along, young lady," he said in a half-mocking tone tinged with more than a hint of triumph at being allowed to have the girl he adored all to himself for the evening.

Still muttering at the injustice of it all, Eileen was packed off to bed with yet another ticking-off for having ruined her parents' day.

As soon as they were out of the house and in the High Street, Joe took her hand, threading her arm through his. "I promised your Ma I wouldn't lose sight of you and I won't, so don't you dare try to get away from me."

"I won't," she whispered shyly.

Touching her cheek gently with a caressing stroke, he said, "Not now, or ever."

Soon they were in a throng again all of them eager to get to the fairground, the bright lights, the garish colours and the musical cacophony from a dozen different attractions.

"The merry-go-round," Joe said, his mighty arms lifting her up as if she were light as thistledown. "I'll sit behind you and hold you tight, so you won't fall off, I promise."

As he swung her up, the eyes of half a dozen of Annie's workmates were on her and the handsome man who was her escort. Filled with envy they watched the couple who had eyes only for each other.

Annie gave a little cry of fear as the huge plaster horse began to rear and plunge in time to the music. Seated behind her with his arms around her waist, Joe bent to whisper in her ear soothing her with words of encouragement. Annie half-turned to feel his breath and his lips brushing hers in the lightest of kisses. Totally lost in the sheer magic of what was happening, she could not drag herself away from the magnetism of his gaze, offering her lips to his again.

"No, Annie. Too many people watching here." She thought she heard him say, "Later," but his words were drowned out by the music. All too soon the ride came to an end, with Joe lifting her down and holding her to him a second or two longer than was strictly necessary.

"You're a crafty one and no mistake." A girl from the factory muttered the words in Annie's ears. "If you get tired of him, I wouldn't say no."

The crude comment left Annie in a whirl of conflicting emotions. What did the girl mean? What if Joe tired of her, wanting a more adult female companion? Her fears were partly allayed by his next remark. "I am the luckiest man here," he told her, "and so glad I gave Eileen the sweets."

"Joe!" She smiled adding, "So am I."

It seemed as if nothing could spoil the pleasure of the evening. Even the nudges and winks of her workmates were ignored. She would have to put up with a fair share of teasing and worse when the holiday was over, but for the moment, she felt that life was a golden glow of happiness and that she was on the verge of experiencing something exciting in its mystery.

"The Gladwell family don't know what they are missing." Thoughts of Anthony and his sister suddenly sprang into her mind. "It's a pity they can't stay and enjoy the fair. It can't be much fun for them, just watching the races and then having to leave."

A muscle in Joe's cheek began to tense. Barely able to conceal his anger, his harsh words astonished Annie. "I'm sick of hearing about Anthony Gladwell. I suppose you'd rather be with that poor excuse for a man than with me."

Shocked at his wild anger, the tears sprang into her eyes. "Oh, Joe, I'm so sorry, I didn't mean anything. I'd sooner be with you than anyone else in the whole world."

Immediately contrite, Joe placed an arm round her shoulders and held her close. "I'm a damned fool," was his response. His mood lightening, he announced, "To make up for it, I shall just have to win you a present. Come on, the firing range. Watch me win the best prize on the stall."

One disgruntled young man had just flung down his rifle. "They're fixed. The sights are all over the place." He took his girlfriend's arm. "Come on, no point on wasting any more money here."

The weasel-faced man in charge handed Joe a rifle, the same one discarded by the previous customer. Joe flung it back at him. "I'll have that one," he demanded, pointing to one partly hidden near the prizes. "That's the one you use to show off how easy it is to hit the bullseye, isn't it?"

"You'll have the one you're given," the man snarled. "I run this stall."

Too late he realised his mistake, as Joe seized him round the throat with one powerful hand, at the same time clenching the other fist ready to strike. "And I say which rifle I want."

Scowling and green with fright, the man handed Joe the rifle he wanted and watched helplessly while Joe knocked up a top score with each deadly accurate bullet.

"You can't do that," the man whimpered. "You can't take all my prizes, I've got a wife and kids to keep."

"One prize will do. The little lady will choose, and you'd better not try any more of your tricks."

Annie chose a beautiful china doll which had pride of place on the stall. "Eileen will love this. It'll make up for missing the fair."

"You're a lovely girl. I wanted you to choose something for yourself. It looks like I'll have to try again."

"Not here you won't," the little man said.

"Don't worry, I'll just go and see if there are a few honest games to play."

The next stall offered prizes for throwing hoops on to hooks. Annie had set her heart on a six-inch high figurine of a nymph dressed in a long flowing diaphanous gown all in glass. The figure seemed almost life-like, the glass so skilfully blown that the drapes appeared to billow in the light evening breeze. By now Annie was convinced that there was nothing that Joe could not achieve once he set his heart on it.

"You see, I always get what I want even if I have to wait for it." He kissed the top of her head, his mouth ruffling her black curls. "And I want you, Miss Annie Claydon."

It was dark with only the lights from the stalls illuminating the area in front of them. In between were unlit sections where several couples were taking advantage of the dark to kiss and cuddle. Annie was only too aware that Joe was pressing himself ever closer to her and she only had to turn her head ever so slightly for him to pull her to him in an embrace.

"A fortune teller! Please, Joe, I must find out what she has to say." Annie pointed to a red and white striped tent. Above the open flap hung a sign with the words, 'Madam Aurora, fortune teller to royalty.'

"Do you think she really is?"

"No, and you don't want to hear what she has to say." Joe's face was a black thunder cloud.

"Why not? If it's not true, it doesn't matter, and if she can tell the future then I have a right to know."

Defeated by Annie's logic, Joe thrust a coin into her outstretched hand. "If she upsets you, come out straight away. I'll be just outside, right here." He pointed to a spot about a yard away behind the tent. "Promise?"

Annie nodded, ready to agree to anything once she had the money in her hand. Would Madam Aurora tell her if Joe was to become her husband or not? Cautiously lifting the flap, Annie entered the tent. At first it was hard to make out her surroundings, but gradually her eyes became accustomed to the shapes cast by the flickering candles.

"Sit down, child," a deep voice in an unknown accent invited.

Madam Aurora, dressed in what Annie could make out to be a red and purple top partly concealed by the many strands of beads in varying colours, was sitting at a round table covered with a cloth strewn with patterns of stars and moons. A crystal ball reflecting the strange shadows cast by the candlelight sat in the centre of the table.

A fear of the unknown turned Annie's whole body to ice. She half rose as if to flee, but curiosity held her down. The gypsy held out her hand for the silver coin which was swiftly placed in the pocket of her full skirt mostly hidden from Annie's view.

"Do not be afraid, my child," she began. Her black eyes seemed to bore straight into Annie's mind. "I can read your heart and your soul." She stared at the crystal ball again. "I see you have two lovers, one close and one far away. One will take your heart and one will take your head. You have many paths to follow. I must not tell you which one that will be. Some will lead to happiness and some to heartache." She shuddered and gripped Annie's hands in hers until the dark knuckles turned white. "There is danger. Someone will want to destroy you. Have a care. That danger is not far away."

"No!" Annie screamed, jumping up and knocking over her chair in her frenzied desire to escape to the safety of Joe's presence. Hearing her cry, Joe held out his arms to comfort the sobbing girl. "Oh, Joe, you were right. She told me the most terrible things."

Joe stroked her hair, soothing her as one would a small child. Gradually the sobbing ceased, but still Joe held the girl close to him in a tight embrace. "I told you not to go in there," he admonished in as gentle a tone as he could manage.

"She said I was in danger."

"Listen to me." Joe held her at arm's length, his strong fingers digging into her shoulders. "There is no danger, my darling girl, not as long as I am here beside you. I should never have let you go in to see that gypsy woman."

Now quite calm, Annie told him the rest of her predictions. "She said I had two lovers, one near and one far away. What did she mean by that?"

Joe swore quietly under his breath. "Nothing. You can't have two lovers. I'm the only one, do you hear? No other man is going to have you. I love you, my darling girl," he repeated between kisses. More endearments interspersed with kisses followed until Annie was bereft of her senses, just wanting this sensation to go on and on forever.

Suddenly Joe pulled himself away. "I promised your ma and pa I'd look after you. I think we'd better make a move." They stood in silence for a while, each wondering what to say next. It was Joe who broke the silence. "You're my girl now, you promised."

Shouts and roars of laughter broke the spell. "The torches! Come and get them!" A group of men by the gateway were dipping huge stakes wrapped in cloth and twigs into vats of boiling tar. The resulting smoking torches were eagerly seized upon by the young men all managing to hold them on high with one hand, at the same time squeezing their girlfriends close with the other.

"Shall I get us one?"

Annie hung back. "No let's just walk along together. I don't want any drips of tar to fall on my new dress." Her real reason was that she did not want Joe's attention taken up entirely by safeguarding the torch.

"You're right. I need both of my arms to hold you tight."

Their kiss was observed by more than one of both Joe's and Annie's workmates, but neither of them cared who was watching.

"I wish this night could go on and on forever," Annie sighed.

"It will, I promise you," he whispered in her ear. "One day, it will."

When the final activities of the August Bank Holiday Gala were over, the last torch plunged into a huge tub of water and the final farewells shouted out, Joe took Annie's hand in his. "Time to go home."

"And then what?"

Joe walked on in silence for a few minutes. "I don't like lies and deceit, so it seems I'm going to have to ask your pa if I can take you out properly."

"Like sweethearts, you mean?" Annie was a little apprehensive. "Do you think they'll mind?"

"Why should they? Your pa said that your ma was only seventeen when they tied the knot and you've passed your seventeenth birthday."

Panic at what Joe was hinting at made Annie open her mouth to explain to Joe that she did not want to get married at seventeen, but his mind already filled with what he had to say to her parents, he seemed not to hear. Excited as she was with this new experience of falling in love and being loved by Joe, still at the back of her mind she could hear her granny's last words exhorting her to make the most of her talent as a painter. She needed someone to talk to who would understand her dilemma. Perhaps she ought to try to find Anthony and ask his advice on the quandary facing her. He would understand her fears and as her good friend he would be sure to give her the right advice.

Annie's parents were sitting either side of the fireplace when she and Joe entered the living room. "Ah, home safe and sound. Had a good time?" The cheerful tone in her father's voice rang false reflecting the anxious look on her mother's face.

"Lovely. Joe won lots of prizes and…" She was just about to say that she had consulted Madam Aurora, but thought better of it. All that talk of lovers near and far would be frowned upon.

"Off to bed with you," her mother said. "Me and your Pa want to have a little chat with Joe here."

Annie longed to hear what was in their minds. From their serious expressions she had been able to glean that they had some misgivings about her spending the evening all alone with Joe.

Eileen stirred in her sleep as Annie undressed, gradually waking and rubbing her eyes. "Was it nice?" she asked. "I missed all the fair and everything."

"You poor thing," Annie commiserated. "Never mind, there's always next year." Her eyes lit up with a mischievous gleam. "And look what Joe won just for you, the very best prize on the rifle range." She produced the beautiful china doll with the golden curls.

Now wide awake, Eileen sat up and hugged the doll. "I've never had anything so beautiful in my whole life. Gladys will be so jealous."

"Just look at her clothes, Eileen, aren't they really special?"

"That was nice of Joe to get a prize for me." She stared hard at her sister in the dim candlelight. "Did he get you anything? I mean, you did go out with him just as if you were his girl, didn't you?"

Annie blushed. "Don't be silly, I'm not really his girl. He won this bit of glass and said I could keep it." Her attempt at sounding nonchalant did not fool Eileen.

"We'll see," she yawned, sliding down under the bedclothes.

Annie placed the glass figurine on the table beside the bed and blew out the candle. Her dreams were a strange kaleidoscope of colours with Joe always there. She fell asleep puzzling about the lover across the seas.

The warm comfortable feeling was shattered when she woke from a nightmare in which she was being pursued by a faceless creature threatening her with destruction. Trembling, she lay wide awake. Who was this enemy?

Chapter 5

The first Sunday after the gala, Annie waited for Joe to call.

"Where are you off out to with Joe?" Annie's mother was keeping an eye on the situation even though permission had been granted for Joe to take her out.

"Nowhere different," Annie said. "I've told Joe that Sunday afternoon is my day for painting, so it won't be any different just because you've said he can take me out."

What she did not tell her mother was that she and Joe had disagreed strongly about the way they would spend their Sunday afternoons from now on. "I can't stop painting, Joe, you must understand that."

"You win, but on one condition." He put a finger under her chin forcing her to look up to him.

Annie hesitated before capitulating. Joe wouldn't suggest anything she wouldn't like. "I'll agree so long as it isn't anything Ma and Pa wouldn't let me do."

"Just say you'll come out with me one night in the week after work."

"But where could we go? It will soon be dark and cold."

Joe had pulled her close in a passionate kiss. "This is what we could do," he muttered.

"Well, I'll have to ask Ma about going out in the evening," was her reply as she reluctantly pulled herself out of his embrace.

And now for the first time ever, Joe had not turned up to take her out painting. Her petulant, "I've a good mind to go out by myself," was met with an equally adamant retort from her mother. "You've promised Joe, so you're going nowhere, my girl."

A sharp rap at the door made them both start up. "Please Mrs Claydon," a child's voice called out.

Beatie opened the door to a small boy, whom she recognised as the son of one of Joe's neighbours. "Joe asked me to tell Annie that his dad is poorly and he can't come and see her this afternoon,"

Her disappointment forgotten, Annie was filled with remorse. "Poor Joe. Should I go and see if I can help him?"

Her mother's shocked response puzzled her. "Of course you can't go spending time alone with Joe in his house. What would people think?" Grabbing her shawl off the hook on the back door, she told the young lad, "I'm coming with you. Joe'll need a woman's hand."

Worried as she was about Joe, Annie fretted about her lost Sunday afternoon's painting. With Eileen out playing at her friend Gladys's house and her father helping a mate with moving house, there was nothing she could do. Resentment that she was not allowed to go and help Joe at his house still rankled. One minute she was allowed to walk out with Joe and the next she was told what to do as if she were a young child. "I'm off out," she said out loud, figuring that she was unlikely to come to harm walking through the streets of Densbury.

Without thinking, she took the path leading up the hill out of the town. Half hoping that she might bump into Isabelle, she paused outside the doctor's house. The large villa, the last before the road gave way to a poorly maintained lane with fields on either side, showed no signs of life. There was no one on the long drive winding up to the front door. Disappointed at having nobody to talk to, Annie continued her solitary walk, her reverie suddenly broken by the sounds of horses' hooves. She turned round and from her position, partly concealed behind the hedgerow, she observed Isabelle and an unknown man descend from the pony and trap driven by the doctor.

"Quick! Inside!" Doctor Anstruther's voice, an urgent whisper, carried on the breeze to where Annie was standing. "Come along, Isabelle."

Isabelle ran up the drive with the man following while her father drove the pony and trap round the side track leading to the stables at the rear of the house. Curiosity got the better of Annie. Why all the secrecy? She retraced her steps to see the two entering the house. A minute later, Isabelle appeared at the bay window of the drawing room at the front of the house and drew the blinds, but not before the figure of a man who, from his collar, appeared to be a vicar, stood beside her to help her. It crossed Annie's mind that it was still the middle of a sunny afternoon and there was no need to shut out the daylight, but she dismissed the scene from her mind as she continued to climb the hill.

Before long, she had reached a vantage point from where she could see Baythorpe Hall.

Sadness, as she remembered the happy hours spent painting with Anthony, filled her eyes with tears. She had to keep telling herself that she was no longer a child and that she was now promised to Joe. The screeching of tyres brought her back to the present day.

"Annie," a familiar voice called out. Anthony was driving his father's huge Panhard. Clouds of dust choked Annie as Anthony braked hard. "I've been looking everywhere for you. I didn't get a chance to speak to you at the gala."

Half afraid of the car and wanting to avoid breathing in the fumes from the engine, Annie shrank back into the shelter of the hedge.

"I can't talk to you above all this racket. Jump in and I'll take you for a spin."

"No! What if someone sees me?" Longing to spend some time with Anthony, yet afraid of the gossip if she were to be seen in Anthony Gladwell's car, she shook her head.

"I'll drive miles away," he promised, sensing her fears. "Right over to Hoverden."

The sun was shining, the sky was a symphony of blue sprinkled with a few white cotton rags of clouds, enough to tempt Annie into agreeing. "I'm all by myself this afternoon, so I suppose I could, but not for long." She pushed thoughts of Joe and his sick father to the back of her mind.

"Wonderful." He jumped out of the car, running round to Annie's side to open the door and get her seated comfortably. "Don't be frightened. I won't drive too fast." With that he accelerated at such a pace that Annie gave a cry of terror. The hedges and trees were moving by her so quickly she felt as if they were about to fall on top of her.

Anthony pulled up once they were some five miles out of Densbury. "Sorry to have frightened you, but I wanted to get well away." He brushed back a lock of his thick fair hair which had had blown across his forehead. "It's a bit breezy up here." Solicitous for her welfare, he reached over to the back seat of the car to find a rug. "I say Annie, you look a bit pale. You're not cold are you?"

Annie shook her head. "I'm fine now." She lowered her eyes. "I was just a bit frightened. I've never been in a motor car before."

"Oh, I am a fool. I should have realised." He bent close to her wrapping the rug over her knees. "There you are." For a brief second, his face was close to hers, as he looked up at her. "Gosh, you're so pretty, Annie." He moved away quickly. "I shouldn't have said that. Please don't be angry with me."

There was an awkward silence broken by Annie. "No, I'm not angry. We're friends, aren't we? I mean, I know you're a Gladwell and I was only a maid at your house, so I don't really suppose I can be a friend really."

Anthony laughed. "Of course we're proper friends. Who else can I talk to? Who else understands about my painting? Certainly no one in my family. I think Mama does, but she can't help much with Papa keen for me to go into the business. As for Lavinia, she's so taken with Miles and getting him to the altar that she hardly notices me." He stared into space half lost in his thoughts before turning to Annie again. "Oh, I wish I didn't have to keep going away. I hate it at Oxford, but I have to do as Papa says. All I want to do is paint and one day I will." This last remark came out in an explosion of anger. "And what about you, Annie?"

His tender concern was so sincere that Annie found it difficult to explain what she would be doing. "I do paint once a week, but it's a bit hard on Joe. All he can do is sit and watch. He's not really interested and I think he'd sooner be doing something else."

Anthony's eyes narrowed. "You're walking out with him?" Anthony had some difficulty in forming the question. Would Annie get married and be lost to him as the only person who understood his aspirations? Deep down he felt she was worth someone better than one of his father's employees even if she was one of that class.

"Well yes, I suppose you could say that." In a burst of confidence, she blurted out, "But I don't want to get married yet, even if that's what everybody expects me to do. I want to learn how to paint properly and be a real artist, but I don't suppose that will ever happen for me." Her last words were lost in a fit of sobbing.

"Oh, Annie, please don't cry." Anthony hugged her close. "You will one day and so will I. We'll show them all." He took a large white handkerchief from his pocket and dried her tears.

"You will, I'm sure," she told him, pulling away from him. It wasn't until later that she realised that his embrace had not aroused the same emotions as when Joe held her close. Instead, she had felt a kind of comfort, of being cherished by a very dear friend and she was going to miss that more than she cared to admit.

"I'd better get you back before your parents wonder where you are." The carefree atmosphere had gone, blighted by their attempts to see into the future.

Annie's mother was back from Joe's house when she returned home. Beatie's sad face told her at once that things were not right. "What is it, Ma?"

"It's Joe's pa. He won't last the night. Joe sent his neighbour for Doctor Anstruther but he must have been called out to some other poor soul, because she couldn't get any answer."

Annie frowned. "That's strange." It was on the tip of her tongue to say what she had seen on her walk earlier, but the implication that she had been heading in the direction of Baythorpe Hall would not have been lost on her mother.

"What's strange about a doctor being called out, my girl?"

"I meant it was strange that Isabelle didn't answer the door, that's all." Changing the subject she asked, "What can I do, Ma?"

"You'll have to get your pa's tea. Eileen is having hers at Gladys's. There's bread and cheese for your pa and there's a bit of fruit cake in the tin. You can get whatever you like, but leave the ham. I want that for dinner tomorrow."

"If it's so bad with Joe's pa, why can't I go with you?" The niggling guilt at having spent the afternoon with Anthony Gladwell was gnawing at her insides, urging her to find a way to make up for her lack of loyalty. All the same she knew that Anthony was just as necessary to her as Joe, if in a decidedly different way.

"Haven't you been listening to a word? That house is not the right place for a girl. Your turn will come once you've been married a while, when you have to see to such things, but for the moment you stay here and do as you're bid. There's a few things I need to take with me. They're a bit short of sheets and towels." She caught sight of Annie's questioning look. "And don't let on to Joe what I'm sneaking in to his house. A man's got his pride."

Her mother was right. She would have been in the way. Besides, would Joe have wanted her to see him struggling with his grief at his father's bedside?

Just as Beatie was about to leave, her husband came in. "I heard about Joe's pa. Do you want me to come and give a hand to lift the old chap about?"

"No, you've been on the go all day shifting furniture and the like and you've got work tomorrow. Besides, Joe won't let anybody else lift his father about. He's had years of practice knowing just what to do so as not to hurt him."

With that Annie was left alone with her father. Conversation was first limited to what he wanted for his tea, but once that had been decided he asked her what she had been up to all day.

"Nothing much. First Joe couldn't come and then Ma went down to Joe's so I took myself out for a little walk."

Her father paused, cup half way to his mouth. "And where was that? Not up to see that Anthony Gladwell, I hope. Funny how your walks seem to end up in that direction."

Annie avoided his scrutiny. "Oh dear, I've slopped my tea in the saucer. I'll go and rinse it out." She turned her back on her father until the tell-tale spots flaring on her cheeks had subsided. "What did you say, Pa? Where did I go? Just up the hill past the Anstruthers."

Fred Claydon was no fool. "Up to Baythorpe Hall?"

"No." In an effort to change the subject, she blurted out. "I saw Isabelle and her father coming home. They had a strange sort of visitor, a man. I think he was a vicar or something, but I couldn't really see because they pulled the curtains when they went in."

70

"Did they now?" Fred nodded thoughtfully. "Tell me more about this man. When you say he was a vicar, what did you mean? Was he dressed like Pastor Briggs or the reverend at the church?"

"Does it matter?" Annie hesitated, guessing that what she had seen had been of some significance which she could not fathom, yet aware that a truthful reply would be disloyal to her friend Isabelle. To her astonishment, her normally meek and mild father thumped the table with his fist. "If I ask a question, I expect an answer, Annie, so out with it!"

"I couldn't really see. He had something long on – I can't describe it. They all rushed into the house and drew the blinds."

"So you stood and watched long enough? Did you think something odd was going on?"

"Of course not, Pa. It was just that I'd got nothing better to do. If they have a visitor it's nothing to do with us."

"It might be. We shall see," was his grim response.

Once Eileen was home from playing with Gladys, he announced that he had to go out for an hour or so. "Tell your ma I'll explain when I get back."

Eileen's excited chatter telling Annie how jealous Gladys was of the doll that Joe had won for her at the fair went straight over her head. Had her news about the doctor's visitor sparked off her pa's solemn behaviour and need to go out? Absentmindedly she began to wash up the tea things and put the food and crockery away. There were so many things she did not understand.

A weary Beatie Claydon dragged herself through the door at eight that evening. Annie had put Eileen to bed and was waiting to hear news of Joe's father. "The good Lord has seen fit to take him and free him from his pain," she said. "Be a dear and make me a cup of tea, there's a good girl."

Rushing around, filling the kettle and getting out the teapot and cups filled the next few minutes while her mother lay back in her chair utterly exhausted. "Still, it's a blessing in more ways than one. Joe'll have a bit more time and freedom. Besides, the cottage will be his to do as he pleases. Mind you, it could do with a woman's hand to get it halfway decent."

Ignoring her mother's searching look, Annie poured the boiling water over the tea in the teapot. She was filled with a faint disquiet, half guessing what her mother was hinting at.

"Well, perhaps the two of us could get it clean and tidy again. I mean we'd have to wait until after the funeral."

"Maybe. That's not what I meant." She took the tea from Annie and drank greedily.

"Shouldn't I go and see Joe, Ma?"

Beatie's cup clattered on its saucer as she placed it firmly on the table. "The only time you'll be on your own in Joe's cottage with him will be when you're wed and not before."

"That'll be a long time then." Much as Annie longed to be with Joe, she was not going to be browbeaten into getting married at eighteen. Anthony and his talk of being a painter had stirred up longings within her of a different nature.

"We shall see." Beatie could be as stubborn as her daughter. She had seen the look in Joe's eyes when he was with Annie and was determined that there would be no hasty reading of the banns followed by a quick wedding. Counting the nine months after a wedding was a favourite pastime amongst the older women. There would be no such gossip about her daughter.

"Of course, if you were married and in your own house, you'd have plenty of time for painting. I'm sure Joe wouldn't want you to go back to the factory."

"Stop it, Ma!"

Beatie thought it wise to say no more. She had planted a few seeds of doubt. Better to wait and see if they took root.

The funeral of Joe's father took place a few days later in the chapel. As was the custom, all the neighbours came to pay their respects to this poor man who had spent most of his life in pain confined to his tiny cottage. There was pity for Joe now left on his own, a pity mingled with speculation as Annie stood by his side. After the brief committal at the graveside, Joe went to shake the hand of Pastor Briggs. Annie and her family went back to Joe's cottage for the traditional wake. The men were offered spirits whilst the women drank tea and generally bustled about seeing to their needs. Nobody stayed long. After offering their final condolences, most left leaving only the Claydons with Joe.

"You've got the cottage nice," Beatie ventured.

Joe nodded, his gaze firmly fixed on Annie. It was true. In the week following his father's death, he had worked like a man possessed, throwing out all the old cheap sticks of furniture and completely refurbishing the cottage. "Well, it is mine now."

"Of course, you will be able to take it over now," Beatie agreed.

"Oh, no," Joe explained. "Pa never had to pay rent. He must have bought it when he and Ma got married. I don't know how he managed it. He never said and I never thought it my place to ask."

"No rent to pay, did you say, Joe?" Beatie fixed Annie with a meaningful stare. A factory worker who owned property was unheard of. Most people in their situation spent their lives worried to death about being able to pay their rent. There was no mercy for those who fell behind. It was not an uncommon sight to see weeping women with their children and a few pitiful possessions being piled on to a cart before leaving for the workhouse.

"I can't understand you, my girl," Beatie said to her daughter as they made their way back home. "A man with his own house and who worships the ground you walk on, and you're still holding back." She stopped and faced Annie squarely. "You're not a child and it's about time that you took note that a man has his needs. If you shilly-shally too long, Joe might start looking elsewhere."

"No!" Annie was horrified. "Joe would never do that to me."

Even so she turned her mother's words over in her mind. She loved Joe so much that the thought of him with another woman was more than she could bear. Would Joe continue to wait for her much longer?

The pressure on her to name the day was relieved as her father and Joe seemed to spend more and more time together apparently in serious discussion which had nothing to do with wedding plans. Night after night, Fred Claydon went out, returning late and not revealing where he had been.

"Nothing to do with womenfolk," was all the satisfaction she got from her mother when she asked. "We don't ask our men questions."

That there was something seriously amiss struck her when she overheard a chance remark. "That doctor and his daughter need teaching a lesson," she heard her father say to Joe. The two men were out in the yard, as Annie stood by her open bedroom window trying to catch the conversation. Annie caught her breath. It was something to do with their strange visitor and worse, it was all her fault for telling her father about him. Isabelle was in danger and she was the cause. How to warn her was a problem with her mother's constant checking of her every movement. The first opportunity arose the following Sunday when her father said that he was meeting Joe and some of the men from the chapel on a matter of business.

"What about me? He said he would call without fail."

"Men's business is more important than courting," she was told. Her father whispered something in her mother's ear and was gone.

"In that case," Annie told her mother, "he needn't think I'm sitting here twiddling my thumbs. I'm going out." She was out of the door and running before her mother could protest. Fear gripped her on seeing several of the men in the neighbourhood, all keen members of the chapel converging on the road leading to the chapel. There were also a number of men from St Michael's joining them. Grim-faced and carrying huge staves they hurried up the High Street.

Rushing in the opposite direction, she was nearly knocked over by these men eager to get to their appointed positions. At first there was no answer when she hammered on Isabelle's door. Finally, the door was opened a crack.

"Annie! Whatever is the matter?"

A voice from the back called out, "Don't let anyone in, Isabelle, come away."

Isabelle whispered, "I'm sorry, Annie, you heard."

"You must," Annie cried. "You're all in danger."

At this, Doctor Anstruther appeared. "Come in, child." He led her through to the parlour where the strange visitor was sitting. Annie hung back in the doorway afraid of this man in what looked like a long robe to her. "This is Father O'Leary. He's a Catholic priest. Tell me, Annie, is this the cause of our danger?"

"Yes, you've got to get away. The men are all up by the chapel waiting for something. I just know they mean something bad. Please, you've got to hurry."

Father O'Leary and the doctor exchanged anxious glances. "Quick, I'll get the pony and trap and take you over to Wendlescany."

The man rose. "And all because I wanted to set up God's House for a few Catholics," he sighed.

Annie gasped. Had she done right in trying to warn this man? Pastor Briggs had dinned into his congregation that the Church of Rome was the mouthpiece of the devil himself and Annie had believed him. She shrank back as the priest patted her on the shoulder. His words puzzled her. "You're a good Christian girl," he said. How could he be so evil if he called her that?

There was no further time for speculation. "Stay here, Isabelle," her father ordered. "And you, Annie had better get home." There was fear in his pale grey eyes. He kissed Isabelle. "I'll be back later tonight, don't worry."

Isabelle watched Annie run down the front path and away to the town. "Please get home as quickly as you can," she implored.

The main street which had been crowded with grim-faced men only an hour before was now deserted apart from one elderly man. "Get yourself home right now. This is no place for girls and women."

Annie made as if to turn off towards the lane leading to her cottage, then took a short cut through a narrow alley behind the factory. Crouched behind a low wall, she could hear the threatening voices of men. "He's sure to drive the trap this way. He can't get it through Finsbeck Lane, so we'll rush out the minute we hear the horse."

There was a sudden roar as the crowd leapt forward brandishing their sticks and hurling huge rocks at the frightened pony pulling Doctor Anstruther's trap.

"No Papists in Densbury!" was the cry from the enraged men.

The doctor struggled to control the frightened beast with one hand, at the same time holding one hand in front of his face. As the blood spurted from a gash on his head, Annie ran forward, until she managed to place herself between the pony and trap and the men. "Stop! Stop! You mustn't."

"Fred Claydon's girl," the man leading the group shouted. "Hold on."

The pause was enough to allow the doctor free passage and escape out of the town. Annie lifted the hem of her skirt to stem the flow of blood from the cuts on her arm caused by a stray sharp stone.

"Annie!" Joe and her father stood accusingly in front of her. "What the bloody hell do you think you were doing?" her father asked.

"How could you!" Joe shouted.

"You were trying to kill two innocent men. You're all wicked!" she screamed at them, turning and running in her haste to get away from them. That she would pay for her actions was clear to her, but for the moment, she knew she had done what she felt to be right. Sitting at home waiting for her father's return, she confessed to her appalled mother what she had done.

Her ma shook her head. "I dunno what your father's going to say, showing him up like that in front of the whole town. We'll have to wait and see."

"If it hadn't been for me, someone would have been killed." Annie still felt that she had been partly justified in trying to thwart the mob's violent intentions.

Her mood of defiance slowly evaporated as the minutes ticked by. She jumped up, startled, on hearing the back door slam. Fred entered, his face black with suppressed fury. Had it not been for her mother's intervention, her usually even-tempered father would have taken the strap to her. "My own daughter in front of the whole town taking the part of the Papists! Wait till Pastor Briggs has finished with you." He went on in similar vein, daring Annie to interrupt him.

The tirade continued when Joe arrived, the two men standing shoulder to shoulder in their condemnation.

"We warned you about that Isabelle, didn't we? We told you she was trouble and we've been proved right." Joe's anger matched her father's. Sickened at what she read as undisguised disgust at her actions in Joe's eyes, she wept and fled to her bedroom.

The week at work was even worse with none of the women speaking to her unless forced to. There were even gibes of "Papist!" hurled at her by the men as she made her way into work and home again. "You'll be lucky if you keep your job," she was told by Zak's wife.

The following Sunday there was no escape from her final humiliation. Pastor Brigg mounted the steps leading to the pulpit placed centrally high above the congregation. First he raised his eyes to those seated in the galleries above, then lowered them to fix them on the Claydon family below. Having seized everyone's attention, he pointed at Annie, who was sitting with her parents, Eileen and Joe. All were forced to listen to a stream of abuse from Pastor Briggs who likened Annie to a scarlet woman.

Her final humiliation came when she was called out in front of the whole congregation and reminded of her duties as a member of the chapel.

"The prosperity of this town was built by good Christian men and women escaping from religious tyranny on the continent. Our good Mr Gladwell's forebears were amongst them and that is why we enjoy our life here today. There'll be no Papists allowed in Densbury." If it was on the tip of Annie's tongue to say that made them just as bad as the wicked men abroad, she felt it wise to keep her counsel. All the while, her parents sat with their heads bowed. She dared not bring any more shame on them. At the end of the service, the Claydon family waited in their seats until the rest of the congregation had left.

"Right, you can walk behind us," her father said.

"I'll walk with Annie." Joe took a firm hold of Annie's arm. "She's learnt her lesson and taken her punishment. As far as I'm concerned that's the end of the matter."

Her parents took their cue from this pronouncement, and if dinner was a quiet affair with little being said, at least Annie was spared any further recriminations.

After dinner, Annie was told that she need not stay to do the washing up. Her mother gave an indulgent smile, as if all the earlier scenes in the chapel had been forgotten. "You two young people take yourselves off. And you can leave your painting behind for once, madam."

Joe leapt to his feet, eager to have Annie to himself again with her full attention. He had read correctly what was behind Beatie Claydon's suggestion. Her rebellious daughter needed to be married, with the firm hand of a husband to keep her in order. There would be no further repetition of this morning's public shaming at the chapel.

Once out of earshot, Joe held Annie's arm tightly holding her as close as he could without actually squeezing the breath out of her. He led her round the fields skirting the lane where his cottage was situated until they reached the fence at the back.

"Quick, through here," he urged, opening first the gate then the back door.

"But Joe, I'm not supposed…"

Her lips were silenced as Joe's bore down on hers in a long almost savage kiss. "God! I've been wanting to do this for so long but we're always with other people." He pulled her down on to the newly bought sofa, laying her head gently on the soft feather cushions. Kissing and whispering they lost track of time. It was only when Joe's kisses became more urgent that Annie whimpered in protest. "No, Joe, we mustn't. We're not married."

It was too late. "Only because you won't set the date," he murmured, still quietly but purposefully undressing her.

What followed was like some wonderful dream come true for the two lovers, locked in one another's arms. Finally, both sated and relaxed they lay side by side, Joe caressing Annie's flushed cheeks.

With realisation suddenly dawning, Annie began to cry as she pushed Joe away. "You shouldn't have, Joe. Isn't this what happens when you want to have a baby?"

Joe silenced her with another kiss. "Hush, hush. I know what to do not to give you a baby. Don't worry, my darling."

Still not totally convinced, Annie finished dressing. "What if someone sees us? Ma says I'm not to come here until we're married."

"Well?" Joe was exultant. "We're as good as now, so when is it to be?"

So what had happened was just what her mother had planned. The feeling that she had been tricked by both her ma and Joe bubbled up inside her until shame and humiliation gave way to anger. "I'll tell you when I'm good and ready, Joe Langmead, so you needn't think that your trick has worked."

"Anyone would think you didn't enjoy yourself this afternoon." Joe threw his head back and laughed. "I know I'm the happiest man on earth. Tell me you feel the same way."

Annie could not deny it. This handsome man with the taut frame of a prize fighter and dark eyes filled with passion just for her, was the only man she could ever love. Her lips held up to his gave him the answer he wanted.

They crept out of the cottage, Annie terrified that the neighbours would see and report her disgraceful goings-on to her parents. Not a soul was about, not one curtain twitched.

"They're all having a Sunday afternoon nap," Joe assured her. "Probably up to the same as us, I shouldn't wonder."

As Joe walked her home, they talked of future plans. "If only we could get away from Densbury, the factory and the Gladwells," Annie sighed.

Joe was shocked. "Whatever for? I've got a house, a good job and I like it here."

"Well I don't." Annie's forcefulness filled Joe with foreboding. "I want to get right away to a bigger town where I could learn to paint properly and live my life as I want."

"Am I included in your great plans?"

The slight pause before she answered was not missed by Joe. "Of course." She stopped to face him. "But you must understand that I can't live without my painting."

"I can wait. This painting thing can't take up your whole life. Being married is more important. I suppose one day you'll make up your mind what you want the most."

Annie opened her mouth to protest, but was silenced by Joe's anguished, "Don't leave me, Annie. I want you here with me."

Chapter 6

How to get Joe to move away to a bigger town where she could achieve her ambition occupied most of Annie's waking thoughts Surely if he loved her, he could get work in another town.

"I'm not leaving and that's that." Joe refused to budge. "I'm beginning to think that you care more about your painting than me."

Annie gasped at what she saw as Joe's attempt to force her into a decision she was unable to make. "That's not fair. You know how much I love you and want us to be married, but…"

"There's always a 'but' with you, Annie." For a moment, Annie flinched as his powerful arms reached out to grip her shoulders. "Name the day before I go mad." He let go of her, sinking back into the armchair and burying his head in his hands.

"I'm here, aren't I? You know what Ma would say if she knew we were meeting at your house."

"You're right. We'd better get you home before someone sees you here." Dejected at his failure yet again to win Annie over to the idea of an early wedding, he led her out of the back door. They left Joe's house with Annie keeping her head down and dashing through the gate which led out of the tiny back yard. Sweet as these meetings were, she knew that if her parents were to find out, she would have no say on the subject of marrying Joe; her parents would insist on a wedding date being fixed before she shamed them further.

These arguments began to cloud their meetings until Annie flatly refused to meet Joe on one of their regular Sunday afternoon walks. After Sunday dinner, she pleaded a headache and said she needed to go and lie down.

"What's the cause of this all of a sudden, my girl? You've never had a headache in your life before."

"Honestly, Ma, I didn't sleep too well last night." That much was true. The latest argument with Joe had kept her awake. Desperate as she was to spend her life with him, a quiet but persistent voice inside her held her back, making her apprehensive of a humdrum life tied down in Densbury.

"OK, Joe," her father said, "let's you and me go rabbiting. Billy Peggle has got the best ferret in Densbury. It can catch enough rabbits to feed a family for a fortnight."

"Why not?" Joe agreed. "Might as well catch a rabbit or two, if nothing else." The morose downturn of his mouth was not lost on Annie.

"I dunno." Her mother shook her head. "Go on then, off to bed with you."

Annie sat on the top stair waiting for her mother to make a move. Once the dishes had been put away, her ma would be off to see Fred's sister Violet, who kept her up to date with the latest gossip. Once silence reigned in the house, Annie crept out of the back door and through the lane leading to the fields behind the houses. A short run and she had skirted the town, ending up at her favourite spot from where she could look across to Baythorpe Hall. It was August and Anthony would be home, she guessed, that was if he hadn't departed on one of his holidays in Italy. She sat down on a little mound just behind the hedge on the Gladwell land, safe in the knowledge that she could not be seen and that she could make her escape if she saw anyone coming.

"No!" Annie struggled as two hands were placed over her eyes. "I'm sorry," she whimpered, terrified that it might be the gamekeeper or one of the other men who worked for the Gladwells.

"It's me, Anthony." He swung her round to face him. "I saw you coming," he told her. "I've been making some sketches down there." He pointed to a dip in the parkland hidden from Annie's view. "Here, let me sit down with you and tell you how sorry I am to have alarmed you and how glad I am to be finished with Oxford."

"You mean you're home for good?" Annie felt her heart lighten at this news.

Anthony made a little moue. "No, not really. Papa has this idea that I ought to be sent to a cousin of his in Australia to learn about sheep and wool."

"Oh, no! You can't go all that way away." She remembered the big globe at school twirled round by Miss Turkentine. Australia might just as well be on the moon. "I'll never see you again. I won't have anyone to talk to about painting. You're the only one who understands what it means to me. Please don't go," she pleaded.

"Well, it's not fixed yet, so let's talk about something else."

Gradually the talk came round to the stoning of the priest and the doctor by the enraged men of the town. "You were a bit of a madcap to take them on." Anthony was not smiling. "I heard about all that. You really must be more careful. There are things you don't understand. Just don't meddle, Annie." His tone was very much that of a disapproving older brother.

"I'm not a child, Anthony, and I couldn't just let my friend's father get hurt. Isabelle hasn't any other family, you know."

"Promise me, Annie, you won't do anything like that again."

Annie had never seen him look so solemn. "Well, it's not likely to happen again, so I promise."

"Oh, God, here's Lavinia!" Anthony leapt to his feet. "Quick, you'd better go!" His warning came too late as Lavinia and Miles Fanshawe reined in their horses in front of them.

Annie shrank back, her heart thumping with terror at the sight of the two horses snorting and pawing the ground within feet of her. "Please, keep them away from me," she begged Anthony, clutching his arm and trying to seek protection behind him.

"Nothing to be afraid of, little one," the man said, swinging down from his mount. "At least not from the horses, heh, Anthony? You're a sly one entertaining the village maidens." His leering face inches from hers sickened her as did his words. "When he tires of you, I'll be waiting."

Lavinia could not catch what he had said, but guessed it was not meant for her ears by Annie's look of revulsion. "Come along, Miles." She turned her attention to Anthony. "Just wait until I tell Papa about what you're doing with the factory hands, you'll be on the first boat to Australia."

"Lavinia!" Anthony protested, his colour stripped from his cheeks. "I'm coming in now. Just give me a minute." He waited until Lavinia and her companion had disappeared. Still ashen, his next words sent a chill through Annie. "Lavinia hates you, Annie, and believe me she'll stop at nothing if something is standing in her way. Don't do anything to upset her whatever you do. Promise me!"

"Please, Anthony, don't worry." Concerned as she was about his warning, she sought to reassure him. "I'm not likely to cross her path, am I? She can't possibly hurt me."

He patted her arm. "You're a good sort, Annie. We'll just have to keep out of her way. I don't care what she says, if I get a chance to see you, I will, but first I've got to convince Father that he doesn't have to send me to the Antipodes."

She watched his tall, lithe figure running towards Baythorpe Hall until he was out of sight. The strange thought struck her that one day he would be married and that perhaps his wife would not want him to be friendly with a girl from her walk of life. She felt a stab of pain at the thought that their happy times together would come to an end.

Having lost track of time until then, she was shocked to feel the coolness of the breeze on her bare arms as the sun lost its early afternoon warmth. She flew back to her house, getting herself up to her bedroom well in advance of her mother's return from the visit to her aunt. As usual, Eileen was out with her friend Gladys. Although both quite grown-up, they still spent their Sunday afternoons together with Eileen staying to tea.

"Annie! I want you down here! Never mind the headache, my girl." Her mother's voice screeching with fury carried up the stairs.

Annie smoothed her hair and tousled her hair as if to show that she had just been roused from a deep sleep. "Coming," she called, wondering what had upset her ma. Perhaps she had seen her running home and guessed that she had lied about having a headache.

Her mother stood by the table. "Sit down and don't say a word. We'll see what your father has to say about this when he gets back with Joe."

The two women sat, neither saying a word. "Would you like a cup of tea, Ma?" Anything to break the uncomfortable silence.

"I told you to hold your tongue, madam. If I want tea, I'll make it." Grim-faced, her mother sat motionless watching the clock.

Annie gazed at the back door willing it to open and admit Joe and her pa.

"Here we are then. Enough rabbits to feed us for a week," Fred Claydon announced, proudly holding up the result of his afternoon's sport. His wife's stony features told him all was not well. "Something happened?"

"Ask your friend Joe here and your daughter," was all the reply he got.

"Out with it, woman, I'm not standing here guessing."

Annie had the uncomfortable feeling that her mother was enjoying being the centre of her little drama. She was unprepared for the onslaught which followed.

"I've just got back from Violet's." Fred's sister's favourite pastime was dredging up gossip and passing it on with embellishments. "Your aunt knows a thing or two about you," she told Annie.

By this time, Fred's impatience was slowly turning to anger both with his wife and Annie. "Get on with it!" he roared.

"It's her, spending her Sunday afternoons in Joe's house, getting up to goodness knows what for all the neighbours to see and laugh about." She dealt Annie a stinging blow across the mouth. "You little trollop."

Joe's eyes flashed fury. He took a white handkerchief out of his pocket to wipe the blood from Annie's swollen lip. "I love Annie and took her into my house so that we could talk about our future together. You will not call her a trollop, Mrs Claydon." For once, he did not address her as Beatie.

She opened her mouth to protest. "Fred, do something—"

He silenced her with a gesture. "I think you've got a lot more explaining to do, Joe. We entrusted Annie to you as a friend and we said you could walk out with her. We didn't expect you to shame her in front of the whole town." Fred's quiet words hung in the air for a few moments.

"I want Annie to marry me soon. I thought if she saw for herself what a nice home I could provide, it might help her make up her mind a bit quicker." He put a protective arm around her shoulders. Tall and proud he stood beside her. "She is more precious to me than life itself."

Tears tumbled down her cheeks as the man she adored made this quiet declaration. Guilt at making him go through this humiliation flooded through her.

"That's as maybe." Beatie Claydon, still fired with the recollection of her sister-in-law's enjoyment at retailing the news about her daughter's shameful behaviour, was not to be so easily placated. "First she shames us in front of the whole town with her Papist friends and now she behaves as if she's no better than she ought to be. I know what I think ought to happen and the sooner the better."

It was Joe who came to Annie's rescue. "Annie and I will marry just as soon as she decides. One thing is for sure; there will be no hasty wedding for the town harpies to gossip and speculate about."

"And there will be no more Sunday afternoons spent with our Annie at your house." If Fred had surmised that the meetings had not been altogether as innocent as Joe had explained, he thought it better to say nothing on that score. No harm done as far as he could tell in that there was no obvious need for a quick wedding. "Perhaps you and Annie had better go out for a walk and have a little talk." He raised a quietening hand to his wife who was about to protest. "It's their decision. I think our Annie knows what she has to do."

In full view of the neighbours, Joe and Annie strolled arm in arm finally wending their way along the main street. "So what was wrong with you this afternoon, Annie?" He gently removed a hawthorn leaf tangled in her soft black curls. "You didn't get this lying on your bed, did you?"

Annie blushed with shame at Joe's easy discovery of her deception. "I felt better so I went for a walk."

"And how is the heir to the Gladwell fortune?" Joe's mouth was twisted in a cruel sneer. "So you went to meet him rather than come out with me." His angry voice caused one lone walker to turn his head. "We're supposed to be talking about our wedding plans and you're meeting another man. You have got to stop seeing Anthony Gladwell." He grasped her arm roughly. "Tell me you love me and no one else," he demanded.

Annie held his hand tightly. "You're my only love and always will be. Anthony is just a friend to talk to about painting. Whatever happens, you must never forget that."

Joe's rugged features reluctantly creased in a smile. "I won't and I won't let you forget it either." He pulled her closer to his side. "So, what shall we tell your ma and pa?"

"Tell them that we're making plans."

Her parents seemed partly satisfied that the wedding plans were moving forward, although her ma was still impatient for Annie to fix a definite date.

"I need to save some more money for my bottom drawer," she was told.

"But you don't need one. Joe's got everything for the house already and it's all new."

"Yes, but I want my own things as well," was Annie's explanation.

It was with this in mind that she took herself shopping the following Saturday afternoon in the High Street. Eileen was working in the wool shop and had told Annie that they were beginning to stock some nice new lines in tablecloths. "Miss Witton's ever so pleased with me and my knitting. I've done a whole lot of jumpers and baby clothes while we wait for customers and they've sold really well." She pointed to her handiwork in the window. "Look, I've arranged the shop window so that we can put other things in it as well. Do you think it looks nice?"

Her appeal touched Annie. Instead of a nondescript pile of knitting wools and allied paraphernalia, the whole window was like a picture in itself with the eye being drawn to the beautifully knitted jackets created from Eileen's original patterns. Their granny's gift had been passed on to both of her granddaughters. "I never realised it before, Eileen, but you're an artist just like me aren't you, just in a different way. The way you've set things out is really clever."

The praise from her elder sister cemented a bond between them. If Annie approved, her window arrangements must be good. Annie left, promising to call in the following Saturday and buy the pretty white tablecloth edged with pale blue cornflowers just like the ones growing in the wheatfields.

Happy at seeing Eileen so well settled in a job she enjoyed so well, she continued up the High Street. Immersed in her thoughts of collecting for her bottom drawer, she did not take note of the sound of a horse's hooves, not seeing the animal until it was within a foot of her. The driver of the pony and trap reined in so close that Annie, in her terror, was forced to cower against the wall of the saddler's shop.

"Here girl, hold these reins while I call into the saddlers." Lavinia Gladwell made as if to toss the reins into Annie's hands.

"I can't, Miss Lavinia." Fear froze her to the spot at the sight of the snorting pony's nostrils near her face. With her hand held up to protect herself Annie turned her head away.

Sniggers from a few lads standing watching the exchange did nothing to improve the Gladwell girl's temper. "Idiot! How dare you!"

One of the lads, eager to earn himself a few pennies stepped forward, but was brushed aside. "She is to do it." Lavinia pointed her whip at Annie,

"I can't, I'm frightened of horses. I'm sorry, honest I am."

Lavinia handed the reins over to the waiting lad. "You will be sorry," she sneered at Annie.

Anthony's words of warning about his sister rang in her head. He was right; Lavinia was never going to miss an opportunity to humiliate her.

The incident was largely forgotten in the ensuing weeks, but a sudden reminder of Lavinia Gladwell's venom came when the factory manager announced that Miss Lavinia was to pay the factory a visit. "Mind your Ps and Qs, if you know what's good for you," Charlie Singleton warned the women and girls. Annie made up her mind that she would be on the lookout and behave exactly as was expected of her.

Later that morning, he told them that Miss Lavinia had had to change her plans. Annie breathed a sigh of relief, continuing to work on a particularly difficult seam. Struggling with the heavy jacket material in order to keep the seam straight, she was totally lost in her task and did not notice the sudden quiet in the workroom. The machines had all fallen silent apart from hers, but still oblivious to her surroundings she battled on.

"Stand up at once, girl," Charlie Singleton hissed.

"What for?" Annie complained. "I've got to get this right."

The gasps of her workmates alerted her to the fact that her minor act of defiance was going to incur severe consequences. She turned to see Miss Lavinia scowling at her. Dressed in the latest silk London creation, a dark blue narrow-skirted dress reaching to just above her ankles, she looked every inch the wealthy daughter of a very rich factory owner. Annie thrust the sewing aside and leapt to her feet, attempting to drop a deep curtsey at the same time. Lavinia had let it be known that she was not visiting that day and had watched from the vantage point of Charlie Singleton's office until she could see Annie engrossed in her work.

Not bothering to go further, Lavinia turned on her heels followed by the manager. She did not need to tell him what had to be done. Within minutes he had returned. "You're sacked," he told Annie.

"Sacked? But why?" Annie's lower lip trembled. "I didn't mean to ignore Miss Lavinia. I just didn't see her."

"That's right," one of the girls said. "Annie was working really hard."

"You shut your mouth if you don't want the sack as well," Charlie Singleton said. His ugly thin lips stretched in a rictus of a smile. He enjoyed taking his revenge on his old rival in love, Fred Claydon. Sacking Fred's daughter was a nice little bonus on top of the tip Miss Lavinia had given him to tell the workers that her visit had been postponed. "It's about time you were taught to respect your betters, Annie Claydon." He spat out the name Claydon, his face a mask of hatred as he pronounced it.

"I'll finish this then, shall I?"

"No, you'll leave now, you impudent miss."

Watched in silence by her mates, who had read that there was something more to Annie's sacking than her failure to stand up when Miss Lavinia entered the workroom, Annie went to the office to collect what was owing to her for the week's work.

"It's not ready. Your father can collect it tomorrow. Don't you set foot here again." Charlie would enjoy handing over to Fred the wages of his disgraced daughter. All in all, a day when the gods had smiled on him at last.

Annie ran home to tell her mother that she was now jobless. If she expected sympathy, she received very little. "Why is it that you always seem to meet trouble head on?" her mother asked. "I might have known that you and that tongue of yours would get you the sack."

"I didn't say anything, Ma."

"In that case, you'd better tell me what happened. You don't get the sack for nothing." She relented a little when Annie had finished explaining.

"I would have stood up, but I didn't know she was there," Annie kept insisting.

"It's still your fault, my girl. It sticks out a mile that she doesn't like you being friendly with that brother of hers. How many times do I have to tell you that our sort can't mix with our betters?" She shook her head from side to side. "You're so stubborn and won't be told and now you've lost your job."

"How am I going to be able to save for my bottom drawer?" Panic gripped Annie at the prospect of having no money.

"I don't know. All I know is that no one will dare to employ you hereabouts now that you've insulted a Gladwell."

Seeking work proved to be just as hard as her mother had predicted, with no shopkeeper prepared to give a job to her. Self-preservation dictated whom they employed, and upsetting the Gladwells was not advisable. It was her Auntie Violet who said that she'd heard of a job going for a live-in maid at the Estcourt estate. The money wasn't much, but as she used to work there as a girl, they might accept her recommendation.

"But I don't want to live in a strange house." Memories of being a daily maid at Baythorpe Hall came flooding back. What would it be like to be at the beck and call of another spiteful housekeeper.

"Beggars can't be choosers," her tight-lipped mother snapped. "You should have thought of that when you were meeting that Anthony Gladwell and upsetting his family." She gave Annie a searching look. "Of course, if you marry Joe as soon as a date can be fixed with Pastor Briggs, there won't be any need to work away."

Annie felt as if the walls were closing in around her. Whichever way she turned, there was no exit of her choice. "I'll take the job and save some money. Like I said, I'm not marrying without a penny piece to my name." Even if she were to marry Joe and stay in Densbury, at least with a little money of her own, she figured, she would retain some independence. Paints and brushes cost money and she was not sure that Joe would indulge her to that extent.

The Estcourt estate was even grander than Baythorpe Hall, having been in the Estcourt family for over two hundred years. It was said to have been given to an ancestor for services to the Crown together with a handsome cash settlement. His descendants had lived comfortably on the income and, unlike the Gladwells, had no need to dirty their hands in business affairs.

"I still can't see why you have to be so damned obstinate, Annie. I can earn enough for the two of us and a family. You'll never have to count your pennies." Anger mounted as he saw that his words were having no effect on her. "Who else in Densbury owns a house? What more do you want?"

"You know what I want, Joe," Annie said softly. "I want some money of my own so that I can buy whatever paints and brushes I need without asking you."

"But I'd give it to you willingly, you know that."

Annie shook her head. Hadn't her granny told her what happened when a woman married? Every penny was needed for the family. With a wisdom beyond her years, Annie knew it would only be a matter of time before Joe began to resent her passion for art. "I don't want to work at Estcourt miles away from you, but I promise that I'll save every penny I earn and then we'll marry."

Joe borrowed a pony and trap to take Annie to Estcourt on her first day. They stopped at the front gates of wrought iron decorated with the family crest. Annie stared in dismay at the long drive bordered by ancient elms leading to the massive front door.

"Round the back with you." A tall figure in black approached the couple outside the gate. "Drive round there to the left. The tradesmen's entrance is clearly marked."

Joe raised his cap in deference and duly turned the trap round. "Don't think I enjoy kow-towing to the likes of him," he explained, "but I don't want to upset the flunkeys you're going to have to work under."

Annie made Joe stop at the tradesmen's entrance and hand her down the small bag containing what she needed for the week ahead.

"I'll be here next Sunday at nine," he promised, holding her close in a final embrace. "Oh, Annie Claydon, why did I fall in love with you?" he whispered.

Annie waved to him as she began the long slow walk to the back kitchen of Estcourt Towers. Her first impressions that this was not going to be a happy time were confirmed when she was greeted by the housekeeper with a taciturn, "You're here at last." She summoned a thin girl with a sallow spotty complexion. "Here, Martha, take Annie to your room and show her where things are." She turned to Annie. "No wasting time either. There's work to be done."

Without a word, Martha signalled Annie to follow her up the first flight of back stairs which was succeeded by two more. "We're at the top," Martha explained. "There's six of us, two to a room."

Annie fought back the tears seeing the sparse room with bare boards for a floor and two tiny beds. She turned down the sheets, which although snowy white were thin, patched and darned long past their useful life. "My ma would have used these for dusters long ago."

Martha's mouth dropped open, ugly red blotches appearing on her cheeks. "Oh, you mustn't say things like that here, not unless you want to be sent packing like the last girl." Her features softened. "I'd like to be your friend," she said shyly. "Here, put on your uniform." She handed Annie a black dress and pinafore. "It looks about your size. Nora, the girl who left, was a bit bigger than you, but I reckon we could fix it with a few stitches."

Annie put her possessions in the cupboard alongside Martha's. She sighed. If she was going to get what she wanted, she would just have to grin and bear it.

Rising early was no problem, having been used to it all her working life, but the sheer drudgery of the endless fires to be lit and kept going, the eternal carrying of coal to each and every room was backbreaking work. The Estcourts, Sir Ivor and Lady Cecilia enjoyed entertaining on a grand scale, particularly their London friends who found that life in the country could be highly amusing with hunting game in the daytime followed by evening parties. This meant that often there were fifteen bedrooms to be kept heated and hot water provided for baths. It seemed to Annie that no sooner had she laid her head on her pillow with every fibre of her being craving sleep, that she had to rise again and begin the endless tasks all over again.

"Are we allowed home for Christmas Day?" she asked Martha.

"Are you daft, girl?" Martha shook her lank locks in astonishment at Annie's ignorance. "There'll be twice as much to do with all the guests they have for the big Christmas Eve ball every year. Really exciting it is with all the ladies in their lovely gowns and all the gentlemen looking so handsome." She beamed proudly. "And we get treated ever so well on Christmas Day. Lady Cecilia comes down to the kitchen to wish us all a merry Christmas and we all sit down to dinner once the family and everyone has been served. They're not at all stuck up." Her smile grew wider at the thought of the treats in store. "You don't know how lucky you are working here."

Annie did not agree. The only times she felt lucky were when Joe came to pick her up in the borrowed pony and trap. He would drive to a secluded spot in the woods a mile down the road where he would hold her so tightly, she could hardly breathe.

"It won't be for much longer," she promised him. "I can't bear to be away from you and everyone."

"And what does that mean?"

"What I said." And with that he had to be content for the time being.

Christmas Eve was as Martha had predicted with all the staff on call. The huge ballroom had to be decorated with holly and mistletoe whilst the dining room was set out with a magnificent choice of meats, sweet dishes and vast bowls of punch. A huge Christmas tree surrounded by lavishly decorated boxes filled the huge alcove by one of the windows looking out over the front lawns. Gold and silver baubles, glittering and reflecting the lights thrown out by the crystal chandeliers, hung from every branch.

At six in the evening, the postman arrived. "Come on in, Albert," the housekeeper greeted him. "The cards will be ready soon."

"Why does he have to come here?" Annie asked Martha.

"Ah, well, the ladies like to give him their Christmas cards so that he can deliver them first thing to all their friends on Christmas morning. It's really his day off, but he can't say no, can he?"

No, Annie thought, when our betters pull the strings, we have to do as we are bid or lose our jobs and starve. "I suppose not," was all she said. Better not say anything which might be passed on and construed as insubordination. Her first big shock came when she was sent to turn down the beds for the guests staying over for the ball and Christmas dinner. The sound of the familiar voices coming from the corridor turned her blood to ice.

"More coal on the fire, girl." Lavinia turned her cold eyes on Annie. "Ah, I see it's you. Mind you behave yourself here. I'll be watching your every move."

Annie banked up the fire before retreating. "Can you see to Miss Lavinia?" she asked Martha. "I think she'd prefer you, knowing the job better and all that."

Flattered, Martha agreed, leaving Annie to see to the other guests. If Lavinia were here, surely Anthony would be too. At least there would be one friendly face.

On entering his room, she smiled happily, ready to greet him. His studied coldness stung her. There was no acknowledgement of her presence, no sign that he had ever seen her before. It was with a shock that she found herself curtseying as he issued his curt instruction to see to his fire and bring up enough hot water for his bath. Fool that I am, she thought, I'm just the maid and here he is, an honoured guest of a titled family.

The final room she had to see to was at the end of the long corridor on the first floor. A hand creeping round her waist and then higher to fondle her breast would have made her scream out loud had it not been for the hand placed over her mouth. "Little Annie, Anthony's playmate." She turned to see the Honourable Miles Fanshawe's triumphant grin.

"Excuse me, sir, I have to go." Wriggling free she ran down to the kitchen. One thing was certain, Miles Fanshawe would hardly be stupid enough to do anything to upset Lavinia, she reasoned. She would try to organise the bedroom duties so that Martha did his as well as Lavinia's.

"Getting a bit choosy, aren't we?" Martha asked.

"I'll explain later," Annie promised, her mind working overtime to concoct a story that would be acceptable to the girl who was not as simple as she looked.

The evening flew past with Annie constantly on call. With the festivities in full swing she judged it safe to see to the grate in Miles Fanshawe's bedroom instead of asking Martha to do it. The musicians in the ballroom were playing an extremely fast Viennese waltz, a great favourite that year, so Annie knew that all the gentlemen would be whirling their partners round the floor. Engrossed in the task of laying coals on the dying embers she did not hear the click of the door behind her.

"The lovely little Annie."

Still kneeling, Annie turned her head to see Miles Fanshawe leaning over her. "Excuse me, sir," she babbled, "I've nearly finished here." She struggled to get to her feet.

"No rush, little girl. How about letting me have a taste of what that young rascal Anthony has tried."

"I don't know what you mean, sir." Terror seizing up her throat, her voice came out in a hoarse whisper.

"Oh, but I think you do," he snarled, pushing her roughly backwards.

Annie struggled to get to her feet but was no match for his strong right arm which pinned her to the floor as the other sought to pull off her clothes. Whimpering, she closed her eyes, calling out Joe's name, as if he could hear her cries for help.

A loud bellow, "What the hell do you think you're up to?" brought the half drunken Miles to his senses.

"Sorry, Anthony, old chap," he muttered sheepishly, "but she just lay down and offered herself, so what was a red-blooded man to do, eh?" He nudged Anthony in the ribs. "You understand, don't you?"

As Annie attempted to smooth down her torn apron, Lavinia appeared in the doorway. Her dark eyes filled with hatred, she advanced on Annie. "First my brother and now my fiancé." She gripped Annie's shoulder, smiling with sadistic delight as Annie cried out in pain.

"I say, old girl," Miles protested. "Don't take this too hard. Just a bit of horseplay. Had a drop too much of the punch." He gave a little whinny.

Lavinia ignored his feeble protests. "Fetch the housekeeper," she ordered him. "This little whore will have to go."

It was tacitly understood that Lady Cecilia would not have to be troubled with the sordid events taking place under her roof on Christmas Eve. It was the housekeeper's job to deal with unsuitable staff whatever the time of year.

Mrs Lane glared at the young maid who had brought disgrace on the house. "Get your things and leave now. There'll be no money owing to you, you understand."

Annie winced. "But, that's not right. I'm owed my wages."

Lavinia sneered. "You heard what Mrs Lane said." Her mission accomplished, she turned on her heels to leave the room. "Don't worry about her," she told Anthony, who had been observing the scene with horror, "she knows how to earn her living."

Annie looked wildly about her, but met only cold hostility in the eyes of the others in the room.

"I mean you leave right now," the housekeeper insisted.

"But it's five miles and it's snowing. Can't I wait until morning, please?" she begged.

"Out right now." The housekeeper steered her towards the stairs. "Go up to your room and be down here in five minutes and out of the house."

Annie straightened herself and looked the woman in the eye. "You're as bad as that Miles and Lavinia. You're all filthy and evil. I wouldn't lower myself to stay here a minute longer anyway." She did not see Anthony's look of horror as he heard her defiant words before he crept out of earshot.

Her defiance evaporated as she began the long trek to the back gates. By now the snow was several inches thick and still falling to create what the revellers in the ballroom would call a pretty Christmas card scene. The story of the sacked servant girl had reached the ears of some of the guests, who continued to enjoy the Christmas Eve party. Apart from a few smirks on the faces of Miles Fanshawe's friends, who secretly admired his failed attempts to rape the girl, most dismissed the event from their minds.

Annie paused for a moment outside the main gates to view the colourful picture of lights, beautiful gowns and dancing. It was bitterly cold and dark with the stars and moon hidden by the thick cloud and driving snow. Her earlier mood of defiance was rapidly diminishing as she felt the cold eating into her bones, the woollen shawl a pitifully inadequate protection against the worst of an East Anglian winter. Annie recognised that she was facing an arduous battle to reach home. Her boots already letting in the snow, her feet were beginning to lose their feeling. Hot tears spilled down her cheeks as she recalled stories of travellers found frozen after attempting to find a way through snow storms. Barely able to see the road ahead, she prayed for Joe's forgiveness. What a fool she had been to think that she could escape the fetters her class placed upon her. She should have given up her wild ambitions and settled down to marriage with the man she loved. Finding a signpost, she leant against it for support. Even in the dark after brushing off the snow, she could see that she had a good five miles to go. The lights of Estcourt still twinkled in the distance.

A sudden noise startled her. The huge Gladwell Panhard driven by Anthony, slithered to a halt. "Annie, quick, get in!" he urged.

Annie remained motionless clinging to the signpost. "I can't move," she managed to whisper.

It was true; she was on the point of collapsing at its foot. Anthony leapt out of the car, cursing Miles Fanshawe and his sister for their callous treatment of Annie. It took all his strength to lift her and place her in the front seat. First he removed her sodden shawl and replaced it with a thick dry rug, wrapping it round her until only her eyes were visible.

"Here, drink this," he ordered, producing a small flask. "It's brandy."

Annie shrank back. "No! What would Pastor Briggs say?" she protested.

"He'll be conducting your funeral service if you don't soon warm up."

Annie took a few tentative sips, gradually relaxing as the alcohol warmed her throat and sent a feeling of well-being throughout her veins.

"There, that's better," Anthony said, relieved at seeing Annie respond. "Now to get you home."

"But how did you manage to get the car? I thought it belonged to your father," Annie said.

"I gave the chauffeur a five pound note and told him to take the night off." He stared straight ahead peering into the blinding white of the snowstorm.

"Won't your father be angry?"

"Very," was Anthony's only reply.

Although only five miles, the journey took several hours with Anthony having to stop and check where the sides of the road ended and the ditch began. He would be in even worse trouble if he wrecked his father's prize possession.

It was three o'clock on Christmas morning when Annie hammered on her parents' back door. Heads appeared out of the windows of neighbouring cottages, angry voices demanding to know who was disturbing their sleep.

"Annie! What on earth are you doing here?" Fred Claydon pulled a blanket round his shoulders before racing down the stairs to let his daughter in.

Close on his heels, her ma rushed to enfold Annie in her arms. "Whatever is it?" she asked as Annie wept unable to speak. "Quick, Fred, put the kettle on. And you'd better see if you can get the fire going again." Whatever had happened to Annie was going to take a while to explain.

It wasn't until Annie came to relate how Anthony had come along in his father's car that her parents' sympathy showed signs of diminishing. "Always that Anthony Gladwell," her mother complained. "Hasn't he caused enough trouble? Where is he then?"

"He's had to try and drive back to Estcourt. Honestly, Ma, I'd be dead if he hadn't come along."

"And none of this would have happened if you'd married Joe instead of letting your head be filled with daft ideas about saving money and being independent." She spat out the last word. "It's about time that you forgot such rubbish. It's the menfolk who bring in the money and the women do as they're bid."

The stubborn set of Annie's mouth infuriated her further. "You stupid girl! When will you ever learn?"

Annie was glad to snuggle up beside her sister in her own warm bed. Her mother was right about one thing; she should never have gone to work at Estcourt. A nightmare woke her once in the night. She felt she could smell the whisky on Miles Fanshawe's breath as he pinned her to the floor. It was with relief that she opened her eyes to see the glass figurine that Joe won for her at the gala. It was still where she had left it, its delicate flowing lines calming and soothing her, reminding her of her love for Joe.

In a few hours Joe would be coming to join the Claydons for Christmas dinner. She would tell him that she had set a date for their wedding. Easter would be a time for renewal, for putting the past behind her and forgetting her stupid ambitions which could never come to fruition.

Joe would be so happy.

Chapter 7

The early days of 1911 did not bring joy to the Claydon household. Word had been spread in Densbury that Annie Claydon had been sent packing from Estcourt. Knowing winks and nods accompanied the information that she had been found in a gentleman's bedroom in highly suspicious circumstances. More than one man had left the factory at the end of a shift with a bloody nose after being unwise enough to say as much in Joe's hearing.

"You fool of a girl," Annie's ma blasted at her when she heard of the argument Joe had had with one man over Annie's dismissal from Estcourt. "The trouble you've caused. One good job after another thrown away and if Joe goes on like that sticking up for you in the factory, he'll be the next one without a job."

"It wasn't my fault," Annie protested. "Surely you don't think…"

"I don't know what to think any more." Her ma's face drooped with weariness. "All I do know is that you've managed to upset the Gladwells yet again. It will be a miracle if your pa gets to keep his job." She flopped into a chair. "Then what will we do?"

Annie was at a loss to know how to comfort her mother. "I don't know, Ma."

Beatie leapt to her feet. "It's all your fault with your fancy ideas. Why can't you be like any normal girl and get married? God knows you've left Joe dangling long enough."

"But I don't want to get married yet. Joe understands about my painting."

"Your painting! I'm sick to death of hearing about your painting," Beatie stormed. "It doesn't put a crumb of bread on the table or pay the rent. You and your fancy ideas, thinking you can be friends with the likes of Anthony Gladwell and that doctor's daughter."

"But they are friends," Annie insisted.

"Well, perhaps your fine friends will find you some work, my girl. One thing is for sure, your pa can't keep you at home here as if you were some fine lady of leisure." She placed two hands heavily on her daughter's shoulders and stared hard into her eyes. "There's the rich, who don't have to worry about where the next penny is coming from and there's the poor like us. We have to work to pay our way or else we end up out on the streets and in the workhouse. Nobody gives us anything unless we work damned hard for it, so you had better think on."

"Right!" Annie jumped up out of her chair. "I'll go and get myself a job right now!" She grabbed her shawl, flung it round her shoulders and flounced out of the house.

Once out of the lane and in the High Street, she considered her options. Surely one of the shops flanking both sides of the street would be in need of an assistant. The first one she tried was the greengrocer, Ebenezer Farlay. She was shocked at his response to her request.

"I wouldn't give you a job if I had one, Annie Claydon." He wiped his hands on his green apron and pushed her out of the door.

The next one was only slightly better. Dick Poley kept darting nervous glances towards the door. "I'm sorry, Annie, but a saddlery is no place for a girl to work. I can't help you." He then

105

gave the real reason for his refusal to give her work. "Besides, Miss Gladwell often drops by. You know how fond she is of her horses."

Once again, Annie found herself being helped out of the door. As a last resort, she decided to try knocking on the door of the manse. Perhaps Pastor Briggs' wife would need someone to help with the rough work.

"I'll work for less than you pay Mrs Main," she pleaded.

"I wouldn't have you in my house if you offered to work for nothing," she said, slamming the door in Annie's face.

The bitter truth of her situation and the unfairness of her treatment burned deeply into her heart. "How dare they!" she muttered to herself. Never a word of criticism of the Honourable Miles Fanshawe or the way she had been thrown out of Estcourt to find her way home on Christmas Eve.

Her head down, lost in her thoughts, she did not notice Daisy, one of the girls who had worked alongside her at the factory. As the two collided, Annie looked up ready to greet her old workmate. "Hello, Daisy."

The girl did not return her smile. She pushed past Annie with a barely audible mumbled, "Hello, can't stop."

Annie turned on her heel to see the hastily retreating back of her old friend. Her eyes burning with unshed tears, she made her way back towards home. It was all so wrong, she told herself. Why should the Gladwells have so much power? At least Anthony was different. Without considering the consequences, he had defied his father by taking her home on Christmas Eve. She allowed herself the tiniest of smiles at the thought of what Lavinia's reaction would have been when she heard that a humble chambermaid had ridden in the family limousine. It crossed her mind that Anthony must have been worried about what his father would say; he had barely given her time to get out of the vehicle that night before turning round in the lane to get back to Estcourt. A hasty farewell and then he was gone.

The clouds full of snow allowed a few rays of wintry sunshine to filter through, giving the false impression that warmth would follow. There is still plenty of time before I go home, she thought. In any case, she shied from facing her ma with the news that nobody would speak to her, let alone employ her.

Annie suppressed her guilt as she turned away from home and began the familiar climb up the hill leading to Baythorpe Hall. She convinced herself that she ought to see if Anthony were about and thank him properly. Halfway up the hill, she paused. The snow cover on the hill had hardened to a gleaming sheet of white ice. With so few travellers, it was still pristine, reflecting diamond flashes in the dying sun. The leaves on the hedgerows decorated with fine snow had the appearance of brides in their finery. Annie stood enchanted by the whole scene; her hands itched to have a paintbrush and easel to commit the scene to a canvas before the coming months melted it away for ever. That particular scene could never be perfectly repeated.

A tiny gap in the copper beech hedge surrounding the high ground at one corner of the Gladwell estate, allowed her to peer through to see the house. Lights were shining at every window, the maids not yet having been instructed to draw the curtains. She scanned the grounds, hoping that Anthony would be out with his easel; if he were, no doubt he would have a struggle to pick up the nuances of white, light and shade which made up the January scene.

Disappointed at not seeing him she was just about to turn away when a movement in a hollow some hundred yards or so inside the hedge boundary made her throw caution to the winds. Easing herself through the hedge, she ran towards Anthony. It was all she could do to stop herself calling his name. The look of horror on Anthony's face when he caught sight of her caused her a momentary feeling of shock.

"Annie! You shouldn't be here! You know what Lavinia can do."

"I just wanted to say thank you properly for bringing me home safely on Christmas Eve." Anthony's lack of enthusiasm on seeing her had upset her. "I'll go now."

"Just a minute, Annie." Anthony looked down towards the house. By now the curtains were all drawn and there was no sign of life. "Well, I suppose we'll be safe. Everyone is sitting cosily in front of the fire with their tea and toasted muffins. He pointed to his canvas. "Tell me, Annie, have I caught the crisp, cold feeling of this winter afternoon?"

"Nearly." Annie's impish grin accompanied her criticism. "Here, give me your brush. See, you need to put some white here to show where the snow is reflecting the sun."

"Ah," Anthony conceded. "Now why didn't I see that? Probably because I haven't half your genius," he finished.

As Annie continued to touch up Anthony's efforts, she asked him if his father had been very angry with him for taking the car.

"Angry?" Anthony rolled his eyes heavenwards. "Angry isn't the word. He's packing me off to Australia at the end of next week to learn all about wool production."

Annie gasped. "Australia! That's the other side of the world!" She remembered Miss Turkentine twirling the huge globe which stood near the blackboard. "He can't! Who will I have to talk to when you're gone?"

A wry smile wrinkled Anthony's smooth cheeks. "I doubt if many sheep shearers will be interested in my artistic leanings, either," he said ruefully. He stroked her face gently with the backs of his fingers. "One year from now and I'll be back. We can carry on where we left off. That is if you're not married to that Joe fellow."

"I'm so miserable," she blurted out. "I don't know what to do now."

"Here, cheer up, Annie. The year will soon pass, you'll see." He removed the painting of the winter scene from the easel, rolled it up and gave it to Annie. "Quick, off you go before you freeze to death." A tender kiss on her cheek and he departed with his long-legged lope towards the house.

Overwhelmed by her misery, she watched him until he was out of sight. He was right about the consequences of her marrying Joe. There would be no more innocent painting sessions together once she was married and Anthony was back from Australia. Lost in her thoughts, she suddenly realised that she had strayed well away from the gap in the copper beech hedge. With the shadows cast by the hedge lengthening in the gathering dusk, the gap was no longer easy to find. Becoming more frantic as her efforts proved fruitless, she began to run.

"Not so fast!" Lavinia's voice carried in the stillness of the late afternoon.

Annie turned to see Lavinia on her favourite mount, a huge brute of a black stallion now bearing down on her. Sitting astride the beast, instead of riding side-saddle, Lavinia leaned forward, urging the animal on with savage blows of her whip.

"No!" Annie screamed, helpless to escape the imminent attack.

Snorting and slavering, the horse galloped straight towards her. As Annie stumbled, Lavinia reined the horse in until it reared, its hooves directly over Annie's face. Whimpering and begging Lavinia to stop, she cowered, protecting her face with her arms. The hooves descended delivering Annie a sharp blow in the ribs. Feeling the bones crack, Annie screamed in pain.

"Get out of here, you slut!" Lavinia yelled bringing her whip down on Annie's face in a savage blow. This was followed by more blows to her arms, legs and back. "Think you're going to marry my brother, do you? Get back in the gutter where your sort belong"

She wheeled the horse round as if to leave, sufficiently for Annie to think that she was to be spared further blows, but Lavinia wheeled round again, spurring the horse on until it gathered speed, bearing down on Annie yet again.

Her eyes burning black with malevolence, she leant over the horse's flying mane. Raising the whip high above her head, she brought it down with the strength of a maniac dealing Annie one more vicious blow just over her left eye. "Get out before I throw you to the dogs," she screamed.

Groaning as each movement stabbed her with a dozen daggers, Annie tried to crawl towards the hedge. Mercifully the gap to freedom lay just ahead of her. The branches tore at her dress and shawl inflicting even more damage to her bruised and bleeding skin, but she struggled on, still fearful that Lavinia would return to the attack. The night was now drawing in. No one was about in this bitterly cold weather, no one to hear her feeble cries for help. Unable to stand, she crawled, inching her way along the lane, until she finally tumbled into a snow-filled ditch. As she drifted in and out of consciousness, she remembered the gypsy at the fair. What was it she had said about two lovers, one near and one far away, and someone who hated her? It was clear that someone was Lavinia Gladwell. Having had her thrown out of Estcourt on Christmas Eve had been Lavinia's first attempt to kill her. Annie gave a little sob. Was she to succeed this time?

"My God! Quick, Fred, wrap my coat round her. I'll lift her. My poor darling Annie."

"Right, Joe, just ease her gently."

I must have died and gone to heaven, Annie thought, as she felt strong arms lifting her and carrying her.

"She's still alive," she heard Joe say, as the two men, half running and half stumbling over the slippery snow in the road, raced towards her home.

"Annie? Annie?" Her ma's voice was added to those of Joe and her pa. "My poor girl, is this really my Annie?"

"Who did this to you, can you tell me?" Half sobbing with anger, Joe caressed the matted dark curls.

"Lavinia Gladwell." Annie's voice came out in an almost inaudible gasp.

"I'll kill her, the evil witch," he roared.

"That'd be no more than she'd deserve." Annie's ma kissed her daughter's bruised cheeks. "Right," she said as anguish quickly gave way to practicality. "Quieten down the pair of you. You know as well as I do, we can't take on the Gladwells, so show a bit of common sense. Into the kitchen with you. Heat some water. Eileen upstairs and fetch towels and an old sheet to make bandages."

Slowly and with infinite patience, Beatie tended to her daughter, bathing each bruise, tearing up the old sheet into strips to make bandages to stem the blood oozing from some of the deeper cuts on Annie's legs, all the while uttering soothing noises.

Once Annie had been dressed in a fresh nightgown and wrapped in a blanket, Beatie summoned the men in from the kitchen. "I think she's got some broken bones. It's hard to tell with her hurting all over. One of you go and get the doctor, quick."

Annie lay on the couch, every inch of her body burning with pain. Any movement triggered pains which took her breath away. Eileen knelt by her sister, dabbing the mass of bruises over Annie's left eye.

"Is that any better?" she asked hopefully.

"Much," Annie replied, not daring to say that she could not bear to be touched even by her kindly younger sister.

Some thirty minutes later the doctor arrived. "Doctor McLeod," he introduced himself.

He needed no introduction. Everyone knew he had come to replace Doctor Anstruther who had been forced out of Densbury following his harbouring of a priest.

"Let me see the young lady. I need…" He stopped mid-sentence, visibly shocked at the sight of the barely recognisable girl in front of him. "How on earth did this happen? How did she come to have such a terrible accident?"

"This was no accident," Joe snarled. "The Gladwell woman rode her horse deliberately at her."

The young sandy-haired doctor coughed. This was his first practice and if he wanted to further his career, it would hardly be prudent to take sides against one of the most powerful families in the county. Ignoring the comment, he asked to be left alone with his patient with just Beatie present as chaperone. Tenderly and carefully, he examined Annie from head to toe. From time to time, he uttered words of sympathy. "You poor child." Peering more closely at her face, he asked, "Can you open your left eye for me?" When Annie shook her head, he opened the eyelid with his thumb and forefinger. "Can you see me?" Annie nodded.

Finally, he stood up. "That's a blessing, at least. I had begun to wonder if her eye was damaged."

"Well, Doctor?" Beatie tried to hide her fear at what damage had been done to her daughter.

"She has a fractured left wrist, several broken ribs and extensive bruising. I'll put a splint on her arm, but there's precious little else I can do. She is going to need weeks if not months of careful nursing." He patted Beatie's shoulder. "Your daughter is young and strong, so don't worry too much. There'll be no lasting damage."

He left with a promise to call again in a week's time. The minute he was out of the door, Joe and Fred came in from the kitchen to hear the news of Annie's injuries.

"Well, he will be able to give evidence when we get that Gladwell woman to court." Joe's mouth was set in a firm, hard line. "I can't wait."

"You'll wait a damned long time," Fred told him. "Beatie's right, you can't win against the likes of them."

A hammering at the back door ended that particular discussion. Fred went to let in PC Stanley Blackthorne, the sole guardian of the law in Densbury.

"Joe! Did you send for the police?"

Puzzled, Joe shook his head.

"I'm here at the request of the Gladwell family. It concerns an incident which occurred at Baythorpe Hall late this afternoon." PC Blackthorne opened his notebook and proceeded to read from it. "It appears that Annie Claydon caused injury to Miss Lavinia Gladwell."

"What?" Joe grabbed the astonished policeman's arm. "Come here and take a look. Who did you say caused injury?"

In spite of himself, the constable muttered, "My God! Is this Annie?"

"Yes," Joe shouted in his face. "So what are you going to do about it?"

The constable was almost six feet in height, but Joe towered above him. "I'll remind you that I'm in charge here, so calm down before I take you into custody." He glowered at Joe who was in no mood to be placated.

"Let's hear what the constable has to say," Fred suggested.

"It appears that Miss Lavinia Gladwell was out riding this afternoon, when suddenly her horse was startled by Annie Claydon, who dashed out in front of her waving a stick."

"Annie! You were on the Gladwell land again?" Joe shook his head reproachfully. Annie had betrayed him yet again, seeking out Anthony Gladwell.

"Miss Lavinia was thrown to the ground, but fortunately has sustained only a sprained elbow." The constable looked up from his notebook. "I have seen Miss Lavinia with her arm bound up. However, Mr Gladwell does not wish to cause any embarrassment to your family and will not be pressing charges for trespass or his daughter's injuries."

"His daughter's injuries?" Joe pointed to Annie. "If she hadn't been so vicious with her whip, she wouldn't have a sprained elbow. What about the injuries Annie got at the hands of that madwoman?"

"Now, now, that's enough. If Annie was stupid enough to trespass and frighten Miss Gladwell's horse, she has only herself to blame. Mr Gladwell is being most generous in the circumstances." He glared at Annie. "Consider yourself lucky that I'm not arresting you here and now."

Joe gave a harsh laugh. "Go on, put the handcuffs on her, if you can."

The policeman wagged a warning finger at him. "There'll be no arrests, Joe Langmead, so long as you can remember who's in charge here."

He took one last look at the girl lying on the couch. "I trust Annie soon gets better," he said as he left.

The doctor was right. It took weeks of careful nursing before Annie could even get up to her own bedroom and that was with the help of her father. The first time she attempted it, each step made her cry out with pain, but gradually as the ribs knitted together and the weals on her legs healed, she was able to move more freely. Still too weak to go out in the biting February winds, she spent her days on the couch near the fire. Eileen had brought her some wool from Miss Witton's shop where she worked.

"You can knit yourself a jumper," she told her, patiently instructing her older sister, who had never taken to knitting before.

Annie could not help smiling. "So are you going to spend the rest of your life knitting in Miss Witton's shop?"

Eileen's eyes opened wide. "What do you take me for? I've got other ideas."

"What do you mean by that?" her ma interrupted. "You've got a nice little job where you are. Look where fancy ideas got your sister."

Eileen sighed, impatient at her mother's lack of understanding. "I intend to have my own business one day. You don't get rich working for other people."

Both girls hid their giggles behind their hands as their ma shook her head. "Where did the pair of you get such mad ideas? It certainly wasn't from me or your pa."

Even Annie was taken aback by her young sister's wisdom. She was not yet sixteen but already planning a future which did not include slaving for someone else. "You do it, Eileen," she whispered when their ma was out of earshot.

Although Annie's struggles to produce a wearable garment with Eileen's wool helped to pass away the long hours, she longed to have a friend with whom she could chat. One of her old workmates from the factory had dropped by once to say that everyone was sorry to hear of her accident, but after passing on a few snippets of news about who was getting married that summer, conversation dried up.

What she looked forward to mostly were Joe's visits each evening. With him sitting beside her, she felt wanted and cherished; this feeling was mingled with a glow of excitement his physical presence always aroused. She longed to be well enough to be allowed to go out and spend some time alone with him.

One Sunday afternoon in late February, Annie's parents had considered it safe to leave the young couple alone for a short time.

"She's hardly in a position now to start humming and hawing," her ma said. "She's got no job and that Anthony Gladwell is on the other side of the world, so there's no one to put daft ideas into head any more."

Her husband agreed. "Let's hope Joe can talk her round, then."

"Will we be married when you are well again?" Joe pleaded. "I want to be there for you all the time." He moved closer to her, bending his head to kiss her hard on the lips.

Annie gave a tiny cry which came from deep in her throat. "Oh, Joe, you don't know how much I want to be with you too." All pain was forgotten in the sheer ecstasy of their physical closeness.

Joe pulled away from her. "Well? Does that mean you really want to fix a date for our wedding?"

Annie closed her eyes, concentrating hard. "I still can't walk very far and some of the scars on my back haven't faded yet."

"I'll carry you down the aisle if I have to and I'll be so gentle with you," Joe promised, his eyes shining.

"No, I have to be really well," Annie insisted. "I want to buy my dress and get my bottom drawer ready." She broke off impatiently. "You men just don't understand. It will have to be the end of June."

"Promise?"

She stroked his lips with her fingers. "Promise."

Beatie Claydon beamed with satisfaction at the success of her little ruse. Two lovers filled with physical longing and left alone for a limited time was a sure recipe for them to name the day.

"So it's to be June, is it? Why wait so long?" she asked.

"June is what we've decided, Mrs Claydon. It will give us all time to make sure it will be a day to remember."

For the first time in months, Beatie Claydon was able to lay her head down on her pillow that night and sleep contentedly.

Eileen was nearly as excited. "Two conditions, sister," she said. "One, I'm to be your bridesmaid and two, you have to finish that jumper. I'm not going to see my wool going to waste."

They hugged and laughed together at the prospect of planning the wedding.

Beatie Claydon's satisfaction that her daughter had at least named the end of June as the date for the wedding was short-lived. It was nearing the end of March when a knock at the door heralded the arrival of an unwelcome visitor. Isabelle Anstruther greeted her with a polite, "Good afternoon, Mrs Claydon, I've come to see how Annie is getting on."

"What are you doing here?" Beatie asked with no attempt at civility. "I didn't think that you or your pa would be setting foot in Densbury again."

On recognising her old friend's voice, Annie struggled into the kitchen to greet her. For one awkward moment she thought that her ma was going to send Isabelle packing. Beatie looked at her daughter's expectant face and relented. Annie had few enough visitors and needed cheering up from time to time.

"Come on in then," she said somewhat ungraciously. "Annie will tell you all about her wedding plans." Isabelle's frown of disapproval pleased her. "I'll leave you two to chat while I do a few errands. I won't be long," she warned.

"I'll be gone long before Mr Claydon gets home from work," Isabelle reassured her. The incident when he had been one of the group stoning her father and the priest did not need to be mentioned specifically. Fred Claydon would not welcome the Papist doctor's daughter into his house.

"How did you know I was ill?" Annie asked as soon as they were alone.

"Papa had some of his colleagues to dine last week and the subject of broken ribs came up. One of the doctors mentioned a girl in Densbury who had had an accident on the Gladwell estate. Knowing your friendship with Anthony Gladwell, I made a few discreet inquiries and came up with your name."

Isabelle was shocked when Annie told her of the two attempts made on her life by Lavinia. "She's a madwoman!" she exclaimed. "So why are you staying in Densbury? You ought to get miles away from her." She laid a hand on Annie's arm. "She's so dangerous I just know she will try it again. Oh, please Annie," she begged.

"You heard what Ma said: I'm marrying Joe in the summer."

"You mean the Joe who used to look after you when you went painting on Sunday afternoons? I thought he was more like an uncle to you."

Annie reddened. "Not really, he is only five years older than me."

"All the same, he seemed a great deal older and he was so severe. He told me off once, do you remember?"

"Oh yes, when we said we were going off to London to make our fortunes, you to be a doctor and me to be a famous artist. Doesn't seem as if either of us got to see our dreams come true." Annie was suddenly quiet.

"What do you mean?" Isabelle was about to give Annie a shake, but thought better of it. "What is to stop you? I've talked to Papa and made him change his mind. He has arranged for me to go to London to study to be a doctor. I shall be lodging with some of his former colleagues."

"By which time I shall be an old married woman with a husband to care for and a house to keep clean."

"Annie, you can't! All those beautiful paintings you've done. You've got to go on. Marriage is for the factory girls who see marriage as a means of escape. At least put the wedding off for a year or two."

Beatie heard the last sentence as she came in through the back door. "What sort of foolish ideas are you putting into her head, young lady? It's all very well for the likes of you. Your pa might be able to keep you up in London playing at learning to be a doctor, but we can hardly get enough money to put food into her mouth here."

118

Isabelle rose to go. "I'm sorry, Mrs Claydon. It is just that Annie is so clever with her painting that I think she ought not to let it go."

"Take a closer look at her!" Beatie shouted. "It was the painting that brought her to death's door, going to see Anthony Gladwell. Hasn't she told you the real reason the Gladwell woman thrashed her? She didn't want her brother mixing with the likes of us." Beatie pointed to the door. "On your way, young lady."

"You'd better go," Annie said quietly. "Please come again soon."

Once she had gone, Beatie turned on her daughter. "If she comes again, I'll be staying right here. I'll not have her filling your head with her nonsense. London indeed!"

Annie pressed her knuckles into her eyes to stop the burning sensation as hot tears brimmed over.

Joe must have been forewarned by Beatie. His first words to Annie when he appeared the next evening did little to reassure her that she would have some measure of freedom once they were married.

"What did you want to entertain that doctor's daughter for? You know she only brings trouble. I don't like her." His forehead creased in a stern, forbidding frown.

"Well, I do like her," Annie persisted. "I will not let you choose my friends for me."

Joe recognised the obstinate set of her mouth. He decided to wheedle her into accepting that what he said made sense. "But she's not one of us, can't you see that? She's going to make you miserable with all her talk of money, living in London and being a doctor. We live in Densbury and I work in the factory. Surely you can see the difference."

Annie could see there was no point in arguing further; Joe would never be budged. He would always be adamant that Pastor Briggs was right: if God placed you in a lowly position in life, you were destined to remain there. Somehow Annie felt that was not what God intended. What about the parable of the talents?

"You're back to your old self again," Fred remarked to his daughter seeing her race up the stairs one day at the end of April.

"I am, Pa," Annie sang out happily. "I think I could almost dance around the maypole." She stopped halfway up. "I do wish I could find some work and bring in some money for you and Ma. It isn't right that our Eileen is working and I'm not."

Fred followed her up the stairs. "Hold on there a minute, my girl. You can't find work in Densbury and we all know what happened when you went away to Estcourt. I'm not letting you run the risk of anything more like that, so bide your soul in patience until you get married. It won't be long now."

Seven more weeks and she would be sleeping alongside Joe every night. With her strength increasing, she was able to walk out on Sunday afternoons again with Joe. Their steady progress along the High Street was noted by those who knew the couple.

"Won't be long now," one of Joe's workmates commented. "Lucky man," he said, winking and giving Joe a dig in the ribs.

"I wish it was right this minute," Joe whispered in Annie's ear. "Come on, let's go to my house, just for a little while." His voice was husky with longing.

Annie hung back. "What if we're seen and Ma gets to find out again?"

"Annie," Joe pleaded. "I'm going mad. We'll be man and wife in a few weeks."

Desire sent her blood pounding through her veins. With Joe's dark, smouldering eyes boring into hers, she was lost.

Within seconds of locking the cottage door behind them, Joe had pulled Annie to him in a fierce embrace. The next hour passed in an ecstasy of mutual passion, giving and receiving until at last, they lay back entwined in one another's arms. Annie had never felt so sure that the only thing that mattered in her life was that she should be Joe's wife.

"Just think, my love, in a few weeks, we'll be lying together every night with me making love to you all night long."

Annie gave a little mocking laugh. "You'll be too tired to get up for work in the mornings. Of course, I'll be able to stay in bed and recover."

"What do you mean, you little hussy? I've had to get my own breakfast long enough. I can't wait to see you cooking for me in the mornings. And then in the evenings, when I get in from work, you'll be waiting for me with my dinner on the table and the house spotlessly clean."

My ma's life all over again, Annie thought, as the cold water of reality dashed out the flames of passion.

The next few weeks passed in a frenzy of wedding preparations. Annie chose a length of ivory silk which her ma could fashion into a simple style. Eileen had asked if she could be dressed in her favourite colour, a light creamy yellow which set off her pretty brown hair. Any misgivings that Annie might have had about her future life as a married woman and housewife were swept away as she was carried along on the tide of enthusiasm engendered by Joe and her family.

By the end of May, the preparations were entering their final stages. Pastor Briggs had been approached by Joe and the third Saturday in June had been fixed for the wedding. There would be no fancy reception afterwards, just a simple meal at home for the family and a few friends.

With no sign of any hitch in the arrangements, Annie was shocked to come downstairs one morning to find her ma looking drawn and unhappy.

"What is it, Ma? Are you ill?" Panic stricken, Annie put her arms round her ma's shoulders. "Tell me you're not ill, please."

Touched by her daughter's solicitude, Beatie patted her hand. "Of course I'm not ill. It's this letter, it's just put me out a bit, that's all."

Annie looked over her ma's shoulder. "Who is this Ivy? I've never heard you mention her before."

"Oh, she's an old friend. We used to work together at the factory years ago before me and your pa were wed. She left Densbury all of a sudden one day and never came back. The last time she wrote was from an address somewhere in London to say she was doing fine."

"So why is she writing now?"

"She wants to come back for a visit for old times' sake. She wants to know if she can stay for a couple of days. I don't like to say no, but what with the wedding and everything, I don't know."

"Oh, let her stay, Ma. We can manage if it's only for a couple of days," Annie said in a tone meant to reassure her ma. Curiosity got the better of her. "Why did she leave all of a sudden?"

Beatie closed her eyes and thought back. "It was strange, really. She was in love with your pa's mate Zak, you know from the factory. We all thought they would make a go of it, but he changed his mind and married Emmy instead. Broke poor Ivy's heart it did." She folded the letter and tucked it into the pocket of her pinny. "Right, I'll tell her she can come next week."

All the same, Beatie had a bad feeling about the visit of this friend from the past.

Chapter 8

"Who is this Ivy?" Eileen asked her sister. "Ma's got a face as long as a fiddle ever since she agreed to let her come and stay."

"Some old friend from her factory days. Seems she left Densbury suddenly because Pa's mate Zak upped and married someone else," Annie explained.

"Poor old thing," Eileen sympathised. "Didn't she ever get married?"

"No, according to Ma, she went off to London to work as a nanny in some posh house."

"How awful." Eileen made a grimace. "Fancy spending your life looking after other people's children." She shrugged her shoulders. "Still, I expect she had to get a roof over her head or else end up on the streets. She must have been very brave to go off like that."

Annie nodded. "Her train gets in at noon tomorrow. Ma's made up a bed for her in the attic. Probably not as fancy as she's used to, but we can't turn the house upside down with my wedding to get ready for."

Eileen gave a little dance round their bedroom. "Oh, Annie, you're so lucky getting married to Joe. He's the best looking man in the whole of Densbury and he adores you."

"I know." Annie smiled, remembering the last afternoon she and Joe had spent together.

Just before noon next day, Beatie told Annie to put the stew on to heat while she went to the station to meet Ivy.

"Can't I come too, to help with her bags and things?" Annie pleaded.

"You're not carrying bags yet, my girl. Besides, it'll give me and Ivy a chance to have a little chat on the way home."

In between giving the stew a stir and laying the table, Annie kept dashing to the front window to see if she could get a glimpse of the visitor. She wasn't sure what to expect. From what Anthony had told her about his nanny and from the one she had seen at Estcourt, she had a mental picture of ferocious females with unprepossessing looks. She was not prepared for the elegant creature walking arm-in-arm with her ma, both engaged in animated conversation.

Annie felt she ought to drop a curtsey when Ivy held out her gloved hand to shake. Tall and with some evidence of the result of too many ample meals beginning to show on her rounded bosom and hips, it was as well that her navy blue suit had been cut to conceal the defects in her figure.

"My word! Beatie Claydon! If you haven't got the prettiest daughter I've ever seen in my life." She patted Annie's shoulder. "You ought to be on the London stage. With your looks, you could end up marrying a duke." She roared out laughing seeing the look of horror on Beatie's face.

"She's getting married to her Joe in a few weeks," Beatie reminded her friend. "He owns his own house, would you believe? Our Annie will be set up for life," she finished proudly.

Ivy's eyes were round and small, but piercing in their intensity. Charcoal black, they reminded Annie of the gypsy at the fair. As if reading right into Annie's heart, she said, "So long as that's the life you want, Annie."

"That's all settled, Ivy. That's what she wants. Marrying a duke, whatever next." Beatie was having no more doubts put into her daughter's head.

With Ivy settled into her room and shown round the house, the three waited for Eileen to appear. Fred had opted to take his snack with him to the factory, correctly guessing that the women would have enough to talk about without him being there.

Eileen came dashing in just as her ma was about to dish up. "Sorry I'm late, Ma, but we had a customer who couldn't make up her mind and Miss Witton had already gone for her dinner." She looked expectantly at Ivy waiting for her to speak.

"So this is your other little beauty, is it, Beatie?" She held out her hand to Eileen. "Pleased to meet you, my dear," she said. There was something awe-inspiring about Ivy's appearance, yet she had the knack of making mere acquaintances feel like old friends.

Eileen blushed at this unexpected compliment. All her life she had become used to people staring in admiration at Annie's black curls and deep blue eyes fringed with long curling lashes. In comparison, her wavy brown hair and hazel eyes seemed very ordinary. She had not realised that approaching womanhood had lent a glow to her perfect English complexion. That and the glint of amber and gold flecks in her eyes had already aroused the seeds of passion in more than one young hopeful in Densbury.

"And have you got a special young man yet?" she asked.

Eileen stared at her plate. "No," she mumbled. Now was not the time to tell her ma that Daniel Parfitt kept stopping and gazing at her through the wool shop window. She was nearly sixteen, so perhaps her ma and pa wouldn't mind if he asked to walk out with her. The elder son of elderly parents who owned the large ironmongery in the town, he was considered to be quite a catch. Besides, although Eileen would not admit it to anyone, his face kept intruding into her dreams at night.

Concentrating on eating meant that conversation flagged for a while. Finally, Ivy laid down her knife and fork. "Your Fred certainly picked a good cook, Beatie," she said.

Beatie murmured a few self-deprecating words as she cleared the plates away and carried them through to the kitchen. "I'll make a cup of tea before I sit down. Our Eileen's got to get back to work as soon as she's downed her tea."

"Not for me," Eileen said, hastily flinging her shawl round her shoulders. With a bit of luck if she made haste, she might see Daniel.

"You've got good taste in art, I see," Ivy called out to Beatie. "I never would have thought you were that interested in paintings."

"Oh, you mean that one?" Carrying the cups of tea into the living room, Beatie flicked her head in the direction of Annie's painting on the wall. "Our Annie did that for us," she said casually.

Ivy gasped. "Annie! You did that?" Mouth open, she stared at Annie. "All by yourself? But there's no art college here, is there?"

"No, of course there isn't. It's just her favourite little pastime. She won't have time for that once she's married next month."

"Pity," Ivy said, her expression serious and a little sad. "You mustn't give it up, Annie," she said.

"I don't want to," Annie said. "What I'd really like to do is learn more about it. Are you interested in art?"

"Oh, yes, you have to be where I work. Mr Salisbury is an art dealer. He has a gallery in Cork Street in London. He buys and sells only the best."

"Really?" Annie's eyes were shining with excitement. "Do you paint too?"

"Me? Goodness no!" she laughed. "But in that house, surrounded by pictures and talk of art from morn till night, you begin to learn a lot, believe me. Take Mrs Salisbury, she's expecting her third in six weeks' time and can hardly sit at her easel, but that doesn't stop her. Then there's young Orlando not yet nine years old – he'd miss going to school if he could, just to sit and paint."

126

Beatie's cup missed the saucer, splashing tea over her clean tablecloth. "Oh dear, look at me," she stammered, glad of anything to change the subject.

"Then there's Katherine, nearly eleven, not so good an artist as her brother, but already keen to learn about her papa's art business. I tell you, I live and eat painting every day of the week." She laughed again. "And I love every minute of it."

"How did you come to work for them?" Beatie asked. "You never said."

"Surely you remember what happened between me and Zak."

Beatie nodded. "That was hard on you, girl," she said, "marrying Emmy like he did. Got her in the family way, we heard."

"That's water under the bridge," Ivy said firmly. "I was hurt at the time and just took the first carrier out of Densbury. I ended up in Aldgate not knowing a soul in London and not much money in my pocket. I found some lodgings and started looking for work, but didn't have any luck. I happened to be walking along Oxford Street one day when a lady stumbled as she got out of her carriage. I managed to catch her and prevent her doing herself a mischief. Her baby was due any minute and as you can imagine, she was very grateful to me. To cut a long story short, she took me on as a nursemaid to help her nanny. When her children went away to school, she recommended me to the Salisburys and that's where I've been nanny since Miss Katherine was born. I reckon I've had a better life than if I'd stayed working at the factory and marrying Zak."

Beatie fidgeted, casting concerned glances at her daughter whose flushed cheeks showed the effect the visitor's words were having. "No regrets then, Ivy, not having a home of your own?"

Ivy threw back her head and laughed. "Not at all. I reckon Zak did me a favour getting Emmy in the family way. What have they got now? A miserable little cottage to live in, a paltry wage with just about enough to cover the bare necessities of life." She leaned forward in her chair and stared hard at her old friend. "And how many times have they been out of Densbury?" She leaned back, a smug, satisfied expression on her face. "I've seen all of London, mixed with clever people, artists and so on."

"It sounds wonderful." Annie was lost in dreams of this fairy tale life that was now far out of her reach. Ivy's summing up of the life led by her old love, Zak and his wife Emmy, was far too close a description of what lay in store for her for her to feel comfortable.

"Why don't you come back with me, Annie?" she asked. "Mrs Salisbury has asked me to find a nursemaid to help me for when the new baby arrives. I know you're a bit older than the usual nursemaid, but you'd fit into the household a treat."

"No! She can't!" Beatie's rising anger at what she saw as treachery on the part of her old friend made her stand, pointing an accusing finger at her. "Annie's promised to Joe and they're getting wed in a few weeks' time. That's right, isn't it Annie?"

Annie nodded bleakly.

Unfazed by Beatie's anger, Ivy was determined to capture Annie's imagination, as she continued to describe the Salisbury home and life. "You'd have a great time with young Orlando. I can just see the two of you painting together and keeping him amused while I see to the new baby. Of course, you'd have to get up in the night to see to the baby. I just do the day duty."

"That's enough, Ivy," Beatie persisted. "It's a waste of time filling her head with such ideas. You'll have to look elsewhere for a nursemaid."

Ivy paid no attention, carrying on with painting the idyllic life waiting for Annie if only she could agree to put off her wedding plans and go to London with her. "They're a very easy-going family, Annie. You would be treated very well. Do you know that there's an art college not far away. I'm sure the Salisburys would give you time off if you wanted."

Annie lay awake most of the night turning over and over in her mind the choice that she had to make. By morning her mind was made up. Her dying grandmother's words urging her to follow the right path rang in her head. I promised Granny on her deathbed, she told herself to justify her decision. "At least I will know whether I am right to want to be an artist. If I'm not, I will just forget all about it," she told her horrified parents.

Her ma's tears and her pa's recriminations did nothing to weaken her resolve. "If Joe loves me, he will wait one more year for me," she reasoned.

"Well, you'd better tell him yourself," her pa said. "You're not getting away with this so easily."

When Joe called to see her after work, he was met with a red-eyed Beatie and a grim Fred. His first reaction was that Annie had been taken ill, or perhaps had suffered a relapse. "Where is she? What's happened?"

"Come down here!" her pa called. "Tell Joe what you've told us. Me and your ma are going for a little walk and you'd better have come to your senses by the time we get back. And that Ivy Goodman can pack her bags and be out of my house by the morning," he added, as the two left the house.

Annie gestured to Joe to come and sit beside her on the sofa. As he held her close to his beating heart, she felt again the magnetism his physical presence had upon her.

"Now, tell me, sweetheart, what is all this about? I haven't given you a child, have I?" Stricken at the shame he might have brought upon her, he held her close again.

Annie pulled herself away. If she stayed in his arms a minute longer, she would give in and carry on with the marriage plans. "No, of course you haven't. If you had, things might be different. I'm going away," she said more bluntly than she had intended. "I want to get away from Densbury and I want to paint."

"You can't! We're to be married, Annie." Full of anger and pain, he seized hold of Annie's arm with more force than he intended.

"Let go, you're hurting me." She recoiled from his touch. "Don't you see what you're doing? All your fine promises of love, but all you want is a wife to do your bidding." It took just a few sentences for her to explain her plans. "I'll be gone by tomorrow. I'll understand if you don't want to see me again."

Joe took one last anguished look at her before turning on his heel and slamming out of the back door. He scarcely noticed Annie's ma and pa as they returned to hear the outcome of the meeting. They did not need to ask. His black, brooding eyes told them all.

Chapter 9

Summer 1911

Following an evening of rows and recriminations, Annie had gone to her bedroom to pack her few belongings. Tears threatening to spill down her cheeks, Eileen went to help her. "You are sure this is what you want, isn't it, Annie?"

Annie opened the door of the huge wardrobe that had once belonged to her grandparents. She pulled out the cardboard box, untied the yellowing string securing its lid and withdrew the contents.

Eileen peered over her sister's shoulder. "Did you do these?" she asked, as Annie unrolled the sketches done by their granny so many years before.

"This is what Granny had to give up when she got married." Seeing Eileen's puzzled expression, she went on, "She told me to choose the right path in life and that if I wanted to paint, I should." Joy lit up her face. "I do believe that it was Granny who sent Aunt Ivy here just to make sure I didn't marry before I'd had a chance to do something with my life. Do you think that is what has happened?"

Eileen shook her head. Rash decisions did not fit into what she perceived as an orderly life. "I don't know about that. I don't know how you can go off and leave poor Joe. Think carefully, Annie. He really is so handsome, most of the girls in Densbury will be setting their caps at him once you're out of the way."

Annie dismissed the suggestion with a confident wave of her hand. "Joe loves me and no one else. He's said that he'll wait for me for a year and if that's what he's said, that's what he'll do."

Eileen shrugged. "Well, it's your life." As tears ran down her cheeks, she threw herself at her sister. "Oh, Annie, what am I going to do here all by myself with no one to talk to?"

"Well, there's always Daniel Parfitt," Annie said with a wicked grin. "I'm sure he'd be only too willing to comfort you."

"Annie! What do you know about him?" Eileen hung her head to hide her blushes.

"Oh, just let's say that I've seen him staring through the shop window at you. Unless, of course, he's a keen knitter and wants to choose wool to knit baby clothes."

Tears and laughter mingling, the two girls hugged one another. "You do what you want, Annie, so long as you write to me every week."

Breakfast next morning was a dismal affair. Beatie slammed Ivy's breakfast of bread and jam in front of her with a, "This is the last mouthful you'll be offered in this house. Taking our daughter away just weeks before her wedding with all your fancy words and promises."

Ivy pushed her plate away and stood up. "We've been through all this, Beatie. If Annie is unhappy, I promise you I'll send her home." Her dark eyes narrowing, she looked at Annie's expectant face. "Somehow, I don't think that is likely."

The train journey to London was spent mostly in silence. Annie watched the green fields of Suffolk and Essex gradually give way to towns which seemed to merge one into the other. "Where do people go for walks?" she asked Ivy.

"There are some nice parks," was the reply.

Panic seized Annie. In Densbury, she was free to wander up and down the lanes, free to gaze at the rolling fields, watch the changing seasons, the partridges and pheasants cavorting in their strange courtship ritual, hear the skylark singing its joyful hymn to the skies and breathe the pure air into her lungs. Already she was beginning to feel smothered as if someone had placed a blanket over her head. And the people! Everyone was in such a hurry, jostling against her with no word of apology. The noise and the heat threatened to stifle her so much that she had the greatest difficulty in not turning on her heel and catching the next train back to Densbury and Joe.

"Here we are," Ivy announced pointing to a flight of wide steps leading up to a grand oak door with a burnished lion's head knocker. "Number fourteen Cavendish Mansions," she said. "Your home for as long as you like, young lady."

It was on the tip of Annie's tongue to say that it would be for one year only as she had promised Joe, but a sudden wave of excitement at the prospect of the new life ahead of her silenced her. She would be living in one of the most beautiful townhouses in London instead of Joe's humble little cottage.

A maid in the traditional black dress with white lace collar and white frilly cap opened the door to them. She bobbed a tiny curtsey before standing with outstretched arms ready to take their cloaks. Annie was used to the ways of staff in big houses, but she had always been the one to know her place, although it had often been a struggle to keep her eyes downcast when confronted by her betters. This reversal of roles was due in no small part to the elevated position Miss Ivy Goodman as Nanny held in the household. Annie reflected that this show of respect might diminish when she began her duties as a lowly nursemaid.

Whilst Ivy and the maid exchanged a few remarks concerning the weather and the train journey, Annie was able to let her eyes wander over the splendid marble hallway from which a magnificent curved staircase wound up to a galleried landing. She was trying to count the number of doors on this top landing, when the drawing room door was opened. A tall, rangy man appeared. His pointed grey beard and stern dark eyes gave him the appearance of an ogre. The moment he saw Ivy, his eyes shone with delight.

"Nanny!" He rushed forward to greet her. "And this is our new nursemaid I take it." He took hold of Annie's tiny hands in his. "So you're Annie. Welcome to the Salisbury household."

Overwhelmed by this show of kindness, all Annie could do was mutter, "Thank you, sir." It was so much in contrast to the treatment meted out to her by the Gladwells and at Estcourt where servants were held to be creatures of such a low order that the ordinary rules of politeness did not apply.

"Diana, come and meet our new nursemaid," Stanley Salisbury called out, turning his head towards the doors leading to the back of the house. "She's probably in the kitchen with Cook," he explained.

"Coming," a voice replied. The doors were flung back revealing a heavily pregnant woman with a small boy clinging to her wide skirts. Behind her, a solemn girl aged about ten with straight brown hair and dark brooding eyes, stared at the newcomer.

Annie's heart sank. How would she win over two children who had been brought up in circumstances so different from her own?

Sensing her feeling of insecurity, Ivy Goodman placed a comforting arm round Annie's shoulders and gently pushed her forward. "And this is Annie, Ma'am, not much experience as yet, but I'll soon make a wonderful nursemaid out of her."

Diana made her way slowly towards Annie. A smile which began in her violet eyes and spread gradually to her fine-boned cheeks, ending in her wide, generous mouth, made Annie feel that she would be happy with this lovely family.

"Welcome, welcome, welcome, my dear." Like her husband before her, she took hold of both of Annie's hands in hers. "We hope you'll be very happy with us." She patted Orlando's head, ruffling his mop of dark red curls, so like her own. "And if this one causes you any trouble, just you tell me."

"I'm sure he won't, Ma'am."

"Not when Annie helps him with his painting," Ivy put in. "I've seen some of Annie's paintings and she is very gifted, Ma'am."

Orlando's eyes opened wide. "You're a painter as well as a nanny?" In his excitement he was barely able to keep still, tugging at his mother's arm until she had to release his fingers before he tore her sleeve. "Did you hear that, Mama? Did you hear that?"

"Now, we're forgetting our manners," his mother reminded her children. "Let Nanny and Annie get settled first." She spoke to her nanny. "Show Annie her room and then come down to the kitchen. We'll all have a cup of tea and a talk."

No one noticed that Mr Salisbury had disappeared, leaving the womenfolk to sort out household matters.

"He's like that," Nanny explained as she showed Annie her room, "always got his mind on the next art exhibition. When you get a day off, you'll have to take a look at his gallery. He's got some studios as well, lets them out to artists if he thinks they've got a future."

She pointed to the cupboards where Annie could put her few clothes. "We'll fit you out with a uniform in a day or two. Mrs Salisbury is most particular that we should be smart." The corners of her mouth turned up in a smile. "She's always covered in paint herself, but she dresses for dinner with Mr Salisbury and when they have friends in. You will eat in the kitchen with Cook after you've brought my dinner up to my room on a tray."

Annie noticed that her room had connecting doors with a second larger room where the children slept. Ivy opened the door to show her the large bathroom opposite.

"There's always plenty of hot water for baths," she explained tactfully. "You'll find that Mrs Salisbury is very particular about such matters."

Annie compared the cold water in her bedroom at home and the copper being heated at the weekend so that they could take it in turns to have what her mother called, "a proper all-over wash." She stifled a feeling of disloyalty picturing the tiny kitchen in Joe's cottage with the tin bath hanging on the wall, although inwardly acknowledging that once she had become used to life in the Salisbury household, it would be impossible to go back.

Opposite the bathroom was another room with huge windows overlooking the garden, which Ivy pointed out was the schoolroom. "It's not used much now," she explained. "Katherine and Orlando both go to a day school. Mrs Salisbury won't have them sent away to boarding school, says it's wrong. It will be your job to take them every morning and meet them later on."

The whole of the second floor seemed to have been designed simply for accommodating children and nannies. Nanny's room was larger than the others, also with an adjoining room. "After a while, once the baby has been weaned, it will spend much of the day here with us. Of course, to start with Mrs Salisbury will feed it herself."

It seemed to Annie that Nanny would not have too much to do and neither would she with the children at school all day. Admittedly, the weekends might become a little more hectic, but with an army of maids and a cook, Annie could see that she would not be the kind of slave she had been before in service.

As the days went by, she found herself fully occupied making sure that Katherine and Orlando were correctly dressed for school each morning, one of her duties being to look after their clothes and schoolbooks. Katherine was neat and methodical; she had obviously inherited her father's business-like attitude, whereas Orlando tended to wander around in a perpetual state of bemusement never remembering what he was supposed to be doing. He was quite surprised when Annie took him to task.

"Just because you think you're going to be a famous artist doesn't mean you can expect the rest of us to run round you all day, young man. Your sister can put things away and so can you."

Orlando stared at her. "But you're our nursemaid. That's what you do, isn't it?"

"Well, if you want me to treat you like a baby who needs a nursemaid, then I won't ask your mama if I can take you out in the park on Saturday. Out of my way, young man, while I pick up your things."

Katherine exchanged a secret smile with Annie. "Quite right," she agreed. "I'll go with Annie and we'll sit and read together."

Orlando's green eye filled with tears. "I'm sorry, truly I am. Please take me out with you," he begged.

This set the pattern for each Saturday morning with Annie taking the children to the park. She did not notice the pursed lips of the starchy old nannies in their grey coats and thick stockings as she played ball with her charges before settling them down on a bench. The one she chose was on a slope leading to the edge of a small, artificial lake with ducks circling the smooth waters, occasionally darting to the edge whenever they saw children with bags of stale bread eager to feed them.

"I'd like to do a picture of that. Do you think Mama would let me?" Orlando asked.

The longing in his eyes reminded Annie of herself the very first time that Anthony Gladwell gave her some paints, paper and brushes. She bent to hug him. "We'll have to ask her, won't we?"

Diana Salisbury's pregnancy had begun to weary her more than she had anticipated, so that with only a week or so to go before her confinement, she spent most of the day in her room resting. Annie's suggestion that she and the children might spend most of Saturday morning in the park painting meant that the house would be blessedly quiet.

"By all means, my dear," she told Annie. "Mr Salisbury will show you where I keep my stuff in the studio in the garden."

This set the pattern for many more weekends both before the birth of Emily Jane and after. Annie loved watching Orlando's natural talent blossom under her tutelage and even Katherine began to join in, quite philosophical about the fact that her efforts were more the result of painstaking work and attention to detail rather than natural genius.

As the autumn days brought squalls, Annie spent time in the schoolroom at weekends, helping Katherine with her reading and writing, while she and Orlando painted. One Saturday morning, all three were totally absorbed in their tasks and did not hear the door to the schoolroom being opened. It was Mr Salisbury's loud, "My word!" which made Annie jump in alarm

Scarcely able to breathe, she waited as he stood towering over her studying her picture of her well-remembered Suffolk meadows. Terrified at the thought that he might be about to sack her for not paying enough attention to the children, she did not hear his next words.

"Who taught you, my dear?"

The blood pounding in her ears, she tried to make sense of his question. All she could do was shake her head and murmur, "I don't understand, sir."

"Katherine, go and fetch Mama at once," he ordered.

Still convinced that he might be displeased, Annie stammered an apology and was astounded when he roared out laughing. "A genius under my own roof, while I go looking all over London. Here, Diana, come and take a look," he said, as his wife arrived.

She too stood enthralled before Annie's unfinished painting.

"I told you Annie was clever, but you didn't listen to me," Katherine complained.

"And I told you her drawings were better than some that Papa has in his gallery, didn't I?" Orlando chipped in.

"My darlings, you are both very clever," their mother said, hugging them both.

It was later that afternoon that Annie felt she ought to see Ivy and apologise to her for the extra work that would be put on her shoulders. The result of Stanley Salisbury's discussion with his wife had been that Annie should attend the local art college for two days a week.

"But I can't have a day off as well," Annie had protested. "It wouldn't be right."

After further negotiations it was decided that she could take her days off in one block at Christmas time which meant that she would have a whole week to spend with her family and Joe.

"Wonderful news," Nanny Goodman said. "When I saw that painting on your ma's wall, I knew you were something special. I've been to all Mr Salisbury's art exhibitions and believe me, I've learnt more than most people would give me credit for." She winked at Annie. "I wouldn't be surprised if Mr Salisbury doesn't give me a rise in pay as a reward for discovering you."

Annie's letter to Joe the following week was one of the longest she had written. It was full of a description of the art college, her tutors and new friends. The sentence, "I've never been so happy in my whole life," filled him with foreboding. Only a short sentence at the end mentioned that she was missing him. And soon she will not miss me at all, the bitter thought cutting his heart in two.

Only Eileen was thrilled at the happiness in her sister's life. She wrote to say that however much she missed Annie, she could not believe how lucky it had been for her that Ivy had come to see them before her wedding to Joe. 'To think that you can have proper art lessons and live in a lovely house," she wrote. Her only mention of Joe was that he called in now and again to see them and that there was talk of promotion for him at the factory.

Joe's letters to Annie were cold and matter-of-fact. Not once did his proud nature allow him to beg her to come back. Each letter ended with the same words.

'I look forward to seeing you at Christmas.
From your ever loving Joe.'

If Annie felt any pangs of guilt, they were soon forgotten in the hectic days in London. Although she had spent many hours producing paintings of country scenes, she had never tackled portraits. The lessons in anatomy were a source of wonder to her. The lecturer showed the class pictures of Michelangelo's sculpture of David. A flash of memory took Annie back to the day Anthony Gladwell sent her the postcard from Florence, the one her parents tore up in disgust. She suppressed a smile remembering how the sensible Eileen had retrieved the torn fragments and the two girls had pored over the picture of the nude male.

No one in the art class flinched at the sight of the picture of the nude male, following the lecturer's explanation of the artist's attention to detail. If anyone had asked Annie to define the moment when she recognised the widening gulf between herself and those she had left behind in Densbury, the moment would have had to have been at that lecture on anatomy. Her first attempts at drawing the human frame lacked life, making her doubt her artistic ability, but with the introduction of live models to work from, she began gradually to breathe life and movement into her subjects.

At the end of one very long day at the college, she was called into the principal's office. Mr Dornway, a man renowned for his scathing comments on students who were wasting the time of his staff, was feared throughout the college. Annie was terrified.

What if he told her that the Salisburys were wasting time and money on her? Would she be sent back home in disgrace?

"Sit down, Miss Claydon," he said. His eyes were on a pile of paintings Annie recognised as being her work. "So what do you think of these?" he asked.

Annie lowered her eyes. "I have tried hard, sir," she whispered. "I know I'm not very good."

A booming laugh echoed round his office and through the walls startling his secretary.

"Not very good? Not very good?" He wiped his eyes with a large red handkerchief. "Oh dear, oh dear, I must remember that to tell Stanley Salisbury."

"Do you want me to leave?" Annie asked. Please get this over with quickly, she prayed.

James Dornway's smile evaporated. He fell silent for a minute, his gaze still focused on Annie's work. Finally, he took a deep breath.

"Miss Claydon, I have been instructing artists for over twenty years, some of whom have done modestly well in their chosen career, but sadly many who have had to come to terms with the fact that they would be better off working in a shoe factory."

Annie waited before asking, "So you think I ought to work in a shoe factory?"

James Dornway's disconcerting laugh rang out again. "Oh, goodness me, no." Suddenly serious, he went on, "What makes my job worthwhile is the hope that one day I will find a student who has that extra talent that lifts him or her way above the rest. Miss Claydon, I have to tell you that you have a great future ahead of you." He wagged a warning finger. "But like all great artists, you will continue to need more study."

Annie gasped. "You think I'm good, really?"

"I think you are brilliant, my dear, and I hope I will have you in my college for some time to come."

Walking back to the house, she scarcely noticed the horse-drawn tram as she crossed the wide street. A warning shout bringing her back to reality made her jump back on to the pavement. Gradually, the euphoria at being praised by the college principal faded, giving way to more practical considerations. For how long would the Salisburys continue to give her time off to study? What if she really could plan for a future earning her living with her art? And would Joe come up to London to be with her? The answer to the last question was not difficult to acknowledge. Joe had always been adamant that, once married, they would live in Densbury, he would work at the factory and she would remain at home running his house and bearing his children.

The Salisburys had already been told of Annie's success and promised that they would continue to support her for as long as was necessary. They were rapturous at having discovered this young genius in their own home, where the children adored her and Orlando in particular was paying more attention to his schoolwork knowing that progress at school meant that he would be rewarded with Annie's help with his art at the weekends.

"But, of course, Christmas is coming," Diana Salisbury reminded her. "You will have a week at home with your family to talk things over." Her deep violet eyes were troubled. Her compassionate nature understood the agonies Annie was suffering. "I know you have a young man waiting for you, and I cannot advise you what to do for the best. Only you can make up your mind what to do." She seized Annie's hands in hers. "You know we love you and want you here with us."

Stanley Salisbury was first and foremost a businessman who, having nurtured Annie's talent, did not accept that she would be unable to resist the pressures of family and sweetheart. He took pride in having discovered this fresh artist and wanted to show her off to the art world. It would not be long before he could display some of her work in his gallery. He did not doubt that both he and Annie would benefit financially before long.

Until then, Annie had painted at college or in the children's schoolroom. It was now time to show her the wider world. "I would like to show you my studios," he told her. "Perhaps if Nanny could spare you, we'll take a cab to Cork Street."

Ivy Goodman did not need telling what her employer was up to. The excitement of having the opportunity to work in a real studio would soon put the handsome weaver out of her mind for good.

"I have already let out part of my studio to a young man," Stanley Salisbury told Annie, "but there is plenty of room for two to work without spilling paint over one another."

The cab being dismissed, he led her down Piccadilly, turning off down a narrow side street. There were a number of houses all with their doors closed apart from one. This door was wide open and the sound of someone whistling cheerfully carried through to the street.

Annie took in the chaos of half-finished paintings, easels, palettes and the smell of turps. Her blood pounded through her veins as she saw the culmination of all her dreams. A real studio to work in with artists who would understand her paintings, instead of the meadow by the river in Densbury with Joe for company. The young man whose whistling had been heard out on the street, turned from his canvas.

"Annie!" Flinging down his brush and palette, Anthony Gladwell rushed to gather Annie up in his arms and twirl her round until she had to beg him to put her down.

"I take it you two need no introduction," Stanley Salisbury grinned. It had been earlier on when Annie had first come to stay and he had seen her first painting of her beloved Suffolk meadows, that he recollected having seen a similar one, albeit not so good, in his studio painted by Anthony. A little investigation and he found that Anthony, too, came from

Densbury, although he had been reticent about his antecedents. Seeing the two young people together, he felt that the latest step in his plan to keep Annie in London was proving to be an even greater success than he had anticipated.

Totally forgetting Stanley Salisbury's presence, Annie and Anthony gabbled explanations of how they both came to be in London.

"After my year in Australia, Papa could see that he was no nearer to turning me into a factory manager or lawyer, so Mama persuaded him to give me my allowance and let me try to make my way as an artist." He held her at arm's length and sighed. "It's so good to see you again, Annie."

Still as boyish-looking as ever, with the lock of yellow hair falling over his forehead, he gazed at Annie. "And what about this Joe chap? Weren't you going to get married? What happened?"

Annie bit her lip wondering how she could explain that her intentions to go home at Christmas and reassure Joe that she would marry him the following summer, were still the same? But memories of Joe and his cottage were beginning to dim as the prospect of painting with her dear friend Anthony drove all thoughts of Densbury and Joe out of her head. A little voice kept telling her that perhaps Joe would wait a bit longer.

"So, how do you feel about sharing this studio?" her employer asked. "You could live with us as before, go to college two days a week, help Nanny with the children in the mornings and evenings and the rest would be spent here with Anthony."

It was as if the door to paradise was being opened wide for her. Granny must be so happy up in heaven, Annie thought, knowing that I am getting the chance to be a real artist.

"Wait until you get back from home after Christmas and then you can give me your answer." Stanley had no doubt what Annie's answer would be.

His smile broadened at Anthony's next suggestion. "I say, Annie, how about if I drive you down to Densbury. Papa gave me a car for my last birthday, so you needn't take the train."

The two friends did not notice Stanley Salisbury leave the studio with a spring in his step. The more that Anthony and Annie were thrown together, the more likely it would be that the London art world would see more of his delightful protégé.

Chapter 10

"Please, Anthony, not so fast!" Annie wished she had turned down his offer of a ride back to Densbury in his car.

"I can't help it, Annie, I'm so excited meeting you again. I can't believe we'll soon be painting together just like old times. And you won't have to keep running away from me, you know like you had to when…" The unspoken, "When you were a servant," hung in the air between them. They both recognised that there had been a shift in their relationship; with Anthony away from Baythorpe Hall and Annie living with the Salisburys, there had been a subtle narrowing of the wide gap in their social status. Aware that he had turned his head to look at her sitting beside him and fearing what she would read in his shining blue eyes, Annie kept her eyes fixed on the road ahead. Anthony had never been able to hide his feelings from her in spite of being reminded that she was engaged to Joe.

"Look where you're going!" she screamed.

Immediately contrite, he turned his attention to the road ahead. In a more sombre tone, he went on, "Of course I realise it will only be for a short time until you get married, that is." The slight inflection in his voice carried the suggestion of the statement being more like a question.

Annie's curt, "Yes," did nothing to lighten his mood and nothing more was said for the last hour of the drive.

"Drop me here, please," Annie begged, as they reached the last few hundred yards leading to her parents' cottage.

"What about going back to London in the New Year? Shall I call for you?"

Annie shook her head. She was finding it hard to explain something she barely understood herself. "I expect Joe will want to see me off on the train when I go back to London. I don't think he would like it if he knew you had brought me home." She did not add that Joe would like it even less when he heard what her employer had planned for Anthony Gladwell and herself.

She waved goodbye to him, lifted her two bags and trudged towards what just a few months before had been her home. A feeling of guilt at the disloyal recognition that the cottage seemed even smaller and shabbier than when she had left, was swiftly suppressed. How quickly she had become used to living in a large house with bathrooms, huge fires lit by maids and all her meals prepared by Cook.

Eileen was the first to fling herself at her sister. "Annie, you look so grand! Where did you get that lovely cloak?"

Her mother's first question after hugging her daughter was to ask where Joe had gone. "He's meeting the train from London, the one you said you were catching when you wrote to him. He said he couldn't wait a minute longer than he had to. He must be still at the station. How could he have missed you?"

Annie gave a cry of dismay. "Oh, no! Anthony Gladwell drove me down. I didn't think to tell Joe."

Her parents' shocked chorus of, "Anthony Gladwell!" was heard by Joe as he came in the door.

Annie ran across the room to hug him. "The people I work for know Anthony Gladwell and he offered to bring me here in his car. I could hardly offend everyone and refuse."

She could see the colour rising in his cheeks, anger threatening to explode at what he saw as his rival's triumph. "Anyway, I've told him flatly that I'm going back by train, so we can forget about him." Pressing herself against him, she smiled up at him, "And now I'm here with you."

Now was not the time to explain the plans made by Stanley Salisbury for her future, especially those which included Anthony. She pushed them to the back of her mind, determined to make the most of the few days with Joe. Their exchanged glances were not lost on her ma and pa. It was as if neither she nor Joe cared whether anyone could read what was in their hearts, the longing to spend a few precious hours together in his cottage away from the rest of the world.

"Just give me minute to unpack, Joe, and I'll be down."

Eileen helped her put her clothes away in their old shared wardrobe, firing questions and dropping hints about her friendship with Daniel.

Annie, too, was breathless with excitement, chatting about the delightful Salisbury children and her time at the art college. "The house is so grand and Mr and Mrs Salisbury treat me like one of the family. And the college! I'm learning so much. It's a different life, Eileen. Oh, I'm so lucky."

Eileen's lip quivered. "I don't think you'll ever want to come back here again, not after all you've got in London."

Annie put her hand in her sister's. "I haven't got my lovely sister in London, have I? I do miss you, honest, Eileen."

Reassured, Eileen went back downstairs with Annie.

"You're having a good time then, daughter?" Her mother's seemingly innocent question concealed a more urgent one. Was she going to be prepared to give it up in the summer and come home to marry Joe?

"I'm very happy, Ma."

Beatie Claydon busied herself in the kitchen. "Dinner won't be ready for a while. Why don't you and Joe take a walk down to his place for an hour or two? Joe tells me he has been working hard to get it nice before the wedding."

Annie was puzzled at this change of attitude. Only a year or so ago, her ma had accused her of bringing shame on the family spending time alone with Joe in his house before they were married. She had been obviously terrified that Annie would get pregnant and had been relieved when her fears had proved groundless.

Holding Annie close to him, as the two almost ran the length of the High Street, Joe whispered, "Just wait until I get you all to myself, Annie Claydon."

Inside the cottage a fire smouldered in the grate throwing out a welcome heat after the icy winds outside. Joe drew the curtains creating a warm private haven. Within minutes, they were locked together, releasing a passion which had been suppressed for so many months.

"My God, Annie! I've been going mad here all by myself. The thought that we should have been married by now has been tormenting me night after night."

"Shh, darling," Annie said, drawing him down to her once again until he groaned out loud again with his longing for her.

It was as they were dressing ready to go back to her home that the significance of her ma's sudden laxity in suggesting that she and Joe should spend time together, struck her.

"Do you realise, Annie Claydon?" Joe said, gently fondling her breasts, "that if we had been married, you might be having our first child?"

So that was her ma's plan! Hadn't she tried that before when she wanted Annie to name the day soon after she was thrown out of Estcourt? Give the lovers enough time alone together and before long Joe would give her a child and they would have to get married. Goodbye to all her London friends, college course and artistic ambitions. Annie was horrified at her ma's devious plans. She could hardly believe that her ma would rather see her disgraced with a hasty wedding than enjoying what she considered to be a life above her station. What else would her mother do to get her back to Densbury as quickly as possible?

That question was soon answered. The day before New Year's Eve, Pastor Briggs knocked at the door, not an unexpected visitor as far as her mother was concerned.

"I'll go into the kitchen and make some tea for the pastor while you have a little chat."

Annie sat on one side of the table whilst Pastor Briggs sat facing her, his fat jowls and loose wet lips as repellent as ever, as he assumed his unctuous attitude.

"You have been a little bit of a rebel, haven't you, my dear? First the business with the Papists, then causing poor Miss Lavinia to fall off her horse, not to mention cancelling your wedding at the last minute."

Annie did not answer for a while. The pastor waited. "And what about Joe Langmead?"

"We're getting married next summer," she said, a stubborn frown creasing her forehead.

He leant back in his chair. "Ah, but is that good enough? A little bird tells me that you are in the habit of visiting him at his house for long periods and with the curtains drawn." He raised a warning hand as Annie began to protest. "No, hear me out. I'm not saying that you are on the road to damnation, but there are those who are pointing the finger. You do not want to bring disgrace on your poor parents, I'm sure." He went on in similar vein for several minutes until Annie interrupted him.

"I'm going back to London in a day or two to work as a nursemaid and study art, so there is no chance that I will be getting married before next summer." She looked up to see her mother carrying in the tray of tea. "Did you hear that?" she said to both of them. "Joe and I have an understanding." Shards of ice penetrated her brain with the fear that perhaps she could not trust Joe to take care of her as he had promised. What if he and her ma had colluded in getting her to spend time with him in his cottage? There would be a niggling doubt in the back of her mind until she was confident that there would be no unwanted child.

Holding her close until the very last moment, Joe saw her off at the station. "I wish you didn't have to leave me again, my love," he whispered in her ear.

"Please, Joe, I promise I'll be back in the summer and we will be married, no more delays." Even as she made the promise, Annie was praying that nothing else would happen to make her change her mind forcing her to stay in London.

The look of relief on Stanley Salisbury's face when she returned was palpable. Had he been afraid that his discovery would decide to give up everything for the love of her Joe? Ivy had already told him that Joe was a very patient man, but that he was so besotted with Annie that he would do anything to make her stay in Densbury and marry him.

Annie, too, was relieved when two weeks later, nature told her that her fears about becoming pregnant were groundless. Of course she should have trusted Joe, she told herself. At heart she was terrified of admitting that the magnetic draw of wanting to stay in London was beginning to win over her desire to be Joe's wife.

The whirl of excitement that was life in the Salisbury household soon made memories of Christmas in Densbury fade. Orlando clamoured for more help from Annie, convinced that she was the best artist in the whole world.

"I'm still learning," she kept telling him, as indeed she was. Although she did not elaborate on what she was doing at the art college, she had shared descriptions of the life class and the lessons on anatomy with Eileen.

"Whatever would Ma and Pa say, not to mention Pastor Briggs?" Eileen had giggled.

Eileen had summed up the chasm between her sister's life in London and that of those she had left behind in Densbury. "Even if you do miss me, I wonder if you will ever want to come back?" she had said.

Joe's final words as he held her close before she boarded the London train, echoed those of her sister. "Promise me you'll come back, Annie. I'm so afraid that I've lost you already. Sometimes, I wish I had never offered to spend my Sunday afternoons watching you paint."

In spite of the disapproving looks from the other travellers waiting on the platform, Annie kissed him full on the mouth. "I can't bear being away from you, my darling Joe. Just wait till June and we'll be together for good."

The next few months flew past, leaving Annie barely enough time to write a scribbled half page once a week to Joe. It had become an effort trying to find news which did not include accounts of the days she spent at the studio with Anthony. How could she tell Joe that Anthony was becoming more and more attentive to her?

"A little bird tells me that young Anthony Gladwell is more than a little in love with you," Nanny Goodman said one day, a knowing twinkle in her eye.

"Well, the little bird heard wrong," Annie insisted, her blushes giving her away. "I've known Anthony for years. He's just about my best friend and that is all. Besides he knows that I'm going home to Densbury this summer to marry Joe."

Ivy gave a sly smile. "Just think of what a life you would have married to Anthony Gladwell, heir to his family fortune. You'd be mistress of the house with an army of servants at your beck and call and you would be able to paint all day and every day if you wished. The only requirement would be for you to provide an heir for the Gladwells."

Annie clapped her hands over her ears. "I'm marrying Joe."

Ivy gave a knowing grin. "Ah, but the thought of young Anthony in your bed instead of Joe doesn't fill you with loathing, does it?"

Alone in her room, Annie thought about the nanny's suggestion. It was true for all to see that Anthony was besotted with her. How many times had Mr Salisbury teased him at the studio. "Come on, Anthony, leave Annie to get on with her landscape."

Anthony would stammer, "I was just interested in her use of colour for that group of ash trees, Mr Salisbury."

It was when Mr Salisbury told them both that he was thinking of putting on an exhibition of work by up-and-coming artists, that Annie realised just how far she had travelled since her granny had given her the little bundle of drawings and since she and Anthony had shared snatched moments together painting at Baythorpe Hall.

Anthony put both arms round her waist, lifting her off the floor. His face flushed with excitement, he exulted, "The two of us, what a team we make, Annie."

"It will mean solid hard work from now until the end of July. I've fixed the last week in July for the exhibition," Stanley Salisbury said.

"Oh, no! I can't do it," Annie wailed. "I've promised Joe we'd be married at the end of June. I'm sorry, Mr Salisbury, I just can't let him down again."

There was a stunned silence, broken by Anthony's discreet cough. "Look, Annie, Joe knows how clever you are and he's already said he'd wait until this summer. Surely a month or two isn't going to make such a difference in the great scheme of things."

Joe's reply to her letter telling him that their wedding would have to be postponed yet again, left her dazed and shocked. There was no opening endearment, simply a cold statement that he released her from their engagement and was cancelling all wedding plans. "You can now stay in London. I wish you success in your chosen life. I do not expect that we shall meet again."

Distraught at the coldness of Joe's response, Annie wept for days, only being tempted to leave her room by Diana Salisbury. "I need you to come out with the children and me this afternoon, Annie, so dry your tears and get ready. We're leaving in half an hour."

This curt order reminded her that the Salisburys were her employers and that she was paid to help with the children and not waste time grieving over her broken engagement.

"Right away," she sniffled.

Diana apologised later for sounding so unfeeling. "I had to think of something to get you up and moving, so I've planned a visit to a new art exhibition."

The gallery was situated in a turning off New Bond Street. Only a small group of visitors were viewing the works of a relatively unknown artist.

"Sylvia Pankhurst," Diana explained. "See, no rural landscapes for her." She paused in front of one study, the head and shoulders of a working woman, whose sad eyes mirrored a life of drudgery. "You know, Annie, I think you would do well to follow her example," She stamped a foot. "It's about time we threw out portraits of the well-heeled upper class ladies and let the world see what we do to our poor sisters."

Annie nodded, remembering the young mothers who worked long hours, breastfeeding their babies in between stints in the factory. A vivid picture of her mother scrubbing the kitchen floors at Baythorpe Hall until her hands were red raw, danced before her eyes. These were real people, not like the pampered Lavinia Gladwell whose portrait hung in the drawing room at Baythorpe Hall.

"I think I'd need more tuition. I don't think I'm very good at people."

"Well, that can be arranged once your exhibition is under way."

Not for the first time, Annie felt a glow of pride at the recognition that she was being treated as a serious artist.

Chapter 11

Brush in hand, Annie stepped back to study her first attempt at portraiture. She had to admit that the result was not a great success. Inexperienced as she was, it was hard to know exactly where she had gone wrong.

Stanley Salisbury smiled. "Full marks for trying, Annie, but I think we need more work on your technique." He pointed to her subject's elongated nose. "See what I mean. I know that your model had a big nose, but it is somewhat out of proportion, wouldn't you say?"

"What you are trying to tell me is that I had better stick to what I can do." Annie tried hard to mask her disappointment with a rueful smile.

"At the moment, yes. There'll be time later to work on your portraiture techniques. We still have plenty of your other work from which we can choose for the exhibition, so you've not wasted your efforts, Annie."

He left his two protégés with a promise to call in on them later that morning. "Someone I have to see."

Annie studied her latest landscape, a study of the riverside view similar to the one she had painted as a girl and which Joe had had framed and presented to her parents. They had been so proud of her talent and yet could not understand her desire to pursue her dream. Her mother's narrow view of what constituted a woman's life was summed up in her constant harping on the fact that Joe owned his cottage and had a job. Annie placed a cover over the unsuccessful portrait. In any case, now was not the moment to discuss her future ambitions. Seeing Sylvia Pankhurst's studies of working women had fired her with a desire to show the world the backbreaking drudgery they endured. Whatever Stanley Salisbury might say about the commercial viability of landscapes which captured the light and the myriad colours of rural scenes, Annie wanted her art to convey more. Deep in her heart she remembered her grandmother's words. Painful as it had been, she had chosen her path, but there were still choices to be made. For the time being, she would carry on with what Stanley Salisbury called her forte.

"Come on, Annie Claydon, stop daydreaming and come and tell me where I've gone wrong this time."

Annie smiled as Anthony frowned, running his fingers through his unruly fair hair. Taking the brush from his hand, she teased him gently. "If I didn't know you better, I'd think you were trying to stop me working, just because you're behind with your schedule."

"That remark calls for punishment," Anthony threatened. Grabbing Annie round the waist, he seized the brush and daubed her nose a brilliant blue. Shrieking with laughter, Annie struggled to free herself from his grip. Twisting and turning, she ended up facing him. "Let me go, Anthony," she begged.

His tight grip relaxed, he placed his hands on her shoulders, gradually drawing her close to himself. The change from childlike play to a lover's embrace alarmed Annie, but she felt unable to stop Anthony as he bent to kiss her. "My sweet, darling Annie," he whispered. "We're not children any more."

So long starved of Joe's loving, Annie was powerless to stem the flood of longing welling within her. She returned Anthony's kisses with a passion that took him by surprise.

"Marry me, Annie!" There was no mistaking the sincerity of his proposal. "I've always wanted you to be my wife, but well, there was that chap Joe and you seemed so stuck on him that I didn't think I stood a chance."

For so long Anthony had been her dearest friend, her soulmate in their mutual desire to portray the beauty of the world around them, that she had never noticed him as a man capable of satisfying more than just her spiritual needs. Now, with his arms around her, Annie realised that the man she had accepted as a loving companion could be what Joe had been and more. Joe had always wanted to dominate her, assuming that once they were married she would devote all her time to caring for him and raising their children. Anthony knew and loved her for what she was, a free spirit longing to express herself through her art. She remembered Nanny Ivy's remarks about her feelings for Anthony. The older woman had been right, seeing what Annie had been blind to; she could very easily enjoy being in bed with Anthony. As she gave herself up to the warmth of being desired again, the reality of their situation struck her, forcing her to pull away from his embrace. "I can't! Your parents would never agree to it. Can you imagine your mother's reaction if you announced that you were marrying their maid?"

Anthony was silent for a moment. "Mother would want me to marry the girl I love," he said quietly.

"Maybe, but what about your father?" Annie insisted. "He'd never agree. I doubt if he would allow me into his house even if I were Mrs Gladwell."

"Be honest with me, Annie, if it weren't for him, what would you say?"

"I don't know if I've gone completely mad, but I'd say yes, Anthony." If she gave any thought to Joe, it was only to confirm that he, in rejecting her and her ambitions, had severed all emotional ties between them, leaving her free to fall in love with whomever she chose.

Any further attempts at completing canvasses for the exhibition were abandoned as the young lovers absorbed in one another forgot the world around them. Unlike Joe, who could not wait to make love to Annie, Anthony was reserved. "I'm so sorry, Annie," he whispered, afraid that his clumsy attempts at caressing her might upset her. "I promise to wait until we're married, so long as it is soon."

Annie could not confess that what she wanted more than anything was for Anthony to forget his gentlemanly instincts and show her the passion she had experienced with Joe. Now serious and composed, Anthony was more concerned with the practicalities of making their engagement public. "I'll write to Papa first and you must write to your parents and then we'll put an announcement in *The Times*. I'm sure Papa will be agreeable, although he might need Mama to persuade him."

Annie was troubled at Anthony's naïve assumption that things would all proceed smoothly. He had left his sister Lavinia out of the equation. After the incident at Estcourt, when Lavinia had blamed Annie for enticing her fiancé Miles, Lavinia had had a blazing argument with Miles and had been astounded when he told her that he would release her from their engagement. That was the end of Lavinia's ambition to marry into the aristocracy. Reports of her virulent temper had spread, leaving eligible but impecunious young aristocrats willing to remain poor rather than suffer her bad temper.

"What about Lavinia?"

"Oh, she won't mind," Anthony said, dismissing her with a broad gesture.

Annie stared at him. Had Anthony really no idea of his sister's vituperative nature? Or was this the way he dealt with difficult situations by pretending they did not exist? On reflection, her agreeing to marry Anthony was already throwing up problems. "If I marry you and Lavinia is still unmarried and at home, that will mean that I will be her superior in rank and she would never agree to that."

Her unhappy frown worried Anthony. "You still want to marry me, don't you?" He drew her to her feet, gently stroking her hair and whispering words of comfort. "Lavinia's bark is worse than her bite," he said.

"No, it's not, Anthony! She hates me! Don't you see?" Memories of the black stallion rearing up in front of her caused her to cry out. "She won't let us marry, I know it."

Further discussion was prevented by Stanley Salisbury's appearance. Taking them out to lunch was his priority. A mutual warning nod made Anthony and Annie keep silent about their proposed marriage.

The proposed exhibition was the sole topic of conversation for days on end. Anthony wrote to his father to tell him of his engagement to Annie and of his intention to put an announcement in *The Times* newspaper. Annie wrote to her parents to tell them that Anthony had proposed and that she had accepted. The reply from Annie's parents was short, telling her that she had their blessing, but that they would be unable to attend the wedding whenever it was planned. Anthony received no reply from his father in spite of sending several letters. Finally, a brief message arrived to say that his sister Lavinia would be arriving in London to view the exhibition and would speak to him about his stupid infatuation.

"I told you that's what would happen." Annie had never shared Anthony's optimism that his father would come round to the idea of his marrying a servant girl, even if she had bettered herself and was now becoming well-known in the world of art.

"Yes, but Lavinia is coming." Anthony's attempts to reassure Annie only served to show her how little he knew about his sister. "I'll soon be able to talk her round, get her on our side. You'll see."

Waking in the night from nightmares in which Lavinia's stallion was rearing in front of her, intent on breaking every bone in her tiny body with its massive hooves, Annie wished she could convince Anthony that Lavinia was intent on destroying her.

As the date drew nearer, Diana asked Annie what she would be wearing "You look pale, my dear," she told her, noting the dark shadows under the girl's eyes. "Let me help. You're going to be in the public eye, so we have to be just right." She stood back and surveyed Annie's dark grey dress. "No, too severe, I think. Something shorter and a little more colourful. What we need is to give the impression of a young fresh talent with just a hint of sophistication. I think I have just the thing." She opened the door of the heavy walnut wardrobe and began to search through the row of dresses. "Ah! This is exactly what you need." She gave a sad little smile as she pulled out a silk dress in midnight blue. "It's too small for me now, Annie, so you must have it."

The art gallery, although small, was large enough to accommodate the thirty or so paintings on show. Art dealers and newspaper critics, all keen to see if Stanley Salisbury's enthusiasm was justified, were among the chosen guests.

Anthony's blue eyes sparkled with excitement when he saw Annie. "You're so beautiful," he whispered as they went up the stairs to the upper floor where the exhibition was being staged.

At six o'clock, Stanley Salisbury signalled to one of his assistants to open the wide oak doors. Annie felt as if her lungs had turned to stone, refusing to be filled with life-giving air. Gasping, she gulped in air, forcing herself to breathe in a huge effort which she hoped would dispel the terror paralysing her limbs as the invited guests arrived. Stanley Salisbury had been careful not to openly compare the work of his two protégés, carefully mixing the positioning of their paintings, but the experts had no difficulty in selecting Annie's work which made Anthony's seem amateurish in comparison. Glasses of champagne in hand, they took up various poses in front of her pictures. Snatches of comments, none of which made any sense to her, floated across the room. Unable to move from the position she had taken up with her back to the wall, she watched Anthony who was totally at ease mingling with the well-heeled, some of whom he recognised as relatives of old school friends. Annie shivered. Had she made a huge mistake in accepting Anthony's proposal? How could Anthony ever think that the two of them could be together mixing socially?

"Quite out of your depth, aren't you?" Lavinia Gladwell had entered the gallery and was standing by Annie's side.

"Ah, Lavinia, how kind of you to come." Stanley Salisbury's intervention saved Annie from struggling to find the right words to counter Lavinia's insults. "But I have to drag my little genius away for a moment," he explained. "Everyone is keen to meet her. They are practically fighting over her paintings." His eyes shining with triumph, he led Annie away. "A wonderful success, Annie."

Surrounded by admiring art lovers, Annie accepted their compliments, all the while looking to see where Anthony had gone. She caught sight of him at last now standing quite alone by one of his paintings. Poor Anthony. Only one or two of his paintings had sold, the London art dealers showing little interest in his work. The ones which had sold had been the ones which had been improved by Annie's touch.

"I'm so proud of you, my darling Annie," he told her, when she managed to escape from her admirers. "I always knew you were the genius." He kissed her lightly on the cheek.

"How touching." Lavinia's voice was soft enough not to be heard by anyone else but Annie and Anthony, yet it carried the familiar ring of hatred and menace. Elbowing Annie out of the way, she placed herself close to her brother. "So, the little slut has wormed her way into Stanley Salisbury's affections. I wonder what she did to persuade him to put on this little show for her."

"Lavinia!" Anthony was shocked at Lavinia's crudity.

Lavinia gripped Anthony's shoulders, causing him to recoil. Her face inches from his, she told him, "I'm not staying. I only came to deliver a message from Papa. If you insist on bringing disgrace on your family by marrying someone from the gutter, you will no longer be considered to be a member of the Gladwell family. Papa will cut you off. You have a choice. Are you going to let this woman destroy our family?"

White-faced, Anthony stared at his sister. His words came stumbling out "I don't understand. Cut me off? What does Mama say?"

"Mama will say whatever Papa tells her to say. I daresay she would have been soft-hearted enough to give in to your little whim, but not Papa and I."

"You'd better listen to your sister," Annie said quietly.

"Ah, the little slut sees sense," Lavinia said. "I'm sure she will keep your bed warm until you find someone of our kind to marry."

"No!" Anthony's vehement denial caused a few heads to turn. Embarrassed at being the focus of attention, Anthony whispered in Lavinia's ear. "I'm marrying Annie and no one else. Tell Papa that."

Lavinia turned towards Annie. Her obsidian eyes smouldered with loathing, contrasting with the forced air of sisterly affection. Any observer would have thought they were engaged in a friendly conversation. "I'll see you dead first," Lavinia said. "I failed before, but not this time." Still smiling, she gave Annie a friendly wave as she left.

Anthony gave a nervous cough. "Take no notice, that's just Lavinia. Her bark is worse than her bite."

Vivid images of Lavinia beating her into the ground with her whip were the last things imprinted on Annie's mind as she sank to the floor in a dead faint.

"It must be all the excitement," she heard Diana Salisbury say as consciousness returned. "You've worked the child too hard, Stanley."

Anthony was cradling her in his arms. "Here, drink this, darling."

The fierce fumes of the brandy he offered, hit the back of her throat, making her cough and splutter. Gradually, her colour returned.

"There, that's better," Diana said. "Let's get Annie home and in bed. You can stay here and take care of the guests," she told her husband.

"No!" Annie protested. "I'm fine now. Please let me stay."

Anthony continued to hold Annie close. "I'll take care of her. She's my responsibility now."

Stanley Salisbury raised his eyebrows. "Is she indeed?" he said, smiling.

"May I?" Anthony asked Annie.

After all the events of the evening, Annie did not have the strength to protest. There was an icy quality in his amazing blue eyes that she had not seen before. She squeezed his hand and smiled. "We're engaged to be married," Anthony said.

Diana clapped her hands in delight. "This calls for more champagne," her husband said. He summoned a waiter. "None of the usual stuff. Bring a bottle of the Moet and Chandon, Premier Cru." His two protégés engaged to be married. What could be better? He could see years ahead of the young couple working together, producing marketable paintings. He congratulated himself mentally on his discovery of Annie's talent. She would encourage her husband and improve his work. Even if Anthony's talent was not in the same class as Annie's, Stanley was confident that with her help Anthony would still turn out better paintings than most of his contemporaries.

Annie remained seated with Diana as the glasses were brought. Onlookers would have concluded that they were celebrating the success of the exhibition.

"Where's your sister gone?" Stanley asked. "She ought to be celebrating with us."

"She had to leave," Anthony explained.

"Yes, but…" Annie changed her mind about revealing Lavinia's reasons for leaving. "I expect she wanted to get back to her hotel."

"Look, I'll get the gallery locked up and we can go over to the studio and wait there for our car. I told the driver to come at midnight and it is still only eleven. Besides, I want to take a second look at some of Annie's paintings." He mentioned a collector who had expressed an interest in buying more examples of Annie's work. "We can't afford to let interested buyers wait."

He and Diana complemented one another perfectly. Both were passionate about art, but whereas Diana would have spent her days painting, her husband had turned their shared passion into a very profitable business. Annie wondered if she and Anthony would make such an ideal partnership.

Stanley Salisbury locked the gallery door. "Must make sure all our treasures are safe," he said, winking at Annie. There was no moon, the narrow street lit only by one guttering gas lamp, barely enough to illuminate the faces of the group walking the short distance from the gallery to the studio. By now, the crowd had dispersed, the carriages having all departed. Stanley Salisbury was adding up the profit he had made on the evening, while his wife was lost in dreams of having her own exhibition once the children were older.

Anthony had already dismissed his sister's threats as idle. That was just like Lavinia to exaggerate and make a drama out of the slightest problem. It was ridiculous to think that his father would disown his only son. They would all come to love Annie as much as he did. He squeezed her hand gently. "Happy, darling?"

At first Annie did not hear his question. The image of the hatred in Lavinia's eyes blotted out Anthony's gentle voice. She felt him nudge her arm. "I asked if you were happy," he repeated.

"Of course. Of course I am." Annie felt that if she repeated it often enough she would come to believe it herself. Only a short while ago she had been feted as a rising young artist, but how far could she go once Lavinia began to spread her evil lies? Lavinia will destroy me, she kept telling herself. And Anthony will not be able to protect me.

Stanley began to study those paintings in the studio which had not been exhibited. With Diana by his side offering advice, the two selected a further two in the style admired by the wealthy collector. Anthony stood behind the pair, occasionally adding his opinion. None of them noticed Annie with shoulders hunched sitting quietly by the door. The evening had been so overwhelming for her, it had left her too exhausted to be able to make any worthwhile contribution to the discussion on the merits of her work. Unthinking, she smoothed the silk folds of the dress given to her by Diana. A vague memory nudged her mind, struggling to remind her that something was not in place. Annie gave a little cry of horror as she realised that she no longer had the tiny silk embroidered bag belonging to Diana. The last time she had seen it was when she was recovering consciousness in the gallery. She was about to ask Anthony to walk back with her to retrieve it, when she noticed Stanley's keys to the gallery lying on a bench beside his cloak.

Too engrossed in one particular landscape, the three did not see Annie creep silently out of the door. It was darker than she had expected as she stumbled along the uneven cobbles. For a brief moment the clouds parted enough to illuminate the gallery door giving Annie sufficient light to see the lock and insert the key. Slightly off-balance with fatigue, she stumbled over the threshold.

"Hello, Annie." In the unlit passage Annie could not see the features of the woman addressing her, but the voice was familiar.

"Lavinia! What are you doing coming back here?"

Lavinia laughed. "I never left. You were all so busy telling one another how wonderful you all are, that you didn't notice me." She gripped Annie's arms with vicious strength. "First I'm going to destroy all your fancy work. Oh, yes, I can see your painting is worth twice that of Anthony's. Poor Anthony! Don't think for one moment that I'm going to let you make a fool out of my brother."

Annie turned to run. "You can't destroy all this," she screamed.

Lavinia was too quick for her, grabbing her by the hair and slamming her head hard against the wall. "The paintings and you," she threatened. Annie's feeble attempt to ward off the blows faded as swirling clouds of blackness overcame her and she slid unconscious to the floor.

In the studio, Stanley called Annie's name. "Tell me what do you think you need to do to bring up the pale green of the meadow behind the church? Do you think a darker shade would better convey the lack of bright sunshine there?" He repeated the question. "Annie?" He swung round. "Where the devil is she?"

Diana shrugged her shoulders. "She can't be far. Perhaps she's gone outside to study the effect of moonlight on the cobbles. You know how serious she is about her painting."

Anthony stared at the two. "She wouldn't go wandering about the streets of London on her own in the dark." He pushed past them, knocking over an easel bearing Annie's latest half-finished painting. "It's all been too much for her."

Calling Annie's name, the two men ran out into the street. "My God! Smoke!" Anthony shouted. "It's the gallery!"

167

The gallery was a two-storeyed building, with the lower storey used as a sales area and the upper used only for exhibitions. Thick plumes of black smoke spewed out of the windows of the upper storey. Tongues of bright orange flames streaked with vivid reds and yellows were already greedily devouring the wooden window frames. They looked up to see a woman's face appearing at one window.

"Lavinia!" Anthony shielded his face from the searing heat as Lavinia hurled a blazing painting down at him.

"You fool!" she yelled. "I told you I wouldn't let that little slut destroy our family. She's dead!" Incoherent with delight at her triumph, Lavinia continued to vilify Annie. With the heat and the smoke choking her, most of what she was screaming out was incomprehensible.

Police whistles drowned out her next words. Suddenly men appeared from neighbouring houses carrying buckets of water with one elderly man struggling to fight his way past the police into the gallery. "I saw the girl go in. Let me in!" The two policemen held him back from performing useless heroics There would be no survivors in that blaze.

"It's Annie! She's in there!" Anthony took advantage of the distraction to push his way through the doors. Once inside, thick black smoke blinded him, filling his lungs with suffocating fumes. "Annie!" he called.

By now, the fire engines had arrived playing spumes of cold water on the building and in particular on the entrance leading to the lower floor. The smoke subsided momentarily, just sufficiently to allow Anthony to reach the stairs leading to the upper storey. Groping his way along the wall, he stumbled over what appeared to be a sack of rubbish. "Annie!"

"Come on, lad." One of the firemen had followed him in. "It's too late to save her," he gasped. "Here, let me help. Get out before you're burnt alive."

"No! I've got Annie! I won't leave her!" He knelt down beside Annie's inert body struggling to lift her. "I've got to get her out." Although tiny, she was a dead weight in his arms. Guided by the fireman, he carried her along the passage to the front door. Just a few yards now, but iron hands squeezed his lungs, driving out what little oxygen he had been able to breathe in. The last thing he heard before he lost consciousness was the cheering of the crowd as he carried Annie through the door to safety. By now, the fierce flames fuelled by the wooden-framed oil paintings had begun to devour the heavy beams supporting the oak floors. The crowd recoiled as the gunshot sounds of cracking timber blasted the narrow street. Anthony recovered consciousness to hear his sister's final words cursing Annie. "I've killed her!" Lavinia's black hair with an aureole of flames was visible for just a few moments before she disappeared into the depths of the fire she had created.

For the next two weeks, Annie and Anthony were nursed at the home of the Salisburys. Both lay in a state of shock, too ill to tell the police what had happened. Stanley Salisbury blamed himself for being taken in by Lavinia's entreaty to send her an invitation to the art exhibition. "If I hadn't encouraged her, she would never have come," he kept repeating. "It is all my fault." He shut himself in his study, refusing to take meals with the family. Under strict instructions not to disturb their father, the children crept about, unable to understand what was wrong.

As her strength returned, Annie's determination grew; she was not going to let Lavinia's act of self-destruction destroy this lovely family. Diana was so preoccupied with her husband's mental state that Annie did not feel she could add to her problems by telling her the extent of Lavinia's warped mind.

"In here, Annie." Nanny Ivy summoned Annie into her quarters. She was not going to see the family torn to pieces any longer. "Here, drink this first," she said handing her a cup of hot chocolate. "Now, Annie, tell me. This Lavinia, what about her? Look at me." Annie read compassion in the dark eyes, but how could she tell Nanny Ivy the extent of Lavinia's obsession with Anthony which aroused such self-destructing hatred and violence?

"She tried to kill me before." Her hands trembling, she reached out to place the hot drink on the table beside her. Gradually, Annie's tears subsided.

"You have to tell me everything, Annie." The older woman took Annie's ice-cold hands in hers. "You can't protect Anthony. He saw with his own eyes what she was capable of even to the extent of trying to kill you. It will take time but he will have to deal with that in his own way. In the meantime, this family has to know that Lavinia was deranged and that Mr Salisbury is in no way to blame. I have to tell Mrs Salisbury."

"I understand." Through her sobs, Annie told Nanny Ivy the whole story. Ivy felt the hairs on the back of her neck prickle as Annie recounted the horror of Lavinia's black stallion rearing over her ready to kill. "And now I've got to tell Anthony." Annie made up her mind that if she and Anthony were to be married, there could be no secrets between them. Nanny Ivy was right; Anthony had to be told the whole truth. But first she had to talk to Stanley Salisbury.

His reaction was first one of disbelief. "Kill you? Surely not, Annie!"

Annie rolled up her sleeve and thrust the arm in front of his face. "One tiny scar is all I have left to show you. My father and Joe found me in a ditch left to die by that madwoman."

"If only I had known. It's all my fault that she nearly succeeded this time. Oh, my God!"

"No, it is not your fault," Annie insisted. "As far as you knew, she was the daughter of a wealthy and respected family and Anthony's sister." Exhausted at having to relive the events of that cold night when Lavinia first attacked her, Annie sank into an armchair and covered her face with her hands.

Stanley knelt down in front of her and gently pulled her hands away from her face. "Now, my dear, it is all over. I am so glad you told me. I must have a word with Diana. She had been blaming herself, too."

Telling Anthony that his sister was a deranged madwoman eaten with a black, corrosive hatred, was even harder for Annie.

His quiet acceptance came as a shock to her. "I think I've known all along. I've never forgotten that night at Estcourt when she had you dismissed."

"And you drove me home in the snow." Annie smiled in spite of her tears.

"Oh, Annie, if I hadn't been there, you would have died." Anthony held her tightly. "You're safe now, my darling. You're with me, remember?"

There was still the unsolved problem of whether Lavinia had been speaking the truth regarding his inheritance. Anthony did not have long to wait for his fears to be confirmed. He received a brief note to say that his sister's remains had been taken back to Densbury and that the funeral had already taken place. He wrote to his father and mother once more. He received a curt reply accusing him of being the cause of his sister's death and informing him that he was no longer to be considered as the son and heir of the Gladwell family.

"My father's disowned me," an astounded Anthony told Annie. He thrust the letter into her hands. "Surely he can't mean it."

The tone of the letter made it clear that the family had summed up Annie as being a scheming woman intent on securing a share of the Gladwell wealth. "Our poor Lavinia saw her for what she was and paid the price with her life." Anthony's father hinted that a complete break with Annie would satisfy the family. "If you were to marry someone of your own standing, then I might reconsider, but it would be only after such a marriage had taken place."

Annie half expected Anthony to show anger or defiance at the outrageous suggestion that he should marry someone else. Instead, she read into his avoidance of her steady gaze a wavering in the aggressive attitude he had shown to Lavinia in the gallery.

"Why don't you go home and speak to your father?" Annie was beginning to fear that Anthony might not be strong enough to defy his father, but in spite of the risks that she might lose him, she had to know for certain.

Anthony shook his head. Defeat and despair weighed heavily on his shoulders leaving him with no energy for challenging his father's unjust decision. "He never concedes." He patted the letter still in Annie's hands. "You've read it; he will give in only when I marry someone else." Suddenly leaping to his feet, he cupped Annie's face in his slender fingers. "I'm marrying you, Annie. I don't need my father's money. We can live in my flat until I make enough money from my paintings and then we'll find a house of our own."

"Who pays the rent on the flat?" Annie asked. The difference in their backgrounds became only too apparent when Anthony started to discuss practical matters such as rent. He would never have known how important the payment of rent had been to those poverty-stricken families in Densbury forced into the workhouse because they did not have the money to pay the landlord. He had never had to worry about having sufficient money to put food on the table or coal in the grate. Trips abroad, entertaining his friends, even being able to buy the materials for painting were never a matter for discussion. There was always money for whatever he wanted to do. At that moment, Annie had to struggle to bury her resentment as old memories surfaced of what she saw as his extravagant, carefree life, whilst she and her family had had to struggle to exist on the plainest of fare and keep warm with one tiny fire smouldering with twigs and the poorest quality coal.

"The flat?" Anthony considered Annie's question. "I didn't have to pay rent, so I suppose Papa must have done." He thought for a moment. "Of course, that's it. My father arranged it all when he finally gave in and said I could come up to London to study art. We agreed that if I didn't succeed in one year's time, I would go and work with him in the family business."

"So, it is possible that your father has cancelled future payments." If they had nowhere to live with no means to support themselves, she would have to remain with the Salisburys helping with the children whilst continuing to work on her paintings at the studio. "Where will we live?" she asked Anthony.

"We'll manage. We've both got money to come from the sale of our paintings." He kissed her lightly on the cheek. "That will pay the rent. We can both spend all our time in the studio painting together." Delighted at having solved all their problems, he went on, "It will just be like old times, when we were children and you told me what was wrong with my work."

Annie was right about the arrangements for paying the rental on his rooms. Anthony returned pale-faced from his discussion with his bank manager. Will Gladwell had not only cancelled the agreement on the rental of Anthony's flat, but also his monthly allowance. Not only was he homeless, he was penniless too. They would both have to work to survive.

Chapter 12

Fully recovered from the effects of the fire at the art gallery, and feeling that he could no longer remain as a guest of the Salisburys, Anthony had returned to his bachelor rooms situated in a three-storey Victorian house just a stone's throw from Marble Arch. The suite of rooms had seemed ideal for his purposes when he had first found it. The sitting room was large with a high sash window overlooking the street. The wallpaper with its flocked pattern of pink roses offended Anthony's artistic eye, but he had kept his opinions to himself when the landlady had pointed it out to him with the proud admission that she had chosen it herself. The bedroom was small with a comfortable double bed which Anthony was longing to share with Annie. Unusually for suites of rooms in that area there was a minute bathroom and an even tinier area which served as a kitchen. Anthony had been surprised at the provision of the latter, and although always having had Cook to wait on him at home, in time he had managed to make a pot of tea. The kindly landlady had seen straight away that Anthony was a gentleman never having had to do to women's work and had offered to prepare an evening meal for when he came back from the studio, an offer which was gladly accepted. Anthony thought he would have to ask Annie if she preferred to go along with this arrangement. His financial problems had been solved for the time being when Stanley Salisbury advanced him the proceeds from the sale of his paintings, two of which had been spared from the fire with the buyers having taken them away immediately after the exhibition. The unexpected windfall had been a bonus, but this would only be in the short term. He would have to think of something to bring in a more substantial return once he had a wife to keep. No longer cushioned by the Gladwell fortune, he was now a young man of very limited means and with no qualifications to earn a decent living. He felt a pang of distress when the hard facts of the situation struck him in that Annie, as the more gifted of the two of them, would be able to earn more than he could from selling paintings.

Whilst he had recovered and was more his old self, Annie had taken longer to get over the shock of Lavinia's attempt to murder her, often being woken by vivid dreams of the moment when she thought she was about to die in the gallery. Physically she was becoming stronger and so able to continue helping Katherine and Orlando. Orlando repeatedly asked her to tell him what had happened to his father's art gallery. Having listened quietly to the adults' conversation, he had formed a picture in his mind of a madwoman setting fire to the building.

"Can I do a picture of it?" he asked Annie. "I could do the fire and all the colours but you'd have to help me with the mad lady. I can't draw faces." At ten years old, Orlando was determined that he could produce a picture to please Annie. Shy but determined, he said, "I want to do it for you."

Annie felt her whole body tense with terror at the prospect of having to relive Lavinia's attempt on her life, one which had almost succeeded. "You can't do it, Orlando. You didn't see what happened, Orlando." As the memory of Lavinia with murder in her eyes swam in front of her, she repeated, "You didn't see it."

"No, but you did, Annie." His eyes shining, he suggested that the two of them could paint it together. "You could easily tell me all about it. I mean you were there and saw everything."

That was not true, since for a part of that night, she had lain unconscious until Anthony rescued her. However, she had recovered to see the gallery in flames and Lavinia disappearing into the inferno she had created. "I'll have to ask your mother." Annie hoped that Diana would veto the project as being too much of a painful reminder of Lavinia's attempt on her life, one which had almost succeeded.

Although she could see the distress in Annie's eyes, Diana was not totally against her young son's idea. "It's up to you, Annie. It will need some courage." With her head on one side, she considered the matter further. "Don't you think it might help to lay a few ghosts?"

Diana was right, Annie conceded. Besides, it was always difficult to deny Orlando his wishes. Orlando babbled with delight when told that he could spend his Saturday mornings working with Annie on re-creating the torching of the gallery. "You'll have to tell me every single bit about it. I want it to be perfect."

Diana and Annie exchanged glances. "You're absolutely sure?" Diana asked.

"Absolutely!" In his childlike enthusiasm to please his adored Annie, he had convinced her that if the only way to cleanse her mind and soul of images of Lavinia was to transfer them on to canvas, then she would have to do so. "I can't wait to get started. Come on, Orlando." With a feeling of gladness, she led the delighted boy off into the schoolroom.

Whilst she and Orlando were deep in discussion focusing on the composition of the painting, Stanley dropped in. He patted Orlando's arm. "You've got a good teacher here, young man," he said. He darted an inquiring glance in Annie's direction. "Have you thought about your immediate future yet, Annie?" He was a little nervous as if not sure whether he ought to say more, then took a deep breath and went on, "Your admirers are still just as keen to buy your work, Annie. Besides, Anthony won't start again without you and since his rift with the family, he has very little in the way of means."

Annie was forced to quell the emotions rising within her. The thought of Anthony being alone because of his love for her, made her confront her problems and accept that it was time to take up where she had left off, time to rebuild and replace her lost work. She would not let Lavinia rule her life from the grave. "I'll tell Anthony. We will be at the studio on Monday morning. But first of all, Orlando and I have some very important artwork to complete."

As the two worked frantically to achieve what Annie needed to depict the heat and frenzy of that night, the picture took shape. Orlando had a gift for selecting and mixing just the right reds and yellows to re-create the flaming orange hues which had lit up the night sky. It was only when they reached the area Annie was dreading, that she had to bite her lip hard to stop herself from screaming out. It took a supreme effort to hold the brush in her trembling hand. She could still feel the terror gripping her stomach as it had when, intent on murder, Lavinia had confronted her in the gallery.

"I'll do the mad lady," she told Orlando. The black hair, the crazed expression in Lavinia's eyes, the engulfing smoke and greedy flames – all had to be there on canvas.

"That's really good." Praise from Orlando made some of the tension relax its grip on her heart, releasing the bands of the emotional straitjacket which had been threatening to crush the life out of her.

"Yes, Orlando, I think we have done a very good job here. We must show it to your father."

"Very good, but not quite ready for the gallery," Stanley said, patting Orlando on the head. "Perhaps I'll put it in my study. It will remind me what a clever son I have."

"And Annie's clever too, isn't she, Papa?"

Stanley's eyes were full of compassion. "Very clever and very brave, my dear."

For Anthony, there was to be no return to happy days spent with Annie at the studio. With the assassination of Archduke Franz Ferdinand in Sarajevo on June 28th 1914, newspaper headlines reflected the mood of insecurity and foreboding descending on the nation. The Salisburys talked in hushed tones about their fears for the possible outcome of this event. Their fears were soon crystallised in reality as Germany declared war first on Russia and France before invading Belgium, the catalyst for Britain to declare war on Germany on August 4th.

Stanley went with Annie to call on Anthony, who was pacing up and down his sitting room in a mood of scarcely controlled excitement. "I've got to volunteer. I'll get my commission straight away, my darling, then we can get married. I'll have my pay and you'll get an allowance as well." The words came tumbling out in Anthony's euphoric state. It was as if he considered the outbreak of war to be a benevolent act of the Fates especially designed for him. "We needn't worry about Papa and the money thing any more."

Her anxiety growing, Annie stared at him. He had the excited air of a schoolboy looking forward to thrashing a rival school at a game of rugby. "Don't you understand, Anthony? You'll be in the front line. You could get killed. Please, Anthony," she begged, "go home, tell your father we aren't getting married. He'll forgive you and you can work in the factory making army uniforms. That way, you won't have to go off to fight." Her head drooped, as she fumbled in her bag for a handkerchief to dry the tears brimming over her cheeks.

Anthony held her close until the crying subsided. "No, Annie." His voice was quiet and firm, the schoolboy enthusiasm gone. "I am determined that I am not going back to Densbury. We are going to get married and I am going to fight for my country."

Her voice muffled as he crushed her to his chest, all she could murmur was, "My dear Anthony."

The wedding was to be a quiet affair solemnised in the tiny church a few hundred yards from the Salisburys' house. Annie wrote to tell her parents and was thrilled when she received a parcel from them containing a small gift of pillow cases, "for your bottom drawer." Her sister Eileen sent a beautifully embroidered tablecloth in which she enclosed a long letter saying how much she missed Annie and wished she could be at the wedding. *"I think it would be better if I stayed here with Ma and Pa. Besides, Daniel and I are very busy with the shop and we are saving up to get married. Joe still comes round, but he is joining up soon."*

The news that Joe, too, could die in the war came as a shock. Somehow, she had thought of Joe as being firmly settled in Densbury working for the Gladwells all his life. She wished with all her heart that he could stay and make uniforms as she had suggested that Anthony ought to do, then suppressed the feeling as being disloyal to Anthony, who was overjoyed to receive a short note from his mother wishing him and Annie happiness.

The letter written in a quivering hand said, *"Your father does not know about this letter, but I could not let my dear son embark on marriage without my blessing. Annie is a lovely young woman and will make you very happy."* Thora Gladwell went on to say that she was worried about the war and would pray for his safe return.

"You see, Annie, everything will turn out fine. Maybe Papa will change his mind."

Annie gave a dispirited shake of the head. "Don't be too hopeful, my love. Remember that your mother does say that she has had to write to you in secret."

There was reproach in Anthony's eyes. "Please, Annie, don't be too hard on Papa."

There were few preparations to be made for the ceremony. Stanley Salisbury was to give the bride away, whilst Hugo, one of Anthony's old schoolfriends was to act as best man. Hugo had been at the gallery on the night of the fire and had volunteered to join the Grenadier Guards on the same day as Anthony. Young Katherine accepted the role of bridesmaid with her usual solemnity, insisting that she be given the chance to practise beforehand in order to be perfect on the day. In spite of complaining that he ought to be given a part in the wedding, Orlando was told firmly that he would sit with his mother and Nanny Goodman and help keep his baby sister quiet.

The words, "Till death us do part," had taken on a greater significance for the many couples rushing to the altar in the early days of August 1914. As Anthony placed the simple gold band on her finger, Annie prayed silently that he would come home to her safely.

Stanley had arranged a quiet celebratory meal in a nearby hotel. There was no wedding cake or speeches; had it not been for Anthony and Hugo being in uniform the other guests would have summed up the group as being an ordinary family out enjoying a meal together. Whilst the grown-ups made conversation covering the possible length of the war, the likelihood of further invasions by the Kaiser's troops and prospective food shortages, the children sat in obedient silence. Having long finished his pudding and bored with the serious talk, Orlando was bursting to tell Anthony about his latest achievement.

"We did a really good painting, Mr Gladwell. Annie had to do the mad lady, because she saw her and I didn't know what she looked like."

"Quiet, Orlando!" his father ordered.

The colour suddenly stripped from his cheeks, Anthony paused for a moment unable to speak. With an effort to appear casual, he laid a hand on Orlando's shoulder. "Come on, then, tell me about it, young man."

Orlando was only too keen to describe in vivid detail the scene he and Annie had painted. "We did lots of black smoke and burning windows, and Annie did the lady with the black hair who was throwing paintings out of the window."

"Enough!" Diana told her son.

"Well done." Anthony could see that the little boy adored Annie. "I'll come and see your painting one day when I get back from the war."

"I'm so sorry." Diana shook her head.

"Please don't be. You should be proud of young Orlando." Anthony placed a protective arm round his new wife's shoulders. "It's all in the past now, isn't it, darling?" He was rewarded with a loving smile. Both recognised that they had come through an ordeal which would have tested more fragile relationships.

"Time for us to go and leave Lieutenant and Mrs Gladwell in peace," Stanley declared. He gestured to Nanny Ivy to gather up the children. A nod from her reminded Katherine and Orlando to shake hands with Anthony before they were firmly ushered out of the door. Near to tears, Orlando shook off Nanny Ivy's restraining hand and raced back into the dining room. "Please don't leave us for good," he wept. "We all love you, Annie, don't leave us."

Annie held him close for a moment. "I promise I'll come and see you every Sunday and perhaps we can do some more paintings together."

Orlando's face creased in a big grin. "Goodbye. I'd better go. Nanny Ivy will be ever so cross."

Alone at their table, Anthony gave an embarrassed cough. "I suppose we ought to be getting back to our home." His boyish cheeks flushed pink, emphasising the brightness of anticipation in his blue eyes. He came round to her side of the table, taking her hand and gently helping her to her feet. "Come on, my love."

Annie had visited Anthony's rooms with the Salisburys when they had helped her take her few belongings the day before the wedding. And now, small as the apartment was, she was to be mistress of her own household. With difficulty Annie closed her mind to the memory of Joe and his cottage, where although she might have been mistress of the household, it would all have been on Joe's terms, stifling her spirit and ambition. This is different, she told herself. I shall have my home and be able to pursue my painting career too. Stanley had told her that she needed to improve her skills in portraiture and that was what she intended to study once Anthony had left for France. The little bundle of drawings left to her by her granny was already in the cupboard beside her bed, a constant reminder of what she intended to do in life. Any tiny doubts as to whether she had chosen the right path were quickly dispelled, anticipating the moment when Anthony would take her in his arms as a lover and not just a friend.

Giving herself to him with the same passion she had felt for Joe, she was disappointed to feel Anthony recoil ever so slightly. "You have to leave it to me," he whispered. "I know you don't know, my darling, trust me." It was clear that his knowledge of passion between a man and a woman was very limited. With no attempt to rouse her, he completed his lovemaking in a matter of minutes. Sighing with satisfaction, he murmured, "My darling wife," before rolling off her He kissed her gently on the cheek and was soon asleep.

Unable to sleep, Annie lay beside him listening to his soft breathing. A chink of light from the street's gas lamps partly lit up the bedroom. She turned to look at Anthony's face. "My darling friend," she whispered. "I've married my best friend, not my lover." Tears streamed down her cheeks as she lay awake contemplating what the future might hold for her. This marriage would not give her the satisfaction she craved. How long would it be before Anthony realised that he was not the man she should have married?

They had only one more night together before the time came to see Anthony off to war. He made love to her tenderly as he had done the night before, still unaware that she found no physical joy in their union. "I'm the luckiest man in the world," he told her before kissing her on the cheek and falling into a deep sleep.

"You will be all right here without me, won't you?" Anthony's solicitude moved Annie to admit again that although she loved Anthony only as a friend, his feelings for her were far deeper, akin to what she and Joe had once felt for one another so long ago. She concentrated on listening to Anthony. "Promise me you'll move back to the Salisburys if you feel too lonely."

"I promise, but I'll be so busy at the college and then there'll be all the letters I have to write to you. I won't have time to be lonely."

Annie made an effort to make cheerful conversation all the way to the station. A big smile stretching his generous mouth, Hugo was there to meet them. Annie did not miss the sly dig as Hugo muttered in Anthony's ear, "Lucky dog. Bet you wish you didn't have to go." Anthony gave a nervous laugh, at the same time warning Hugo with a frown not to say any more.

The crowds of men in uniform being hugged by tearful women pressed on all sides. Annie was grateful for the noise. At least it meant that conversation was confined to the banal with no mention of what had happened between them in their marriage bed. Anthony held her close. "I'll soon be back to my beautiful wife." The longing in his eyes filled Annie with a mixture of guilt and resignation. Her role would be that of the faithful wife ready to please her husband without making demands of her own. She suspected that not only would Anthony fail to understand her desires, he would be shocked to learn of her deep sexual feelings which he could not assuage.

Men in uniform struggled to lean out of the carriage windows waving farewell to wives and sweethearts. "Back home for Christmas," was the shout from one young soldier, which was taken up by hundreds more, confident of the strength of the British army to defeat Kaiser Bill. Desperate for a last glance at Anthony, Annie ran the length of the platform pushing her tiny form against the crowds of mothers, wives and sweethearts all equally determined to remain close to their beloved menfolk. Annie waved until the train disappeared in a cloud of steam. As the steam floated away on that warm August day, the excited shouts and cries died away to be replaced by a general feeling of dismay and foreboding. Who could know how many of the men on that train would never return?

Stanley Salisbury was waiting outside the station to meet Annie. "Diana insists that you join us for dinner. I'll see you back home afterwards." Sensing her hesitation, he went on, "The children would love to see you, Annie."

Touched as she was by their kindliness, Annie's first reaction was to refuse, but whether from the fear of having to face up to living on her own for the first time in her life, or not wishing to offend her friends, she said she would love to come. Instinct told her that the Salisburys would be lavish with their invitations and unless she was very firm, would suggest that she stay with them while Anthony was away. Her premonitions proved to be right.

"Your old room is still ready for you," Diana mentioned as she passed round the coffee. "It seems a pity for you to be all alone while Anthony is away. Besides, Stanley could take you to the studio in the mornings on his way to the gallery. It would all be so convenient."

Annie hesitated. "Well, I don't know," she began. "If Anthony gets leave unexpectedly, I want to be there for him." The reason sounded unconvincing even as she voiced it.

Diana touched her hand. "I understand. You have so many adjustments to make. It must be so hard for you, but if at any time in the future you need to come here and be cared for, we will be ready and waiting."

The significance of Diana's offer did not surface in Annie's mind until much later. Undressing for bed, she remembered the two nights she and Anthony had spent together. Ignorant as she was about many aspects of married life, she remembered with a pang of shame what Joe had said to her the first time they made love. He had said that he knew what to do not to give her a child. What about Anthony? Had he made her pregnant already? Was that what Diana had meant when she hinted at caring for Annie later on? Lying face down on the bed, Annie wept into her pillow. Please God, she prayed, please don't let me be carrying Anthony's child. That was not the path she had chosen.

It was a struggle to get to the studio the next few mornings and start work on replacing the paintings destroyed by Lavinia. Stanley watched over her carefully as she prepared to try to recapture the scene depicting the Densbury river banks splattered with tiny but sturdy yellow wild celandine firmly established amongst the grass.

"There's something missing, Annie. What is it?" Stanley stood back from the painting. "Hmm, can you see what it is?"

Annie had to agree. The glint of sunlight on the river failed to bring the picture to life as it had done in her original work. "I think it's me," she admitted. "I'm the one who's lacking life."

Stanley firmly took the brush from her hand. "Go home. Take yourself round an art exhibition, go shopping, but don't come back here until you get that burning feeling you have a message to convey and you simply have to get it on canvas."

Annie knew that no art exhibition was going to cure the pain in her heart. Even wandering round an exhibition of Sylvia Pankhurst's famous paintings of working women did little to inspire her. A sudden pang made her catch her breath and hold on to a railing for support. The well-known artist had a message to convey about the drudgery of the lives of working class women. Annie felt ashamed of what she was producing; some pretty rural scenes to grace the sitting room walls of the well-to-do. Was that really worthwhile? Soon men would be dying tended by nurses who ignored their own safety in order to carry out their duty. Perhaps Anthony would be one of the men needing skilled care. And Joe, she thought. What if both of them were to die? Wrong as she knew it to be, she could not dismiss Joe from her thoughts. Restless and disorientated, she wandered the streets of London. Lost in thought at one point, she was almost crushed under the hooves of a horse, one of a pair pulling a carriage.

"Look out, young woman!" an irate driver shouted.

Annie was too mesmerised by her memories to reply. Standing on the edge of the pavement, she could still see Lavinia's stallion rearing in front of her, but the memory held no terror for her. The blackness of the stallion had faded to grey. The hatred in Lavinia's eyes had been replaced by a melancholy longing. "It really is over," she whispered to herself, as with renewed purposefulness she crossed the road.

The poster, "England needs you," brought her up with a shock. It was on a hoarding outside St Margaret's Hospital and the finger seemed to be directed at her. "Me?" she asked herself.

"Yes, you," a woman's voice answered, startling her first by its familiarity.

It lifted her, immediately transporting her back through time to Sunday afternoons in a meadow painting pretty watercolours and giggling with her dearest friend as they made plans for the future, all under the disapproving eye of Joe Langmead.

"Isabelle!" Anne flung her arms around her old friend. "Oh, Isabelle, I never thought I'd see you again!"

Isabelle Anstruther's unruly curls were still just as bright a red as Annie remembered, but were now tamed by being firmly tied back in a neat bun. No longer a teenager dressed in flowered muslin, she was formally attired in a smart black suit with a long skirt and a jacket buttoned up to her neck.

"You look so grown up!" Annie blurted out in her astonishment at seeing her old friend.

"We both do." A serious expression in her eyes, Isabelle took a step back and surveyed Annie. "So you're married, I see. Not to Uncle Joe, though. I saw the announcement in *The Times*."

Annie forced a smile to crease her cheeks. "No, not to Uncle Joe. I'm Mrs Gladwell now."

Isabelle glanced round. "Look, we've so much to catch up on and I'm so excited at finding you again, I don't know where to start. How about we go back to my lodgings and I'll get my landlady to make us tea and buttered scones?"

"I... er..." Annie hesitated.

Isabelle picked up the signals of distress in Annie's reluctance. "Just some tea and a bit of reminiscing," she urged.

Annie's downturned mouth turned up in a flicker of a smile. "Yes, that would be lovely, Isabelle. I need someone to talk to."

The two walked along the Embankment purposely keeping the subject of the conversation away from Annie's marriage, Isabelle chatted about her work a trainee doctor. "It's a lot harder than I thought. Years of study and then having to convince my male colleagues that I can actually treat women. And, what is even worse, having to convince some women that I know what I am doing. You know there are still some men who won't let their wives be treated by a woman doctor." A smile lit up her freckled face, a sudden echo of the enthusiastic girl who had declared her ambition to be a doctor so many years before. "Do you remember your Joe's look of disapproval when I told you what I wanted to do when I grew up?"

Annie bit her lip, trying to hide the pain of remembering how hard it had been leaving Joe in order to fulfil her childish dreams. "He didn't want me to come to London either."

Isabelle's sharp eyes detected that there was a story concealed behind the fleeting shadow crossing her friend's face. She was saved from having to comment on Annie's last remark as they approached a fine Edwardian house in a wide avenue. "This is where I live," she announced. "The house belongs to a former colleague of my father. He and his wife have let me have a couple of rooms on the second floor." She took a key out of a capacious black leather bag and beckoned Annie to follow her up the white stone steps leading to the substantial front door. Once inside, Annie was astounded at the apparent wealth of the house owners. It reminded her of the Salisburys' house, but here there was no evidence of children. A massive arrangement of red and pink tea roses spilled out of a huge epergne in the centre of a highly polished oak table just inside the door. The overpowering perfume filled the entrance hall.

"Just a minute," Isabelle told Annie. "I'll just let the housekeeper know that I have a guest. She'll have the tea and crumpets brought up to my rooms."

Isabelle's sitting room was lined with bookshelves. "All medical, I'm afraid. I don't have time for anything else. I want to specialise in children's illnesses. So many of the poor families in the East End can't afford doctors for their children and by the time we get them in hospital it is too late to do save them. If I could work with these families, I could make a difference, I know I could." Catching sight of Annie's sad smile, she paused. "Forgive me, Annie. Here am I talking about myself as usual. Come on, sit down and tell me what you are doing in London."

It was warm and comfortable in Isabelle's room and soon Annie found herself telling the story of how she had broken off her engagement to Joe to follow her dream of becoming an artist. Isabelle was shocked to hear of Lavinia's mental breakdown culminating in setting fire to Annie's work and almost killing her.

"But why? What had you done?"

The gulf between Isabelle's background and her own became more apparent as Annie tried to explain why the Gladwells did not want their son to marry a former maid. "The fact that I was having some success in London in the art world counted for nothing. I was merely the daughter of a factory hand and a lowly cleaner."

"Well, Anthony married you, so clearly he did not agree with his family."

Tears spilled down Annie's cheeks. "And now Anthony has gone off to fight this war in France."

For a minute or so the two young women sat in silence which was eventually broken by Isabelle. "So, what are you going to do while he is at the Front? Will you carry on with your art and do another show?"

Annie shook her head. "I don't know. Suddenly it all seems so pointless. I feel I ought to be doing something to help."

Understanding dawned in Isabelle's eyes. "So that was what you were doing looking at that poster outside the hospital where I work."

Annie nodded. "But what use would I be? I can't tell one end of a bandage from another."

Isabelle grinned. "It doesn't need much skill to empty a bedpan," she said. "If you want to train as a nurse, I'll introduce you to Matron tomorrow morning."

Chapter 13

Isabelle's enthusiastic, unexpected offer nearly had Annie agreeing with her at once. "That sounds wonderful, Isabelle," she agreed. "It's just what I need, that is, I mean, to feel I am doing something useful while Anthony is in France." Suddenly remembering her last conversation with Stanley Salisbury, she shook her head. "Oh, no, not so fast, Isabelle. I can't start at the hospital, at least not yet. I'll have to talk to the Salisburys first. You must realise I do owe them so much. Stanley took a chance with me and invested a great deal of money in my first show." A sudden sadness touching her eyes, she went on, "I can't help feeling it was my fault that Lavinia destroyed the gallery. If only I'd known that Lavinia had been invited, I could have warned Stanley. I should have guessed."

"But you didn't know," Isabelle reminded her. "So why the guilt?"

Annie's hands trembled as she plucked at the folds in her skirt. "It's no good. Before I do anything else, I've just got to replace the paintings lost in the fire, but somehow I can't recapture the colour and light I created in the originals. Everything seems so flat and dead. I'm so afraid that it's not just the paintings that were lost in the fire, it's as if I've lost whatever it was that made me a good painter."

Isabelle took her friend's hands in hers. There was a depth of sympathy and understanding in her advice. "You need to get away from London and the bad memories. Anthony won't be getting leave for a while, so why don't you go home to Densbury? You'll be able to relive old memories, revisit the places you painted before. I'm sure it will all come back to you." A slow smile spread across her face. "Go and take a look at the river bank where we used chat and dream of what we were going to do when we grew up. I've never forgotten how happy we were." She gave a little laugh. "Perhaps Joe will go with you, then it really will be like old times."

The heat from the glowing coal fire was not sufficient to bring back the colour to Annie's suddenly pale cheeks "Oh no, Isabelle, I couldn't do that."

A quick exhalation of breath showed that Isabelle had realised the extent of her insensitivity. "Oh, Annie! I forgot for a moment that you were once engaged to him. How stupid of me!"

"That's all in the past," Annie assured her. "I'm now the wife of Lieutenant Gladwell, remember?"

Isabelle flinched slightly at the over emphatic assertion. "Of course, Annie." She stood up. "Come on, I'll walk a little way with you back to your rooms. It's too soon for you to make up your mind whether you want to carry on with your art or take up nursing while the war is on, but I'm sure you will make the right decision once you have had time to think."

Letting herself into her rooms, Annie was not so confident about her ability to choose the right course to follow. She would wait until the morning and see what Stanley Salisbury had to say.

The studio was empty when she arrived early next morning. In spite of the warm summer sun filtering its light through the high, wide windows, Annie felt a sharp chill piercing her bones. The half-finished paintings, some covered carelessly with white cloths had an air of sadness and neglect. She stood facing the copy of the scene painted on the Densbury river bank. Joe had liked her interpretations of the meadows there, she recollected.

It was strange how he admired her talent, yet expected her to put it on one side once they were married. Guilt kicked her in the stomach as images of herself as Joe's wife hammered themselves into her brain. "No!" she whispered. "He wouldn't have let me do this. I just have to do my painting."

"Who says you can't?" Stanley Salisbury's voice boomed out from the doorway.

Paintbrush in hand, Annie swung round. Babbling, "I don't know," Annie faced him. "Me, I think. I just don't seem able to paint like I did before."

"Hmm. What you need, Annie, is time to step back and look at where you are going."

He paused. "I've been thinking." Annie was half afraid he was going to say that she ought to give up and try something else. He pointed to her latest picture. "It's all there, my dear. What is missing is inspiration, something to kick-start it into life."

"I can see that, but how do I do that?"

Stanley beamed. "Easy, my dear. You need to go back to Densbury, forget about London and all the dreadful events associated with these paintings. Go back in time and absorb the atmosphere which first inspired you to put brush to canvas."

Annie drew breath as if to argue with him, then paused. "How strange. That's exactly what Isabelle said." Seeing the look of puzzlement, she explained, "Isabelle is an old friend from when we were children. She's a doctor now at St Margaret's."

"And a very good doctor by the sound of it." A smile hovered round Stanley's mouth. "So, it's settled then. I'll close down the studio for a couple of weeks or for however long you feel you need." Sensing her reluctance, he patted her hunched up shoulders. "Come on, Annie, take my advice. Get back to your rooms, write to your parents and Anthony, of course, and just pack your things."

A week later, she received a letter from her mother to say that they were all looking forward to seeing her again. Hearing nothing from Anthony, her anxiety grew. During the third week in August there had been reports of fighting between the Germans and the Russians, but the rest of Europe had remained strangely quiet. What if the fighting in Europe intensified while she was in Densbury? What if Anthony were to be wounded and sent home? "I don't know if I can leave London," she told the Salisburys. "I'm so worried about Anthony."

"I will look in on your rooms every day and check to see if there are any letters from Anthony," Stanley promised. "Diana has your Densbury address. If need be, I will get on the train and deliver any urgent communications in person."

Faced with such kindliness, Annie relaxed. She would take the early train the following morning and be in Densbury before midday.

With a wardrobe full of smart outfits including several skirts whose fashionable length ended just above the ankle, Annie had no difficulty in finding sufficient clothes for her projected two-week stay in Densbury. Going through her collection of clothes, Annie felt a sense of shock, struck by the difference between her life in her parents' cottage and her present life in London. She agonised over whether she should dress exactly as she had become accustomed to or choose older and more serviceable clothes which would not cause heads to turn. In a sudden act of defiance, she set out on the bed all her favourite outfits. She decided on a couple of simple tailor-made suits in navy and dark green. The hems of the full skirts stopped just above her ankles whilst the long belted tunic-style jackets came almost to mid-thigh. These suits accompanied by her favourite blouses with high necks and ruffed collars would show Densbury that little Annie Claydon, the one who had been sent home in disgrace from Estcourt and whom no one would employ, had risen above them all. Surely her ma and pa would be proud of her.

Rummaging through the drawers of the huge chest in the bedroom, Annie came across the notice in *The Times* advertising Stanley Salisbury's gallery and the exhibition of the work of two young artists. Her name was there alongside Anthony Gladwell's. She would take that too. Gradually, the capacious suitcase began to fill to overflowing, yet Annie could not decide on what items to discard. In the end, she bounced up and down on its lid hoping that her slim figure would help her close the case. Dismayed at its weight as she dragged the heavy case off the bed, she hoped that she would be able to find a porter to help her not only with her suitcase but also with her canvases and paints.

The rhythmic clicking of the wheels of the train triggered a hammering in Annie's brain, reminding her not only of the pain she had suffered on leaving behind her family, but also the distress she had inflicted on Joe. It had been so difficult to understand her mother's initial coldness and refusal to accept how much her art meant to her. A roof over one's head and money to buy the bare necessities were the sole ambitions that Beatie Claydon had ever been able to allow herself. In that lay the motivation for her not forgiving Annie for giving up the chance of marriage and living in comfort in Joe's tiny cottage. Still, Annie consoled herself with the recollection of the wedding present sent by her mother when she married Anthony. She had never been sure if her parents had come to terms with the knowledge that their daughter was the daughter-in-law of one of the wealthiest men in Suffolk. What if her parents asked if she intended visiting her in-laws at Baythorpe Hall? Annie had not yet told them of Anthony's disinheritance, but speculated that the rumour must have reached the ears of the workforce in the Gladwell mill. Watching the fields roll past, she was struck by the full import of the difficulties she would have to face over the next few days.

Densbury station had changed. In a spirit of defiance at Germany's militarism, the porters had set summer flowers alongside the platform. Lupins, delphiniums and dahlias greeted the passengers alighting at this tiny Suffolk backwater. Annie's spirits surged at what seemed to be a harbinger of happy days to be spent with her parents and sister, Eileen. A porter whom she recognised from her days at Baythorpe Hall helped her with her cases.

"It's me – Alfie," he reminded her. "Don't you remember when we had to beat those carpets out on the lawns at Baythorpe Hall?"

"Of course." Annie's eyes sparkled as she teased him. "And a fat lot of good you were, as I recollect. You said it was women's work."

Suddenly defensive, he went on. "I volunteered to fight for my country, but they said my eyes weren't good enough. Some people say I'm a coward, but honest to God, I'm not."

"Of course you aren't, Alfie." Annie felt compassion for the young man, who would have been one of many to receive white feathers in the post. "We need men at home to do men's work."

Alfie's gratitude touched her. "Listen, Annie, I mean Mrs Gladwell, I'm off duty in a few minutes, so if you wait I could carry your cases up home for you."

"That won't be necessary." The familiar voice, deep and slightly husky, carrying the length of the platform startled her as Joe strode towards her. "Allow me, Mrs Gladwell." He stooped to pick up the heavy suitcases, "Welcome home, Annie," he whispered in her ear.

Annie could feel the colour surging into her cheeks. "Joe! I didn't expect you to meet me." His physical presence was stirring up memories she had worked so hard to forget. Seeing Joe's muscular physique as he towered over her by more than a foot, Annie suppressed the disloyal thought that he made Anthony seem like a boy in comparison.

Suddenly conversational, he explained, "Your ma told me you were expected today, and as I was passing the station, I thought I'd check and see if you were on this train." He gave a warning look at young Alfie, who had seen him pacing up and down the platform for the past two hours.

"Here, take my arm, Annie."

Annie took a sharp intake of breath. "It wouldn't be right, Joe. I'm married."

"Afraid?" The dark eyes mocked her.

"No, sensible." She would not allow him to dominate or humiliate her. Her show of defiance helped hold in check the maelstrom of emotions which were threatening to destroy her outwardly calm demeanour.

Joe's hurt manifested itself in further mockery. "So how do you like being Anthony Gladwell's wife? Does it make you feel superior to me now, Annie? Are you satisfied with what you have? You made it plain that I couldn't offer you enough." They had left the station and were descending a curved path flanked by tall hedges. Joe dropped the cases and seized Annie roughly. He pulled her face towards his and kissed her hard on the lips. Annie's response brought a triumphant smile to his face. "As I thought," he said.

Annie reacted with a swift smack to his cheek. "Leave me alone, Joe Langmead. I don't belong to you any more. The past is over and done with." Without looking back, she struggled on with her cases, not seeing the look of agony and longing on his face.

"Please, Annie, forgive me." Joe was at her side. "Let me walk you home."

"I can hardly stop you, I suppose. Here, take this then." She handed her case back to him. "I can manage my painting materials." For the moment at least, she had her emotions under control. Once home, she told herself, it would be like old times with talk of Eileen's business and wedding plans sufficient to crowd out from her brain the meeting with Joe. With a promise to see her again before she went back to London, Joe left her a few yards from her door.

Eileen rushed to fling herself at Annie. "Oh, Annie, I've missed you so much." She drew back to admire Annie's smart navy suit. "Heavens! You look so, so London," was all she could say to describe her older sister.

"Come here, love." First her ma, then her pa, held her in a tight embrace. "You've done well for yourself and that's a fact." Annie took that as a sign that she had been forgiven for deserting Joe. "I'll put the kettle on and then you can tell us all your news."

Eileen was still dancing around like a child. "Here, let me take your things upstairs. You're in Granny's old room." Her eyes twinkled. "Now that you are a married woman, you can't be expected to share with your little sister." She stopped halfway up the stairs. "Daniel and I are getting married before Christmas. Please say you'll come, Annie. I've got to have my sister here with me."

"Just you try to stop me," Annie declared. "I want to know everything there is to know about this wedding."

The two continued to chat happily while Annie unpacked. Seeing Eileen's envious appraisal of a dark grey silk blouse lying on the bed, Annie offered it to her. "This will suit you better than me, that's if you'd like it, of course."

Eileen held the blouse to herself seeing her reflection in the long mirror on the front of the walnut wardrobe. Her eyes filled with tears. "It's beautiful and you're so kind. I've missed you so much, Annie."

"Come on down, you two." Their mother's voice carried up the staircase.

The sisters stifled their giggles. Eileen put her hand up to her mouth. "Just like old times," she whispered. "We'd better get a move on before the tea goes cold."

Conversation was strained and unnaturally formal as they ate lunch. Beatie was nervous, frequently asking if the roast beef or the vegetables were cooked to Annie's liking. "Your pa grew the carrots and potatoes. He helps old man Farrow with his garden and shares the vegetables. Well, the old man can't eat them all himself and you can't beat home grown."

Annie recognised that her ma was working herself into what her Granny would have called, "a right stew." She laid down her knife and fork and leaned across the table to pat her mother's arm. "This is the best dinner I've had in months. Food is never fresh in London. Besides, the air is always so full of smoke and soot, you can hardly breathe let alone taste what is on your plate. I've missed Densbury and everybody." The last stammered confession was true in part. London was simply a means to an end.

It wasn't until the plates had all been cleared away that Beatie nodded to her husband, giving him a prearranged signal. Fred Claydon came out with the question that had deliberately been avoided throughout dinner. Now that they were all feeling more relaxed, he spoke up. "You can tell me and your ma to mind our own business, but we've heard that old Mr Gladwell didn't take too kindly to his son marrying their former servant."

Annie had already decided that it would be pointless to hide something that was patently known by the whole of the Gladwell workforce and therefore the rest of the town. She described her engagement to Anthony and the events of the night of the fire at the gallery. From her parents' shocked reaction it was plain that her parents had not heard of the last attempt on Annie's life by Lavinia.

"Annie! You could have been burnt to death!" Eileen ran to her sister's side.

"My Lord!" White-faced, Beatie held on to the edge of the table for support."I always said she was mad." Beatie struggled to overcome the memories of seeing her daughter's broken body before. "Just like that time she nearly killed you with that horse of hers." Her slender body sagged in despair. "Oh, why did you ever have to get involved with the Gladwells, Annie?"

Annie ignored the question and went on to explain in a detached voice. "Well, the truth of it is, that Anthony refused to give me up and so his father disinherited him. Simple really." Her attempt to play it down did not fool her father.

"So, what do you and Anthony propose to do now that he has no Gladwell money?"

Annie tried not to show her impatience with this last question. "I get a good allowance from the army and besides that I'll soon be selling more paintings." Now was not the time to talk about her plans to take up nursing to help the war effort. It would be difficult to mention hospital work without informing them that she had met Isabelle Anstruther again. Reviving memories of the incident when Isabelle and her father were run out of town would be too painful. "So you see, once the war is over, Anthony and I will continue to paint together and Mr Salisbury will sell our work."

"That sounds wonderful. Who needs the Gladwells?" Eileen picked up her sister's defiant mood.

"Never mind talking like that. We all do," her father told her. "I work in their factory. It's just as well that Joe has taken over as manager. It's good to have a friend like him. He's done very well for himself." Annie wasn't sure if she detected a slight note of criticism in the last statement, as if her father were hinting that she would have done just as well for herself by staying in Densbury and marrying the factory manager. "Old Mr Gladwell doesn't come in very often these days. He seems contented enough to leave it all to Joe."

"So, what about this wedding?" Annie felt it time to divert attention from herself and her problems.

"Well, Daniel thinks we ought to get married in case he gets called up. It's August now and I reckon we could be ready by the end of October. I'll still run the wool shop and we'll live in the rooms above his parents' shop."

"Quite the woman of business." Annie was pleased that Eileen's life was working out so well. Daniel had adored Eileen from the day she had begun work in the wool shop. Life would never present Eileen with impossible choices. A happy marriage with children, a successful business and respect from the local community; it was all mapped out for her. Not that Annie envied her; she had chosen her path for better or worse. Perhaps she was not destined to be content with all her choices.

"So why have you decided to come home now?" Eileen had detected a shadow of sadness in her sister's eyes.

"Trust you to see right through me." Annie smiled at Eileen's direct question. "Simple really. I lost all my paintings in the fire."

"Oh, Annie, I didn't mean to remind you of that. I'm so sorry."

Annie tried to reassure her. "No, don't be. I need to take a new look at the places where I used to paint."

"Like the one you did for us?" her mother asked, pointing to the painting on the rough plastered cottage wall. "I'll never forget the day Joe gave it to us."

So, Joe was still very much in her mother's mind. Annie's forced, "Yes, that was very nice of him," took an effort, but she went on quickly, "Eileen, would you like to come with me this afternoon?"

Within minutes the girls were out of the house and into the town. Annie felt vaguely guilty seeing the shabbiness of the poor cottages neighbouring her old home. Had she become so used to the smartly painted houses and air of wealth which surrounded her in London? Passing the little shop where she had been happy to buy the blue dress for the gala, a ball of pain gathered in her stomach. Memories of the gala and the fairground where Joe had first made his declaration of love washed over her, threatening to drown her in feelings of regret. That is past, she told herself firmly.

Eileen chattered merrily, pointing to her future in-laws' shop and the rooms above. "We're going to be so happy."

"Of course you are." Annie hardly dare ask if Daniel was going to volunteer for the army. So many young men, fired with patriotism were lining up at recruitment centres.

"I just hope that Daniel doesn't get called up. I couldn't bear it if anything happened to him." She clapped a hand to her mouth. "Oh, I'm so sorry. You must be worried sick about Anthony." With an air of forced brightness, she added, "Of course, everyone says it will be over by Christmas."

The two made their way through the town past the church of St Michael and All Angels until they came to the Old Independent Chapel. Eileen broke the silence. "Daniel and I are getting married at the church. His parents are church people, you know. Anyway, I don't like Pastor Briggs. I'll never forget how horrible he was to you, just because you tried to help your friend Isabelle."

"You remember that? You never told me." Annie stopped and stared at her kind, loving sister.

"I couldn't, not with Pa being in such a state over it. Joe stuck up for you, didn't he?"

Yes, Joe had supported her after she had been harangued by Pastor Briggs in front of the whole congregation. She had not forgotten that the price of his support had been her firm promise to marry him. In spite of the warm summer sun, ice encased her heart. It was not until they reached the meadows bordering the Densbury river bank, that Annie began to relax. "I just want to sit down here and take it all in again."

The gold of the buttercups thrusting through the rich green meadow grass, eager to face the warmth of the sun, made Annie want to reach for her palette. "This is just as I remember it." She listened to the faint rushing sound of the river as it made its way over the age-old boulders on its banks. Dark green reeds were forced to bend gently in deference to the power of the water being pulled inexorably towards the sea many miles away. Annie had never ceased to be enchanted by the scene. "I can't wait to get started. I'll bring my things here tomorrow." The heavy stone which had been weighing down her heart was gradually lifting, leaving her with a breathless feeling that she was once again ready to translate the beauty of the meadows of her home town to canvas.

"Oh, Annie, I promised to meet Daniel and his parents after chapel. Should I tell them that you need me to help you?"

"Always thinking of everybody else, aren't you? Of course you don't have to spend your Sunday afternoon with your old married sister. I'm quite capable of carrying a few things." She pondered for a moment. "There is just one problem. Did Ma and Pa keep my easel after I left?"

Eileen nodded. "I think Pa put it up in the attic. Well, what else could they do with it apart from burn it, and Pa wouldn't allow Ma to do that. I think he was really quite proud of you and your painting." She stood up. "I'll tell you what we can do. Daniel and I will carry your paints and stuff down here tomorrow for you and then we will leave you in peace."

"You're a born organiser," Annie said, smiling at the kindness of her young sister. "One day you will be a very wealthy business woman."

"And you'll have your name in all the papers," Eileen replied.

Sunday morning brought problems. Annie had already read what was troubling her mother. "So, what time do we leave for chapel?" she asked, casually pouring herself a second cup of tea.

Beatie's eyes opened wide. "You mean you want to come with us? I thought that perhaps…"

"Ma, why shouldn't I? If old Mr Gladwell is there and chooses to ignore me, so be it, but I will not hang my head in shame for anyone in Densbury and I mean it. Oh, I know some of them looked down on me in the past, especially after Lavinia Gladwell had me thrown out of my job at Estcourt, but I'm doing better than the lot of them now. Believe me, I'm more than ready for them all."

Her mother was astounded at this unexpected outburst. "You won't cause any trouble, will you?" Beatie Claydon was never sure of what Annie would do. First the incident with Doctor Anstruther and the priest, then visiting Joe alone in his cottage before breaking off her engagement and suddenly running off to London. She sighed. Thank goodness Eileen did not take after her sister.

"Of course I won't cause trouble. The wife of Lieutenant Gladwell knows how to behave in public." One look from her and they would not dare to pass derogatory comments.

Heads turned as Annie followed her parents into the Old Independent Chapel. She had deliberately chosen her latest fashionable summer dress to wear. In a dark blue cotton with a modest high neck and wide sleeves gathered into deep cuffs, Annie had achieved the look of understated prosperity. The hat, a simple navy blue straw with a small brim complemented the dress perfectly. Holding her head high, she and Eileen followed their parents to their usual pew. For one brief moment, her sangfroid faltered on seeing Joe sitting in the pew on the opposite side of the aisle. Aware that the eyes of the Densbury chapel worshippers were on her, Annie followed her parents' example, acknowledging his greeting with a slight inclination of her head. To her relief, old Will Gladwell was not there, confined to his bed with a slight chill according to Pastor Briggs who urged his congregation to pray for him. On hearing this request, Annie crossed her fingers when the prayers were said. It would have been hypocritical to pray for Will Gladwell, a vindictive old man who had deserted his brave soldier son and was now too cowardly to face his daughter-in-law.

Pastor Briggs, florid and round-faced, struggled to avert his eyes from Annie Claydon, or rather he had to think of her as she was now, Annie Gladwell. Mr Gladwell had told him that his reason for not coming to chapel was in order to avoid an uncomfortable meeting with Annie. Pastor Briggs felt the bile rise in his throat at the realisation that this upstart little madam could now claim to be superior to him. By the pert tilt of her pretty black curls, he could see that she would no longer maintain a mute silence if crossed as she had done in years gone by. And to think that there had been that time when Mrs Briggs would not let her over their doorstep even to do a little scrubbing. Even as he urged his flock to pray for humility and forgiveness, resentment built up inside the mean-minded cleric.

On the way out, Annie stopped to chat to some of her former workmates from the factory. "You've done all right, my girl," was the usual comment. "Fancy you marrying young Mr Gladwell. He's an officer, we hear."

"We did wonder why you broke off your engagement to Joe Langmead." The young woman gave a meaningful glance in Joe's direction. "Never mind. At least it leaves the field clear for one of your old workmates." She nudged Annie in the ribs. "If you know what I mean."

Annie smiled. "Well, he is free, I suppose, now that I'm married to Lieutenant Gladwell." If she repeated it often enough, she might wipe out the memory of the blissful afternoons spent in Joe's cottage. Unthinking, she put her hands up to her face as if to erase images of Joe with another woman.

"Are you all right?" Eileen asked, happy once Annie assured her that it was just an insect that had flown into her eye.

"Come on, the sooner we get dinner over, the sooner we can get out again."

Impatient to resume her painting, once the dishes had been put away, Annie hustled Eileen up to her room to get ready.

"Stop rushing me," Eileen protested. "I want to look nice for Daniel."

Daniel was in awe of his future sister-in-law. He stood in the doorway twisting a handkerchief first one way and then the other. Eileen had told him that not only was Annie married to a Gladwell, but that she was now a famous London painter with her name in the papers. It took all Annie's charm and gentle teasing to get him to come in and sit down. A typical East Anglian with his short stature, broad shoulders and light brown, almost fair hair, he could not be called strikingly handsome, but he had the kind of comfortable attractiveness and dependability that would appeal to most young girls looking for a husband. Annie concluded that her sister had found the perfect man. The adoring look in his eyes when Eileen finally burst in through the door, confirmed her view.

"Right, I'll take the easel," Daniel volunteered. "You girls can bring the other bits and pieces." His pleasant features creased in a frown. "But how are you going to get all these things back on your own?"

"Oh, you'd be surprised how tough I am," Annie assured him.

Finding exactly the right spot beside the river took a little time. Annie needed the correct angle if she were to recreate the landscapes destroyed in the blaze. "Right, you two, off you go and have a lovely afternoon." There was a tingling in her fingers as she laid out her brushes. This was what Stanley had meant about getting inspired. The atmosphere of her own lovely home meadows was firing her with the desire to surpass the beauty of her original paintings. A few couples out for a Sunday afternoon stroll, paused at a respectful distance to observe Annie's work. The comment that the buttercups looked so real that you could almost pick them off the painting lifted Annie's spirits. That was what had failed to achieve in her work in London after the fire. There would be no looking back, she told herself. Without being aware of the identity of one couple who had sat down on the grass just a few yards to her right, she carried on.

"Oh, Joe, can't we go somewhere a bit quieter, if you know what I mean?" The nasal tones of the girl who had spoken to her outside the chapel carried clearly on the still summer air.

Annie froze. The picture on her easel became transformed into a meaningless jumble of colours tumbling and twisting blown in all directions by the force of her wild emotions. She sank on to the grass, busying herself with the pretence of wiping her paintbrush. So, Joe had guessed that she would not be able to resist returning to her favourite spot and had deliberately brought one of the factory girls along to remind her of their Sunday afternoons. Well, if Joe thought that he could will her into turning round and acknowledging his triumph, she would show him how wrong he was. Steeling herself to remain steady, she rose to her feet and pretended to stand back in order to appraise her work. Gradually, the kaleidoscope of swirling colours began to take shape once more.

"Mrs Gladwell, may I assist you in carrying your easel and paints home?" Joe was standing behind her. He touched her shoulder lightly.

Annie shrugged, just sufficiently to show that she did not welcome his physical nearness. "No thank you, Mr Langmead. My father will be along shortly. Don't let me keep you." With an effort, she dabbed an unnecessary dash of white on one cloud. "Please don't interrupt my work, Mr Langmead."

"Come on, Joe. I've got to be 'ome in 'alf an hour." The girl was not pleased at Joe's angry reaction to Annie's coldness. She did not want to have to tell the girls at work on Monday that Joe was not really interested in her, not after she had hinted that he might be popping the question before long.

"Just you wait, Annie Claydon," Joe muttered in Annie's ear.

As soon as the couple was far enough away, Annie gathered up her easel and paints. She knew that Joe would have seen through the lie about her pa coming to meet her. It was going to be a long, hard walk home with no help. As she struggled with the cumbersome equipment, Annie felt peeved at her naivety. She had not reckoned on Joe's persistence in pursuing her in spite of her married status, which she interpreted more as an attempt to get revenge than a manifestation of his continuing love. She consoled herself with the knowledge that next day he would be at work as manager of the factory during the daytime, leaving her free to wander at will.

"So where are you off to today?" her mother asked, once her husband and young daughter had left for work on the Monday morning.

"Baythorpe Hall," Annie announced. "I won't be able to visit, of course, but I will be able to look across at the views from the slope where Anthony and I used to paint."

"Annie! You can't go there!"

"Ma, I can go where I please. Lavinia and her stallion won't be there to savage me and I doubt if old Mr Gladwell will stir from his bed to berate me."

Beatie shoulders sagged. "Just don't do anything to annoy them up there. Remember your pa's job depends on the Gladwells."

Annie placed both hands firmly on her mother's shoulders. "Ma, do you remember when you and I were slaves to that family? Well, I'm a Gladwell now, and even if Anthony has been disinherited, I promise you that it will not be for ever. I am determined that one day Anthony and I and our children will live at Baythorpe Hall."

Icy diamond glints in her eyes, Annie thumped her hand on the table. "And you and Pa will dine with me off Gladwell china one day. I shall make it happen, I swear."

Chapter 14

"Wonderful! What a transformation!" Stanley Salisbury's satisfied smile filled Annie with delight. She had been back at the studio working for a month on replacing the landscapes lost in the fire. "If going back to Densbury is what it takes to inspire you, we shall have to make sure you make the trip regularly."

"Just one more to complete, and then…?"

"And then you can make a start on perfecting your portraiture techniques as we discussed a while back. I want to see you go on and develop your skills. In spite of the war, there are still plenty of art connoisseurs in London keen to see more of your work. I know you could go on with similar paintings which would sell, but I won't let you waste your talents. You must go back to college and study as well as spend time here at the studio."

Annie put to the back of her mind her earlier intention to tell Stanley that she wanted to give up full-time painting to concentrate on useful war work such as nursing. Disloyal as it seemed, she could not help resenting that the war had made little impact on his way of life. Whilst appreciating his drive in wanting to develop her talents, Annie could not get out of her mind that with Anthony daily risking his life, Stanley should be doing something to help the war effort.

"I have to go home again in the middle of October," she explained. "My sister Eileen is getting married in the third week and I must be there."

"Of course you must go home for your sister's wedding." He laughed out loud. "Who knows what inspiration that will bring?" He closed his eyes as if in deep thought. "So if you have to be home for the third week in October, that should give you time to finish this last picture before you go. Excellent!"

Lost in her work at the studio, Annie had little time to think about life outside. Occasionally, she would give a little sigh of satisfaction as she breathed life into the landscape on her easel. The satisfaction partly arose from the feeling that the green meadows and gently rippling waters of the River Dene would be admired by people who would never dream of stopping off at Densbury station to see for themselves the natural beauty of the small town. Only she and Anthony had seen what was to be admired in this rural gem. She closed her eyes, lost for a moment in memories of golden summer afternoons spent with Anthony painting the lush fields and burgeoning hedgerows. If only Anthony could be here to see what she was achieving once again following her last visit home.

The next day, she received a letter from Anthony saying how much he missed her and that he hoped soon to get some leave.

I miss you so much, my darling Annie, he wrote, *that I can't wait for us to be together in our own little home. Those two days and nights we had are constantly in my mind. It won't be long now. Everything is quiet. We are digging in and waiting for the Germans to make a move.*

I loved hearing about your visit to Densbury. If only we could be there now painting together with no one else near. One day we will, my darling.

Yes, one we will, Annie thought, just as I told Ma and Pa. First, though, she had to get ready for Eileen's wedding. She had arranged to arrive in Densbury a few days in advance of the big day in order to give Eileen and her mother a hand with the preparations. Stepping off the train, she was ashamed to experience a pang of disappointment seeing no sign of Joe on the platform

"Do you need a hand with your case, Mrs Gladwell?" It was Alfie. "I expect Mr Langmead is at work today, so he won't be here to help." Alfie whistled cheerfully as he picked up the case. "The next train isn't due in for a couple of hours, so it's no trouble."

Hoping that Alfie had not noticed the pink flush spreading over her cheeks at the mention of Joe's name, she pretended not to have heard. "Thank you, Alfie, but I've only brought a smaller case this time, so I can manage. I mustn't tear you away from your work."

Still annoyed with herself for half wishing that Joe had been at the station to meet her, she struggled with the heavy case which contained her own wedding outfit plus some expensive lingerie for Eileen bought in a flash of extravagance in Bond Street.

"Annie! Where did you buy these?" Eileen fingered the beautiful silk underwear laid out on Annie's bed. She picked up a delicately embroidered white nightdress "I can't wear this nightie." She blushed. "You can nearly see through it."

"Well, it's only nearly, so stop worrying," Annie giggled. "If a bride can't wear something special for her wedding night, when can she? There'll be plenty of time for sensible warm nightgowns when you have to get up in the middle of the night to feed the baby."

"Annie!" Eileen protested, a warm smile lighting up her eyes. "We want to make sure the business is running well before we start a family. In any case, we intend to wait until the war is over." Still clutching the lacy nightdress, she sat down on Annie's bed. "It might be different if Daniel gets called up and sent to France. We might want a child then in case he gets…" she sobbed, the tears spilling over her cheeks. "Don't you feel the same way

210

about Anthony? Don't you wish you could at least have his baby if anything happened to him?"

Stroking her sister's shiny brown hair, Annie muttered a few soothing words. How could she explain that even if Anthony were to be killed in action, she would not want to be left to mourn with his child? She reflected on the happy times shared with Anthony, acknowledging in her heart that maybe they were more like a couple of children playing their favourite game innocently oblivious to the grown-up world outside. Once the war was over, she would see things differently, Annie kept telling herself. Hadn't she told her parents that one day she intended bringing her children up in Baythorpe Hall?

"Sorry, Annie," Eileen said, wiping her tears. "It must be ten times worse for you not knowing if Anthony is safe."

"Now, important matters," said Annie, pretending to be stern and sensible. "Isn't it time we had a look at your wedding gown? We can't have you going down the aisle looking a mess."

That set the pattern for the days leading up to the wedding. Danny's parents had wanted the Gladwell Memorial Town Hall for a sit-down reception for the hundred or so guests expected. As important members of the business community in the town, the Parfitts had intimated that they had to invite many of their friends and acquaintances. There had been some delicate negotiations leading up to the booking, with Fred and Beatie Claydon insisting that it was their responsibility and not that of the bridegroom's parents to pay for the reception. Beatie felt that a more modest affair in the church hall would not only have been more appropriate but would have been just what Fred could have afforded. The matter had finally been settled when Joe had offered to pay for the reception as his wedding present to Eileen. The only condition was that it should be kept a secret, leaving guests to assume that the father of the bride had paid.

"Joe's a friend in a million offering to give our Eileen a proper wedding. He wouldn't hear of us paying him back bit by bit. He's done really well for himself, has Joe." This was accompanied by a meaningful glance in Annie's direction. "With the factory turned over to making army uniforms, he'll be in a safe occupation, so there's no danger of him getting called up." There was a slight but intentional emphasis on the 'him'.

"That's nice for Joe." Annie struggled to keep the bitterness out of her reply with the ever present thought in her mind that at this very moment, Anthony might be facing danger and possible death. Even though she had no intention of arguing with her mother, Annie was beginning to feel her anger rise at the frequently repeated references to Joe's prosperity. On the defensive but with a defiance not missed by her mother, she added, "Anthony's a true patriot. He volunteered to serve his country. He didn't wait to be called up." She hoped that her ma had picked up the intended insult.

The morning of the wedding, everyone in the Claydon household was up by six. Sufficient water had to be heated in the copper for all to take turns at bathing in the old tin bath hung behind the outhouse door and used once a week. Determined that on this special day Eileen was to be treated like a princess, Annie took her sister breakfast in bed at seven.

"There's toast and jam and a cup of tea and I'm not leaving until every last crumb and every last drop is cleared, do you understand?" Annie placed the tray on the bedside table. Hands on hips, she faced her sister. "No argument, do you hear? We don't want you falling down in a dead faint in church right in front of everybody, although why shouldn't they all get a chance to admire those fancy knickers I bought you?"

Spluttering toast crumbs all over the patchwork eiderdown, Eileen burst into giggles. "I'm so glad you're here, Annie." Suddenly serious, she added, "You mustn't take any notice of Ma going on about Joe. It's only because she misses you and wished you'd married Joe and stayed in Densbury."

"I know it must be hard for her and Pa. All the same I wish she wouldn't keep going on about Joe. I'm married to Anthony and that's what I want. I don't want Joe now."

Eileen was too busy wiping the jam from around her mouth to see the defiant but desperate blaze in Annie's eyes.

"Right, I'll fetch the water up and we'll make a start on getting you ready." Annie was once again the efficient and slightly bossy older sister. "Stay where you are until I get back, then I'll set all your things out on your bed." She took the tray and moved towards the bedroom door, turning to say, "My sister is going to be the most beautiful bride Densbury has ever seen. Daniel is a very lucky young man."

Beatie was already fussing about in the kitchen. Still in her everyday brown cotton dress, she was flicking imaginary flecks of dust from windowsills.

"Ma!" Annie set the tray down before taking the duster out of her mother's hands. "No one is coming back to the house, so just get yourself and Pa ready. By the sounds of things, he's having a hard time trying to do up his shirt collar. Go and give him a hand while I see to Eileen."

Eileen's dress was a simple design in white brocade with the modest high neck finishing in a tiny Medici collar, whilst the long full skirt reached to her ankles. The veil prettily embroidered with white lilies, had been lent to her by Daniel's mother, who had worn it on her wedding day. Annie brushed Eileen's newly washed golden brown hair until it shone, falling in gentle waves to her shoulders.

"Now, you don't put that dress on until I say so, Eileen Claydon, do you hear? I've got to get myself ready first, then I'll be back to do up the hooks and eyes down the back. It'll be Danny's job to undo them later." She grinned at her sister.

"Annie!" Eileen's eyes lit up with a mixture of embarrassment and excited anticipation.

213

Annie had chosen a fashionable narrow-skirted dress in her favourite dark blue. The matching wide-brimmed hat trimmed with a single white feather and due to be put on later completed her outfit. The image of a smart young married woman gazed back at her from the mirror on the wardrobe doors. Sadness tinged her eyes as she reflected on how different her own wedding had been with no mother or sister to help and guide her. With just the Salisburys to lend support, her marriage ceremony had been overshadowed by the memory of Lavinia's final descent into madness, the Gladwells' disapproval and, worst of all, Anthony's departure to fight for his country.

At nine o'clock, Alice, Danny's younger sister arrived. It was Annie's job to transform the plain fourteen-year-old with a pasty complexion and lank hair into a passably pretty bridesmaid. Annie's announcement that the first job was to wash the girl's hair met with a howl of dismay.

"What's wrong with it? I hate having my head all wet and cold. Once a week is enough and the week isn't up yet." Skinny and pale, defiance lit up Alice's spotty face.

Annie was torn between wheedling and bossiness, finally deciding to try flattery first. "I know exactly how you feel, Alice, but your brother will expect to see his sister looking as pretty as his bride, won't he? I've just washed Eileen's hair and she looks a picture." She took hold of a greasy lock of hair. "Hmm, this will not look nice under your blue headdress."

The child's lower lip began to tremble. "I'm sorry, Annie. I didn't want to be Eileen's bridesmaid. I mean she's so pretty and I'm so …" The tears came in huge drops spilling out of the round brown eyes. "I wish I could go home."

Annie held her close in a loving hug, "No you don't. Just think, once Danny and Eileen are married, you and I will be sisters."

"Sisters? Will we really?" The tears ceased as suddenly as they had started.

"Well, sisters-in-law which is the same thing really, so let's pretend I'm your big sister and I'm telling you what to do."

Alice tried a brave smile. "If you say so," she said. "I expect I would look better if you washed my hair."

One hour later, punctuated by Alice's cries that the water was either too hot or too cold, Annie transformed the child into a passably pretty bridesmaid. She pulled the pale pink dress over Alice's head before giving the straight brown locks a final brushing. "We'll do the headdress in a minute once we see what Eileen has to say. Come on up to Eileen's room and we'll see how she is getting on."

A faraway look in her eyes, Eileen was sitting on her bed gazing at her reflection in the wardrobe mirror, when Annie and Alice entered the room. Without turning round, she said, "Do you think that Danny will think I look nice?"

"Oh, Eileen, you look so beautiful."

The breathless tones of the little girl made Eileen turn towards her visitors. "Alice, come here and let me look at you." Astonished and delighted at what Annie had achieved with Alice, she went on, "I don't believe how pretty you look, Alice. I can't have that. Everyone will be staring at you and not me. Come here and let me give you a big hug."

"No!" Annie yelled. "It's taken me ages to do Alice's hair No one is to touch her."

Feeling suddenly part of this grown-up alliance of sisters, Alice's mouth broadened into the happiest of smiles. "Annie is so clever at doing hair," was all she could manage to say.

"Now, you two, I am going to check on Ma and Pa before I finish getting ready, then it will soon be time to leave. It's the bride's privilege to arrive at the church a little late, so if we leave here at, say eleven, you'll be about ten minutes late. That should be enough to keep Danny on his toes."

"I don't want to be late," Eileen complained.

"I think we have to do what Annie says," Alice solemnly advised her soon to be sister-in-law.

At the sound of the latest outbreak of laughter, Beatie called out to the girls. "Are you three ready yet? We don't want to be late." Her comment was the trigger for yet another outbreak of laughter. "Settle down now. Your Pa's getting quite worried, so behave yourselves."

"Won't be long, Ma," Annie reassured her mother. "I'll have them downstairs in five minutes."

The plans were for Annie, her ma and Alice to go ahead in the pony and trap. Once they had been deposited at the church, the driver would return to pick up the bride and her father. It was one of those golden October days when the sun gave a defiant breath of warmth before losing its heat to cold November. The excitement of the occasion kept at bay the hint of coolness in the air. All the neighbours had gathered outside to cheer on the bridal party. Annie felt a glow of happiness seeing her mother enjoying the attention, confident in the knowledge that her younger daughter at least was making a good and safe marriage to the son of a comfortably off business family.

Eileen would never leave Densbury to seek a new life. The little rural town held all that she would want. Annie guessed what was in her mother's mind. "You'll have both your daughters here one day. I'll be back, Ma," Annie told her mother as they neared the church. "I've said that Anthony and I will take our rightful place one day at Baythorpe Hall and I mean it."

Beatie sighed. "We'll see. Let's just get our Eileen safely married off."

The church was almost full by the time they arrived to stand in the porch and await the arrival of Eileen and her father. Annie felt an anticipatory thrill at the thought of seeing Joe again, a thrill she struggled to suppress. She was about to peep inside the church to see where he would be seated, but the sea of massive hats festooned with enormous feathers in all colours obscured her vision. Danny's parents and relatives were in the first few rows on the right, whilst the Claydons were on the left, leaving the front row for Beatie, Fred and Eileen. Annie guessed that Joe would probably be in the second or third row. She only hoped that he wasn't seated too near Aunt Violet, the one who had told her ma about the secret Sunday afternoon meetings at Joe's cottage. Shame mingled with desire flared within her at the memory of those passion filled encounters.

The arrival of the pony and trap put an end to those thoughts. Assisted by her father as she stepped down from the pony and trap, Eileen looked exactly what she was, a virginal bride about to marry her childhood sweetheart. Alice was standing patiently inside the church porch waiting to be told when to take her place behind the bride. She had been carefully instructed to walk behind the bride and carry the long train without pulling too hard which would have displaced the headdress. Having been elevated to the position of being Annie's sister, she was taking her responsibilities very seriously.

"Just let me have a look at you." Annie fussed round her sister in an attempt to keep busy and stem the flow of tears threatening to cascade down her cheeks. If anyone had asked her the reason for the tears, she would have had difficulty on pinpointing one particular cause. Eileen was so content to be making her future life in Densbury that Annie envied her serenity. Joe could have made her choose to stay perhaps, but he could not compete with the magic attraction of London and the opportunities available to a young aspiring artist. She wanted to weep for Anthony, so sensitive and yet, no doubt desperately trying to hide his fear in the face of the enemy, whilst she was here laughing and rejoicing in the safety of an English country town. Most of all, she wanted to weep for her own disloyalty in thinking about Joe Langmead and the precious moments they had spent together.

"Right, come along now, Annie." Beatie had finished straightening her husband's tie. "Ebenezer will start playing the minute we get to our places. We don't want to keep people waiting." She hustled Annie to the front row, ordering her to move along a few places to make room for Fred once he had fulfilled his duty of handing his daughter to the care of her new husband.

Annie prayed that Eileen would soon appear so that Ebenezer Gilford could start the Wedding March. At that moment, she felt as if the eyes of Densbury were on the wayward factory girl who had married the son of the wealthy mill owner. More than anything, she could feel Joe's eyes on her from where he was seated in the third row behind Aunt Violet. She had deliberately tried to avoid his gaze as, escorting her mother to her place, she had passed by him, but at the last minute had given him a covert glance from under the brim of her hat. That brief glance had told her that, tall and self-assured, Joe was no longer merely a humble factory hand. Respected and admired now that he had risen to the position of manager, he had lost that earlier diffidence and self-deprecating air which had allowed him to let Annie slip through his fingers. His head held high, he had the look of a man intent on getting his own way.

Thankfully, the thundering tones of the organ alerted the congregation to the arrival of Annie. As one, a sea of feathered hats turned towards the aisle, where, proud of his lovely daughter, Fred held his head high as they approached the altar. Little Alice seemed to have been transformed from a plain, frightened child into a confident young woman. Now that she had Eileen and Annie for sisters, she felt the weight of responsibility bearing down on her and was determined not to let them down. She permitted herself the tiniest of smiles hearing one of her father's business acquaintances say, "My! Doesn't little Alice look a picture!"

Concentrating on the lavish altar arrangement of lilies, Annie was able to prevent herself from dwelling on the difference between Eileen's marriage and her own. Annie had gone to

Anthony's bed already aware of the joy of passion between a man and a woman, whilst Eileen, still a virgin, had confided in her sister her fears of what was to come. Annie had held her close and had done her best to reassure her, even raising a smile as she reminded Eileen of the postcard of Michelangelo's David which Anthony had sent so many years ago from Florence.

Following the ceremony, there was a noisy gathering outside the church before everyone walked to the Memorial Hall. Fortunately, the wind which had threatened to portend disaster to some of the more extravagant millinery creations, had dropped, much to the relief of the wearers.

Rows of tables covered with crisp damask tablecloths had been laid with shining cutlery. An army of waitresses stood by ready to serve the guests. The top table was reserved for both sets of parents, Danny's brother Aaron, Alice and Annie. There were three sprigs of tables, the nearest set out for uncles, aunts and cousins. Although not a member of the family, Joe had been placed at the head of one of these tables. With Annie at the end of the top table, she found herself sitting at right angles to Joe, so close that it was impossible to prevent her knees from touching his.

"How are you, Annie?" The formal greeting from the man who had once been her fiancé and lover shocked her.

"Fine. Worried about my husband of course. Who knows what is going to happen in France?" Perhaps a dig at Joe for not being as brave as Anthony was justified.

Joe's dark eyes were smouldering. He gave a wry smile. "Perhaps you will be able to worry about me next week. I intend to volunteer. The factory is on its feet now, turning out army uniforms." He glanced towards Annie's father deep in conversation with Danny's mother. "I think I can recommend my best friend to Mr Gladwell to take over while I am away."

Annie struggled to find the right words. "But why? Do you really have to go, Joe?"

"Oh, yes." The laugh held no warmth. There was more than a touch of bitterness in his question. "Why do you ask? Would you miss me, Annie?"

Fortunately, at that point, Aaron rose to make his speech as best man and Annie was able to turn away from Joe's intense gaze. How could she tell him that the thought of losing him in the war was more painful than she dared to admit? 'I'm married to Anthony,' she kept repeating to herself until it became a dull beat hammering inside her head.

As food, drinks and finally wedding cake were served, Annie fought to suppress the feeling of a lead weight in her lungs restricting her breathing, a sensation which had been threatening all morning. Unnoticed by the guests all engaged in excited chatter, Annie left her seat to go outside for a breath of air. The back door of the Memorial Hall opened out on to a small garden set out with lawns and seats. The faint buzz of conversation was still audible from behind the old oak at the far end of the garden where Annie had hoped to find refuge. A few more days and she would be back in London, safe in her studio and possibly working all God's hours in a hospital with Isabelle. That way she would be safe from the power of Joe's physical attraction.

"Running away again, Mrs Gladwell?"

Anger burning her cheeks, Annie turned on Joe. "How dare you follow me out here, Joe! Leave me alone."

"You know, Annie, if I thought that you really wanted me to go away, I would."

"Please, Joe," Annie begged.

Suddenly compassionate, Joe took her arm. "I'm sorry, Annie." He turned on his heel to go back into the hall. Half way, he stopped. "Oh, Annie, why did you have to leave me?"

It took all Annie's self-control not to run and throw herself into the arms of this man whose agonised cry told her how much he wanted her still. Struggling to calm herself, Annie waited a few more minutes until trusting that her absence had not been noticed, she took the side path to the front of the hall. Correctly surmising that Joe would have been seen going in by the back door, she hoped that her entrance by the front door would not give rise to gossip. By now, many of the guests had left their seats and had begun to mingle exchanging good-natured chatter. Likewise, the two families at the top table were standing and making a move to thank their guests personally for coming. Eileen caught sight of Annie and waved, beckoning her sister to come over. Next to Danny and Eileen, her father and a solemn Joe were standing, with their heads together clearly having a serious discussion.

Thankful that Joe was too engrossed in his conversation with her father, Annie hugged Eileen and her new brother-in-law. Although they had already made arrangements concerning the newly-weds' departure and return to their flat above the Parfitts' shop, Eileen was full of excitement, reiterating the details over and over again.

"Right," said Annie, amused at Eileen's insistence on going over the details. "Anyone would think that you couldn't trust your older sister. Tomorrow morning I will go over to your rooms, tidy away your wedding things, set the presents out for display, and leave everything ready for when you get back from your honeymoon in Lowestoft. Yes, I've got the keys, so there's no problem."

"I hope you don't mind, Annie. My mother would do it," Danny explained, "but my parents are staying up in Yarmouth with my grandparents for a few days, so I'm afraid it will all fall on you."

"Stop worrying, Danny, I'd love to help you." Leaning towards him, she gave him a kiss on the cheek. "I'm so glad you're married to my little sister."

Danny's cheeks turned a bright shade of red. "Gosh! Thanks, Annie."

By four o'clock the hall had emptied and Eileen and Danny had been seen off at Densbury station. After waving them goodbye, Annie walked back home with her parents.

"All I want to do is sit down with a nice cup of tea," Beatie declared once they were indoors. Although her cheeks were lined with fatigue, she had the look of satisfaction of a mother who has seen the last of her chicks nicely settled. "Our Eileen is set up for life," she declared. "Isn't that right, Fred?"

"Er, yes." Fred's eyes were fixed somewhere in the distance. "Joe's coming round later. There are one or two things we need to discuss."

Annie felt a sharp stabbing pain in her ribs. Facing Joe under her mother's sharp gaze would be too much of an ordeal. She knew that Beatie would not miss the anguish in her elder daughter's eyes. "I'll just go up and start on my packing. Once I've seen to Eileen's flat in the morning, I want to take the one o'clock train back to London. The sooner I get back, the sooner I can decide what I need to do next. In any case, Anthony must be due for some leave soon and I want to be ready for him."

Steadfastly shutting her ears to Joe's voice downstairs as he discussed his plans with her pa, Annie busied herself with her suitcase. Only after she heard the door slam on his departure did she go downstairs. Her parents stopped talking as soon as she entered the room.

"Joe's off to join up," her ma volunteered.

"And not before time. Isn't that what every man should be doing? I'm proud that Anthony was one of the first to go."

"No need to talk like that, Annie. Joe's had the factory to run making uniforms for our boys out there." Her pa looked across the table at his wife. "In fact he's going to put a word in with old Mr Gladwell. Joe thinks I could take his place as manager for the duration."

Beatie's face was pink with pride at the possible promotion. "Just think how well off we'll be." She frowned at Annie. "You might look pleased for your pa."

Annie fidgeted with the buttons on the front of her blouse. "Of course I'm pleased." How could she tell them, that ever since Joe had told her that he was joining up and going to recommend his old friend as his successor, she had been agonising over what old Will Gladwell would do? Would he give the job of factory manager to the father of the servant girl who had been the cause of his daughter's death and his own estrangement from his only son?

"I shouldn't count on it, Pa," she said. "You know what the Gladwells are like." She did not have to say more.

"Not a word to anyone until we know one way or the other," Beatie ordered. "If the Gladwells don't like us, too bad. We've managed before and we'll manage now." As far as she was concerned that was the end of the matter.

Next morning, Annie cried off going to chapel. Not only would Joe be there, but it was possible that Will Gladwell would attend. She told her parents that she had decided to tidy up Eileen's flat while they were at chapel. That way she would be sure of avoiding not only Will Gladwell but also Joe. Once her parents were out of the house, she took the familiar route to the High Street, pausing only once as she reached the saddlery where Lavinia Gladwell had terrified her with ordering her to hold her horse while she went inside. Taking a deep breath, she was relieved to find that the shop held no more fears for her. There was not even one hint of Lavinia's ghost to bring shuddering fright to her whole body.

The Parfitts' shop being closed, Annie had to cut through the alley leading to the back of the premises, where a gate opened into a small enclosed yard. There were no buildings behind the yard, only a wide road leading to the water meadows. Taking the key out of her bag, she opened the back door and went up the stairs to Eileen's new home. On the left of the passage was a tiny kitchen. Annie went further along to a tiny living room which had been newly furnished. On the right of the narrow passage were two bedrooms, one of which was as yet unfurnished. Annie went into the larger bedroom almost filled by a double bed with a modern walnut headboard. Annie smiled seeing her sister's wedding finery strewn on the double bed. The couple had been in such a hurry to get to the station that neither had noticed that the veil belonging to Danny's mother had slipped down on to the floor. It took Annie just a few moments to gather up the scattered clothes and hang them in the closet. Humming to herself as she arranged the clothes so that Danny's were on the right and Eileen's on the left, she did not hear the sound of the door being closed behind her. As she stood back ready to leave, she turned to see Joe leaning against the door. "Joe! What are you doing here? You mustn't."

"Next week I shall be in France, Annie. Did you really think that I could leave without seeing you just once more time? Everyone is at chapel, so nobody knows I am here."

Annie pressed her back against the wardrobe door. "No, Joe, please go. You shouldn't be here. What if someone sees you? Please, Joe, you've got to leave me alone," she begged. "I'm married."

Joe took hold of her gently in his arms. "To the wrong man, Annie. You're mine and you always will be." Lifting her up in his strong arms, he laid her down on the new eiderdown. "Just once before I go," he begged.

Longing to feel Joe making love to her, Annie made no attempt to stop him from beginning to unbutton her blouse. At the first kiss, the guilt which had made her tell Joe to leave was swiftly dissipated. It was only the sound of a horse's whinnying outside which brought her back to reality. "No!" she screamed, hastily scrambling off her sister's bed. "We mustn't, Joe."

Shaking with unfulfilled desire and with his eyes black with anger, Joe stood back from her. "You want to. Oh, yes, you want to, Annie. One day we will be together, I promise you." He turned to look at her a last time. "You're mine, Annie."

Dizzy with pounding noises in her head telling her that Joe was right, she had lain back on the bed for almost an hour until she felt able to creep back home.

Chapter 15

Annie was relieved to find an empty carriage on the train taking her back to London. The encounter with Joe had overwhelmed her with guilt and disgust. It was the recognition that Joe was not entirely to blame which was the most difficult to bear. Had it not been for the sound of the horse's whinnying outside which had penetrated a mind filled with passion and longing, would she have given in to Joe and enjoyed the fulfilment Anthony could never give her? No! Annie glanced round the empty carriage, grateful that there was no one there to hear her protest. Desperate to leave Densbury and its memories behind her, she willed the train to speed faster and faster towards London. The green fields and grassy meadows by the river no longer held any fascination for her. London's noise and fog-filled days suddenly seemed like a promise of paradise. At least there she could concentrate on her work.

What kind of work would that be? Could she really lock herself away in her studio, painting bucolic scenes which had no relevance in a world where men were dying in their thousands gunned down by heavy cannon fire or choked to death inhaling lung-destroying mustard gas? As the leafy suburbs gave way to crowded tenements, Annie came to a decision. Not until the war was won, would she resume her painting. The agony she felt was akin to tearing herself from the arms of a lover, but it had to be done; for Anthony's sake, she told herself. As soon as possible after getting herself settled again in her apartment, she would see

Isabelle and ask her help in getting her into St Margaret's to train as a nurse. Most importantly, though, Stanley Salisbury would have to be consulted. Although his art dealing business had brought him substantial wealth, he would not be too pleased to see one of his investments collapse if Annie were to reject the art world. Annie made up her mind to go and see him the day after her return from Densbury.

The letter from Anthony delivered the following morning drove all thoughts of future plans out of her mind.

My darling precious girl, he wrote, *life here is becoming rather more difficult with the ever worsening weather no help. I miss you so much that it is hard to keep one's spirits up. The memory of our brief honeymoon sustains me during these dreary days and nights. Please God this wretched war will soon be over and we can be together once again.*

Your loving husband
Anthony

On reading the letter, Annie was wracked with remorse. The thought that she could have been lying on her sister's bed with Joe at the very moment that Anthony was fighting for his life, was what she needed to wipe out memories of Joe's powerful magnetism. Shame swept over her in ice-cold waves, cleansing and liberating her from her past. Love for Anthony filled her with renewed determination. Dear, sweet Anthony, her husband and her best friend needed her now more than ever. The best way to prove to him that she shared in his struggle was to work with Isabelle in St Margaret's. That would be her war effort.

Her chance to speak with Stanley came the following Sunday at lunch. The children were delighted to see her, dragging her off to the schoolroom to show their beloved nanny their latest achievements. It was Orlando who would not let her go, demanding her advice on his half completed painting of a war scene complete with horses, soldiers and cannon. There was little he had left out of what appeared to be a realistic representation of a battlefield. Annie tried to suppress a shudder as she studied Orlando's picture in which he had even managed to include the bloodied body of a soldier.

"Don't you like it?" he asked anxiously.

Annie hugged him. "I'm going to have to look out, I can see. One day you will be painting with me in the studio and everyone will want to buy your work instead of mine!"

"Do you mean that, Annie?" he asked, suddenly serious.

"Oh, yes," Annie replied. How could she say that his work already displayed more talent than some of Anthony's art which had sold?

"Lunch is served." A voice boomed out from downstairs, alerting Annie and the children.

It was not until after lunch when the children were banished to the schoolroom, that Annie was able to explain her plans to the Salisburys. "With Anthony away fighting, I just cannot go on indulging myself. At least if I work in St Margaret's, I will be doing something to help the war effort. I owe it to Anthony."

Stanley put down his coffee cup. For a moment he studied Annie's serious face. "Of course you must do what you think is right," he told her. "There will be plenty of time for you and Anthony to resume your careers once this wretched war is over. A break away from your painting will not diminish you as an artist." He turned to his wife. "Is that not right, Diana?"

Diana handed Annie a cup of coffee. "Quite right. We can't go on pretending that life can go on exactly as it did before the war. We all have to do something. This hospital work sounds perfect, Annie. You must get started at once, then you can come and tell me all about it." She gave a little smile. "You may not believe it, but I've taken up knitting pullovers for our boys in the trenches to keep them warm this winter."

The image of the fey-like Diana wielding something as prosaic as a pair of knitting needles had Annie and Stanley laughing out loud.

"You didn't tell me," Stanley protested.

"No, and I can see now why I didn't. I knew you would find it funny." Diana pretended to be annoyed, but Annie could see that this couple complemented one another so perfectly, that neither could be angry with the other for long.

When the maid came in to draw the heavy crimson velvet curtains, Stanley glanced at his fob watch, "Good heavens!" he exclaimed. "Hardly tea-time and here we are settling in for the night. "Fetch Mrs Gladwell's coat," he instructed the maid. "I must see you home," he told Annie.

"You've both been so kind and understanding," Annie said, as Stanley helped her on with her ankle-length brown woollen coat. "I was so worried in case you wanted me to carry on painting. I owe you both more than I could ever repay."

"Nonsense, my dear," Stanley said briskly, bringing that subject to a close. "I think you have chosen very wisely. Come to think of it, Annie, it will do your art a power of good experiencing new scenes. I wouldn't be at all surprised if your work after the war doesn't prove to be the next step in your development."

Annie smiled to herself. Trust the businessman to see the profitability in even the most calamitous of situations. "That's right, let us see the bright side of this horrible mess."

It was with a feeling of immense relief at the success of this first part of her future plans that Annie sat down to write to Anthony.

My dearest Anthony,

I have been so busy with Eileen's wedding and everything that I have not written for over a week. It is not that I haven't thought of you every minute of every day, my darling Anthony.

Annie's hand trembled as she struggled to wipe her memory clean of the shameful moments spent with Joe when she would have given herself to him completely.

Sorry about the blot! I am writing to tell you what I intend to do until you are safely home here with me.

I cannot carry on at the studio where we were so happy together. That will still be there for us when this war is won. Instead, I am going to train as a nurse at St Margaret's. At least I will feel that I am doing something useful while you suffer in the trenches.

Take care, my love. I count the days until we are together again.

Your devoted Annie

Even as she sealed the envelope, Annie fought to suppress her misgivings about life with Anthony after the war. There was no doubt in her mind that she loved him, but a sharp needle repeatedly probed her heart opening painful wounds that kept reminding her of what she had thrown away with Joe. The only way was to see Isabelle at once and tell her what she intended doing. Only by throwing herself into hard physical labour could she expunge guilty memories.

Isabelle was overjoyed at Annie's decision. "I'll take you to see Matron in the morning. Wear something dark and sensible. I must warn you that it will not be easy. For a start, I believe all the new recruits have to undergo a talk by one of the top doctors." She gave a little giggle. "It's Professor Newton and he always starts by dragging out Bonypart; that's the hospital skeleton. He spends half an hour telling the new nurses the names of every bone in the body. It's a wonder some of the ladies don't walk out there and then. Don't let him put you off though, you'll be given plenty of useful training in emptying bedpans, washing patients and generally helping on the wards."

"Oh, I think I might be able to manage that," Annie said, a feeling of excitement sending a tingle of anticipation rushing through her veins at this new challenge.

Isabelle paused, staring hard at her friend's animated face. Suddenly solemn, she asked, "Have you ever seen a child dying in pain because his or her parents have put off calling in the doctor because they have not had the money to pay his fee? Have you ever seen a mother die in childbirth leaving half a dozen little ones to the tender mercies of a drunken father? I tell you, Annie, nursing at St Margaret's is not an exciting game, something to fill in your time while Anthony is away."

"I'm not doing it for that," Annie protested, then seeing Isabelle's raised eyebrow, added, "Trust you to see through me. Honestly, Isabelle, my first thought was that it would help me feel a little less guilty knowing that I was doing something useful while he was in the trenches. Somehow my heart isn't in my art and won't be until Anthony is back home."

"Good!" Isabelle seemed satisfied with Annie's answer. "I'll take you along to Matron and leave you to her tender mercies." She gave one of her cheeky smiles. "Actually, she is neither tender nor merciful with nurses who make mistakes. You'll soon find out."

Sitting behind a huge mahogany desk in her office, Matron looked up as Isabelle introduced Annie to her. "Another volunteer. Well, we can use all the help we can get." She gave a long appraising look at Annie's brown woollen coat, its perfect cut outlining the wearer's neat figure. Definitely Bond Street, Matron concluded with a sigh. Not another of these well-meaning wealthy housewives who were looking for something to do to talk about at their dinner parties. She had had to suggest to several that they ought to look for war work more in keeping with their station. Some had moved away to the country where relatives had opened up their grand houses as convalescent homes to officers recuperating after care in hospital. All that was needed there was the ability to dispense tea and cakes and indulge in a little pleasant conversation and innocent flirting to help keep up the spirits of these wounded warriors.

"I'll come straight to the point, Mrs Gladwell," Matron said. "Your husband is an officer in the Grenadier Guards fighting in France, I understand." The underlying meaning was that here was yet one more spoilt upper class wife.

"Yes, Matron." Annie could not see where this questioning was going.

"I also understand that you have made a reputation for yourself as one of our gifted younger artists. Are you sure that you want to end your time here with swollen reddened fingers which might compromise your future career?" This question carried more than a hint of venom.

"I can cope with that," Annie replied.

The matron leaned forward in her chair. Clearly she was not getting through to this young woman. Tapping the desk with her pen to emphasise the sharpness of her words, she asked, "Do you know what it is like to empty bedpans or clean up after a patient who is incontinent."

The colour rose in Annie's cheeks as the thrust of the matron's message sank in. The triumphant look in the narrowed eyes conveyed the contempt this hardworking nurse felt for women who had always had other women carry out unpleasant tasks. "Oh, I do assure you, Matron, that I have scrubbed floors, washed filthy laundry, emptied chamber pots and generally cleaned up after young gentlemen who have not been able to hold their liquor. I have worked from six in the morning until midnight with scarcely a break, insulted, yes, and even beaten. And I've had to curtsey to whoever was inflicting the insults." All this was delivered in a quiet monotone. Annie might have been reciting her two times table.

Isabelle drew her breath in sharply. Whatever was Annie thinking of speaking to Matron like that? Annie might be sent on her way with a flea in her ear, but what about her own position? Belonging to a generation which firmly believed that men were born to be doctors and women nurses, Matron would be only too pleased to find something to criticise in this red-haired Catholic woman doctor.

"I've no doubt that you will do well enough here then," Matron answered, a hint of a smile turning up the corners of her mouth, "though I promise you that we do draw the line at beatings and you will be allowed a tea break."

"Thank you," Annie muttered, ashamed at her outburst.

"Right, I'll take Mrs Gladwell to see Sister," Isabelle said hurriedly, grabbing Annie by the arm and dragging her out into the corridor. Breathing raggedly she leant against the wall. "Honestly, Annie Claydon, will you never learn? We were lucky to get out of there in one piece. Come on, I'll take you to Sister, then I've got to get back on the wards."

The rest of the day passed in a blur as Annie was handed over to the sister who was to be in charge of her training. As Isabelle had already forewarned her, the programme was designed to be thorough and punishing. There were to be lectures interspersed with sessions of practical training with barely a moment for the cup of tea which Matron had hinted at in the interview. Sister McFarley, a kindly Scot, ran through Annie's employment history to find out if she had any practical knowledge of basic first aid.

"Sorry," Annie had to admit. "I'm going to be a very difficult pupil. The only bandages I've come across are the ones the doctor put on me, when, er, when I had an accident with a horse." The explanation came out in a whisper.

"Riding were you?" Sister McFarley asked, a hint of amusement in her keen blue eyes. This new recruit was a bit of an enigma. There was a faint hint of the country girl in Annie's speech, yet the carefully enunciated educated accent led her to assume that this officer's wife was a member of the hunting, shooting and fishing classes.

To her surprise, Annie found herself able to reply calmly, "No, I just got in someone's way who was riding."

Isabelle had already left the hospital by the time that Annie had completed her first day. "She likes to visit some of the families in the East End," Sister McFarley told her. "Between you and me, she takes on far too much. Reckons she can cure the ills of the world all by herself." She shook her head. "When you've been nursing sick folk as long as I have, you get to accept that the good Lord isn't always too fair in who he chooses to take."

At the end of a punishing day, it was as much as Annie could do to get herself home to a meal prepared by her landlady. Every muscle in her body screamed with fatigue, telling her to take a hot bath and get into bed, but Annie could not rest until she had written to Anthony to tell him about her day. With her eyelids drooping, it was an effort to push the pen across the paper. Anthony had to understand that she was doing this out of love for him. She dared not admit to herself that the motivating force behind her decision was a gnawing sensation of guilt.

The relentless drudgery of the next few weeks left Annie mentally and physically exhausted. Certainly, the work was no harder than when she had slaved as a domestic at Baythorpe Hall or at Estcourt. "I was younger then," she admitted to Isabelle, when the two met one Saturday for tea in Isabelle's rooms. "Besides, I hadn't got used to a life of standing idly in front of an easel with no one to threaten me with the sack if I didn't complete my jobs."

"Are you telling me that life as an artist and an officer's wife has made you too soft for the real world?" Isabelle's gentle, mocking tones brought a smile to Annie's lips.

"Not at all," she protested. "I'll soon get back to my roots and remember that at bottom, I am still little Annie Claydon with ideas above her station."

"Oh, no, not you!" Isabelle told her. "You've long moved away from your roots. You're the wife of a Gladwell now. There's no going back."

"You're right, as usual. Isabelle. We just have to move on," Annie agreed with a sigh of resignation. "But sometimes I'm not always sure of what I am." Rejected by the Gladwells and with her own parents displaying signs of awkwardness, she wondered what the future held.

As each day passed with its round of cleaning up after incontinent patients and scrubbing floors interspersed with long theory lectures, Annie began to have doubts about her impulsive decision to take up nursing. Certainly, she was becoming more accustomed to the monotony of the tasks assigned to her, but frustration built up inside her having to accept her inability to change the inevitable outcome of many of the hopeless cases in the wards.

A letter from Eileen was waiting for her one evening early in December. Eileen's tears had smudged some of her words telling the sad news that Aaron, Danny's older brother had been killed in fighting at Ypres. Annie wept remembering Aaron as best man struggling to find the right words to describe his younger brother Danny at the wedding just two months previously. Danny was broken-hearted and having difficulty in comforting his parents. What was even worse was that Danny had been receiving white feathers in the post since being turned down for military service due to his poor eyesight.

My Danny is not a coward, Eileen wrote. *More than anything he wants to fight for his country. It is making us all so unhappy. I do miss you having you to talk to. Please come and see us soon.*

Torn between her duties at the hospital and Eileen's plea, Annie spoke to Isabelle. "I know I'm needed here, but I am so worried about my sister."

Isabelle held up a warning hand. "Stop right there, Annie. Eileen is a married woman with a husband, your mother and her in-laws to give her support. Let her grow up and find her own feet. You have had to, isn't that right?"

"Right again, Doctor," Annie agreed reluctantly.

"Listen, I have to visit some families in the East End on Saturday. Would you like to come with me? The children were in St Margaret's a little while back and I promised I would look in on them if I got the chance."

Annie had been looking forward to spending a quiet weekend recuperating from an exhausting round of duties at the hospital. There were so many letters waiting to be written. The most difficult one would be to Mr and Mrs Parfitt sending them her condolences for the loss of their dear son Aaron. How could she tell them that dying for his country had made him a hero? All they would know was that they would never see Aaron again and that his body lay somewhere in the mud on the battlefield, perhaps never to be found and given a Christian burial. Then there was Anthony who would be looking forward to receiving a long account of her routine at St Margaret's. He had been delighted to hear that she had found her old friend Isabelle.

"Oh, come on, Annie, you've got all day Sunday as well to do what you have to do." Isabelle's enthusiasm finally won Annie over.

"You win," she agreed. "Just tell me where and when and I'll be there."

They agreed to start out from Isabelle's lodgings at ten in the morning, take a bus and then walk the rest of the way to the address in Bethnal Green. Annie had seen run-down housing in Densbury with most of the working class living in tiny two-up and two-down cottages cheek by jowl. Standpipes for water shared between ten cottages were commonplace, but the children had rosy cheeks from running around in the fresh air in the open countryside. However limited the family income with no money to spare for the smallest of luxuries, no one starved as long as fathers and sons caught rabbits and game for the stewpot. Here in London, the smoke from thousands of coal fires hung like a leaden pall veiling the sun in a dirty orange glow. Ragged children played in the streets, jumping in and out of the gutters where foul water flowed, a breeding ground for rats.

Annie had been warned to wear her oldest coat and shoes in order not to stand out too much in this area of unrelenting poverty. Looking at the women standing on the doorsteps clutching the latest unplanned addition to their brood, Annie could see that whatever she had worn, she would have been conspicuous.

Isabelle looked at the address in her hand. "Number ten is what we want, Annie. It must be along here somewhere. Ah, over there, come on." She looked hastily right and left before crossing the road in front of a huge dray carting a load of beer destined for the local alehouses. The drayman leant over to swear at her for frightening his horses, but Isabelle was too intent on getting to number ten to take any notice. Annie hung back until the carthorses were out of sight before joining Isabelle.

"Come on, slowcoach. It's nearly midday and I promised that I would be back in time for lunch."

Although the door to number ten was wide open, Isabelle knocked, calling out, "It's Doctor Anstruther here. May I come in?"

A weary voice called back. "Upstairs, Doctor."

Isabelle gave Annie an anxious look. "Quick, upstairs!" Taking the stairs two at a time, she raced up to the landing where a pale, worried woman in her forties was waiting.

"I'm glad you've come," she said. "It's our Sarah. Burning with the fever she is and can't speak."

The little girl lay on top of a pile of filthy blankets. Bright spots on both cheeks bore out her mother's description. Isabelle examined Sarah's throat before covering her own mouth and standing back from the bed. "Have you called the doctor?" Isabelle asked.

The despair in the woman's eyes told her the answer even before she spoke. "It's my old man. Gone off down the pub with what few coppers I'd got in me purse. 'ow can I pay for doctors?"

"Right," Isabelle said to Annie. "There's a doctor's surgery at the end of the road. They will have a telephone. Ring for an ambulance straight away. I'll stay here." She followed Annie downstairs. "It's diphtheria. We may be too late, but if we don't get her into hospital at once, she doesn't stand a chance."

Annie's first breathless attempt to get the surgery to call an ambulance nearly ended in disaster, the receptionist telling her that she was just about to lock up and that the doctor had gone to lunch and would not be back that afternoon. "You can't expect doctors to work all weekend, you know," she said.

"Unfortunately, children get taken ill on Saturdays, so kindly call an ambulance for Sarah Mulvaney at number ten," Annie ordered.

The grey-haired woman bristled. "That feckless lot! No, I will not. Never pay their bills, but there's enough for that drunken ne'er-do-well of a father to spend on drink."

Annie slammed a sixpenny piece down on to the counter separating herself from the woman. "Make that call or else I'll let the whole street know. If that child dies, I wouldn't want to be in your shoes."

Fear at what this angry young woman could do by unleashing the collective fury of the street, made the receptionist unhook the receiver and ask the operator for the number. After a short conversation, she replaced the receiver. "The ambulance will be at number ten as soon as possible." Struggling to regain some of the dignity lost in the exchange with Annie, she buttoned up her coat tightly. "We don't all have time to play at visiting the sick," she said, a sneer on her thin, pale face. "I have to go home and look after a bedridden elderly mother. Your sort don't know what life is." She pointed to the door. "Now, if you don't mind, I need to lock up."

Mumbling deliriously and still wrapped in the same filthy blanket, Sarah was carried out to the ambulance. Every door in the street was open as anxious mothers stood on their doorsteps watching the child being taken to hospital and praying that their own offspring hadn't been playing with her recently.

"Get inside!" one mother yelled at a scruffy lad peering over his mother's shoulder. "I don't want you catching the fever."

The night of December the twenty-first was one which Annie would never forget. The news earlier that little Sarah had lost her fight against diphtheria had disturbed her more than she could have imagined.

"I tried to warn you," Isabelle said gently. "Children die from so many diseases, but we have to have hope, Annie, that one day we will win the battle."

Heavy with sleep that night, Annie's eyelids were closing when the first loud explosions were heard. Imagining that she was dreaming of Anthony in the trenches, she paid no attention to the noise. It was not until the agitated voice of her landlady penetrated the fog of fatigue which had engulfed her that she managed to rouse herself.

"Mrs Gladwell! Get up! It's the Germans! It's an air raid. Quick, get up and come down into the cellar. Our policeman says we'll be safe down there." The frightened landlady continued to hammer at the door until Annie replied that she would be up and dressed in a few minutes. "Where are you going my dear?" she asked, as fully dressed in outdoor clothes, Annie ran down the stairs towards the front door.

"The hospital, they'll need me," Annie called out. Dashing through the deserted streets, Annie began to despair of ever reaching St Margaret's, as it soon became clear that public transport had come to a standstill. A loud explosion set off the frantic whinnying of a horse directly behind her in the street. "Please," she called out to the cabbie. "I'm a nurse. I must get to my hospital."

The cabbie gave Annie a helping hand into the cab. "We'll do our best, old Hector and me, but hang on tight, 'cos he ain't too 'appy with these bangs. All the same, we ain't gonna let the Kaiser beat us, are we?"

The ride was bumpy with Hector getting more and more agitated with each bang. Finally, the cabbie said, "I'm sorry, luv, but I'll have to let you off 'ere before Hector takes it into 'is 'ead to go off at a gallop. We ain't too far off the 'orspital now. Good luck, dear. You're an angel, you are." Refusing to take any money, he waved goodbye to Annie just as Hector set off at a cracking pace heading for the safety of his stables.

"Good, you're here. We need all the help we can get." Matron was standing inside the main entrance of St Margaret's supervising the admission to the wards of those injured in the air raid. "See Sister McFarley in Nightingale. She'll give you your instructions."

Breathless after her dash through the streets, Annie managed a hoarse, "Yes, Matron, at once."

Every bed on Nightingale ward was occupied with patients still waiting to be seen by the army of doctors who had all left their beds to tend the sick and dying. Two of the auxiliary nurses were busy making up extra beds to accommodate the influx of victims of the raid. Annie was instructed to wash and bandage the wounds of those with more superficial injuries. Once seen by a doctor they could be discharged. It was while Annie was putting the finishing touches to the bandages of one elderly patient, that Isabelle came into the ward and began checking on the occupants of the beds. Knowing that it was contrary to hospital protocol for a nurse to leave her duties to address a doctor, nevertheless, Annie stared hard at her friend hoping for a response. She was shocked at Isabelle's haggard appearance. Tired and ill-looking, going from bed to bed, Isabelle worked with a frenetic haste. When she reached Annie's patient, she drew Annie to one side.

"I've just been to see Sarah's mother, but she wasn't there." Isabelle's eyes were red with weeping. "The whole street has gone. Just a flattened area where once whole families lived." Unable to say more, she returned to her task, gently admonishing her patient for getting in the Kaiser's way. "You're lucky to be alive," she told him.

As morning broke, the newspaper boys were out on the streets selling newspapers full of the account of the first air raid on London. Annie bought one to read after she had had a bath and a few hours' sleep. No one mentioned the optimism of the early days of the war, when the cry that it would all be over by Christmas was on everybody's lips.

Annie's heart froze at the premonition that the war was only just beginning.

Chapter 16

It was easier for Annie to spend that first Christmas of the war working at St Margaret's than having to choose between celebrating it with the Salisburys or her parents. She wrote to her family to say that she would visit Densbury for the New Year, using her duty rota at the hospital as a reason for not joining them for the holiday. She remembered how Christmas morning had always followed the same pattern; early breakfast, preparation of vegetables for dinner and the goose put in the oven. Once dinner had been organised to Beatie's satisfaction, it would be time to set out for chapel. The attendance at chapel was the problem. Annie knew that she could not have borne having to accompany her family there, where the Gladwells, as benefactors of the chapel would be lording it over their employees. The sight of the Gladwells being curtsied to would have been too much for Annie.

"I think if I were there, I would want to show them up in front of the whole congregation. Singing hymns and praying while all the time they are ignoring their only son out there in France fighting for his country." Annie's cheeks were bright pink with fury as she spoke to Isabelle.

"It certainly would brighten up the proceedings," Isabelle said. "I can just see you telling old Will Gladwell exactly what you think of him just as everyone is singing Hark the Herald Angels Sing!"

Annie giggled. "And what about the expression on Pastor Briggs' face!" Suddenly serious again, she went on, "All the same, I want to see Eileen. Things have not been easy for her with Danny's brother Aaron being killed at the Front and Danny being turned down for active service."

"You and Eileen were always so close." Isabelle blinked away a few tears. "I wish I could have had a sister."

Annie gave her a hug. "You've got me instead, Isabelle, so stop bemoaning your fate. Remember, it's my turn to make tea today after this shift, so don't waste time stopping to chat to that nice doctor you always seem to be with."

Isabelle blushed. "We only talk about the patients," she protested.

In a spirit of defiance, the nurses had put up a few brightly coloured paper chains to decorate the wards. Matron had strongly resisted at first, but relented when the senior doctors assured her that hygiene would not be compromised and that a little boost to morale was all that was needed to put some of their patients on the road to recovery. In spite of the fact that the food shortages were beginning to impact upon the rations allowed for each patient, the hospital cooks managed to make puddings and mince pies, admittedly not quite as good as homemade Christmas fare, but tasty enough to bring a glow to thin, pale cheeks.

Remembering that she still had to visit the Salisburys, Annie called round on Boxing Day morning with presents for the children. She had bought a book for Katherine, some expensive paint brushes for Orlando and a doll for little Emily Jane, the baby of the family. Diane insisted that she stay for lunch. "Just the remains of yesterday's goose and pudding," she explained when Annie began to protest.

"And we've got presents for you," Katherine explained shyly.

"She's made you a scarf and I've painted you a picture," Orlando announced loudly.

Katherine stamped her foot and lunged at her young brother ready to box his ears for giving away her secret. He was saved only by his father taking hold of his collar and leading him out of the room with the promise of a good ticking-off.

"Nothing changes then, Diana," Annie commented with a smile. It was so warm and comforting being with this delightful family that she had to suppress burgeoning regrets about her decision to relinquish her painting to take up nursing. Diana's next question, however, banished them.

"How is Anthony? Have you heard from him lately?"

Annie was silent for a moment. "He always says he is fine, but he can't be, can he? He's not like other men. He's kind and gentle. I can't see him killing other human beings even if they are Germans." Her voice quavered as she added, "I don't think he is one of those tough soldiers who can survive in the trenches."

Diana was too sensible to try to offer meaningless words of comfort. She took Annie's cold hand in hers. "You may be right about Anthony, my dear. All we can do is hope."

Annie left the Salisburys with a promise to visit again in the New Year. "First I have to go to Densbury for a few days, then it will be back to St Margaret's, but I promise that I will come and have lunch with you the very first Sunday after that."

"Right, we'll hold you to that," Stanley said. "Come along, let me see you safe and sound in a cab."

Their kindly solicitude for her welfare filled Annie with a sensation of being soothed, ready for sleep, as if comfortably wrapped in a warm, fluffy towel after a hot bath. But before allowing herself the luxury of falling into bed, she had to write to Anthony to reassure him that she was coping well with her work at St Margaret's. She did not tell him the real reason for staying away from Densbury at Christmas.

The train to Densbury on New Year's Eve was half empty, the few passengers on board displaying no sign that this was the beginning of a year of hope. The air raid on London in December allied to reports of casualties sustained in France had effectively dampened the earlier mood of optimism in the country, replacing it with a quiet spirit of determined patriotism. Filled with patriotic fervour and a spirit of adventure, young men, who had never travelled further than their neighbouring villages were still volunteering in their thousands.

There was no one to meet Annie as the midday train drew into Densbury station, apart from young Alfie on the platform, eager as ever to help his former workmate. He now treated Mrs Gladwell with an air of deference as he approached to help carry her suitcase. "Just me here today, I'm afraid, and I can't leave my post."

Annie struggled to hide her embarrassment at what she took to be an innocent reference to Joe Langmead. "I wasn't expecting anyone," she said lightly. "I can manage. It's not too far."

A light rain threatening to turn to sleet made her wish that she had written to ask her mother to meet her with an umbrella. Instead, it was a breathless Eileen who came running up the slope towards the station. She flung herself into her sister's arms with a cry of delight. "Sorry I'm late, Annie. I've shut up the shop. I'm not missing a minute of having you here. I'm having dinner with you and Ma and Pa." Remembering why she had come to meet Annie, Eileen opened up the huge umbrella. "Quick, you don't want to spoil your nice coat."

Arm in arm, the two young women made their way to what had been their home. For a few minutes, both seemed to be afraid to say what was in their minds. It was Annie who broke the silence. "How is Danny?"

Eileen sighed. "It's so hard for him not being able to join up. He feels it even more after losing Aaron. It's eating away at him not being able to avenge Aaron."

"But it's not his fault that he's unfit. Besides, he is needed at home here." Annie did not want her younger sister to suffer the apprehension she felt whenever the postman called. "Come on, cheer up, let's hope the New Year brings us all good news."

Enveloped in clouds of steam, their ma was stirring the contents of a huge pan on the stove when they arrived. She greeted the girls with, "Speak to you in a minute, I don't want the stew to burn." Once the stew was safely simmering, she ushered the two into the living room, then stood back waiting for Annie's reaction.

"Ma, what a difference!" Annie exclaimed. "Just look at that new sofa! And the rugs, they're lovely."

What had been a shabby little cottage living room poorly furnished and lacking comfort, had been transformed thanks to her pa's promotion to factory manager. She was pleased to see that the painting she had done and which Joe had had framed for her parents was still proudly displayed.

"Well, it's all thanks to your pa," Beatie said proudly. "And we mustn't forget Joe. It was Joe who talked Mr Gladwell round to giving your pa the job. I don't think Mr Gladwell was too pleased about it, you know what with the trouble over you and Anthony getting wed against his wishes."

"He'd have been a fool to have given the job to anyone else, Ma," Annie protested. "The Gladwells are out to make money for themselves, so he was hardly likely to cut off his nose to spite his face."

"That's as maybe," her ma said. "Your pa's just coming up the path, so let's all sit down and have a nice hot dinner. I'll dish up the stew, Eileen, while you make haste and dish up the vegetables."

Annie's plea to be allowed to give a hand was met with a sharp reminder that she was a guest. So, Eileen is the daughter who stayed at home and I am to be treated like a virtual stranger, Annie thought, just because I'm married to a Gladwell. "I'll set the table," she insisted. "I've not come to be waited on hand and foot. I do know where everything is kept."

She was rewarded with a brief smile of relief from her ma.

A huge hug from her pa the minute he set foot in the door, told her that she was once again back home with her family. Fred Claydon was looking well. His promotion had taken him away from the drudgery of the factory floor into the more mentally demanding environs of the manager's office, where he had been surprised to find the responsibility invigorating.

"So how is Anthony?" he asked, forking a mouthful of cabbage and mashed potatoes.

"As far as I know, he is doing well, but of course I am worried."

"Not surprising," he went on. "We've just had word that Joe has been wounded and is in a field hospital behind the lines somewhere in France, no one seems to know exactly where."

"Is he going to be all right, Pa?" Eileen asked, trying to avert her parents' attention from her sister's ashen face.

"We understand that he has been shot in the leg. Once they've patched him up, I expect he'll be sent back to fight again."

Annie pushed her chair back from the table with a muttered, "Just a minute, Ma. I must get a glass of water. I think I swallowed too much hot stew all at once."

Eileen attempted to make a joke of it. "Serves you right, Annie. You've forgotten how good Ma's cooking is. You shouldn't eat so fast."

"Oh, leave your sister alone," her mother admonished, blushing at her younger daughter's compliment.

Grateful for the diversion created by Eileen, Annie fled to the kitchen where she found herself a glass. Still shaking from the shock of hearing about Joe, she turned on the tap with a trembling hand.

"You all right out there?" her mother called.

"Fine, Ma." Annie smoothed her hair back and rejoined the others. "I'm sorry about that," she said. "The stew's lovely, Ma. Any chance of a second helping?"

Eileen gave her a sideways glance. Annie was behaving very oddly. Surely she could not have been affected so keenly by news of Joe's injuries? Perhaps she was thinking that it might happen to Anthony. Poor Annie.

New Year's Day provided more stress with Fred's sister Violet invited to dinner. Annie had never forgotten that it was Aunt Violet who had told her ma that she had seen her enter Joe's house on Sunday afternoons. Annie tried to ignore Aunt Violet's pointed remarks as she turned her boiled gooseberry-coloured eyes on her niece. There was malevolence in her gaze as she said, "So, Mrs Gladwell is it? And to think that by rights you should have married Joe Langmead." She tapped the side of her nose as she emphasised 'by rights'. "Funny how things turn out. Aren't you the lucky one!"

"Very lucky, Aunt Violet," Annie agreed coldly. She stood up to help her ma carry plates out to the kitchen. Thank God she would be returning to London next morning. Densbury contained too many memories of Joe, memories which she had carefully struggled for so long to shroud in thick veils. Constant reminders of him tore tiny holes which if allowed to continue might threaten to tear the veils to shreds.

Thoughts of Joe were banished when she received a letter in March from Anthony to say that he would be home on leave the first week in April. With news of the battle at Neuve-Chapelle in which two thousand casualties had been sustained out of a force of fifty thousand, Annie feared desperately that she would never see Anthony again.

She was not prepared for the thin, grey-faced Anthony who waved to her as the train pulled into Charing Cross on that April morning. Hardly recognising the stranger who was her husband, she waved back. Carriage doors were being flung open with little regard for those waiting on the platform by men eager to feel the healing warmth of wives and sweethearts, a warmth they hoped would ease away the horrors they had left behind. Annie ran to Anthony to be gathered up in his thin, wasted arms.

"My darling girl," he murmured. "My beautiful Annie."

Annie was glad that she had kept her cab waiting outside the station to get Anthony home as quickly as possible. Clinging to him as the cabbie urged his horse on, Annie choked back the tears. Anthony's ill appearance had shocked her more than she dared admit. His lovely blue eyes, once shining with boyish eagerness were now sunken and dull as if hiding memories of unspeakable nightmares. The vibrant young man who had run across the fields with his great, loping stride to greet her only a few short years ago was now a listless shadow.

Her whispered, "We'll soon have you well again, my darling," was met with a look of such despair, that Annie feared she had lost forever the Anthony she had once known.

Their landlady was waiting with a tray of tea. "I've taken the liberty of lighting fires in both of the rooms." Her shocked reaction to Anthony's drawn appearance was not lost on Annie, who thanked her for her kindness before ushering her husband into their rooms.

"Help me undress," Anthony begged. "I'm so tired, my darling." Leaving Annie to pull off his boots and gently ease off his uniform, he lay back on the bed and closed his eyes. Annie pulled the sheet and blankets over him, tenderly tucking him up in bed as a mother would a child and left him to sleep.

For the next few days, he stayed in bed, waking only to eat light, nourishing meals of soup, before lapsing back into a deep sleep. Occasionally, Annie heard him call out in anguish, but these episodes gradually ceased and his sleep became more like that of a contented child. Exhausted herself, Annie slept late one morning, waking to find Anthony standing by their bed with a tray of tea, which he placed on the bedside table.

"We'll just let the tea cool for a while," he said, pulling off his pyjamas and getting back into the bed beside her. "You don't know how many times I've dreamt of this moment, my precious darling." His thin body pressed against Annie, he eased himself on top of her and took her with a savage intensity, which left her both horrified and unsatisfied. Still unaware that his lovemaking was in any way lacking, he kissed her. "You make me so happy," he said. "I'm the luckiest husband in the whole world." He smiled, his blue eyes once again alive and sparkling. "Now, my darling wife, your tea is going cold."

Annie told herself that he was a hero and that it was her duty to keep him happy before his return to the trenches, but how long could she keep up the pretence of returning his passion? Sometimes as he lay awake beside her, Anthony would describe men dying, choking to death as they inhaled the dreaded mustard gas. It was at moments like these that Annie felt full of guilt even contemplating putting her needs before Anthony's.

As the day approached when he had to rejoin his regiment, Anthony's maniacal, joyous mood disappeared to be replaced by one of sombre melancholy. Even Annie's gentle words, soothing and encouraging him as he lay in her arms, did little to lift his spirits. He clung to her in silent desperation as they parted at Charing Cross station, finally managing to say, "If I don't come back, remember you're the only girl I have ever loved." Her reply, "You will come back, my love, you will," was lost in the cries of farewell all around her.

In April 1915, London was attacked five times by Zeppelin airships, with the result that Annie and the other nurses at St Margaret's were called on at short notice to tend the injured and dying. As the year went on, Isabelle remained a constant friend in spite of her ever-lengthening shifts, the two of them meeting regularly in Isabelle's rooms for tea and a chat. She provided a sympathetic ear whenever Annie expressed her fears for Anthony's safety.

"He'll come home for good one day, but remember, he will be changed by all that he is going through. No man can endure what our men in the trenches are suffering. He won't be the light-hearted boy you married."

"I know," Annie agreed. "It is like having to get to know a stranger each time he comes home on leave. I still see something of the old Anthony and yet, I don't know, it is all being submerged under a sea of depression, as if it is something he can hardly bear. He won't be home for Christmas and he was so looking forward to it. You hear of men coming back with shell shock, hardly able to recognise their loved ones. Do you think Anthony will be like that?"

"Annie, he is still in the front line. If he were so ill, he would be sent home." Even as she uttered the words, Isabelle did not really believe them herself. She had seen men sent home too shell-shocked to know where they were, calling out in the night, fighting imaginary battles, convinced that they were still in the trenches.

Going back to her lonely rooms that evening, Annie could hear the sound of singing coming from inside one of the public houses. "Keep the Home Fires Burning," was being chorused by the half-drunken customers. Further along the road, she glimpsed inside the open doors of a large restaurant. Well-dressed wealthy men and women, oblivious to the deprivation of the rest of the population, were eating and drinking. Corks were being pulled on bottles of champagne as waiters bore mountainous plates of food to the tables. There were many for whom the war had proved to be a gold mine as they collected their profits from their munitions factories.

Her heart breaking, Annie asked herself, "Is this what Anthony is risking his life for?"

Chapter 17

The letter from Anthony with the news that he had been promoted in swift succession first to Captain and then to Major arrived in July just as the bloody battle of the Somme was beginning to rumble. With massive casualties, the young officers going over the top leading their men were dying in their thousands, with the result that survivors were being rapidly promoted. Annie scanned the newspapers each morning with feverish anxiety, which increased as rumours spread of nearly twenty thousand casualties being sustained on the first day. It was the announcement in *The Times* that Major Anthony Gladwell had been awarded the Military Cross for outstanding gallantry in battle, saving the lives of many of his men with no regard for his own safety, that filled her with a quiet pride.

She was congratulated by doctors and patients alike as she went from bed to bed. Even Matron called her into her office one morning. "You must be very proud of your husband, Mrs Gladwell. I should like you to know that all of us at St Margaret's are honoured to know that we have the wife of this gallant officer working here." She then turned her attention to the papers on her desk and Annie was dismissed.

Annie waited in vain for some communication from the Gladwells, who surely must have seen the announcement in *The Times*. Furious at their callous disregard, Annie wrote to her sister.

Dear Eileen,

I am enclosing a cutting from The Times. As you can see, it gives a full account of Anthony's bravery and how he won the Military Cross. Would you take it to the offices of the Densbury Clarion and give it to the editor and explain that Mrs Gladwell would like to see it printed. Let me know what he has to say!
Your affectionate sister
Annie

Almost by return, she received a letter from Eileen.

Dear Annie,

I did as you asked. That silly Mr Pooley was a bit concerned at first. He thought he ought to wait until the Gladwells made the announcement. I told him that if he did not put it in, the Parfitts would withdraw their advertisements from his paper and that I would inform The Times editor that a country publication was insulting one of our famous war heroes.

He soon saw sense and promised a full front page coverage. I will send you a copy the minute it is published.
Your affectionate sister
Eileen

Annie had not told Eileen that one of the reasons for having the announcement put in the *Clarion* was to shame Anthony's father into admitting that he had a son. She could picture the scene in chapel the Sunday following its publication, with everyone rushing to congratulate him. How would he react? She soon found out, when her ma wrote to say how pleased they all were at the exciting news which Pastor Briggs read out on Sunday morning.

Mr Gladwell seemed a bit dazed by all the attention, but I expect he was pleased, she wrote.

"I expect he was more than dazed," Isabelle said. "What does he do now? Do you think he will acknowledge Anthony as his son again and you as Anthony's wife?"

"I just don't know, Isabelle. He's a stubborn man and he won't be too happy that I have deliberately forced him into a corner. I wonder if I did the right thing."

"You have to stand up to bullies," Isabelle told her.

"You mean like you did to that horrible Professor Gearly when he wanted to turn that poor sick woman and her family away, accusing her of looking for free board and lodging?"

Isabelle looked sheepish. "A bit like that, though I have to admit that I think he was right in the long run. Still, it was a health issue, wasn't it? I mean, the woman and her children were in need of attention with the youngest one suffering from rickets."

"You don't have to justify yourself to me," Annie said. "But I think you ought to grovel to Professor Gearly if you want to keep your job. I might have to do the same with Anthony's father."

The opportunity arose sooner than Annie had anticipated and in circumstances which she had dreaded. The news arrived that Anthony had been invalided out of the army following one particularly vicious battle during the course of which his gas mask had been damaged and he had breathed in the deadly fumes of the enemy's gas. The official communication informed her that he was to be repatriated on September 16th and taken to recover at a hospital in Surrey. He would be arriving at Charing Cross station and she would be able to meet him there and see him briefly before he was taken to hospital.

She rushed to the station entrance crowded with relatives also eager to see their husbands, sons and brothers being invalided out of the army. In her haste she collided with a paper boy selling the *Sunday Pictorial* shouting out the banner headlines announcing, *All Goes Well for Britain and France.*

The ambulance men were standing at the station ready to carry the injured men to the ambulances lined up outside the station. Annie was not prepared for the sight of the hundreds of casualties being lifted off the train. Many had lost their sight and with bandages swathed round their head were being led like babies to the ambulances. Others with the tell-tale pinned up sleeve or trouser leg were struggling along the platform accompanied by medical men. Annie made her way along the platform until she found Anthony with a doctor and a nurse tending him.

"Poor chap," she heard the doctor say. "His fighting days are over. He will never be the same again." He shook his head. "I pity his poor young wife."

"What is it?" Distraught at seeing Anthony wrapped tightly in blankets and almost lifeless, Annie tugged at the doctor's sleeve.

"I'm sorry my dear," he said. "Major Gladwell has suffered severe breathing problems following the inhalation of gas and, I have to tell you, he is also suffering from shell shock." He placed his hand gently on her shoulder. "We'll do our best to patch him up, but he will need a lot of care once he leaves hospital."

Annie bent over the stretcher to kiss Anthony's cold cheek. He gradually opened his eyes on feeling her warm lips. "Annie? Is it you?" A tear rolled down his cheek.

"Sorry, we must take him now," one of the men told her.

Annie stood motionless as he was carried away. She had got Anthony back alive, but as an invalid who was going to need all the loving care she could give him. How could she tend him single-handed in their small suite of rooms? Once home, she paced up and down trying to picture herself here with a disabled Anthony and had to finally admit that it would be impossible. This was no time for pride either on her part or on Will Gladwell's. She would have to swallow her pride and write to Will Gladwell to tell him the extent of Anthony's injuries. She would have to risk being rejected by her father-in-law. The question was, would he risk public scorn and criticism by rejecting a war hero invalided out of the army. If he had any feeling for his hero son, surely he would offer help of some kind. She was surprised to hear by return of post.

Dear Annie,

Thank you for your letter. My wife and I are naturally saddened to hear of Anthony's injuries sustained in defending his country. In the circumstances, we feel that we must offer all the assistance in our power.

You will need a home where you will be able to nurse Anthony other than the rooms in London, which are most unsatisfactory. My wife will ensure that the Dower House will be made ready for you once Anthony is discharged from hospital. I understand that you have been nursing in London and will therefore have the necessary skills. Any further support will be available to you.

Yours sincerely
W Gladwell

The following Sunday, Annie took the train to Morbridge to see Anthony in the hospital which, set in its own leafy grounds, was situated a mile or so out of the town. It was of those pleasantly warm early autumn days with the sun filtering gentle rays through the branches of the lime trees lining the long drive leading up to the main building. Nurses were chatting to the occupants of wheelchairs as they pushed them slowly along the gravel paths. Annie scanned the faces of the soldiers hoping that Anthony would at least be well enough to be taken out into the fresh air, but was told by one of the male orderlies that Major Gladwell was in bed in the ward at the end of a long corridor. She finally found him lying asleep at the end of a half empty ward.

Stroking his pale cheeks and brushing a lock of his still golden hair away from his forehead, she whispered, "My dear Anthony. It's me, your Annie."

Anthony stirred in his sleep, gradually opening his eyes. At first, he seemed bewildered, unable to recognise Annie. "Is it really you, Annie?"

"Yes, my darling, of course it is."

He held out a painfully thin arm in an attempt to hold Annie close as she leant towards him and kissed him tenderly on the lips.

"I've such wonderful news," she said. "I've had a letter from your father."

"From Father? He's written to you?" Disbelief followed by sheer joy lit up the faded blue eyes. "Oh, Annie, I've wanted this so much." It hurt Annie to realise how much Anthony had sacrificed in loving and marrying her as the words came tumbling out.

She went on, "We're going to have the Dower House all to ourselves, my darling, and once you are well, we'll be able to paint together."

"Just like we did when we were children," Anthony said, lifting his head slightly. "Oh, Annie, it will be so wonderful to be home."

"He's getting on like a house on fire," the doctor told her two weeks later. "I think the prospect of going home to the country has worked wonders. Some good fresh air will help his breathing too."

"He is going to feel guilty not being able to carry on fighting. He will think of himself as a coward," Annie said. "That is going to be so hard for him to deal with."

"We must never forget what he has done," the doctor said. "Major Gladwell is a hero. He will return home to a hero's welcome, I'm sure. He can do no more for his country."

It was the second week in October before Annie received news that Anthony was to be discharged from hospital. Once again, she wrote to the Gladwells to inform them and received the reply that a car and chauffeur would be at her disposal to collect them both and bring them back to Densbury.

On a cold foggy morning, Annie went to see her old friends, the Salisburys to tell them that she was leaving London. "I don't know what the future holds," she explained. "It will be some time before Anthony is well enough to be left. Perhaps, once the war is over, I'll be able to come back and work again." The reality that she might never paint again in Stanley Salisbury's studio was too much for her. Harsh sobs shook her tiny shoulders as Diana enfolded her in her arms as a mother would a child.

"Give it time," was all Stanley could say. "When the time is right, my dear, you will start painting again. Talent like yours can only improve with the passage of time." In his heart, he was afraid that once Annie was back in Densbury nursing Anthony, she would find it even harder to leave than she had the first time.

The next few days were spent in packing her clothes and the few belonging to Anthony. She examined one of his jackets, holding it close to her, before rejecting it. It had been tailored for him when he was a healthy young man with the muscle to fill it out. It would be too cruel to give it to him to wear now, showing as it would the wasted body that was his. Her landlady promised to dispose of any items left behind by donating them to the many charities for the poor and the homeless.

As she went from room to room, Annie remembered the feeling of optimism she and Anthony had shared as they began their married life and their career as new artists. Was it really just a few short years ago? Now, Anthony was an invalid and she was having to put thoughts of the London studio behind her.

When the Gladwell car drew up on the Saturday morning with Stokes at the wheel, Annie was ready and waiting for him. He stowed the suitcases in the boot of the car and stood to attention as he opened the rear door open for her. "Allow me to wrap the rug round you, madam," he requested. "It is a raw, cold morning to be out and about."

Annie was not used to such deferential treatment, especially as she remembered Bertie Stokes from her days as a servant at Baythorpe Hall. He must have recognised her, but was sufficiently aware of the change in their status not to make reference to it. If Annie was not yet mistress of Baythorpe, that day would surely come. It was not for him to criticise the changing order which allowed a servant girl to rise to become an equal of families such as Will and Thora Gladwell.

By the time they reached the hospital at Morbridge, it was almost noon and they arrived to find Anthony being served lunch. He was almost too excited to eat, wanting to leave at once, but Annie insisted that Bertie Stokes as well as herself had to be allowed something to eat before starting back to Suffolk.

"Can I sit in the front with you, Bertie?" Anthony asked the chauffeur busily attending to folding the wheelchair in order to accommodate it in the already full boot. "It will be just like old times when I was a boy."

"That's right, sir, you were always keen on motor cars."

Annie forced herself not to complain, pretending not to be disappointed at having to sit in silence alone in the back of the car, recognising that Anthony would have to be spoilt. The doctor had said that his illness sometimes manifested itself in fits of temper if Anthony were to be thwarted in any way. This was just the beginning.

The drive back to Densbury took nearly three hours, by which time Anthony had fallen fast asleep without addressing one single word to her throughout the journey. It was with a sigh of relief that the streets of Densbury came into view. With darkness fast falling, the gas lamps had been lit giving the town an almost festive appearance. A little like the night of the gala when Joe had declared his love for her. I was just a child then,

Annie thought, and now I have all the cares of an old married woman.

The lights outside Baythorpe Hall were all alight with the front doors being flung open as the car began the long approach along the drive. As if by magic, all the staff appeared outside the door ready to give three cheers to the returning hero and future master of Baythorpe. Anthony was determined to enter his old home on his own two feet with the aid of crutches and with no one to support him He made his way slowly towards his parents, leaving Annie standing by the open car door. Will Gladwell took hold of Anthony's hands in his and held on to them.

"Welcome home, my son."

Thora hugged him as if she would never let him go. "Don't you ever go away again, do you hear?" she admonished him as if he were a little boy.

Still ignoring Annie, the assembled servants led by the butler gave three hearty cheers for the returning hero. The spiteful Mrs Golding gave a malevolent smile seeing Annie treated as if she did not exist.

Annie's anger slowly spread throughout her whole body. She was no longer the little skivvy who had married above herself. She was a successful artist, feted by the London critics, not the little Annie Claydon they remembered. She took a deep breath and, hand outstretched, advanced on Will Gladwell. "So kind of you to send Stokes to pick us up, Mr Gladwell. Anthony and I are so looking forward to taking up residence in the Dower House." Had she said, "I am Mrs Anthony Gladwell and I am no longer your servant and you will not treat me as such," her message could not have been clearer.

There was a barely audible gasp from the line-up of servants. Will Gladwell paused, staring at Annie's offered hand. She returned his stare with cold determination daring him to insult her.

"Welcome to Baythorpe Hall, Annie," he said, taking her hand.

The significance of the welcome was not lost on Annie. His greeting implied that this was her first visit to Baythorpe, as if she had never entered its doors previously. Was it that he did not want to acknowledge that Annie had ever been there as a servant, something shameful he would prefer to forget? Annie did not care. She had won her first battle to be accepted.

He was followed by his wife who held Annie in a brief but warm embrace. "It will be lovely to have you both so close to us."

After dinner, Annie and Anthony were taken to the Dower House which stood a little way back from the main gates of Baythorpe Hall. A one-storey building, it was ideal for accommodating Anthony's wheelchair. Even though he was beginning to take some steps with the aid of crutches, he had to accept that in his weakened state, he needed the support provided by the wheelchair. There were three bedrooms, a tiny sitting room, dining room and kitchen. Annie could see where the grass surrounding the house had been disturbed when the builders had erected an extension providing a necessary bathroom. Under the guidance of Thora Gladwell, the house had been so tastefully furnished in gentle colours restful to the eye that Annie wondered how she had managed to avoid the red carpets and heavy furniture of the time. It was clear to see from whom Anthony had inherited his love of art.

"It's really beautiful, Mrs Gladwell," Annie said. "Anthony will be so happy here."

"I hope you will be, too, Annie," came the quiet reply.

The first few weeks were not easy with a constant flow of servants sent to clean and meals being sent down from the kitchens of the big house. This meant that Anthony had to stick to rigid meal times, often when he would have preferred to sleep. In the end, Annie had to convince her mother-in-law that Anthony could not adhere to the mealtimes dictated by the main kitchen and that, although cold pies and cooked meats would be welcome, she would attend to Anthony's main meals. There were a number of minor battles to be won before Annie could begin to feel that she was mistress in her own home, but gradually things settled down.

It was as she was preparing afternoon tea ready for Anthony when he woke, that she noticed one of the china cups had a tiny chip as had its matching saucer. Checking the rest of the tea service, which appeared to be intact, it was clear that Mrs Golding had chosen to show her contempt for Annie by including a faulty tea service in the crockery sent down to the Dower House. A telephone having been installed so that Annie could call the doctor for Anthony without having to run up to the house, Annie picked up the receiver to speak to the butler.

"Kindly send Mrs Golding to the Dower House at once," she ordered.

"I will see if she is available, madam," he replied.

He was not prepared for the sharp reminder that Mrs Gladwell was not enquiring whether Mrs Golding was available. This was an order and Mrs Golding would present herself at the Dower House within the next five minutes. Annie did not have to add, "Or else."

Exactly five minutes later, the woman appeared at the back door. "You called, I believe, madam." Her expression of contempt for this servant who now called herself Mrs Gladwell was barely concealed.

Annie pointed to the chipped cup and saucer on the kitchen table. "Explain this," she demanded curtly.

"It's only the one," she said, her thin lips curled in the beginnings of a sneer.

"I see," Annie said. "So you consider it your duty to deliver this rubbish as being good enough for the Major to use. I really will have to inform his mother of your insolence and you will have to suffer the consequences."

Seeing where this was leading, Mrs Golding began to apologise for her mistake. "It won't happen again," she said. "I will make sure that the tea service is replaced."

"Oh, before you go," Annie told her, "I understand that it is still the policy of Baythorpe Hall that servants have to pay for breakages." She smiled briefly seeing the memory dawn in the woman's mind of the day she had sent Annie on her way with half of the wages due to her, because Lavinia had said that Annie owed for breaking the best china.

"Yes, madam," the housekeeper confirmed.

"In that case, I will see that the correct amount is deducted from your wages. You may go." Before long, the servants at Baythorpe would know that the new Mrs Gladwell had arrived.

Will Gladwell called one Saturday afternoon to visit his son a few minutes after Annie's parents had come to have tea with their daughter and son-in-law. Although Will Gladwell considered himself to be an enlightened employer, this did not extend to meeting his factory manager in what might be considered to be a social setting. Embarrassed at the situation, Fred Claydon leapt up from his chair, spilling his hot tea over Annie's white starched tablecloth.

"I'll call back later," Will said. "I apologise for the intrusion." Clearly annoyed that he felt forced to leave, he turned on his heel and with exaggerated swings of his walking stick, stalked off in the direction of the Hall.

"Oh dear, we're in the way, we shouldn't have come. Perhaps it's better if we don't come again. We don't want to upset Mr Gladwell, do we, Fred?"

"Sit down, Ma," Annie told her mother. "This is my house. I'll just take this wet cloth off the table and fetch some fresh tea and then we'll talk about it."

While her ma gave her a hand to dry the table and floor, Fred Claydon chatted to Anthony, an easy exchange of views which brought a smile to Annie's lips. She nudged her ma. "See, you belong here as much as old Will Gladwell." She made this point later to both her parents. "Don't you see that this is my home and Anthony's? No one will dictate to us who visits and when."

"I agree," Anthony said. "Papa can come and visit me whenever he likes, but I'll explain to him that Annie's family and friends can only come after their work is finished at dinnertime on Saturday, so he is quite likely to find a house full of people on Saturday afternoons."

Annie kissed Anthony on the cheek. "Always the peacemaker." Recognising the signs of fatigue in the strained eyes and pale cheeks, she took hold of his arm. "I think it's time for your afternoon rest."

"Let me help," Fred said and was pleased and surprised when his son-in-law smiled and thanked him.

As her parents left, Annie said, "I think I'd like to drop in on Sunday afternoons sometimes, that is, if you're not going out. I can have Anthony taken up to the Hall to spend some time with his parents."

This set the pattern for the weekends leading up to Christmas, by which time the uneasy truce had developed into what might be called a friendly routine. For Annie it was a welcome relief from the daily round of caring for Anthony. He slept late in the mornings, often after a night of sleep broken by nightmares. Sometimes, his lungs damaged by gas, left him struggling for breath in the middle of the night. The panic induced by these attacks meant that Annie had to sit him up in bed and help calm him until he was able to breathe more easily. When the Gladwells heard of one such episode, they tried to insist that Annie and Anthony come to live up at the Hall where he could be properly cared for, a suggestion which both Annie and Anthony resisted.

Day after day, Annie worked from morning until night and often during the night. It was with a shock that she realised that she had not unpacked her paints and easel, which still lay in their wrappings in the small third bedroom. Life had become a dreary round of chores from which there was no escape. Sometimes, as she lay in bed beside Anthony, he would turn towards her, but any attempt at making love always ended with him saying, "Sorry, my darling, I can't," before falling asleep. Watching Anthony sleeping one afternoon, she could see her future life mapped out before her; she could see only a vast monotonous desert with no relief in the landscape.

Was this what she had left Densbury for? She remembered with bitterness telling her Ma that one day she would be mistress of Baythorpe Hall and that she and Anthony would raise their children there. Now the reality was that there were to be no children, ever. For years to come she would be nursing an invalid husband.

She raised her eyes and looked up at the wall where a Victorian sampler worked by a ten-year-old little girl, decorated the plain cream wall. She read:

I slept and dreamt that Life was Beauty
I woke and found that Life was Duty

Annie laid her head on her arms and wept until she had no more tears to shed.

Chapter 18

Annie's depression gradually lightened as Christmas approached. Anthony's breathing seemed to be easing with the medication prescribed plus the good food not enjoyed by the rest of the population. With business-like foresight, Will Gladwell had instructed his head gardener not only to turn over the flower beds to growing more vegetables, but had set some of the men to constructing hen houses and pigsties in order to provide a nourishing and varied diet for the family and in particular, Anthony.

"Let's do some painting just like we used to do," Anthony begged. "If you wrap me up well in my rugs, I am sure I could sit outside for a while with you."

The morning sun having warmed the paved area just outside the kitchen, Annie agreed to setting him up with his easel and paints. He had decided on painting the view of the Hall across the grassed area where he and Annie had first met to paint as children, whilst Annie had opted for a view of the long beech hedge. The memory of Lavinia's violent onslaught would never leave her, but it no longer had the power to grip her in a spasm of terror waking her in the night.

An hour or so passed quietly by as the two tackled their chosen subject. Annie was so absorbed in her theme, she did not notice that Anthony's rugs had slipped to the ground as he drifted into a deep sleep. It was only the sound of the living room clock chiming twelve that reminded Annie it was time for her to prepare lunch. She looked over to where she had placed Anthony's wheelchair. Slumped motionless in a foetal position, his lips blue with cold, he was scarcely breathing.

"Oh, my God! No!" She knelt by his side, rubbing his hands to restore some circulation, before struggling to manoeuvre the cumbersome wheelchair over the threshold into the warm kitchen. Gradually, his eyes fluttered open as the heat breathed life into his thin frame.

"I'll call the doctor," she said, holding his body close to hers.

"No, don't leave me, Annie. I was having such a lovely dream. We were painting together just as we did when I was a schoolboy home for the holidays. Do you remember how I was painting the grounds in front of the house and you came along and somehow made the picture come to life? You were the prettiest girl I had ever seen." He held her hand in his. "And you still are, my darling."

"Is that what you were doing, painting the same scene?"

Anthony nodded. "I'd nearly finished it when I must have fallen asleep."

Annie cradled his head in her arms. "We were painting together again, just like old times," she said. "Wait a moment and I'll see if yours is dry." She left him smiling at his memories while she went to his easel. Shocked at what she saw, she stood and stared in horror. It was not the painting he had described. The scene he had depicted was like something out of Dante's *Inferno*. Dead men being devoured by rats, mutilated men, their faces contorted in agony stared back at her from eyeless sockets from the canvas. All his suffering in the trenches was there. Not only was his once handsome body eaten away by corrosive gases, his mind was now eroded by his anguish. Suddenly ashamed of the self-pity which had caused her to weep with regrets at her bleak future, she returned to the kitchen.

"Not yet dry," she told him with a forced air of brightness. "Now let's see what we can find to eat. I won't call the doctor so

267

long as you promise to eat your lunch." She was a mother talking to her child.

It had been planned to spend Christmas Day at the main house with Annie and Anthony sleeping there over the holiday. Annie agreed with Thora that Anthony's worsening breathing problems would have been exacerbated if he had had to leave the overheated rooms at the Hall to be wheeled across the lawns in the cold night air to return to the Dower House. Exhausted herself, through nights of broken sleep nursing Anthony, Annie agreed was relieved at Thora Gladwell's practical suggestion. They would have separate, but adjoining rooms with Anthony being cared for by a nurse hired for the holiday.

"You have done so much for Anthony," her mother-in-law said. "It is time you had a rest. There's a long way to go before Anthony will be well enough to do much for himself."

The two women understood that this game of pretence had to be played, the pretence that one day Anthony would be fit and strong. To have openly admitted and accepted the inevitable would have been more than either could bear. Thora had already lost her daughter and now had to watch her precious son deteriorate gradually before her eyes.

"My parents would like me to spend Boxing Day with them," Annie explained. "I know Anthony will be fine here, but if he needs me, you will send for me, won't you?" She gave a little laugh. "Anyway, I expect he'll be so busy enjoying himself in his old home, he won't give me a second thought."

"But if he insists on your presence, we'll send Stokes to fetch you."

One of the reasons Annie did not want to spend too long over Christmas at Baythorpe were memories of herself and her ma having to work whilst their betters ate, drank, laughed and danced with no regard for the fact that their servants had to desert their families on this special day. She may have married into the Gladwell family but, deep down, she could not accept their callous attitude towards the women who worked for them.

It was with some relief that she kissed Anthony on Boxing Day morning telling him of her plans. "I'll be back later, my love," she promised. She called in at the Dower House on her way to pick up the presents she had wrapped for her ma and pa, Eileen and Danny.

When she walked through the door of her old home, Eileen had already arrived with Danny and was busy helping her ma in the kitchen. "No, you are not lifting a cup," her sister told her. "You look worn out as it is nursing poor Anthony." During her visits to the Dower House Eileen had not missed the daily drudgery that was now her sister's life. "It's a good job Anthony's up at the Hall with his parents. It gives us a chance to see our Annie, doesn't it?"

Her ma's absent-minded agreement caused Annie to raise an eyebrow. Why was she constantly glancing out of the kitchen window? Her pa provided the explanation. "Joe's joining us for dinner. He's home on a spot of unexpected leave, so we had to ask him, didn't we? Otherwise, he'd be all on his own."

A little flutter of happiness rose in Annie's heart on learning that he had not found another girl to take her place. "He's not married then?" she asked.

"Don't be daft, girl," her ma said. "We'd have told you if he was getting wed." With a toss of her head she went to rejoin Eileen in the kitchen.

Annie made an effort to carry on a conversation with her pa about Anthony's health and the Christmas she had spent at the Hall, all the while listening for Joe's knock at the door. Aware that her mother's eyes would be observing her keenly, she greeted Joe with a friendly, "Hello," adding that he looked well and it was nice to see him again.

"And it's nice to see you," he replied, a mocking smile lifting a corner of his mouth and creasing the fine lines round his dark eyes. "I do hope that you are settled in nicely at Baythorpe Hall with your family."

Annie met his scornful gaze with a direct stare. "My family is here, Joe. It is my husband who is at the Hall."

The exchange did not go unnoticed by Beatie. This was not the time for Joe and Annie to start arguing about things that should have been buried in the past. "Come along now, let's all make a start on our dinners before they go cold." She was relieved to feel the atmosphere lighten as all carefully avoided subjects which could cause pain. How could Danny bear to hear from Joe how bad things were at the Front when he had lost his brother? Joe kept up a flow of questions about the factory to which Fred replied at length.

"I don't miss the factory," Joe said. "In fact, I doubt if I shall return to Densbury after the war."

"I didn't think you ever wanted to leave Densbury," Annie could not hide her bitterness. It was Joe who had refused to move away and let her expand her artistic talent in a larger town. If only he had agreed, she would never have been lured away to London. "You always used to say everything you ever wanted was in Densbury, or have you forgotten?"

At that point, Eileen and her ma began to clear the dinner plates in readiness for the pudding, the clatter drowning Joe's whispered response to Annie.

"It still is, Annie."

As the afternoon wore on, Annie felt that she could not bear Joe's powerful physical presence any longer. "It's getting dark, Ma. I think I'll get back to Anthony. I've been out long enough." She stood up to kiss her parents and sister goodbye. "It was a lovely dinner, Ma, and it was so nice to be home again for a little while."

She was disconcerted to see Joe stand up at the same time. "I've got things to attend to before I go back," he said. "I'll just see Annie safely back to the Hall first. We don't want her wandering around in the dark." There was no request, just a simple statement which he did not expect to be challenged.

"You don't have to see me back," Annie told him when they were out of the house.

"Stop pretending, Annie." His voice was thick with emotion. "You know where we're going first."

In the faint light she could see the outline of his features, the high cheekbones, the set jaw and sensuous mouth as he bent to kiss her with a gentle savagery which left her breathless.

"No! We might be seen," Annie protested. "Please take me home."

"That is exactly what I intend to do," he told her, guiding her to the familiar back entrance to his cottage. "I've waited so long for this, little Annie Claydon, and so have you."

Annie knew that she should protest and tell Joe that she did not want him, but her whole body was aching with desire for the man who had always filled her with longing. As the couple went into Joe's home, the curtains twitched in the upstairs bedroom of the cottage opposite. Aunt Violet smirked. Her long vigil had borne fruit. She had known all along that her niece would soon be betraying her marriage vows to young Anthony Gladwell once Joe Langmead got anywhere near her. Watching the lights first switched on and then turned off, she did not need to guess what was happening between the two lovers. She considered the situation. Although it would give her great pleasure to tell her sister-in-law Beatie the news about her high and mighty daughter, she might be able to make more capital out of it at a future date. She noted the times of arrival and what Annie was wearing as evidence in case that young madam tried to deny it. A waiting game, that was what she would play.

Oblivious to the fact that they had been observed, Annie and Joe were lost in their love for one another. Joe was exultant at Annie's response. "I knew that Gladwell could never be enough for you," he repeated as Annie held on to him as if she never wanted to let him go.

When finally they left the cottage, Aunt Violet made a note of the time before answering her husband's call from downstairs, "What are you doing up there all this time, woman?" Violet grinned. He would not have understood what she meant by, securing our future.

"Oh, Joe, what have I done?" Annie was distraught and overcome with guilt as they approached the gates of Baythorpe Hall.

Joe held her roughly in his arms. "What have you done?" he asked. "You've shown me that you have married the wrong man and that we should be together."

"No! Anthony needs me!"

"He's got his family now. What are you to him? His nurse? Can he show you what love is between a man and a woman?"

Even as she acknowledged that much of what Joe said was true, she could not forgive herself for betraying Anthony. "My husband is a hero and he is dying. Do you really think I would sink so low as to leave him for you? I'm so ashamed! Go away, Joe Langmead. I never want to see you again!" Without turning her head, she ran towards the lights of the house, where Anthony would be waiting for her. She did not stop running until she reached his bedroom.

Bathing his forehead with a cool flannel, his mother was sitting by his bed. She turned on hearing Annie enter the room. "Annie! Whatever is it, child?"

"I was just so worried about Anthony." She pointed to the bowl of cold water. "Has he got a fever? Do we need to send for the doctor?"

Thora shook her head. "You are so good, Annie, but there really is no need to worry." She busied herself with placing the bowl on the washstand before sitting in one of the armchairs in the bedroom. "My husband and I have been talking. We think it would be better for Anthony, and you of course, if he were to remain here where we can give him full-time nursing care." She looked across to her sleeping son and her voice was full of sympathy for Annie as she said, "I don't need to tell you that he is not getting any better, Annie. You cannot make yourself ill trying to nurse him twenty-four hours a day."

Joe's words came back to her. 'He's got his family now.'

"Have you told him?"

"No, my dear, you must talk to Anthony. He will understand that you are not physically capable of nursing him night and day." Her eyes were moist with sadness. "My poor dear boy." She tiptoed across the room and was gone.

Annie sat for what seemed like hours watching Anthony's chest rise and fall with each difficult breath. How could she explain to him that he was so ill that they could no longer live in their own home? He would understand, but it would surely take away what hope he had for the future. She thought of the plans they had made before he went off to France, the plans to paint together in Stanley Salisbury's studio and become wealthy, famous artists. All that had been blown away with one breath of deadly gas. And what was to become of her? If Anthony were to die, would she be expected to be the dutiful daughter-in-law remaining at Baythorpe Hall? Since she and Anthony had had no children, it was more than likely that they would prefer to gently ease their former servant girl out of Baythorpe Hall back to where she belonged.

Anthony stirred in his sleep, opening his eyes and gazing round the room trying to fathom where he was. "I'm home," he said, a smile lighting up his drawn cheeks. "I'm home."

"Yes, and this is where we are going to stay," Annie said.

Anthony frowned as his mind absorbed what she had said. "You mean we aren't going back to our Dower House to paint together?" Now fully awake and aware of what she was saying, he tried to sit up in the bed, his agitated hands pushing back the bedcovers. "But I want us to be together, just the two of us."

"We will be, my darling, I promise, but you've been unwell and we need to stay here just for a little while so that your mother can help me."

Partly placated, Anthony sighed and lay back on his pillow. "You promise, we will go back?"

Annie smoothed back his damp hair from his hot temple. "Just let me bathe your forehead and then you'll feel better," she said.

"Will you stay with me tonight, Annie?" He gave a sigh of contentment as Annie nodded.

When night fell, Annie undressed and crept into bed beside her husband. Anthony held her hand for a while before closing his eyes and falling into a deep sleep. Annie lay awake most of the night, recalling the hours of mutual passion she had spent with Joe. Guilt washed over her in waves as she felt Anthony beside her, his ravaged lungs fighting to keep him alive. He was the bravest, dearest man in the world and she had treated him with contempt by going with Joe, but try as she might, deep inside, she could not deny the truth that she was still in love with Joe Langmead and wished with all her heart that she had never left him.

With each passing day, the doctor's visits became more frequent, often taking place during the night, with the result that Annie had to sleep in the adjoining bedroom. She could hear Anthony calling out her name in his fevered sleep and would come rushing through to him, only to be told by the nurse that he was sleeping peacefully.

It was the second week in March on a fine spring morning as the daffodils began to open their buds to the pale sun that Anthony died in Annie's arms. He had been awake most of the night, managing to talk to her and tell her of his love, reminding her of when they first met and their wedding day. That final burst of strength was his last before he fell into a deep sleep, his breathing becoming increasingly shallow until it ceased altogether.

Annie was scarcely conscious of the events of the next few days. Addressing her in whispers, red-eyed servants went round the house drawing all the curtains. The funeral arrangements were taken care of by Will Gladwell, who, as head of the household, barely consulted either his wife or Annie, merely informing them of what was to be. He had contacted Anthony's regiment so that his son would be buried with full military honours as befitted a decorated soldier of his rank. Annie was pleased when she heard from Hugo, Anthony's best man at their wedding that he was to come. Having seen the announcement in *The Times*, she had heard from the Salisburys and from Isabelle. Stanley and Diana sent their condolences, but would not able to attend the funeral. Apart from her family, it was Isabelle she needed to be near, and with this in mind informed Thora Gladwell that she would be putting Isabelle up in the Dower House. She did not say that the oppressive atmosphere in the Hall was driving her into a deep depression.

"It is all so gloomy and my dear Anthony was always so full of light and happiness," she told Isabelle once she had seen her friend settled into her room. "I can't tell you how glad I am that you are here."

Isabelle could see that it was only to be expected that her dear friend would look ill and exhausted after months of caring for Anthony knowing that he would never recover, but she felt there was something about Annie's pallor for which she, as a doctor, should be able to find a reason.

The day of the funeral, everyone was up before seven. Annie's breakfast, brought by Tilly, lay untouched on the table in her bedroom. After her bath, Maud, one of the older maids, lay out

Annie's mourning clothes on the bed. A long black skirt topped by a hip-length jacket, a hat with a heavy veil designed to conceal a widow's grief, were all there. As she surveyed herself in the long mirror of the wardrobe, her face seemed to have lost its pallor and was tinged with an unhealthy yellow. Her dear Anthony would have hated to see her swathed in the conventional black trappings of mourning.

My darling Annie, he had said in one of his letters from France, *when I think of you, I see colour and lightness and beauty. It is this vision of you which fills the dark days here with a shining brightness.*

"I'm so sorry, my love," she said, "for so many things." For taking him away from his parents, for alienating from his sister, and worst of all for betraying him as he lay dying.

It was as she sat sobbing on her bed, that Thora found her. "My poor dear girl. We know how much you loved our son and that is something we can never forget. You made him very happy. Come now, be brave a little while longer." Proud and upright, she took Annie's hand and helped her to her feet.

As a mark of respect, all the shops in Densbury had closed for the day as had the factory. Caps off, the men lined the street as the black-plumed horses drawing the hearse passed. The only sound was the occasional muffled sob from women who had suffered the grief of losing their own men in the trenches and for whom there would never be a funeral.

The cortege passed the fields on the right where the galas had been held for years until the outbreak of war. Annie glanced to the right once again seeing Anthony, his thick corn-coloured hair blown across his forehead as he drove into the grounds, while Joe, frowning at the attention paid to her by the son of the factory owner, clung jealously to her. It was there Joe had declared his love for her. Thankful for the thick veil concealing sad memories, she dragged her eyes away and tried to concentrate on the ordeal ahead of her.

The seats in the chapel had been allocated in order, first to members of the family, including Annie's parents and sister, and also to the men from Anthony's regiment. Friends such as Isabelle were seated towards the back of the chapel. Once all the allocated seats had been filled, the patiently waiting crowds were admitted.

Anthony's coffin, draped with the flag for which he had given his life, was carried into the chapel by six men from his regiment. Annie had asked for her wreath to be fashioned from spring flowers from the gardens at the Hall, a request which had at first taken his parents by surprise. "I don't want flowers from some strange hothouse," she had insisted. "I want him to feel surrounded by his home."

The hymns had been chosen by Anthony's mother, who knew what his favourites as a boy had been, a fact which caused Annie some pain. Coming from such different backgrounds, she had never known Anthony as a boy; her first meeting had been with the shy seventeen-year-old who had helped her down the backstairs to the kitchen when she had been trying to balance a bucket of coal and Lavinia's morning tea service.

The brief committal at the graveside was restricted to close family members only, the remaining mourners waiting at a respectful distance until the Gladwells had departed for the Hall. There were to be the usual refreshments provided at the Hall, with more set out in the Town Hall for workers at the Gladwell factory. Old Will Gladwell had made sure that the death of his only son would be marked by the whole town.

Once inside, she told Thora that she was going up to her room and that she would come down after removing her heavy hat and veil. "I feel a little unwell," she explained, "but I must thank everyone, especially Anthony's friends from his regiment. I don't want them to see me hiding behind this veil. Anthony would not have liked it."

"As you wish, my dear," Thora said, admiring her daughter-in-law's courage.

The large dining room and adjoining drawing room were filled with the invited guests talking, eating and drinking. There was a sudden hush as Annie appeared and began to circulate amongst the groups. Making polite conversation and replying suitably to words of condolence was made easier with Hugo and Isabelle supporting her and moving her on when some guests tried to monopolise her.

"Have I spoken to everybody?" she asked Thora. She did not hear Thora's response as black circling shadows swirled in threatening patterns in front of her eyes, nor did she hear the anxious cries, as she sank to the ground.

Isabelle and Anthony's doctor were hovering at her bedside when she surfaced from her dead faint. Isabelle was applying a cold compress to her forehead, while Doctor Sharman talked in quiet tones to Anthony's mother. He was asking her to remain while he examined Annie more closely. "I have some idea of what caused her to faint, but I need to speak to her first."

Annie was too weak to protest as Isabelle helped Thora to undress her. The doctor's questions puzzled her. No, she had not suspected there was anything physically wrong the past three months, attributing changes to fatigue and worry over Anthony's state of health.

"You're three months pregnant, my dear," he said. "A cause for celebration on such a sad day, I think."

"I can't believe it," Thora Gladwell said. "Oh, Annie isn't it wonderful? You're giving us Anthony's child." The agony of losing her only son and the pain of seeing him buried in the cemetery half a century before his time was all washed away on hearing that there would be Anthony's child at Baythorpe Hall. "I must tell Will."

One servant girl who had brought hot water to the bedroom rushed down the back stairs to convey the news to the cook and

278

housekeeper. "I tell you, it's true, cross my heart," she kept saying.

"Well, we'd better not say too much until Mrs Gladwell tells us for sure, so keep your mouth shut for the time being," Cook instructed her.

Many of the guests had left discreetly seeing Annie's obvious distress. Those who remained were astonished to see a happy, smiling Thora Gladwell whisper in her husband's ear and they were even more amazed to see his features light up as he swept his wife up in his arms and kissed her in front of everybody.

Annie lay in bed hardly daring to speak. She could not tell Isabelle that the child in her womb was Joe Langmead's and not Anthony's. Counting back the days and checking her dates, it was all too obvious what had happened on Boxing Day. How could Joe have let her get pregnant! Anthony had not been able to make love to her ever since he had returned from the trenches, yet she was going to have to pretend that it happened once at Christmas. Worse than that, she was going to have to spend the next few months watching the Gladwells happily looking forward to becoming grandparents. After that, she would spend the rest of her life living a lie.

As the date of her delivery drew nearer, she came to a decision. Since Joe had left Densbury for good, he would never see the child and in any case would never know that Anthony was not the father.

She remembered what she had said to her ma. "One day, I shall be mistress of Baythorpe Hall and bring up my children there."

Annie's pregnancy proceeded with no health problems and on September the twenty-sixth, nineteen hundred and seventeen, young George was born, heir to the Gladwell fortune.

Chapter 19

At a year old, George proved to be the miracle who brought a smile to the face of his elderly grandpa. With the factory still being capably managed by Fred Claydon, Will Gladwell had an excuse not to follow the routine he had followed for over forty years. "I may drop in this afternoon," he would tell his wife, then a game on the carpet with his grandson would make him forget his previous intentions.

"George has brought this house to life again," Thora said to Annie one morning. Her smile faded as she went on, "It's you I am worried about, Annie. What has happened to your painting? You can't spend all your time caring for young George."

Annie shrugged her shoulders in an attitude of resignation. "What else can I do? He's my child."

"Yours and Anthony's." Annie winced at these words. "Anthony wouldn't want you to give up your wonderful painting to care for his son twenty-four hours a day. We've been thinking about this." Presumably Thora meant herself and her husband, Annie thought. "I can't manage that lively little boy on my own."

Thora's eyes lit up. "He's so like Anthony when he was a baby, always full of life. I know he's dark where Anthony was fair, but he brings back so many happy memories." Remembering why she had decided to speak to Annie, she went on, "What I'm trying to say, Annie, is that we need a nanny, someone who can look after him while you get on with your painting in the Dower

House." Seeing Annie's questioning look, she added quickly, "It will be your decision, Annie, but do think about it."

"You mean I could get back to work again for part of the day?" Any feelings of guilt at having to desert her baby were swept away as she looked at her fingers itching to hold a paintbrush again. "I think it is a wonderful idea. Oh, Thora, you and Will are so good to me!" It still felt a little uncomfortable calling her in-laws by their first names, but both had insisted on it soon after Anthony's funeral, saying that it would seem odd for their future grandchild hearing his or her grandparents addressed so formally.

"Of course, it will have to be someone you approve of. We'll start looking right away. I'll get the Dower House aired and cleaned in readiness for you." Neither referred to the fact that Annie had not set foot in it since Anthony's death. "It will be a new beginning for you."

There was an element of selfishness in Thora's efforts to make Annie feel settled and contented at Baythorpe Hall. Her daughter-in-law was still a young woman and if she were to marry again, would take their beloved little George to live with her and her new husband. Having lost both their daughter and son, the Gladwells had made George the centre of their lives, effectively dulling the pain they had thought would never ease, and now neither could contemplate losing their reason for living. He brought light to the whole household with the servants having to be reminded to get on with their tasks instead of cooing over this dark-eyed mischievous little boy.

The nanny appointed had been recommended by one of Thora Gladwell's friends, her own grandchildren now away at school. Sarah Catchpole, a sensible woman in her mid-thirties seemed to be perfect. With mousy hair pulled back in a tight bun, glasses which kept slipping to the end of her nose, and a thin, bony frame, she was not beautiful, but when she smiled, everyone else had to smile too. Little George was captivated the moment she picked him up and said, "You and I are going to get along fine, young man."

Will was not quite so pleased with the arrangement, feeling that he was going to be pushed into the background. "A boy needs a man's influence," he insisted. "We don't want him growing up to be a mother's boy." Annie felt a cold chill grip her heart as he went on, "I'll put his name down for his father's school. Boarding school is the making of a boy."

"Not so fast," Thora chided him. "Annie will have the last word on where he goes to school."

Annie was not so sure. When Will Gladwell wanted something, he was master. There would be some battles ahead.

These battles were ended when the joyous news rang out that the war was over, with the Germans conceding defeat and laying down their arms on November the eleventh and agreeing to sign the armistice. Armies were disbanded and soldiers sent home to seek work in civilian life. Those obviously shell-shocked were cared for in hospitals, but the majority whose symptoms were not so marked, were demobilised with no possibility of ever working again.

Will Gladwell departed for the factory to give Fred Claydon instructions for the factory to be decorated with the national flag. All workers were to be given a day off with pay so that they might celebrate the good news. The main beneficiaries of Will Gladwell's goodwill gesture were the landlords of the public houses, who having had a thin time during the war, were loud in their praise of this generous employer.

For Annie, the ending of the war did not signal a great change in her situation. Her routine remained much the same, with part of the day devoted to her art, part to spending time with her young son and visiting her parents with him on Sunday afternoons. It was during one of these visits that her pa mentioned Joe.

"We had a letter from Joe just after he got demobbed. He says he's not returning to Densbury. Well, there's nothing to keep him here, I suppose. And he's landed on his feet. Apparently, his old colonel has taken an interest in him and is lending him the money to set up a gents' tailors in London. We'll supply the cloth, so it seems that the factory will get some benefit. With no more uniforms to be made, old Mr Gladwell will be pleased to get his customers where he can."

"That's nice for Joe," Annie said. "What about the cottage?" Why was it she had mentioned that? Did she really want to remind herself of that afternoon when George had been conceived and when she had told Joe that she never wanted to see him again?

"He's selling it. He's asked your pa to see to it. He just doesn't want to come back here, though I suppose he might come and see us one day."

The conversation then turned to Eileen and Danny expecting their first child in the New Year. "It'll be nice for the Parfitts, what with losing their Aaron in the war. A bit like it is for Mr and Mrs Gladwell, having young George to remind them of Anthony," Beatie said. "Oh, sorry dear, I didn't mean to upset you," she added, seeing Annie's stricken expression.

It seemed to Annie that everywhere she went, there were constant references to Anthony as father of her child. How was she going to get through each day living a lie? Yet, to tell the truth would rob him of the comfortable life he would have as Will Gladwell's grandson.

Her only relief came in getting back to her painting. With Sarah Catchpole safely settled into Baythorpe Hall, Annie felt able to spend more and more time at the Dower House. Now that it had been aired and cleaned, it was once again a pleasant haven where she could invite friends such as Isabelle to stay away from the main house free from the constraints of having to make polite conversation with the Gladwells. She had not seen Isabelle since the day of Anthony's funeral and although Isabelle had been present when Annie's pregnancy had been diagnosed, had been so involved with her hospital work that she had not seen her old friend with her baby son.

"I've told Sarah to bring him down from the house at three o'clock. That will give me time to settle you in, get some lunch and make us a pot of tea," Annie told Isabelle when she met her off the midday train. "We've got so much to catch up on."

At three o'clock promptly, the high pram wheeled by the cheerful Sarah was seen descending the driveway. Annie rushed outside to pick George up. "Come back in an hour," she told the nanny. "That will give you time to give him his tea and bath him. I'll come and say goodnight to him at six."

Proudly holding him in her arms, she went back into the tiny sitting room where Isabelle was waiting patiently to see her friend's baby. "Here, take him."

As Isabelle cradled the little boy tenderly, she stared hard at him as he opened his dark brown eyes and frowned at this stranger who was holding him. "My God!" Quickly regaining her composure, she said, "He is a lovely little boy."

"You mean he doesn't look like Anthony, don't you?" Annie could read what was going through Isabelle's mind.

"No, he's got more of a look of you and he is beautiful." Isabelle was not going to be drawn into making Annie confess a secret that should not be shared, but how many times had she seen those dark eyes and that frown when Joe was watching her painting on the meadows with Annie?

The two women played with George until it was time for his nanny to collect him and take him back up to the house. With the baby to distract them, there was little opportunity for the two to discuss what was happening in Isabelle's life.

"What about that nice young doctor you were friendly with?" Annie asked.

Isabelle was silent for a moment or two, struggling to think of the right words. "I really did love him, but I just could not marry him. He wanted to get out of London and set up his practice somewhere in the country. Besides, one of his conditions was that I should give up being a doctor. Can you imagine that? I would have had to go and live in the country and play the doctor's nice wife. I just couldn't, Annie."

Annie nodded. That was how it had been with Joe. He wanted her to give up her painting to stay at home as a compliant wife. In spite of what she had suffered, she knew she had chosen the right path and so had Isabelle. She understood what a difficult decision it had been for Isabelle. "I know, Isabelle. Do you remember when we planned what we were going to do when we grew up? You were going to London to be a doctor and I was going to be a famous artist."

"Yes, and Joe was so cross with us," Isabelle recalled. "But we did it, didn't we?"

Half laughing and half crying, the two girls hugged one another. "Yes, we did," Annie said. "And now I'm back here in Densbury where I started. If it hadn't been for the war, Anthony and I would have stayed in London."

"Yes, and Anthony would have remained estranged from his family and you wouldn't be living at Baythorpe Hall with your beautiful baby boy."

"If, if," Annie repeated. "You know, I've heard from the Salisburys. Stanley wants me to spend some time in London partly at the studio and partly studying portraiture. I'm very tempted. I'd love to do a portrait of George, but I couldn't do him justice. Besides, it wouldn't be fair on the grandparents leaving them with such a young child."

"Well, they wouldn't be on their own with the capable Sarah to hand, would they? Come on, admit it, you can't bear to leave him," Isabelle teased.

The decision was taken out of Annie's hands the following February during a bitterly cold spell. Thora had taken to her bed complaining of a bad headache and feeling feverish. It was while Annie was sitting talking to Will in the drawing room after dinner that Thora's personal maid knocked at the door.

"It's Mrs Gladwell, sir, she's not at all well and she's talking all sorts of nonsense."

"Quick, Annie telephone the doctor," Will instructed. "I'll go up and see what's to be done."

It seemed like ages before Annie could get through to the exchange and then to the doctor. His wife told her he was out. "It's influenza. My husband is working day and night, but I'll tell him the minute he gets in." She didn't add that most of his patients were dying from what was proving to be a particularly vicious form of influenza and that the whole country was in the grip of a killer.

It was in the early hours, as Will held his wife's hand and while Annie tried to cool her with a cold compress, that Thora gave a little sigh and died. In the space of two years Will Gladwell had lost his wife and his son.

"If I didn't have you and young George," he said to Annie once the last of the mourners had left, "I think I'd want to follow my Thora. The two of you make my life worth living." For the first time, Annie noticed how deeply etched were the lines running from his nostrils to his chin, so deep that his once ruddy cheeks now sagged in a grey expression of defeat. She realised that Will Gladwell had become an old man overnight.

Her dreams of spending two days a week in London were once again postponed.

She wrote to the Salisburys to tell them that she would have to wait a little while longer before she could take Stanley up on his offer to help her resume her career In the meantime, she would continue painting in her Dower House studio.

Stanley's reply delighted and surprised her.

Dear Annie

You may not believe this, but I have acquired a motor car and have now become a reasonably competent driver. Would it be possible for me to come and visit you in Densbury? I am hoping to stage a vernissage very shortly and would be grateful if I could collect some of your work. Many of my customers have been inquiring about you, wondering when you will be exhibiting once more.

Yours affectionately
Stanley Salisbury

Annie wrote straight back to invite him as well as Diana and the children, but Stanley decided that talk of business matters would not be possible especially with an excitable Orlando who would now be about sixteen years old and wanting to know everything about Annie's life in Densbury and demanding that she return at once to London. Will Gladwell agreed that he would look forward to meeting Stanley Salisbury, who through a mutual acquaintance had first taken on young Anthony to learn the skills of an artist.

A week later, Stanley drew up in a large black motor car, which caused a little flurry of excitement amongst the younger men working at Baythorpe. Will went out to greet him and take him into his study for a drink. Very politely, Stanley indicated that he needed to see Annie as well and it would be as well if the three of them met together.

The lunch party went very well, with Will becoming quite animated hearing Stanley praising Anthony's work. "I was looking forward to promoting him after the war. He had a promising career ahead of him."

Although not strictly true, it caused Will to shake his head ruefully. "You know, I never really believed he had it in him. Perhaps we don't know our children well enough."

"Stanley wants me to go back to London for two days a week," Annie explained to her father-in-law, "but I don't like to leave you and George."

"What?" Will was astounded. "But he will be well looked after what with me and Sarah. And if it's only for two days a week, he will hardly know you're gone."

"There you are, that's settled then." A beaming Stanley raised his glass. "Here's to Annie and a brilliant future."

Annie then took Stanley down to the Dower House where he chose half a dozen of her canvasses to load into his car. He pulled a face on seeing her attempt at capturing George's likeness. "A little instruction in the art of portraiture is what is called for. I will organise that for your first few sessions in London."

"Just one favour, Stanley," Annie begged. She went to a cupboard and took out the last of Anthony's paintings. "I have added a few embellishments here and there, but it is the last picture Anthony painted and I think everyone should see the horrors that our soldiers saw every day. Maybe it will help men to find other ways of solving the world's problems."

Such a serious speech from Annie surprised Stanley who studied the painting carefully. "I will see that this is exhibited for everyone to see," he said. "It will be our tribute to a very brave young man."

He placed the paintings in his car, leaving with Annie's promise to start soon after Easter. She watched in amusement as he manoeuvred the car through the gates of Baythorpe Hall. The rest of her life was about to begin and Annie was elated. At last, she could return to the life she had hoped would be hers. "I'm going to be famous, Granny, just as I promised you I would be."

She was about to go back into the Dower House to tidy up before returning to the house when she heard a familiar voice. "Aunt Violet, what are you doing here?" It was understood that the only members of Annie's family to visit the Hall were her parents, her sister and Danny's family.

"I see you are still entertaining your gentlemen friends." Violet's spiteful, boiled gooseberry eyes mocked Annie as she followed her into the Dower House.

"What do you mean?"

"Well might you look worried, you artful madam." She waved a bundle of papers in front of Annie's nose. "See, I saw you and Joe Langmead go into his house on Boxing Day. I've written down the times and what you were wearing, so you can't deny it. That baby is his. Your little George is no Gladwell."

Annie felt icy fingers running down her spine as it became clear that her father's sister was intent on destroying her and her baby. "Who is going to believe that?" This was said with more bravado than she felt.

"Mr Gladwell might. He wouldn't be too pleased that the lad who he thinks is his rightful heir is the son of one of his factory workers. You'd soon be thrown out and back on the streets where you belong."

"So, you are the only one who knows?" Annie asked.

"Yes, and I have my price," her aunt said. She named a huge sum. "Should keep me and my family comfortable,"

"So, if you are the only one and the story gets out, then Mr Gladwell will know it is you who has spread this disgraceful rumour. How dare you come here with your filthy lies!" Annie was now in a fighting mood. No one was going to destroy what she had fought for.

"What do you mean?" Violet gave a cry of protest as Annie grabbed the papers and flung them on the fire.

"If this story gets out, then I shall make sure that Mr Gladwell knows who is responsible. I do believe your husband and son both have jobs at the factory – for the moment, is that right?"

Grey-faced, Violet nodded, beginning to see where the conversation was leading.

"And I believe you rent your cottage from Mr Gladwell, or have you forgotten? Perhaps you would like to start looking for somewhere else to live, Aunt Violet. Of course, if you would like to end up in the workhouse, please go on up to see Mr Gladwell, tell that proud man he is being made a fool of and see what he does. He'd never believe the likes of you, especially when I tell him you're trying to get money from me." Hands on hips, Annie was triumphant.

"You! Little Annie Claydon! Who would have thought you had it in you!" Her aunt was furious in defeat.

"Ah, but you forgot one thing, Aunt Violet. I'm not a Claydon. I'm a Gladwell now and it has taught me one thing and that is that a Gladwell never loses."

After the terrified woman had left, Annie sat down for a good half hour and considered the interview she had had with her aunt. With the evidence reduced to ashes, and Violet terrified of retribution, she was confident that the issue had been settled, but she had to acknowledge that her aunt had had the means of destroying what she had carefully built up. With Joe permanently in London now that his cottage had been sold, no one was going to see him in Densbury to compare likenesses and speculate.

Joe Langmead was out of her life for good.

Chapter 20

Leaving George for two whole days while she was in London was going to be painful, Annie knew and could not be compared with leaving him for a few hours while she worked in the Dower House, but she had promised Stanley that she would start after Easter. She gave instructions to her father-in-law and to her nanny that if George were to fall ill, she was to be sent for at once.

"Of course," Will assured her. "In any case, if Sarah here thinks that we need to call the doctor, we will, there'll be no shilly-shallying."

"There is one more thing I would like us to agree on. I would really prefer George to have the company of other children." Seeing Will's look of disappointment, she went on, "It's wonderful that he has you giving him so much attention, but he does need to be with children now and then." Annie paused, as a chill reminder of her situation threatened to bring tears. "Remember, Will, he is never going to have any brothers or sisters, but he does have a cousin."

"Ah, yes, your sister's little boy. I remember now. I bumped into the Parfitts only the other day and they were telling me about their grandson, young Aaron, named after their boy they lost in the war."

"Well, it would be nice if they could spend some time getting to know one another. George is two and a half and Aaron is two so they should be able to play together. I don't want George to grow up thinking he is the centre of the world. He has to learn to share," Annie said.

"Hmm, you're right," Will conceded. "Why don't you ask your sister to bring her boy up to the Hall on the mornings that you are in London."

Anne was surprised and thrilled that Will had agreed without placing obstacles in her way. "Wonderful!" She clapped her hands. "I think two hours would be plenty before they start fighting."

"Don't worry, Mrs Gladwell," Sarah said, her twinkling smile showing that she knew what two-year-old boys could be like. "I won't let that happen. They'll both have to learn to share."

Annie's first visit to London in April was to be a settling in and taking stock time. It was almost like going home being welcomed into the Salisbury house once again, except that Katherine and Orlando were no longer little children in need of an nanny. Emily Jane the baby of the family was coming up to her ninth birthday and insisted that she was to be treated just like her older brother and sister. A very determined little girl with her mother's violet eyes and long-fringed black lashes, very much like Orlando, she looked as if she had inherited Diana's artistic talent together with her father's drive and determination.

They sat in the comfortable drawing room drinking tea and eating muffins on the first afternoon of Annie's visit, after she had unpacked her things and settled herself into the pretty bedroom made ready for her. "So, tell me, what are you all doing?" she asked.

Katherine had taken a secretarial course in order to help with her father's business. With her long brown hair now worn in a fashionable shorter cut and her high-necked white blouse and ankle-length skirt, she was every inch the modern secretary.

"She keeps me in order," Stanley laughed. "I do believe the profits have doubled since Katherine took over. I don't know what I will do if that young art dealer, Frank Devonshire wins her heart. If she starts to work for a rival in business, I'll go under."

Katherine blushed at the reference to her admirer. "Papa!" she protested.

Orlando was studying at Art College. "It's really fascinating, Annie. You know, I thought I could paint and now I find I don't know anything." Huge round eyes mirrored his amazement at this discovery. "One day I'll be as good as you, Annie."

"I think you are already better, Orlando. I've got to go back to school to learn about portraiture. My portraits have no resemblance to the sitter. Either their noses are too big or their chins too pointed, but somehow they are all wrong."

"Which reminds me, Annie," Stanley interrupted. "I've arranged for us to meet your tutor first thing tomorrow at the college, so that we can work out a schedule to fit in with your visits." He closed his eyes for a moment, as if seeking inspiration or perhaps courage for what he had to say next. "The studio." He studied Annie's serious face, uncertain of her reaction. "That is where you will be working."

"I know that, Stanley, and I know what you are going to say. It was where I met Anthony again and where we spent so many happy hours together. I won't feel sad there, I promise you. Quite the contrary, I'm sure it will make me want to achieve more for Anthony's sake."

Stanley coughed. "You're quite sure, Annie?"

"Of course she's sure," Diana said. "Annie's looking to the future especially now that she has George, isn't that right, Annie?"

Annie smiled and nodded. "I can't wait to get started." As the maid came in to clear away the tea things, Annie asked about the old nanny, Ivy Goodman. "I'd love to see her again. If it hadn't been for her, I would never have met all of you."

"Ah," Diana explained. "When she came to retire, we gave her the choice of staying here with us or moving out. It so happened that an old friend, also a retired nanny, was interested in buying a little house down by the sea in Sussex, so the two moved in together there. She does come and visit us from time to time and we've been to see her. Once she hears about you, she'll be on a train right away."

Annie was hardly able to sleep that night. Would the college tutor think her good enough? Would she worry about George too much to be able to concentrate on her work? All her fears lifted faster than the morning mist once she had seen her old principal, James Dornway. He had been at the exhibition destroyed by Lavinia Gladwell and had seen Annie's talent for himself. "I wondered what had become of that promising young artist and here you are. Welcome to the college."

Stanley took her to lunch at a small Italian restaurant in Bond Street, encouraging her to try at least one glass of the excellent red recommended by the proprietor. "Now the war is over, we are finding so many good wines kept to celebrate the peace, that we are having difficulty in getting through them," he laughed.

Annie was not too sure about drinking before facing the studio. It was not as if she needed alcohol to bolster up her courage. On the contrary, she felt that the visit would remind her of some of the happiest moments of her life. When Stanley handed her the keys to the studio, saying that he had some business to attend to at the gallery and would she let herself in, she was content to do so. "I'll be with you in half an hour or so," he said. "Have a good look round and see if there is anything lacking. I want it to be just right for when you start next week in earnest."

The massive plain oak door was as she remembered. Once the door was unlocked, it needed a hefty push to open it. How many times had she meant to tell Stanley to get the locks and hinges oiled? Anthony was always promising to do it, but somehow once they were both engrossed in the excitement of completing a picture, everyday problems such as rusty hinges had been forgotten. For a full minute, Annie stood in the doorway. The easels were exactly as she remembered, the paint-spattered cloths covering half-finished works, the rickety chair on which she used to sit warming her fingers round a cup of tea, while she considered what to do next – nothing had changed. Was that still the same cobweb hanging like a fragment of torn lace on the high window? Feeling an exhilarating lift throughout her whole being, she rejoiced; it would be just like old times, she told herself. Just as swiftly, a dark corrosive blackness descended on her. No! How could it be the same? There was no Anthony to swing her round off her feet whenever he was in a happy mood. She walked over to the easel where he used to stand struggling to find the right mix of shades to bring his canvas to life. It was as if she could hear his voice again, "Annie, what do you think I should do with this?"

She collapsed on the bench just inside the door. Whatever madness had come over her to think that she could recapture those carefree days, days filled with hope for a bright future as one of London's rising stars in the art world? Seeing Anthony's easel, she would be reminded daily of their marriage, of how she had betrayed this dear kind friend, and how she was still betraying him and his father with George, Joe's son. "I can't do it," she said.

"Annie!"

"Oh, it's you, Orlando. What are you doing here? Shouldn't you be at college?"

The young man beamed. "Guess what, Annie, Papa says I can spend an afternoon at the studio when you are here. He says it will be good experience for me watching you work. I can't tell you how lucky I feel. It will be like old times when you and I used to paint together in the schoolroom. Do you remember, Annie?"

"But, I don't know," she began to explain to an excited Orlando who was trying to take in all the sights of this workshop where he would be working with his beloved Annie. "I've got to…"

At that moment, a shaft of bright sunlight pierced the dusty window pane turning the fragile grey cobweb into a curtain of delicate golden lace. Standing with his back to the window, eager and joyful, Orlando was surrounded by this halo of sunshine. Touched by his charm and enthusiasm, Annie recognised in him the young schoolboy Anthony had once been and knew then that the sorrows of the past would be gently laid to rest once she took up her palette.

"I hope Orlando hasn't been annoying you." Stanley Salisbury's voice echoed from within the high studio walls. "I'm so sorry to have left you for so long," he said.

Annie shook her head. "He's been delightful company." Did Stanley really think that she had not recognised his ploy in sending Orlando in to talk to her, knowing that she would be seeing ghosts from the past and questioning her wisdom in returning to London? "There is one condition, though. Once I've honed my portraiture skills, I would like to have Orlando as my first subject. If I can capture his joy of living on canvas, then I will carry on doing more."

"I think we can agree to that, can't we, Orlando?" Stanley was satisfied that his innocent deceit had worked.

In the following weeks, there were times when Annie questioned her wisdom in attempting portraiture. To her it seemed that there was always something lacking in the eyes of her subjects; technically accurate with the colour of the irises correctly transferred to canvas, there was an air of lifelessness about them.

"I can't do it," she complained to her tutor. She placed her palette on the stool beside her. "I might just as well stick to turning out pretty landscapes."

Harry Bailey, her tutor, laughed. "A little self-criticism is always a good sign. I can't bear arrogant students, but don't you think you are taking it a little too far?" He pointed to her subject's eyes. "Now, tell me, what is this model thinking? What sort of a life does she lead? Is there joy, misery, or just a fatalistic acceptance of the life of a model who has to sit still for hours in order to earn a few shillings? I can't see any of these things in her look."

Annie stared at him as understanding swept through her. She remembered Diana taking her to visit the exhibition of Sylvia Pankhurst's portraits of working women. It was the expression of total acceptance of a life devoid of hope for the future in her subject's eyes that the artist had conveyed. It told the world that this woman had to work long hours of drudgery, was concerned for her children left in the care of a cruel childminder, and knew that most of what she earned would be seized upon by a bully of a husband to spend in the alehouse. "I know what I have to do now," she said.

First, she would have to go back to Densbury and ask Will's permission. His blank refusal shocked her. "It would disrupt work," he grumbled. "No, it wouldn't do at all. Can't you see all the other women gawping at what is going on instead of paying attention to their machines?"

"If I could just sit in my father's office and take a look at some of the women and then choose one woman, I could do some preliminary sketches." Seeing him waver, she went on, "There's a tiny area at the back of the manager's office where I could set up my easel and no one would be any the wiser."

"Ah, but what if your chosen subject doesn't want to be painted?" Will raised his black eyebrows.

"Hmm, I hadn't thought of that." Annie considered the problem. "I could give her a fee equal to her wages, then the factory would not lose, the other women would not feel that she was getting paid for sitting around doing nothing and I would get my portrait done."

Will nodded slowly seeing the logic of her argument. "Right, Annie, on one condition. If there are any complaints from the workers, then your father will be duty bound to inform me and it will have to stop. Is that understood?"

Annie understood perfectly. The project was going to need careful preparation. Her father would have to be consulted about the use of his back office and also about taking one of his machinists out of the line. He was not in a position to refuse once he knew that Will Gladwell had given his grudging permission, but made it clear to Annie that she would have to abide by his rules. Annie agreed that she would be as unobtrusive as possible, if she could just sit in his office on the first morning and watch the women working.

The ages of the women machinists ranged from teens to late forties, the former group cheerful, exchanging whispered gossip about their latest conquests, whilst the older ones had an air of resignation about them as they began one more week of monotonous drudgery. Annie's attention was drawn to one woman who appeared to be in her mid-twenties.

"That's Daisy Blakey, lost her husband in the war. She's got two young children. I believe her ma looks after them while she's here, but her ma's not too sharp and has been known to let them wander off. What she'll do when her ma has to be taken away, I don't know." Fred Claydon shook his head. "There are more than a few like her."

It was not Daisy who raised objections, but the new forewoman. "So, who's going to do her work while she sits up here?" A nasty sneer twisted the woman's mouth.

"You are," Fred told them. "She'll be up here with Mrs Gladwell for one day and provided that Daisy's work is covered too, you will all receive some extra in your pay packets." This suggestion had come from Annie and had been grudgingly accepted by her father-in-law, who had had to concede that she was a very determined young woman.

With lank, brown hair tied back hastily in a bun, tired hazel eyes underlined with fine lines and dark blue shadows, and a pale, pasty complexion, there was little to be seen of the pretty twenty-year-old who had married her soldier sweetheart before he went off to war, returning only once on leave to impregnate her with a second child before he was killed. Worried at being singled out by Mrs Gladwell, yet aware that it was an honour, Daisy sat with hands folded in her lap unable to look Annie in the face. If she had, she might have shown some resentment at the difference in their situation. Annie Claydon, once a machinist like herself and just a year or two older, was now mistress of Baythorpe Hall with servants to wait on her and enough money to sit around painting all day.

"Look at me, Daisy," Annie told her. "Tell me about your family."

Shy to start with, Daisy began to pour out the story of her marriage to Albert, the birth of the children and how hard it was with her mother not being "up to the mark", as she put it. "It's a real worry." The changing colour of her eyes reflected the tragedy of her life, as the green and gold flecks became dull giving way to a muddy dark green in which there was no ray of life or hope. A glow of excitement lit up Annie's face as the full impact of what her tutor had said, hit her. To get the sadness of the muddy green colour of Daisy's eyes on to canvas and yet convey the once happy girl was a challenge she was determined to win.

By the end of the day, Daisy admitted that it was easier working at her machine than sitting still all day for an artist. "I feel as if I ache all over."

"There are some people who pose as models at the art college for a living," Annie told her.

"Poor things!" Daisy looked shocked. "I wouldn't want to change places with them." A little shyly, she asked if she could see what Annie's sketch looked like. Peering over Annie's shoulder, she gasped. "Oh, Mrs Gladwell, to think that you were once..." she began, then corrected herself. "It looks just like me. You're very clever, aren't you?" With Annie's money tucked into her pocket, she let herself out of the office and back on to the factory floor where her workmates were just covering over their sewing machines prior to digging out as much information as they could about Mrs Gladwell.

Annie watched the young widow rushing out of the factory eager, no doubt, to check that her babies had come to no harm. She wondered what would have happened if she had married Joe and been left as an impoverished widow to bring up his children. Would she now look like Daisy, drab, with no hope or ambition for the future, except to get through each day with barely enough money to put food on the table?

Her priority now was to complete Daisy's portrait. "I'll start on Orlando," she told Stanley, "once Harry Bailey has said that this one is acceptable."

Stanley did not need to ask her tutor what he thought. Annie had captured the essence of Daisy, the vestiges of a happy young girl now trapped in the body and the world of a careworn mother with no one to share her responsibilities. It was all there in the sad eyes looking out at the world. A few more like that one and the exhibition he was planning for November nineteen-hundred and nineteen would be a post-war success which none of his business rivals could match. Once again, he blessed Nanny Ivy Goodman for finding this treasure in Densbury, a dear sweet girl with an abundance of talent.

"I promise I'll do Orlando as soon as I've completed a few more women's portraits," Annie had assured him. Finding suitable subjects was not easy, but Isabelle promised to ask some of her poorer patients if they would be happy to sit for her friend for a fee. The first three were not suitable. Annie could read cunning and avarice in their eyes and that was not what she wanted to portray. The fourth was a middle-aged grandmother left to rear four lively grandchildren after the death of her son in the war and that of his wife killed under the hooves of a runaway horse.

"I love them all, but it is so hard. Our local church helps out a bit with food and clothes, but they're growing so fast, I can't keep up with it all. I used to have a little cleaning job. I can still do a bit if my neighbour keeps an eye out for the kids while I'm at work." Aggie was exactly the subject Annie needed to add to her growing collection of portraits of working women.

Back at Baythorpe Hall, Annie spent her time playing with George, who had now become accustomed to the pattern of his mother's absences. One Saturday afternoon, she asked Sarah to bring him to the Dower House and stay with him to keep him amused. Although she had not mentioned her plan either to Will or Stanley, Annie had decided to paint a picture of George. More than anyone, she would know whether she could capture better than any camera the real essence of the human being who was her own child.

With Sarah to amuse him, George played happily with his toys while Annie made some preliminary sketches, many of which were discarded with a, "No, that's not right." One by one, they were thrown on to the fire. "Where is George?" she asked herself out loud.

At that moment, George looked up at his mother and frowned, his big dark brown eyes puzzled at her words. "Here, Mama, I'm here."

"Of course you are, my darling," she said, gathering him up in her arms and kissing him. That frown and the puzzled look were just what she wanted to capture. "Here, Sarah, take him back up to the house and give him his tea. I'll be along shortly."

It was past eight o'clock when Will sent a message to the Dower House to remind Annie that dinner was about to be served. Annie had just cleaned her brushes and was looking at the portrait of her little boy. His dark curls were rumpled, falling over his forehead, Annie having forbidden Sarah to brush his hair before she made her sketches. She gave a little laugh delighted that she had captured his puzzled frown at her words. His dark brown eyes seemed to be looking right into her, reading her innermost thoughts. With a sigh of absolute contentment at her achievement, she packed her easel and brushes away and made her way to the house for dinner. "Just wait until Stanley sees this," she said to herself.

Stanley was indeed overwhelmed when he saw it. "I must get Diana to come and see it," he said, "but I warn you, she will want one of Katherine and Emily Jane as well as the one you are doing of Orlando."

"I can't wait to get started," Annie promised. With the landscapes completed at the outbreak of the war and now the collection of working women's portraits together with those of the Salisbury family, she felt that there would soon be enough for Stanley to stage the exhibition before Christmas as he had planned.

It was Diana who threatened to spoil his dream of keeping Annie longtime as his protégé. "Have you ever considered that Annie might remarry and want to give up painting to have more children? You seem to have the mistaken idea that she is not a normal young woman and that she has shut herself away from the world for good."

Stanley patted his wife's shoulder. "Don't worry, my dear. The only man she would ever have married apart from Anthony was that Joe fellow she was engaged to. You can hardly see her with him now, can you? Annie has moved on to a different world."

Chapter 21

Annie took a deep breath before mounting the long, winding staircase to the first floor of the gallery where the exhibition was to be held. This was her first visit to the building since the interior was totally destroyed in the fire on that terrifying night when Lavinia had tried to kill her. Under Stanley's instructions, the architect had created a design with no reminders of the original, so that Annie's first impression was that she was in an entirely new gallery. The stairs had been widened and were now covered with a moss green carpet in contrast to the previous highly polished wood, so dark that the entrance hall and stairs had engendered a gloomy and oppressive air, far different from the present soft, warm welcome which now pervaded the area. Although the dark wooden floor of the gallery itself had been replaced with a similar one made of oak, the tiny chairs and small wrought iron tables where guests could sit and place their glasses of wine, gave an air of light and elegance.

Annie gave a start as she heard the main doors being opened, but it was only Stanley's men about to bring the paintings upstairs and hang them on the walls under his instructions. A breathless Stanley appeared a few minutes after Annie, explaining that he had been talking to the art critic of *The Times*, who had promised to attend the exhibition and write a critique of Annie's work in his weekly column.

"Oh, no! What if he thinks all of this is worthless?" Annie was shocked that Stanley had not consulted her beforehand. "I'm so afraid of letting you down."

"You could never do that, my dear. When he hears all the connoisseurs praising your work, he won't dare go against them for fear of looking foolish."

Having read some of this journalist's critiques before, Annie could only remember how acid his comments could be if he decided that the work he had seen was weak and showed little talent or potential for development. It was with her enthusiasm dampened by this news that she helped Stanley with her views on where each painting should hang, as he spent what seemed like hours, telling the men first to hang one picture in a particular spot, then changing his mind, once he had scrutinised it yet again. With quiet resignation the men obeyed his orders with only the occasional muttered comment to one another that he was the boss and they supposed he knew what he was doing. It was almost three o'clock before everything was to his satisfaction and he dismissed the men. "Katherine has arranged for our visitors to be served with wine and canapés," he explained to Annie.

He gave a delighted roar of laughter at Annie's "Do you think they will need to see my paintings through an alcoholic mist in order to appreciate them, then?"

"Not at all, but this is in the way of being something of a social occasion, a very special event to re-launch your career. Now, you are to go home and rest until dinner. Diana has asked Cook to serve a light meal early so that you will have plenty of time to get ready for the eight o'clock grand opening. We have to be here early. Katherine has seen to the advertising and I am expecting a large attendance. Now, off you go."

Diana was shocked at Annie's pale cheeks and dark-ringed eyes. "My dear, just look at you. Right, off to bed at once," she ordered. "I'll have something to eat and drink sent up to you later, but you are to lie down and not move, or else you will be exhausted this evening. You are going to need all your strength, Annie."

It was so unlike the gentle Diana to be forceful that Annie felt she had better obey her instructions. Besides, she had to acknowledge that Diana was right, and in spite of all the tension she was experiencing was asleep before she had been in bed many minutes.

When the girl who helped the cook arrived with a tray of tea and a light meal at five o'clock, Annie had woken feeling refreshed.

"Madam says you are to eat this and then I will run your bath and set out your clothes for this evening," Millie said, eying the green silk dress with its matching hat. The flared skirts of the war years had been replaced by designs more flattering to a young slim figure. The green dress with its tubular skirt finished several inches above the ankle, so that Annie had had to buy new black patent shoes with the latest slim strap showing off her trim ankles. Trying to maintain the decorum expected of a domestic was not easy for Millie. "Oh, Mrs Gladwell, it's so beautiful. When you look at it one way, it looks green and then it seems to change to blue." Suddenly remembering her place, she excused herself and fled.

Annie's earlier feelings of apprehension had faded, giving way to a rising excitement at the prospect of her paintings being on show to people who would really understand her work. Singing happily, she bathed, dressed and went down to meet Diana and Stanley.

"Well, well," Diana said. "No one will want to look at the paintings, they won't be able to take their eyes off you!"

Her prediction proved to be very nearly correct as the fashionably dressed wives of the art experts climbed the stairs to be greeted by Stanley and Annie. Once inside, the women whispered to one another, amazed that this beautiful young woman should be exhibiting what their husbands were describing as work possessing an outstanding maturity. "Where did Stanley Salisbury find her?" was the question being posed.

Being interested only in the reaction to her work, Annie was not aware of the women's gossip. She had planned with Isabelle that her friend would not greet her; instead she would mingle with the crowd and listen in to the conversations taking place about her work. After thirty minutes or so, there appeared to be no further new arrivals, so Annie joined Diana and Isabelle at one of the small tables, where Isabelle recounted some of the flattering remarks she had heard on her spying mission.

"Oh, Stanley needs me." Annie had seen Stanley beckoning from the doorway. "There must be some latecomers. I'd better go and greet them. I'll be back in a moment."

Some friends of Stanley who lived close by had arrived late and were apologising to him. Annie turned to show them into the gallery, at the same time summoning a waiter to bring them some wine. She did not notice the couple who had been waiting halfway up the stairs and who had now arrived at the door just as she was making her way back to her table.

"I think that must be everyone," she said to Diana and Isabelle before she sat down. "Any more and there won't be room to move."

"I trust there will be room for us." The sensuous voice with its deep resonant tones could belong to only one person.

Annie turned round slowly to face Joe and the woman who was clinging to his arm. Joe's dark eyes were teasing her with a mocking intensity which brought the colour to her cheeks. "How nice to see you again after all this time," she said. Joe's half smile turned to a simmering anger on hearing her banal greeting. "Do introduce me to your friend." Annie took in a short, plump woman in her forties who more than adequately filled the unbecoming red dress she had chosen to wear that evening. What was Joe doing with such a woman?

"Mrs Gladwell, my fiancée, Mrs Clara Lowndes," he announced, a brief upturn of his mouth showing that he had registered with some satisfaction Annie's fleeting look of dismay.

"How do you do?" Annie extended a gloved hand to this woman with whom Joe had chosen to spend the rest of his life.

Clara, too, was enjoying the moment. "My late husband Colonel Lowndes was able to give Joe financial backing for his London businesses and that is how we met." Her coy smile met with a stony look from Joe. Clearly he was not pleased at her reference to his being beholden to her financially.

"Do join us," Diana invited.

"Yes, please do, Joe," Isabelle chipped in.

For a moment, Joe appeared not to recognise her, but once he did, the animosity between the two was palpable. "Ah, Miss Anstruther."

"No, Doctor Anstruther, now Joe. Don't you remember all those years ago when I said I was going to be a doctor and Annie said she wanted to be a famous artist? We've both achieved our childhood ambitions. Aren't you pleased for Annie?" Isabelle's wheedling tones did not conceal the underlying triumph in her words, her revelling in this confrontation with Joe.

"I remember very well, and I can see that Annie has everything she has ever desired," he said quietly. Only Annie detected the hint of bitterness in his reply. "Thank you for the invitation to sit with you, Mrs Salisbury, but I think that my fiancée and I would like to see what Annie has achieved."

Mesmerised, Annie watched as the couple began at one end of the gallery, frequently stopping as Joe exchanged a few words with businessmen with whom he was acquainted. Please don't get to the other side, she prayed silently, as he turned from time to time to give her a look filled with longing. Annie's terror as he and Clara Lowndes crossed the floor to study the exhibits on the opposite wall fortunately was missed by Diana and Isabelle, both engrossed in talking to a guest. She stared in horror as Clara

Lowndes pointed to a portrait before glaring at Joe in fury. Motionless, Joe stood for several minutes in front of the portrait Annie had painted of George. How proud she had been to capture George's dark eyes and puzzled frown, that same frown which was creasing Joe's forehead as he stared at Annie in silent condemnation.

"We're leaving," she heard the woman hiss.

Joe appeared hardly to hear her as he made his way across the floor to Annie and bent to whisper in her ear. "How could you, Annie? He's mine."

The rest of the evening passed by in a blur of congratulations and some chaos as dealers fought to outbid one another in an attempt to secure one of Annie's paintings. The only one not for sale was the portrait of George. Even the dreaded critic from *The Times*, came up to her and kissed her hand. "You came, you saw, you conquered," he said.

It was after midnight when Annie finally fell into bed, tossing and turning as the nightmare of Joe's discovery filled her brain with images of sharp stabbing pain. When morning came, she struggled to maintain a façade of happiness.

"You poor child, you must be exhausted," Diana said at breakfast. "Why don't you go back to bed and rest? Stanley won't miss you; he's too busy with Katherine in his study going over his accounts."

"I'm so glad I didn't let him down after all he has done for me. I'm very relieved, but all I want to do now is get back to see my little boy." Annie did not add that she was afraid of what Joe would do next. "I need to collect some things from the studio. I've left one or two brushes I need. If I pick up a cab when I leave there, I can get to the station in time to catch the midday train to Densbury."

There was a cold, hostile feel to the studio as she entered on that dank November morning, a morning when she should have been enjoying the warmth of being feted as a promising young artist. Sitting on the rickety chair in front of a half-finished canvas, she agonised over what Joe would do. A pain that was almost physical forced a cry of anguish from her lips as she admitted to herself that it was Joe she loved and wanted. Seeing him with that woman, his fiancée, Annie now had to accept that whatever Joe had felt for her was now dead. Even worse, he must hate her for what she had done in concealing the truth about George. Would he now seek to destroy what she had built up for herself and, most importantly, George?

"Mrs Salisbury told me I might find you here." Filling the doorway with his massive frame, Joe paused. "I assume I am permitted to enter."

Annie shrugged her shoulders in an attitude suggesting defeat. "I've no doubt that you will do whatever you wish, Joe Langmead, even if it means tearing down your son's future."

Joe strode across the room and knelt at Annie's feet. He took her frozen hands in his. "Oh, my precious darling Annie, I've never stopped loving you. How could you hide our son from me? We made him together with our love." He was so near, she could feel the warmth of his breath close to her face.

Anger at what she saw as his self-righteous attitude made her retort, "What else could I do? You had gone off to London to start your business. I was left expecting a baby which the Gladwells assumed was Anthony's. Did it never occur to you that you might have given me a child or was it simply that once you had succeeded in making love to Anthony Gladwell's wife, you had got what you wanted?" Wrenching her hands free from Joe's grip, she stood up. "If I had told the Gladwells the truth I would have been thrown out in disgrace. My son would have been labelled a bastard and I would have ended up in the workhouse." She punched Joe hard in the chest. "I did what any woman would do to protect her child, so don't you come here telling me that I have done anything wrong just because your pride is hurt." She choked back a tear. "You've got your wealthy widow. The only reason you want to lay claim to George is because she can't give you children, but you want her money, don't you?"

Joe pulled Annie close to his chest, holding her tightly. "I never did want her. We are not engaged and I shall not be seeing her again. I have never loved anyone but you, Annie, and now I want us to be together as a family."

Her heart beating so loudly she could hardly hear what she was saying to Joe. "I love you, Joe, but I do not intend to be the wife you want. I made that clear when I first went to London. I made my choice to be a painter and that has not changed."

His jaw set in determined lines, Joe played his trump card. "I have sufficient money to support a wife and child. Once old Will Gladwell learns the truth, he won't have you or George at Baythorpe Hall. If you love me, you will go and tell him that the grandchild is not his. Tell him that George is mine."

Annie's tiny shoulders sagged in defeat. "You again, Joe, wanting the world to fit in with your desires. It will break Will Gladwell's heart, Joe, if I tell him the truth. He has nobody in the world now with Lavinia, Anthony and his wife all dead. George is his life. And what about George? He adores his grandpa."

"He is not his grandpa," Joe insisted.

"I will tell him, but how, I do not know," she promised. "Just give me a day or two to break the news to Will."

All the way back to Densbury on the train, Annie rehearsed in her mind the words she would use to tell Will that his adored grandson was not his and that Joe Langmead, his former factory manager, was the father. Would he be angry? Would the news cause him pain? Would he tell her to leave Baythorpe Hall at once? All three, she decided. And then what? It was strange, but she had to admit to herself that she had become used to living at

Baythorpe as if she belonged there. As Anthony's widow, it had always seemed right that she should live in his family home. Besides, she had grown rather fond of the autocratic man who was her father-in-law, although why she should after the way he had objected to her marrying his son and disinheriting him puzzled her. His motives became clear once she had become a mother. Will had been protecting his son, just as she now wanted to protect George. She tried to imagine what would happen once she had told Will the truth. George would be unhappy to leave his grandpa and the house which was the only home he had known, but children adapt and Joe would be able to provide them with a good standard of living in London. Best of all, she would be able to marry the man she had loved all her life, the father of her darling George. Weighing the arguments was easy; what was difficult was knowing what to do in the end, when at the back of her mind was the feeling that she did not want to live in London. Densbury was her home, the very town she had found stifling and which she had left in order to be in London. She wished that her granny could be here to help her choose which path to choose.

It was cold and dark when she alighted from the train at Densbury station. Not having notified Will that she would be returning late that afternoon, there was no Stokes to pick her up in the car and take her back to Baythorpe, which meant a long and lonely walk up the hill, a walk which would take her more than half an hour burdened as she was with her case. More time to think, she told herself as dark grey fog blankets wrapped themselves round her head and body freezing her to the depths of her soul. Barely able to struggle up the drive, she finally found the strength to pull the bell rope and lean against the door, praying that someone would hear and help her inside. It was Sarah, just about to take George his tea in the nursery who heard the bell and the cries for help.

Without waiting for the butler, Sarah placed the tray on the bottom stair and opened the huge doors. "Mrs Gladwell! Whatever has happened to you? Quick, into here." She helped Annie into the library where a huge fire was blazing in the wide hearth and settled her in one of the leather armchairs either side of the fireplace. "I'll get Cook to bring you a hot drink while I see to George," she said.

Will Gladwell, reading his newspaper seated in the other chair snatched his spectacles from his nose and leapt to his feet. "My dear girl! Don't tell me you walked all the way from the station with your suitcase on a night like this. You should have let us know. Stokes could have met you. Here, put this round your knees." He took the rug which had been on his lap and arranged it carefully round Annie's legs. "I'll make sure that a hot drink is on its way."

His kind solicitude for her welfare brought bright spots of stinging guilt to her cheeks at the thought of what she was about to say to him would crush the remaining hope he had for the future. It was a struggle to drink the hot tea and nibble the muffin dripping with butter, but gradually hunger and the realisation that she had had nothing since one slice of toast at breakfast, forced her to finish.

"There you are, Annie, I'm sure you feel better now." He waved his newspaper at her. "I've just been reading about your success last night. Listen to this." He proceeded to read out the glowing report of the art editor of *The Times*. "How proud Anthony would have been. And there's a special mention of a painting done by Anthony of his time in the trenches. It's in an exhibition of war artists. You didn't tell me about that."

"I didn't know that Stanley had succeeded in finding it a gallery," Annie told him.

Without thinking, Annie replied, "If it hadn't been for this wretched war, his other paintings would have been on show too, not only now, but for years to come."

"There, there, don't upset yourself, my dear. Just tell yourself that you are carrying on with your art for his sake and his son's."

With a jolt, Annie remembered the reason for her urgent return to Baythorpe Hall. She could not listen to Will referring to George as Anthony's son one second longer. She jumped up out of her chair and began to pace up and down the room. Where could she begin? Unable to face him, she walked over to where his mahogany desk stood underneath the window and leant heavily on it. "Will, there is something we need to talk about. Please don't judge me too harshly."

Very quietly, the old man said, "Tell me and we will see."

What he was about to say next was interrupted by the clanging of the doorbell and the butler's voice addressing whoever was at the door. Annie started hearing the butler say. "I will see if Mr Gladwell will receive you, Mr Langmead."

His smart coat spattered with mud where he had run up the rutted road leading from the station, his thick black hair dishevelled and falling over his eyes, Joe burst into the room. "Well, have you told him?"

Will Gladwell glared at the intruder. "Joe Langmead. I would remind you that this is my house and if you continue to address my daughter-in-law so rudely, I will have you thrown out. Sit down and mind your manners." Old age had not robbed the old autocrat of his authoritarian bearing. "And you, Annie, come along and sit down. It seems that you both have something to say."

Joe's attempt to begin was interrupted by the sound of a child shouting, "Mama! Grandpa!" as George came running into the room. The three-year-old ran across to Annie to be held in a tight embrace and kissed, before climbing on to his grandfather's lap for a cuddle.

Sarah went over to George to pick him up. "I'm so sorry. He heard voices and wanted to see his mama and grandpa. Now come along, young man, bed!"

Will scrutinised Joe's anguished face as George was taken away protesting to his bed by a determined nanny. "What was it you wanted to discuss, Joe?" He bent over to place a log on the fire. "Come along."

Joe clasped his hands in his lap. "There is no easy way of saying this, and I am sorry to cause you pain, but I now know that George is my son."

The old man nodded slowly as Annie and Joe waited for the expected outburst denying the claim. "Oh, yes, I know that," came the almost nonchalant reply. He leaned forward and patted Annie's hands. "You were a wonderful wife to my son. You cared for him night and day and made his last months on earth truly happy. When your pregnancy was announced, I knew that it was unlikely that Anthony could be the father. He had already confessed to me that his wretched illness had diminished him as a husband."

"But, why didn't you say anything?" Annie wept at the years of deceit. "You could have thrown me out."

"What, and see you and my grandson penniless and homeless? Do you really think I am so heartless, Annie?"

Joe leapt to his feet and thundered. "But he is not your grandson, so why this pretence?"

In reply, Will went over to his desk, took a key from his waistcoat pocket and unlocked one of the drawers, taking out a box, which he brought to show Joe. "Here, Joe, look at this photograph."

Joe studied the faded picture of a young man. It was an early one of Will Gladwell. Annie peered over his shoulder. "Why have you got this picture of Joe?" she asked.

"It isn't Joe, it is me as a young man, Annie."

Annie looked from one to the other. The dark eyes, the thick black hair and the touch of arrogance. She saw two men, both powerful and striving to be in control of others and yet who both possessed compassion and a capacity for love.

"I'm your father, Joe," Will said quietly.

"No!" Joe roared, leaping to his feet and kicking over a velvet-covered chair in his rush to seize the man who was claiming to be his father. He grabbed the lapels of Will's jacket. "I don't believe this stupid story. It's just a trick to prove you are George's grandfather so that you can keep him here." He released the old man. "You disgust me." He turned to Annie. "You don't believe it, do you? If I am his son, why did I spend my life living in that tiny cottage while Anthony lived like a lord, went to the best schools and never had to do a day's work, while I put in all God's hours at the factory to help keep him? No! I don't believe him, because if I did, it would mean that as my father, he rejected me and left me to live in poverty. Is this the sort of man you want to raise our son, Annie?"

Will took one more item out of the box and handed it to Joe. "Look at this, Joe, and if you say anything against the woman who wrote this, I will have you horse-whipped." His grim features quietened Joe.

Joe looked carefully at the photograph of a smiling young woman dressed in the uniform of a lady's maid of her time: long black skirt, high-necked black blouse and white cap. "My mother?" His hand trembled as he fought to control his tears. "So you gave her a child and left her to slave all her life in that cottage. And I am supposed to be pleased to learn that I have you for a father?"

"Read the letter," Will instructed.

My dear Will,

We have had many happy times together, but now that I am with child, they have to end. I will not marry you as you have asked. It would not be right. All I want is a home to rear me and my child. Ben Langmead has asked me to marry him and I have said yes to give our child a name.

I will have left your mother's employment by the time you receive this and will be married the day after.

315

Yours affectionately
Charlotte

"So you see, Joe, I did not abandon you and your mother. I bought the cottage and gave it to Ben Langmead together with an allowance. It was her wish that you should be brought up in ignorance."

"I don't understand. Why should she have done this?" Joe buried his head in his hands.

"For the same reason that Annie wants the best for her son," Will said. "Your mother did what she thought was best and Annie has done the same."

"But I want her and George in London with me." His tone became bitter, as he added, "I've got to go back, don't you see? I want to pay back Clara Lowndes every penny that Colonel Lowndes gave me to set up my business."

"That won't be necessary, Joe," Will said. "I met the colonel when he and his wife were guests at Estcourt and persuaded the colonel to be my agent in financing you, Joe. You owe Clara Lowndes nothing. I'm sorry to have deceived you, but it has been so difficult watching you grow into a man and not knowing how to help and how to comply with your mother's wishes at the same time."

Each wondering what to say, the three sat in silence staring at one another. The silence was finally broken by Will.

"I suppose we had all better go into dinner before Cook starts to complain. I rather think we have a wedding to organise. I am quite sure that if we can get the banns read this coming Sunday, we should see you two married in time for Christmas."

Chapter 22

"Before Christmas?" Annie had echoed, but Will Gladwell was adamant.

"I want everything settled. You two being wed will be the right way to start the new decade. Besides, Joe and I have a number of things we need to discuss and we can't do that with him running his business up in London and me here."

"And I want to make up for lost time with George," Joe agreed. "In any case, what is there to arrange? We've only got to go and see Pastor Briggs." He avoided Annie's eyes. This was not the time to add that this would not be the first occasion that he and Annie had been to arrange a date for a wedding with the pastor. "All you need is a new dress and ask Eileen to be your bridesmaid and that is it."

"There are one or two people I would like to invite. And, Joe Langmead, I won't be told what I need for my wedding." Annie's clipped tones told Joe that she was not going to be the compliant girl he had once wooed at the Densbury Gala.

"You go ahead and plan whatever you desire, my dear," Will said, "and I'll make sure that Cook gets in the extra staff to deal with the reception here at Baythorpe." A shadow crossed his face as he recalled the previous occasions when the house was filled with guests at Anthony's and his own wife's funerals. "I want this to be a day for rejoicing and putting some of the events of the past behind us."

"Just one thing." Annie was lost in thought for a moment. "I have to see my parents and tell them, but what do I tell them? That Joe is your son, Will, and that I deceived Anthony? How can I tell them that?"

Joe and Will exchanged glances. "Is there any need to explain at this point?" Will asked. "I've no doubt that there are some in this town who have already guessed the truth about Joe's father and as soon as they see Joe and George together, will piece the rest of the story together."

Annie remembered Isabelle's reaction the first time she had held George in her arms. Her Aunt Violet, too, had seen the resemblance and tried to make capital out of it.

"I insist on telling my parents. They are George's grandparents and have a right to know everything."

"As you wish, my dear," Will agreed. "Maybe it is better to be open without actually shouting it from the housetops."

Determined as she was to be honest with her parents, it took all her courage to visit them and tell them the truth. Her mother was busy in the kitchen making a batch of pies when Annie walked in the door and was not inclined to follow Annie's instructions to leave her pastry and come and sit down in the living room. "Leave it, Ma, it's important..You've got to be told right now."

Beatie sighed wondering what trouble her elder daughter was in now. Just when she thought that Annie was nicely settled at Baythorpe Hall, she was here now looking as unhappy as she had ever seen her. "Fred!" she called to her husband who was out in the back yard. "It's our Annie and it looks like trouble again."

The two sat side by side at the table waiting for Annie to speak. "Out with it, Annie, her father ordered."

Quite simply and starting with Anthony's final months, Annie recounted events leading to George's birth. "I couldn't tell the truth. It would have hurt the Gladwells so much. Besides,

318

apart from bringing shame on my family, who would have supported me?"

Beatie dabbed her eyes with the corner of her pinafore. "To think that you carried on with Joe when you were married to Anthony. I told you that you should have married Joe in the first place, then all this would not have happened, bringing shame on us even now."

"Perhaps it would not have happened and perhaps I would have been unhappy not being able to follow my heart and Granny's advice, Ma, so let's not rake up the past." She paused. "There's something else I have to tell you."

"Oh, no!" Beatie protested.

Annie's shame at admitting breaking her marriage vows were forgotten as she explained that Will Gladwell was Joe's father. "That is how the cottage came to be owned by Joe, Ma. Will had given it to his mother."

"Well, well, I never!" was all that Beatie could manage.

"Now," Annie breathed more easily now that she no longer had to conceal anything from her parents. "Joe and I are getting married and I want Pa to give me away."

Her father gave her a hug. "Come here, my girl. We're very proud of you and we will be there whatever folk have to say."

It was Pastor Briggs, who saw the interview with Joe and Annie as a god-given opportunity to exact his revenge on Annie. Jumped-up little Miss, marrying a Gladwell then passing Joe Langmead's child off as her husband's. He had seen George out in the car with Will Gladwell and had guessed that Joe was the child's father. "Well, you have placed me in a difficult position, Mrs Gladwell," he said. "I don't wish to say too much, but you can hardly expect me to conduct the marriage ceremony of a woman who has already made a mockery of her marriage to Anthony Gladwell."

Joe put his hand on Annie's arm. "Let me deal with this." He leaned forward to stare hard at the pastor. "This conversation is at an end, Pastor. I will inform Mr Gladwell of your views and we will arrange for the marriage to be conducted elsewhere. Of course, you are at liberty to express your views, but do remember who the chief benefactor of this chapel is." Joe stood up to leave. "And by the way, Mr Gladwell has now made me his heir, so I shall be advising him not to be so free with his gifts in the future."

The significance of Joe's words gradually sank in. "You his heir?" His bulging eyes threatened to part company with their sockets. "Oh dear, oh dear," he kept repeating.

"Indeed," Joe said. "Shall we start again?"

Grateful for the reprieve, Pastor Briggs almost fell to his knees. "Just name the day, Mr Langmead. Oh, and my most sincere congratulations to you both. Please convey my warmest wishes to Mr Gladwell on such a happy outcome."

It was true that Will had persuaded Joe to install a manager to run his shops in London, while Joe was to take over the factory as managing director once Fred retired in the New Year. "I shall be seeing my lawyer," he said, "and you will be named as my heir, so all that I have will be for you, Annie and our little George."

Not just for George, Annie found out a few months after the wedding, but also for his next grandchild due at the end of October. She had once promised her mother that she would be mistress of Baythorpe Hall and raise her children there, not realising that Fate would take a hand and bring her dreams to fruition in a way which she could never have predicted. And yet, when she should have been happier than she had ever been, there was a dark cloud threatening her rainbow.

Joe sensed her discontent as they lay in bed wrapped in one another's arms. "What is it, Annie?"

Annie buried her face in his shoulder. "I don't know. I have everything a woman could want. I have a darling husband, a lovely son and a wonderful family. I must be the envy of every woman for miles around living as we do in this beautiful house, so why is it that I feel that something is not as it should be?"

Disturbed at what she had said, but having no answer, Joe could not reply.

It was the same during the daytime. Sometimes, when she sat alone painting in the Dower House, which had had larger windows fitted to let in more light, Annie felt these stirrings of discontent. She had everything she had ever craved. The paths she had chosen long ago had seemed to be leading in different directions, first leading her away from Joe and Densbury to a land where she had fulfilled her passion for painting and on the way had had the love of her dear, kind friend, Anthony, and then these paths had, in a strange twist, converged into one path leading her back to Densbury. There were no more choices to be made and yet she needed to talk to someone who would understand. She wrote to Isabelle.

Dear Isabelle
Please say you can come and stay for a few days. I have some news for you and I need your clever advice again.
Your affectionate friend
Annie

Isabelle replied by return.

Dear Annie,
I am due some leave next week so can be with you on Monday morning. I simply cannot wait to hear your news!
Your dear friend
Isabelle

"That will be company for you," Joe said absentmindedly. Since taking over the factory again, he had found many problems, not the least of which was finding customers in the post-war years. So far, by seeking ways to expand the tailoring side of the business, he had not had to lay off any of the workforce as neighbouring businesses had had to do. The result was that he and Will spent many hours devising plans to maintain the prosperity of the business. Joe's London shops had proved to be the lifeline in this manufacturing area, taking and selling the suits and overcoats now made in Densbury.

"You will be nice to Isabelle, won't you?" Annie was always conscious of an underlying current of animosity running between the two, Joe always convinced that it was Isabelle who had put the idea of London into Annie's head, whilst Isabelle was just as sure that Joe had wanted to stifle her friend's genius.

"Of course. Just you enjoy yourselves." He kissed the top of her head. "But promise me that you won't let her talk you into any mad schemes." Always at the back of his mind was the fear hovering that Isabelle would take his precious Annie away from him.

Isabelle did not have to be told Annie's secret, her doctor's eye detecting Annie's glowing complexion as well as her rounded figure. "Wonderful! When?"

The next two or three days were spent chatting, playing with George and walking in the grounds of Baythorpe Hall. Isabelle finally spoke what was in her mind. "So, what is there that is not quite right in your world, Annie? I see a wonderful home, a delightful little boy with another baby on the way, an adoring husband and a reconciled father-in-law, but you don't seem as contented as you ought to be."

"Trust you to guess there is something wrong," Annie said, not quite sure how to begin. "It's this feeling that I have too much. Why do I need such a big house for just Will, Joe, George and me, plus the new baby?" She waved her arm encompassing the acres of gardens. "Everywhere is empty, isn't it? Come, let me show you round the house again. I don't suppose you remember it from your last visit." She led Isabelle back into the house, taking her from room to room on the ground floor, then up the grand winding oak staircase.

Isabelle could not see what was troubling her friend until Anne stopped outside the sixth bedroom on the first floor, before taking her up to the second floor. "Do you see, Isabelle? When I was a servant here, I used to spend my working days cleaning all these rooms, laying fires and taking meals up to dozens of visitors, most of them disgusting, lazy good-for-nothings. Well, neither Joe nor I would ever contemplate being hosts to such people, but…"

"But what?"

"I feel as if I am living in a museum with all the ghosts of these people in these empty bedrooms. I don't want to live anywhere else and yet I don't like the house as it is."

"I can't say I find all these heavy furnishings and gloomy carpets and curtains to my taste," Isabelle said. She stopped suddenly on the staircase as the two went down intent on ordering tea in the library. "I may be able to help you out there," she said.

"That's what Joe was afraid of," Annie said, laughing. "He warned me not to let you talk me into any of your plans."

Isabelle pretended to look hurt. "But this one will make you so happy, Joe won't be able to oppose it." Suddenly serious, she went on to explain. "Listen to me for a moment, Annie. Every day I have to send sick children home after an operation or a serious illness. Home is often an overcrowded insanitary couple of rooms with shared sinks and lavatories. What these children need is a week or two of wholesome food, a breath of fresh air, and freedom to roam. You know they have never seen a blade of grass or heard a skylark singing high in the sky over a green meadow." Isabelle's heart was afire with compassion for her little patients.

"And I have all these empty rooms just waiting to have those horrid velvet curtains ripped down and replaced with pretty floral ones. The gardener complains that he has to throw away most of the vegetables he grows and Cook says we don't eat half of what she prepares for us. We need to turn this house into a home filled with the laughter of children." What she was about to agree to would change her whole life once again. Annie hesitated, considering her options. Should she remain mistress of the Baythorpe Hall she had known as a girl or should she agree to the huge changes which would ensue if she changed the status of the house?

Thinking that Annie was about to turn down her suggestion, Isabelle gave a nervous cough. "What do you think?"

"We could easily take a few children at any one time." Annie frowned, working out the logistics of housing her own family and a group of convalescent children. "We would have to block off part of the house and convert it into a separate convalescent home for sick children, if this is to work."

"Of course, this is your home. With a separate wing for the children, my colleagues and I could visit our little patients and see how they are getting on." She stood up and began to pace up and down. "This is something I've longed for ever since I started work at St Margaret's."

Annie fetched some paper out of Will's desk and the two started work in earnest on some preliminary sketches. "I'd have to talk to Joe and Will about the cost of it all. I'm afraid that the whole scheme is going to prove to be very expensive."

"There are charities which help. I could get money from one of them for all this," Isabelle said. "Oh, I can't tell you what this means to me, you've made a dream come true."

"What dream is this?" Joe asked on entering the library. "Don't tell me Isabelle has been filling your head with foolish ideas again, Annie." Seeing Annie's look of alarm, he smiled at her. "Just teasing my darling wife," he said.

He looked over their shoulders at the sketchy plans and thought for a minute. "Well, well, this certainly is a big plan.

Come, let me have a closer look" The two friends held their breath. Finally, he struggled to find the right words to express what was in his heart. "Yes, it's a wonderful dream. Annie and I have so much here which we would like to share and this scheme is perfect. It will make us happy as well as your little patients, Isabelle." He smiled at Isabelle. "And on this occasion, Isabelle, I think I agree that you have found the perfect solution. He bent to kiss Isabelle's cheek. "So, now Annie, do I tell Will or will you, that Baythorpe Hall is about to change its name to Baythorpe Children's Convalescent Home?"

Annie gave a huge sigh of contentment. She laid her hand on Isabelle's arm.

'Oh, I think we ought to allow Joe to do that, don't you agree, Isabelle?'

On hearing news of the plans, a slow smile spread across old Will Gladwell's face. He nodded.

"A future with the sound of children's voices echoing with laughter. Just what this old house needs."